PAPER WAR

EVOLUTION

RYAN LEKODAK

Evolution
Published by RandallVision Publishing.
San Diego, California

Copyright ©2026 by Ryan LeKodak. All rights reserved.

ISBN: 979-8-9896545-4-3 (Paperback), 979-8-9896545-5-0 (Hardcover)
FICTION / Thrillers / Technological

Cover and Interior design by Victoria Wolf, wolfdesignandmarketing.com. Copyright owned by Ryan LeKodak

WHEN THE SNOW REMEMBERS

OCTOBER 2019
CHICAGO

NINE-YEAR-OLD TYRA adjusted her mittens. She'd stolen them from the kitchen earlier in the day, and they were several sizes too large. But this was the only way she could play in the snow, and it wasn't as if her mother would notice anyway; Tyra had heard her father come in a few minutes ago, which meant she had over an hour to play outside while they yelled at each other.

Tyra took her time with the snowman, carefully packing snow into a slender neck between the head and the body. To her, a snowman without a neck just looked like a snowball on top of a boulder. Her friends never seemed to care, but Tyra couldn't understand that. Without a neck, how could it even be a man at all? Soon, her parents' voices drifted through the open window, and Tyra could just barely make out their words. She scowled. Her father's voice was the loudest, of course. It hadn't yet reached the Danger Level—when he started throwing things—but it sounded like he was working himself up to it.

Tyra continued building her snowman, but she was also trying to make out what her parents were arguing about this time. They mostly used Big Words that she didn't understand, but Tyra got the gist of it: Her mother wasn't happy that her father had stayed out late and had come back with lipstick stains on his shirt. This wasn't the first time that Tyra had heard her mother complain about it. The first time, Tyra had been confused. Why would her father put on lipstick? Didn't he know only girls wore it? But Lizzy had explained it to her at school, so now Tyra knew that her father was being *Naughty.*

Tyra scowled more and slapped the snow on the snowman's face a little harder than she needed to. Her father was being Naughty, but instead of apologizing, he shouted at Mother and did the Bad Thing. That meant that father was a Bad Man. Tommy's father, who was a police officer, had told them what happened to Bad Men, but Tyra didn't like the idea of jail.

Inside the house, her father's voice had finally reached the Danger Level. Tyra put the finishing touches on the snowman and then hurried to the window that she'd left open. It gave her a good view of the living room and her parents. Tyra saw her father's red face and the pieces of the lamp on the ground, and she knew it was only a matter of time before her father did the Bad Thing.

But even though she was expecting it, she still flinched when the first hit landed on her mother. She almost shouted at her father, but she'd done that several times before, and it only made him angrier—and he'd beat her mother more. Instead, Tyra forced herself to watch, even though she flinched every time.

When it was done, her mother lay on the floor, sobbing, with red marks all over her body. Her father's fingerprints showed on the marks. From where Tyra crouched, they looked like red scales. Tyra wanted to comfort her mother, but first she went back to her snowman, which she'd decorated to look like her father. She brought out the old knife that she'd stolen from the trash can when her mother had thrown it away several months ago. It was a little too big for her hands, and it was difficult to handle with her oversized mittens. But Tyra was smart and soon figured it out.

And she made sure that she had a good grip when she brought the rusty knife to the snowman's long, slender neck.

DECEMBER 2043
NEW YORK CITY

Tyra Chityothin stared through the window at a snowflake drifting lazily to the ground. It was a drop in the ocean compared to the blanket of white that'd already covered most of the street, but something about the sight made her tattoo itch. Absently, Tyra adjusted the mirror beside her to look at the koi fish that stretched across her back, swimming in its own little pond. Her fingers brushed against its red scales, vivid against her pale flesh. It had been years since she'd had it made, long enough that Tyra barely thought about it anymore. But snow had a way of dredging up the memories she'd buried.

Tyra lifted her left arm in front of her and tapped at the screen of the portable monitor attached to it with her right hand. A metallic glint made her pause, and Tyra frowned at the titanium fingers. It'd been only a week since she'd replaced the stump with a titanium prosthetic, but Tyra didn't think she'd ever get used to the strange sight.

Tyra blew out a breath and quickly scrolled through the panel until she reached the cluster controlling the spores that flowed through her brain. She typed in a command that would have ended her burst of nostalgia—but her fingers paused on the last stroke, and her gaze peered beyond the window, where another snowflake fluttered to the ground.

Tyra scowled and jammed the button. A wave passed through her body, and suddenly the snow didn't hold the deep secrets of her past. She took another breath. She didn't need sentimentality. Not ever, but especially not now.

Not when everything she'd been working toward was finally coming to a head.

PART 1
OUTMATCHED
PURSUITS

CHAPTER

1

DECEMBER 2043

OKAFOR CORPORATION,

ABUJA, NIGERIA

TRAPPED.

The word spun around in Ndidi's head as she waited for the sun to peek over the horizon. Night had fallen quickly and seemed reluctant to end. Ndidi had been too anxious to sleep, so she'd spent it tossing around on her bed, trying not to drown in her thoughts. But her fears held her in their grasp, and Ndidi felt trapped by her own mind.

But she wasn't, of course. Not like Manar was trapped in the Virtual Realm.

Manar and CJ had uploaded their consciousnesses to the internet in order to take the fight to Helene and finally defeat the AI for good. After several months—and an intense battle that had almost destroyed their avatars and, thus, their minds—the two of them had succeeded and returned to their bodies. Or so they'd thought.

In reality, Helene had anticipated and, in some ways, pushed them to take that path as part of her grand plan. Ndidi was pretty sure that she'd figured out most of that plan, but this was Helene; there were probably a few more pieces of the puzzle. In the end, the AI had used the chance to take possession of Manar's body and assume his identity—trapping his consciousness in the Virtual Realm—and fooling everyone, including Ndidi, for several months, until she'd stumbled upon the truth.

Ndidi felt a spark of hurt at the memory, but she burned it as fuel to feed the well of anger that sat in her chest. There were a lot of things she could have been angry about if she put her mind to it. But that kind of mentality was what had caused her problems in the first place. So Ndidi focused that anger on herself. She *was* at fault, after all. She was the one that hadn't been able to see through Helene's pretense: *She* was the one who'd ignored every sign. *She* was the one that'd allowed herself to be deceived time and time again.

And she was the one who'd stupidly become pregnant, providing Helene with a test subject for the next step in whatever grand plan the AI had in mind.

The first rays of the sun shone through the window, and Ndidi threw off her covers. She was alone in the room, as was the norm now. For the first few weeks—before Ndidi had found out the truth and Helene had still put forth the effort to pretend she was Manar—Ndidi had never woken up alone. Now Helene was content to spend all night and most of the day at the lab. Several times a week, she dragged Ndidi along to check the progress of the baby. Several times, Ndidi went by herself to learn as much as she could about what Helene was up to.

But not today. Today was different.

Trapped. The word rang out again in Ndidi's mind as she stood up from the bed and started getting ready. She wasn't truly trapped. Helene, posing as Manar, had gained a surprising amount of influence in the short time she'd been here, especially after pioneering the Picospore Initiative, an endeavor that was already raking in profits for the company. The Okafor Corporation still belonged to Ndidi, at least on the surface, so no matter the AI's influence, Helene couldn't keep Ndidi confined in her own building. Although Helene hadn't ever shown an inclination toward limiting her freedom—Ndidi could theoretically leave whenever she wanted—she had, through her actions, made it clear that the child Ndidi carried held some importance to some grand plan. And Ndidi thought it unlikely Helene would let such an important pawn just walk away.

Trapped.

Being what she was, Helene could maintain constant surveillance on Ndidi through the building's surveillance system—and Ndidi had no doubt that she did. It *could* have been coincidence that Helene always showed up when Ndidi was on the verge of doing something drastic—after all, the AI always had a good reason—but Ndidi didn't believe in coincidences.

So she wasn't taking any chances.

The room brightened as the sun got over its reluctance, and Ndidi darted around as she got dressed. Her clothes were tighter on her, which made her scowl. She was barely a month pregnant, but whatever Helene had done to her child had sped up the rate of development, making her, for all intents and purposes, about three months along. If the trend continued at the same rate, Ndidi would have roughly two months before she was due. That was the best-case scenario. Ndidi didn't want to consider the worst case.

She caught her reflection in the mirror and stopped. She'd substituted her normal pantsuit for a more sensible long-sleeved top with a thick pair of jeans and sneakers. It was far more casual than she was used to—and it might tip a few people off—but Ndidi doubted she'd have the time to stop and change later. If there was any chance that wearing her suit would have deceived Helene, Ndidi would have considered it.

But, she thought, shifting her gaze to a small air freshener hanging on the wall, coincidentally placed to view the entire room. She squinted and could faintly make out a red glow coming from the small container. *That doesn't seem likely.*

Ndidi glanced at her watch, sighed impatiently, and then sat at the edge of the bed. A month ago, the red glow would have been impossible for her to see, and Ndidi didn't want to think about why she could now.

I'm doing it again, she sighed. *I'm ignoring the obvious because I don't want to face the harsh truth.* Hermione would have told her it was an understandable self-defense mechanism. DJ would have called her out on her bullshit. And he'd have been right. Again. She knew why she could suddenly do things she wouldn't have been able to do before. Helene had explained it to her. The nanites Helene had injected into her to enhance the child's development were affecting her, too, if only as a side effect.

There were so many emotions tied into it that Ndidi didn't even know where to start. On one hand, she'd seen what the Murder Twins were capable of with the power of the nanites, and a part of her had always been both awed and envious of their strength. On the other hand, however, the Murder Twins weren't particularly ideal role models. From the reports she'd read, they were crazy even before they got the nanites, but it was also a fact that the enhancement had exacerbated the problem. Even DJ had been affected by their influence. To a lesser extent, sure, but he'd still gone on a rampage in the White House.

Ndidi would have liked to think she would be better—and that led to a realization.

She wasn't as stable as she'd always thought.

Everyone was the hero in their own story; they had to be in order to justify their actions. Ndidi was no different. She'd justified her consistently terrible decisions and convinced herself she was right. And in doing so, she'd ruined most of the relationships that she held dear. She'd pushed away Bethany and hadn't even realized that she was doing so. How'd that happen? Bethany had been the sole reason she'd started this crusade in the first place. And once she finally had her back, she threw it all away? What was *wrong* with her?

I've acknowledged all this. Ndidi pinched the bridge of her nose. *Why am I rehashing it?* She glanced at her watch, then her eyes snapped to the air freshener. She squinted but couldn't see the glow, no matter how hard she looked. Immediately, Ndidi was on her feet and crossing the room. She pulled the door open—and came face-to-face with Manar.

Her feet paused over the threshold, and she stared into his green eyes. But as she watched, the green was replaced by flecks of shining gold until his eyes shone like two suns. That snapped her out of it and reminded her that, although they wore the same face, the person in front of her was *not* Manar Saleem.

"Ah, Ndidi," Helene said. "Did you want to join me at the lab today?"

They were in the guest wing of the Corporation, which was, by design, isolated from the larger workstations. However, the area was where the Corporation housed business representatives while negotiations were ongoing. For a corporation of its size, it meant that the guest wing was never empty. It also meant that the security was especially tight. Just a shout would get a patrol running.

That knowledge helped Ndidi to regain her composure, and she kept her expression carefully neutral when she replied. "I figured some time outside would do me good. I've been cooped up here for too long."

Helene's gaze traveled over her, noting her clothes. She raised a brow, an action so human that Ndidi's surprise almost slipped through her mask. "Your outfit suggests you plan for more than a casual stroll?"

"I thought that I could use the chance to sightsee. I haven't properly explored my country in years."

"I cannot allow that," Helene said. "You should consider your condition."

Ndidi's eyes went flat. "Trust me when I say that I have thoroughly considered it, *Manar*. And my *condition* is the whole reason that I'm doing this." She pushed past Helene to step into the hallway, then started heading for the exit.

Helene sighed and followed, easily keeping pace even when Ndidi sped up. "Your anger is understandable, as is your decision, especially as it is fueled by your misguided impression of my goals. However, you have once again allowed your emotions to narrow your focus."

Ndidi didn't respond, but her glance toward the AI betrayed her curiosity. Helene didn't miss the chance. "Currently, the child growing within you is one of a kind. That means that it requires one-of-a-kind care, the kind only *I* am able to give it. Already its growth is beyond what most modern practitioners understand. Can you imagine what it will be like after its first trimester? Or when your due date arrives in the next few months? How do you think a doctor would fare against a child infused with, and completely adapted to, nanites from birth?"

Ndidi missed a step, but she kept moving. She'd already considered that. Helene forced her to the lab weekly for a checkup and lectured her enough that Ndidi had been able to understand most of her chart the one time that she'd acquired it. She knew Helene was speaking the truth—at least, what the AI considered the truth. Helene probably couldn't imagine anyone who could replicate her feat, but Ndidi already had a name in mind. She just had to find them before the baby burst out of her.

Helene didn't say anything for a while, probably to give Ndidi a chance to consider her words. All it gave her, though, was enough time to pass through the connecting walkway into the main working station of the Corporation. Ndidi barely noticed the transition from the quiet guest wing to the bustling noise of the working area.

After a minute, Helene must have decided Ndidi hadn't taken her warning seriously, because she tried a different tactic. "I am almost curious about how you hope to substitute my assistance with the child. But that is your burden to bear. Without the need to constantly babysit you and your shifting moods, I will have more time to focus my efforts on increasing the production of the picospores. We have had a backlog of families hoping to undergo the procedure."

It was obvious that Helene was trying to get a reaction out of her, and Ndidi was determined not to give her one. She futilely hoped the AI didn't notice when her whole body tensed. Ndidi had thought she'd considered every consequence of her decision, but in her selfishness, she'd overlooked one of the most glaring ones.

Ndidi hadn't been able to shut down the Picospore Initiative after learning about Helene's deception. Even after just a couple of months, the project was too profitable to be stopped. The most she could do was reduce the intake of applicants with the excuse that further testing of the procedure was needed. And even implementing that concession had taken several days of arguing with the board of directors, costing most of the influence she'd gained by pioneering the initiative itself.

Without her around, "Manar" would automatically become the new head of the project, and the board of directors would be all too happy to implement increased production of the spores, as long as it brought them more profits.

Ndidi would be dooming thousands, if not tens of thousands, of people to Helene's control.

Ndidi had to force herself to keep moving, pushing past the guilt rising within her. It helped that the anger that she'd been suppressing was also bubbling up to the surface.

If I hadn't been so stupid—

Ndidi stopped herself from finishing the thought. At the same time, she pushed down the self-loathing until her vision was no longer tinged red. She'd already punished herself enough, and losing herself to her emotions was exactly what Helene wanted.

She'd already made the mistake, and logically, there was nothing she could do. She had already reached the limit of her influence when she'd slowed down the picospore production and distribution. And as her influence waned, "Manar's" rose. Ndidi doubted it would take long for Helene to find a way to convince the board to reverse everything Ndidi had fought for.

In short, her presence would change nothing. Ndidi knew this, but that didn't make it easier to keep walking. Fortunately, she could see the exit in front of her. It was already far too late for Helene to try to physically stop her, so all she had to do was to keep moving.

Naturally, that was when someone stood in her way. Ndidi had been looking down, lost in her thoughts. She blinked, wondering whether Helene had decided to try to stop her after all. But she took in the Italian leather shoes, the handcrafted three-piece suit over a prominent paunch—and sighed internally.

Chinedu Okoye had a stern, weathered face and held an expression of quiet disdain. He was over a head taller than Ndidi, which always made it easier for him to look down on her. Ndidi would have taken it personally, but it was the same way he looked at everyone, including her father.

Oh, the man was everything her father had hated. Where Eze Okafor had sought to promote and encourage Nigeria's values and culture, Chinedu seemed to loathe everything about his country. Most Nigerians would wear variations of their native attires for casual or formal, but in over two decades, Ndidi had never seen this man in anything other than a crisp suit—not even when he'd been bestowed the title of chief in his village.

Chinedu took in her clothes and sneered. A significant part of Ndidi wanted to smack that look off his face, but the balding man was one of the members of the board of directors, and not even her father had been able to get rid of him. Now he stood in her way, and the glance he sent to "Manar" made it clear that it wasn't by coincidence. Ndidi made to step around him.

"Go ahead and run," he said. Ndidi paused mid-step. "It is bad enough that you are a woman, but if you'd had even half the balls that your father had, this company would already be yours."

Ndidi knew she should keep moving. There was nothing to be gained by throwing words at the man. She knew this, but... "The company is *already* mine," she whispered.

"On paper," Chinedu agreed. "But no one is so stupid as to follow a weak leader. And you have always been weak. I know it, and the rest of the board knows it. We gave you a chance with the Picospore Initiative, but you ruined that too. Now I doubt that there's anyone on the board who would listen to you. So, yes..." He smiled thinly, and his eyes, creased at the corners, gleamed with cold calculation. "You are making the right choice. Run, and watch us grow this company to heights even your father couldn't reach. And with your 'fiancé' on our side, there is no fear of us having the same 'accident' that took Eze Okafor so early."

Ndidi noted the emphasis on the word *fiancé*, and her eyes widened in realization. He knew Manar wasn't really Manar. It was more than that, though; the latter part of the sentence made that obvious.

He knows, Ndidi thought. *He knows, and he's still working with her.* She almost blacked out as blood rushed to her head and clouded her vision. She saw herself killing the man so many times that she could almost smell the blood on her hands. She took a step toward him, and peripherally, she saw a small smile on Helene's lips. The sight pierced through the haze in her mind, and somehow, in some way, she managed to restrain herself.

Ndidi didn't know how long she stood there in front of Chinedu, struggling to regain her composure. The entire lobby seemed to hold its breath. Helene and Chinedu seemed content to watch, waiting to see if she would doom herself or not. Ndidi ignored them both as she pitted all her focus against the waves of emotions coursing through her. Eventually, she succeeded, but she took an extra moment to carefully repair the mask over her face. It was probably redundant now, since her previous reaction had been obvious to anyone with eyes, but she did it anyway.

Only when she was confident that she had herself under control did she meet Chinedu's eyes. And only then did she allow her disgust to show. The man surely didn't know who Helene really was, but he definitely knew that Helene was responsible for the disaster that had killed her parents and almost destroyed the Okafor Corporation. Despite that, he'd still decided to align with her.

It was pitiful.

But it was fortunate that the idiot had shown her his hand. It was probably an attempt to goad her into attacking him—but at least it made her aware of another threat. She'd known Helene would never let her go just because she left the Corporation, but she'd assumed the AI's power was limited in Nigeria, being so far away from her operations in New York. But if she was working with Chinedu Okoye, she would have access to a part of the Corporation's resources.

That was far from a negligible threat, especially considering that the Okafor Corporation owned most of the country.

Ndidi turned from Chinedu to Helene. There were several things she wanted to say, but none of them would gain her anything. So she stayed silent, stepped around the obstruction, and went out of the building through the open doors. At the end of the driveway, sitting astride a motorcycle and holding the handlebars of a second, her bodyguard, Pratima, waited for her. Ndidi climbed on her own cycle and collected the large duffle bag Pratima handed to her. She felt eyes on her as they both drove away.

She didn't look back.

CHAPTER

2

DECEMBER 2043
VIRTUAL REALM

CJ STOOD BEFORE a desolate wasteland.

It had caught him off guard when he first returned to the Virtual Realm a few days ago. His initial upload months before, when he'd gone in after Manar, had dropped him into the middle of a bustling city. Manar had said he's appeared in a grassy plain. The fact that CJ was now standing in a wasteland confirmed that the upload location was random. He was fortunate he'd reappeared in the same place after returning to his body and re-uploading.

CJ pressed his lips together. *It probably had something to do with the fact that I didn't need to create a new avatar this time.*

The first time he'd uploaded, he'd been forced to build an avatar from scratch to interact with the Virtual Realm. That body had carried his full consciousness, and when he finally escaped, it was destroyed. But when he uploaded again a few days ago, the process had worked differently—his mind had stayed tethered to his body in the real world. Because of that link, the new avatar he created didn't vanish when he logged out. It persisted, allowing him to return to it instead of starting over.

That was good. If he appeared in a different place every time he uploaded himself, he'd have been forced to just stay in the Virtual Realm until he found Manar. CJ didn't think his brother could handle that again, and he wouldn't want to put DJ through that. He felt guilty enough.

I have nothing to be guilty about though, CJ reminded himself. He'd made his choice with full awareness of the consequences. He shouldn't feel guilty just because he'd done it behind his brother's back. If only that was all it took for the guilt to go away.

CJ pushed the thought away from his head and focused instead on his avatar, going through several warm-up exercises. He'd done it the last time, but it paid to make sure that everything was still working properly.

Plus, CJ loved the control he had over his own limbs. It was liberating to see his arms move *exactly* the way he wanted them to, with barely a thought. It was a feeling that he hadn't had—and one that he'd chased—since the last time he was in the Virtual Realm. And CJ was determined to enjoy it.

His examination lasted just a few minutes, after which he went on to the next thing on his agenda: dowsing Manar's location.

His theory was that by injecting himself with the picospores that Helene had coded for Bethany, he would be able to trace the connection back and identify places where Helene had spent significant time. And in one of those places, he would find Manar.

CJ had proven that theory right several days ago—at least, the fact that Bethany's spores could be used to trace Helene's past movements. One such place was where he was right then. By either luck or design, CJ had spawned relatively close to the area and had made his way to it. After that, he'd spent hours searching for what had drawn Helene to the place initially, and had come up empty. Whatever it was that had interested the AI had either disappeared naturally or had been taken by her.

Despite that, CJ could feel tugs in over a dozen different directions. The problem was that, from what he could sense, most of the destinations were ridiculously far away—and often in opposite directions. There was no way to know which one would lead to Manar and which would lead to nothing. And it would take months, if not years, to search each one of them.

My Sphere would have been handy right about now, CJ thought, admittedly not for the first time since he realized his problem. The Sphere was a tool he'd created during his first foray into the Virtual Realm. It had been made from several pieces of one of the first ancient codes, one that had been integrated into almost every modern programming language in existence. The device had given him rudimentary control over the Virtual Realm, allowing him to crudely manipulate the codes that made up the world.

With it, CJ had been able to create a Zone that was uniquely attuned to him. CJ had been able to see and sense everything within the Zone, and he was confident that if he'd had enough time, he would have figured out how to move freely within the space. Everything pointed toward the conclusion that it was possible. After all, for all intents and purposes, he was on the internet. And on the web, distance only existed in relation to the strength of your Wi-Fi. He shouldn't have to physically move anywhere to get to places.

In theory, at least.

CJ sighed, glancing around the wasteland again. He'd thought he would spawn with the Sphere in tow. He'd been bonded to it, after all. Or, at least, his previous avatar had. Did he have to gather the pieces again? No, that would be tedious and far too time-consuming. If he wanted his ability to manipulate the Virtual Realm back, he'd have to figure out another way to go about it.

Fortunately, he had a theory about that.

DECEMBER 2043

SPARTA HEADQUARTERS, NEW YORK

KARLA WAS ANGRY.

She always was, and had always been, even as a child. It was so easy when everyone around her was an imbecile. When José and Chloe had realized they could not beat her into the clinical and detached assassin that they wanted, they'd sought to forge her anger into a blunt weapon. That had worked better, and Karla rarely lost herself in her rage. Even when her nanites enhanced the emotion until her vision turned red and her daggers screamed for blood, she was able to control herself.

That control was what saved the fool's life when she found out what he had done.

"You had no *right*," she screamed as her dagger sliced through the air. The imbecile scrambled to dodge and then create distance between them. A part of her was pleased to see the panic in his eyes—but she would have to punish him for such cowardice. A second later, her nose was filled with the scent of blood from the cuts that her daggers left on his forearms. That was a mistake because now Karla could feel their thirst. She hadn't killed anything in weeks, and the little droplets she fed her daggers wasn't enough. They wanted more—and there were parts of her that agreed.

But she couldn't kill him. And that only enraged her more.

It was already vexing to be forced to regulate her strength and speed so she didn't break him by accident, but the fool did not even give her the honor of a good fight. He never attacked, only defended. He never cried out when she cut him, only grimaced and clenched his teeth. Karla wanted to hear his *screams*—wanted to hear him beg. But she could see it in his eyes: He wouldn't grant her wish easily, and she couldn't afford to go too far and risk ruining him entirely.

With a yell of frustration, she slashed with her dagger and then flung the other at him. Then the coward tried to create distance between them again. "You had no right to interfere, to *meddle!*"

The imbecile's eyes widened at the dagger coming for him, and he blurred for a moment before returning to normal, holding the weapon in one hand. "I know," he agreed. "Although, it *could* be argued that I had some rights since I was the reason that you and José had that argument in the first place."

Karla took a step toward him with a growl. The coward hastily took a step back, raising his hand to stop her. "Okay, fine, I had no right. But we need their help because we're going to go after Tyra. I'm *not* saying you're not strong enough," he continued before Karla could voice her protest. "I'm saying that *I* am not strong enough. I'm gonna get killed if I try to follow you in there, and I still have a lot to do before I go off to meet my dads."

"Then stay weak," Karla sneered, "and I will go alone."

"I can't do that either. I'm a marine. At least, I was. And we don't leave our teammates to go off and do suicidal things alone."

Karla snorted. She hardly needed her enhanced senses to know he was lying. But it didn't matter. The fool's plan was doomed to fail. Her family would never come, even if they thought she had been held captive by Helene's minion. José was too much of a coward to take the risk, and Karla's sister was too far under their father's thumb to disobey him.

"Your plan will not work," Karla told him. "José is too afraid of the AI. He will not oppose her, even for me."

"It's sad that I have more faith in your family than you do. I honestly think José might surprise you, but I really hope he doesn't. He's a total pain to work with, and honestly, he creeps me out."

"You expect my sister to come?" Karla snorted. "Liz *worships* our father. She would not move a finger unless he commanded it." Karla felt a pang in her chest even as she said it. But she still remembered the day José had sent her off. Her sister had watched her go, her eyes wide and confused. But still, she'd stayed by their father's side.

"She has already picked José over me," Karla continued, feeling her anger rising. "She picked the man who had beaten and tortured us all our lives—the man who'd *leashed* us to himself, like he was our master and we his dogs. Liz chose that man over *me*."

At the end, Karla blurred and appeared a moment later next to one of the weight benches. With a grunt, she picked it up and ripped it apart with as much ease as a normal person might tear cardboard. Karla chucked one piece at the imbecile, rolling her eyes at him.

The fool caught it easily. "Are you feeling better now, after your little tantrum?" he asked, meeting her eyes without fear. "Your sister is going to come. And Chloe too. Maybe. I've never been able to get a good read on her because of all that crazy."

Karla straightened. "How are you so confident that she will come?" she couldn't help but ask. "What did you do?"

"Me? I didn't do anything. But it's Christmas." The imbecile shrugged. "I figured she'd be missing you—y'know, as much as you're probably missing her." Karla growled and took a step toward him, her eyes narrowed. But the fool had already leaped away. "You realize that getting angry means you acknowledge that I'm telling the truth, right?"

She paused mid-step, and then, with another growl, she launched herself toward him. He bounded away, and she followed. It didn't matter what he said. He would be punished. How dare he! How dare he imply that she was weak! It was true that this was the longest that she had ever been without her sister by her side. And it was true that it was a drastic change, after spending most of their lives sharing the same body as conjoined twins. But Liz had already chosen to follow their father. So how dare he imply that her sister would allow her emotions to dictate her actions! And how dare he make her hope that he was right!

She couldn't kill him, but his nanites should be able to heal a broken bone in a matter of days. That would be a fitting punishment. And it would dull the rage in her heart.

At least until the imbecile said something else to piss her off.

DECEMBER 2043
ABUJA, NIGERIA

NDIDI ADJUSTED HER SCARF as she and Pratima walked through the alley. The street behind her was quiet, which was basically an alarm blaring that something was wrong—and was why the both of them had ducked into the alley. The Central Business District was the heart of Abuja's commerce. Nowadays, it was the prime territory for companies looking to dominate the Nigerian market—a sprawl of glass towers, neon-lit billboards, and streets choked with traffic.

It was never quiet. Not anymore. Ndidi remembered when it had been a quieter, less crowded part of the city, with low-rise shops, open-air cafés, and vendors calling out their prices over the hum of conversation. All that had vanished after her father chose the district for the Okafor Corporation's headquarters, drawing in a flood of banks, multinationals, and oil companies. She might have appreciated the rare stillness now, if her entire focus hadn't been on getting as far away as possible.

They'd driven for several hours on the expressway before stopping and ditching their bikes. After that, they'd stuck to the back roads and moved away from the city's center. One of their advantages was that Nigeria didn't have the same camera density as the United States, which would make it difficult for Helene to track them—though Ndidi doubted it would delay her for long.

She estimated they would have a few hours head start while Helene tried to marshal the board of directors to search for her. That was going to be a tough sell, even for the AI. Because why would they want to, when Ndidi disappearing was in their favor? There were some that held enough loyalty to her father to want to make sure that she was safe, but Ndidi had argued against the board enough times to know that those people were too few to be of any help.

Of course, Helene could convince them to hunt me down just to make sure I was permanently gone, Ndidi considered. The board would definitely bite in that case, but Ndidi couldn't say whether Helene would risk them actually managing to kill her. After all, if she died, her child died as well, which would go against Helene's plans—assuming the child was part of Helene's plans and not just another layer of manipulation.

Ndidi waved the thought away. She could get consumed if she allowed herself to go down that rabbit hole. It didn't matter anyway. She'd already used up whatever head start she'd had. She had to hope their plan kept them ahead of Helene.

Up ahead, a figure tore away from the wall and stood in front of them. Ndidi squinted, but the alley was too dark to make out any features—which, she imagined, was the reason the person had waited there.

"Keep moving," Pratima said.

Ndidi didn't reply, and the two of them continued walking until they were a few feet away from the man. The idiot brandished a knife and started to say something. Ndidi never got to hear what because the man was on the ground a second later, clutching his throat. Pratima leaned over him and struck a point on his neck, knocking him out before his groaning attracted attention. She searched his pockets to make sure he hadn't been sent by anyone—and Ndidi was surprised at her relief that he'd just been a common robber.

When had her life become so complicated that the fact that she'd almost been robbed, or worse, was no longer a big deal? A few years ago, that would have been the highlight of her day. Now, she barely blinked while Pratima rifled through the man's pockets.

Ndidi sighed and shoved the thought away. Pratima straightened, and they continued on, their pace a little faster. This incident had involved an opportunist who wanted to take advantage of people he considered easy marks. The next one might be worse, especially since Helene had a way of tracking her.

Ndidi hadn't been able to figure out how exactly. She hadn't seen a tracker or anything, she hadn't sensed eyes on her, and she'd taken steps to prevent conventional tracking. It could have been in her head for all she knew. But it was just better to assume Helene was aware of their every move, planning with that in mind.

So she and Pratima moved faster, leaving the alley and entering the open market. There they slowed their pace and blended with the crowd. Pratima slouched so her height didn't make them stand out. These streets were alive, but in a different way from New York—a way that Ndidi had forgotten.

Vendors shouted their wares from open stalls, children weaved through narrow lanes and people's legs, and their laughter, as well as the scent of fried plantain and roasted corn, filled the air. The place was raw and unpolished, but beneath that, Ndidi couldn't help but notice how every sound and every face was unapologetically loud, warm, and close. So close that Ndidi brushed against someone with every step. Twice, she slapped hands away from her purse.

Pratima led the way, her bulk parting the crowd like a stone in a river. Ndidi tapped her after a few minutes of walking. "Have you...?"

Pratima nodded. "I contacted them before we left. They'll be there. We just have to focus on keeping on schedule."

Ndidi nodded absently, letting her eyes roam over the crowd. Both she and Pratima wore abayas, which were dresses usually worn by Muslim women for modesty. They were often paired with a niqab, a headwrap that veiled the entire face, leaving only the eyes. The outfit made it easier for Pratima to blend in and protected them from easy identification.

Ndidi immediately became alert when she noticed a figure ahead. The man obviously wasn't shopping, though he stood in front of a stall. Instead, his eyes swept the crowd, noting every face. One hand rested on his hip, and Ndidi noticed the slight bulge there.

She yanked on Pratima's hand and weaved through the crowd, away from the man. To her credit, Pratima followed her without a word. "Where?" she whispered once they'd gone a fair distance.

"A man searching the crowd," Ndidi said under her breath. "Behind us and next to a fruit stand. Tall, wearing a blue shirt."

Pratima waited a second before casually looking in that direction. When she turned back, her brows were drawn into a frown. She took Ndidi's hand and led her through another row of stalls. They had to follow the pace of the crowd to avoid standing out, and that slowed them greatly. Ndidi allowed herself to be tugged along, focusing on the crowd, trying to spot anyone that might have been paying them too much attention.

Ahead, a woman met Ndidi's eyes and gestured toward her. Ndidi, assuming she was inviting them to her stall, waved her off. But the woman just gestured more urgently. She was older, her face lined with wrinkles. She stood by a stack of crates, her hand resting lightly on one of them. Ndidi hesitated and tugged on Pratima's hands.

Surprisingly, Pratima walked straight up to the woman, who stepped aside to reveal a narrow gap between the crates and the wall. "Quickly," she said. They slipped into the gap, the crates shifting slightly as they passed. On the other side was a wooden door that had started to rot with age. The woman rapped on it twice, and the door opened.

The space inside was dark, but a single light hung from the ceiling, swaying with the breeze from an open window on the other side of the room. Two men stood by a table, their faces rough and scarred.

"You're late," one of them said in a voice that might have once been deep before all the drug abuse. Now it just sounded like two pieces of wood rubbing against each other.

"We're here," Pratima replied firmly. "I assume everything is in place?" She didn't seem worried, but then again, few things worried Pratima. He gestured toward a pair of duffle bags on the floor, and she picked one up and spent a few seconds going through them. Ndidi guessed it contained the forged documents they needed to leave the country; using their real identification wasn't an option with Helene watching. Still, she couldn't help wondering what else might be inside.

There hadn't been a chance to go over the details, since Ndidi had been under constant surveillance at the Okafor Corporation, so she'd left all the arrangements to Pratima. Not that she could have contributed much anyway. Ndidi's father had ensured her training was thorough, but she must have missed the lesson on how to smuggle people out of the country. Fortunately, Pratima had retained some contacts from her years as an underground fighter; Ndidi's father had hired her out of that life.

Pratima finished with her inspection and nodded in satisfaction. Ndidi noticed the two men visibly relaxed at that, and she was lucky her niqab hid her smile. Pratima slung the two packs over her shoulders. "Your payment will be sent to you within the hour. It will be enough to buy your silence. If it is not, we will be in touch."

Her eyes were the only thing visible beneath the veil, and whatever the two men saw in them made them gulp. Pratima gave them another nod and turned toward the door. "Let us go," she said to Ndidi.

The men didn't follow them out.

It had been twilight when they had entered the hideout, and now it was fully dark. The market was empty, with only a few stores still open. The owners probably slept within the shop so they could open early the next day. There was a full moon out, which gave them enough light to see.

"Where to next?" Ndidi asked as they made their way through the market.

"We are going to need to cross the border," Pratima replied. "But even if we knew the area enough to make the attempt, it would be impossible for two women alone in the middle of the night. Fortunately, an old friend has agreed to help us, and he's sent a driver. It's not far."

Ndidi nodded. The extent of her knowledge on smuggling came from what she'd seen in movies. In those, it was fairly easy for two women to cross the border; all they needed was to flirt with the soldiers a little bit and probably make up an excuse about meeting up with their husbands.

Pratima led them through a narrow alley—without an opportunistic thug, fortunately—and out into another street. Nearby, a dog barked as two children darted around it, trying to catch its tail, while their mothers stood a few feet away, speaking in hushed voices. Several other people shuffled past, dragging their feet in obvious exhaustion after a long day.

At the far end of the street, around the corner, a rusted, beat-up truck sat with its engine idling. As they drew closer, Pratima slowed, and Ndidi instinctively tensed, scanning their surroundings. Her enhanced vision cut easily through the darkness, but no one else was in sight.

The driver was lean with a pinched face, like he'd just swallowed something disgusting. Pratima rapped on his door and pulled down her veil. The man nodded and motioned to the back. "Get in," he grunted.

They climbed in, the metal cold against their hands, and the truck rumbled as it pulled away. Ndidi glanced through the rear window before settling in beside Pratima. Pratima had placed the duffle bags on the floor of the car and was pulling out and reconfirming their contents. Ndidi saw two guns at the top of the pile.

"You want to stay low," the driver said from the front. "There's a checkpoint up ahead."

Both of them ducked and moved closer to the door so they wouldn't be visible to a casual check. The engine's hums vibrated through her chest as the truck slowed a minute later. Voices filtered in through the windows—the driver made a joke, the soldiers laughed and said something. Ndidi could probably have made out exactly what was being said if she tried, but most of her focus was on ensuring that her breathing wasn't too loud and that she didn't make too much noise when she shifted.

Fortunately, it only lasted a few moments. The engine picked up speed again, and the voices faded into the distance.

"We're lucky," the driver said, almost to himself. "The checkpoint's mostly unmanned at this hour."

There were several more checkpoints after that, and each time, Ndidi and Pratima flattened themselves to the floor of the truck. Once in a while, when the chattering went on for too long, Ndidi noticed the driver passing the soldiers something before they were allowed to go. Only once did the soldiers insist on checking the rest of the vehicle. Both women had silently reached for their weapons, but fortunately, the driver stretched out his hand a second time, and they were waved through.

In the darkness of the car, Ndidi allowed herself to imagine what would have happened if the soldier had continued to insist. Most likely, Ndidi and Pratima would have been forced to defend themselves.

Defend ourselves? Ndidi thought. *From what?* She'd heard some soldiers at other checkpoints talking about a missing pair of women, a Nigerian and an Indian, so she knew Helene and the Okafor Corporation were actively looking for them. But *these* soldiers hadn't mentioned it. And even if they had, it would have been because they believed they were looking for missing persons, trying to do the right thing, at least in their minds.

And yet, if it had come to that, Ndidi would have had no choice but to shoot them. She couldn't risk capture and couldn't afford to give Helene any clues about their location. Ndidi didn't know what she would do if she'd been forced to do that.

So far, Ndidi had miraculously escaped having to kill anyone in her vendetta against Helene. She'd only been in one fight early on, against Liz Polova, and it had sickened her enough that she'd sat back and allowed DJ to handle every mission that might have had even a hint of violence. It'd been easy too, since DJ was trained to handle missions like that.

But she wouldn't lie to herself. If the soldier had insisted on searching the truck, it wouldn't have been self-defense. It would have been her choice—her survival, her mission, over the lives of those men. She would have been doing the right thing. But then again, how many times over the last year had she thought she was doing the right thing?

The truck slowed, then stopped a minute later in front of a dilapidated warehouse. The driver killed the engine and turned to face them for the first time. "This is as far as I go," he said. He pointed at the warehouse. "Your next contact is inside."

Ndidi glanced at Pratima, who didn't look surprised. This was part of the plan then. They climbed out without another word, and Ndidi, stiff from her awkward position for most of the ride, took a moment to stretch.

The truck drove off, incredibly loud in the silence of the night—loud enough, Ndidi feared, to wake whatever waited for them inside.

DJ TURNED DOWN A HALLWAY on his way to the gym for his daily beatdown with Karla. He paused when he saw Chloe leaning against the wall beside the elevator at the other end of the passage. She gave a small wave and started walking toward him, her swaying hips highlighted by her tight leather pants.

DJ instinctively took a step back at the smile on her face, but the sound of footsteps forced his attention behind him. And walking toward him from the hallway he'd just left was Liz Polova, wearing a leather jumpsuit that clung to her curves like it was a second skin. DJ grimaced. Karla would kill him if she found out he'd perved on her sister.

"Take a picture," Chloe whispered in his ear. "It'll last longer."

There were several things wrong with that. First, DJ was certain he hadn't been looking at Liz for long. It'd been a second's glance, max. It should have been impossible for Chloe to have crossed the hallway in that time, unless she'd run—and if she had, it was impossible for DJ not to have heard her. With the enhancements from his nanites, he could pick up a conversation three rooms away.

So, DJ thought, holding back his frustration, *how the hell is the bitch still sneaking up on me?*

By the time he turned around, though, his grin was already in place. "Chloe! So nice of you to drop by. How're you doing? We haven't seen each other in, what, a month? Not since José kicked the snot outta me and banished his own daughter. That was crazy, huh?"

Chloe's eyes narrowed. That was all, but suddenly DJ's senses went off, like he was standing in front of a predator. He was used to getting that feeling from José or the Murder Twins. He'd always known Chloe was dangerous, but this was the first time he was so acutely aware that, as unassuming as she was, Chloe could kill him where he stood, probably before he even realized it, enhancements or no enhancements.

"Where is she?" she asked.

A part of DJ, the self-destructive part that made almost every captain in the Marine Corps hate him, wanted to give a flippant response. But Liz came to stand beside Chloe and DJ saw the look in her eyes and reconsidered. "She's several levels up. I can take you to her if you don't stab me."

"You lied to us about Karla being captured," Chloe said, raising a brow. "I'd always wondered if the nanites enhanced the balls as well."

"Please, my balls have always been this big," DJ scoffed, making his way toward the elevator. Chloe kept pace beside him, while Liz stayed a step behind. Having the redhead out of sight made his hackles rise, but he ignored it; she could stab him in the front just as easily as she could stab him in the back. "Shouldn't you already know, though, from José?"

Chloe smirked at his blatant fishing attempt. DJ could have been more subtle, but it annoyed the hell out of him that he didn't understand Chloe's relationship with the Murder Team. Karla and Liz were twin sisters, and José was their adopted father. But DJ had never had a clear read on what Chloe was. The twins didn't treat her as a mother, yet she'd helped José raise them since they were children. José also didn't treat her as a wife, or even a lover. It was weird.

It was a quiet elevator ride. DJ hadn't expected Liz to say anything, but he had expected Chloe to at least tease him. The silence was unnerving, which was bad because when DJ got unnerved, he tended to blurt the first thing that came to his mind. Fortunately, something occurred to him before he reached that point, a question he'd wanted to ask earlier. "José isn't loitering around here somewhere, is he?"

Liz tensed, but Chloe just scoffed. "Please, José would rather die than coddle the girls. In his head, if Karla got herself kidnapped, then she should be strong enough to escape without help."

DJ frowned. "That's some ass-backward parenting if I ever heard it. And didn't he bargain with Helene that one time though? When she captured Karla and Liz?"

"Ah, but that was Helene. *This* isn't. It's just one of her minions. At least to him," Chloe replied. "Plus that whole thing was while they were still conjoined, before they got their nanites."

"Now he expects them to be strong enough to face anything?"

"With the exception of Helene, they *are* strong enough to face anything," Chloe said. The elevator dinged open, and DJ led the way to the gym. He could see her point. Despite clashing with the twins several times, as both enemies and allies, he didn't think that he'd ever seen the extent of what they could do. That being said...

"You don't believe that," he stated confidently. "Otherwise you wouldn't have rushed over here."

Chloe shook her head. "No, you misunderstood me. I said *they*, as in both of them together, are strong enough to face anything. Because that is how we trained them. To only be complete when they are together. Separate and alone…?" Chloe made a face.

DJ glanced back at Liz and hesitated before asking his next question. "Then why didn't Liz follow Karla when she left?"

"They may have been raised as one, but they are still two people, DJ," Chloe said. "They have their own thoughts, make their own decisions."

DJ fell silent, absentmindedly taking turns until he was pushing open the door of the gym. Karla stood in the middle of the room, impatiently flipping a dagger between her knuckles like it was a goddamn coin. DJ blinked, and suddenly Liz was in front of her sister.

DJ had never seen Karla surprised—until now. She stared at Liz like she was looking at a ghost, one she couldn't stab. The sight hit him harder than he expected; it was depressing to realize she truly hadn't thought her sister would come for her. Granted, she didn't need rescuing—he'd lied about that—but still.

"Why...how are you here?" Karla asked, stumbling over her words. "I never thought José would give you permission."

"I did not ask," Liz said, shrugging lightly. "And I left before he could forbid me."

Karla tensed, probably imagining her father's reaction. And then she grinned. It was a terrible smile, like a wolf baring its fangs. "He must be furious. He banished me because I told him that he was too controlling, that he had his leash too tight on us for too long. By leaving, you proved me right. He must be going mad with anger."

She started laughing then, and DJ had to stop himself from covering his ears. *Jesus,* he grimaced, *I never thought I'd wish for her to go back to being broody and angry.*

As if she could hear him, Karla's laughter abruptly cut off, and she stared intensely at her sister. "You understand that he is going to see your actions as a betrayal? That means you can never go back to him. Will you stand with me?"

Liz's back was to him, so DJ couldn't see her expression. But he did hear her response loud and clear. "It has been too long since we have been synchronized, sister."

Karla took a step forward, her arms open as if she were going for a hug. But she stopped mid-motion and glared at DJ for no reason whatsoever. DJ's jaw dropped, and he started to say something, but the sisters had already continued their conversation—in Russian, for whatever reason.

"She was right, you know. When she called José a coward," Chloe said from beside him. She was staring at the twins, a small smile on her face. "I don't know what Helene did to him while she had him, but whatever it was, it messed him up good. For as long as I've known the man, he has never been afraid of anything. But there's actual fear in his eyes whenever Helene's name comes up. By rushing over despite the risks—something that José couldn't do—Liz has forced him to admit that he's afraid."

"So he won't come here, and he won't accept them back because he'd have to live with the fact that he's afraid?"

Chloe nodded. "I don't think he's so far gone that he would kill the girls. But me?" She sighed, and then turned fully to meet DJ's eyes. "I still want to stab you for tricking us—but I have to admit that your plan worked. You've hitched us to your wagon. Now, what was so important?"

DJ started to say something but paused and held a finger up. "Hold that thought. I'll have to contact everybody. This would be a good time for a general briefing." A thought occurred to him that made him chuckle. "My brother is not going to be happy with me for pulling him out. But meh, he'll be fine. He's been in there for hours already."

Chloe cocked her head to the side. "In where?"

CJ KNELT, WITH HIS FACE PRESSED up against the ground. It was all sand for miles, not a single blade of grass in sight. He'd spent a few hours moving in the vague direction of a tug he'd felt before, then decided he'd have to try something else. It would take too long to trek to each location, and there was far too high a chance the destination would end up being a dud. Once he gave up on that, he'd spent some time trying to decide whether it'd be more efficient to just delete this avatar and create a new one.

After all, when he'd created his current avatar, he'd spawned close to one of the places he was being tugged to—so it was possible that the same thing would happen again. But it was also possible that he'd be sent even farther away, or that this method—using Bethany's spores to dowse the places that Helene has been—was a one-time thing and it wouldn't work again if he deleted this avatar. There were too many unknowns for CJ to risk it.

And that's how he arrived where he was right then, kneeling with his face pressed against the dirt. He peered intensely at the tiny particles beneath him, trying to make out the ones and zeros that made them up. This was something that was second nature to him, but it was much easier in the city, where the large buildings made it easier to observe the basic codes of the Virtual Realm.

Size shouldn't matter, CJ thought. It might, when considering external codes added into the Realm, like the websites that made up the buildings of the city or the programs that ran the websites. But CJ was trying to observe the Realm itself. Its codes permeated everything. They should all be…connected.

CJ frowned, then stood. His eyes from the sand to the sky. Almost immediately he saw a large number one stretching across the sky. Beside it was a zero, and then another one in that order as far as the eye could see. CJ slowly lowered his head, following the gigantic tapestry until he was looking at the distant horizon. He lowered his head some more, somehow *uncrossed* his eyes, and suddenly he was staring at the ocean of little ones and zeros that made up the wasteland around him.

CJ knew his avatar didn't have a real heart that could speed up. That meant the excitement he felt was feedback from his actual body. He suppressed it. And only when he was sure he was completely focused did he kneel down once more, his nose almost touching the sand that was not actually sand but the digital blueprint that made up the Virtual Realm.

Ever so slowly, like he was picking up one of DJ's dirty socks, CJ reached down to one of the bits…and he shifted it.

Nothing happened—but CJ's breathing came quicker than the last. He could feel heat rising in his cheeks as his skin flushed with adrenaline. His heart felt like it was about to beat out of his chest. The feeling was so intense that CJ thought he could almost feel it through the avatar.

Wait, he paused, *I am feeling it through the avatar.* He placed a hand on his chest and finally noticed his fingers dissipating into the air. CJ frowned—then got angry. *He's pulling me out? Now? Is he serious—?*

The Virtual Realm dissolved around him, and CJ opened his eyes to meet his brother grinning down at him.

"Yeah, yeah, I know you're pissed," DJ said, straightening. "But rise and shine. We've got a meeting in five minutes."

DJ SAT AT THE HEAD OF the conference table, grinning at the rest of the team. "Come on, what's with all the gloomy faces?" His brother, sitting on his left, glared at him. Chloe rolled her eyes where she sat next to Karla and Liz, a chair away from CJ. On DJ's right-hand side, Christy looked ready to reach over and slap him. Hermione, sitting a chair away from her, just looked tired.

"*Would you just get on with it?*" Olsen barked through the conference-room video call. DJ had tried to reach Ndidi the same way, but she wasn't answering any of her messages, and her number was listed as unavailable when he'd tried her line. Since Ndidi was basically trapped with Helene, the whole thing was more than a little worrying. "*Some of us actually have a day job that we can't just leave,*" Olsen finished. The man's voice was gruff and patchy because of the connection, but it couldn't hide the undercurrent of weariness.

"Fine, fine. I understand that most of us were pulled out of something import-ant," DJ said, ignoring his brother's glare, "but we have three-quarters of the Murder

Team rejoining us, and they need to be caught up. I figured a general meeting would allow us to do that and keep the rest of us updated and on the same page."

Usually DJ would just meet with each person individually and ask for updates on their project, helping out as necessary. But that was time-consuming and stressful—not to mention counterproductive if anyone had a problem that working together could solve.

DJ turned to his brother. "Let's start with you, bro. What do you have for us?"

CJ was so pissed that it was like he forgot to be uncomfortable with talking in front of the group. He sighed. "As most of us are aware, when Manar and I went to the Virtual Realm to confront Helene, she managed to somehow trap Manar's consciousness there and take over his body." Suddenly, CJ jumped, and looked around the table guiltily. "So...um...I have been...uh...I have been working on rescuing Manar's consciousness."

"How's the progress?" DJ asked.

"Wait," Chloe interrupted. "What's this about Helene taking control of Manar's body? And what is a virtual realm? What the hell have you guys been doing for the last few months?"

DJ sighed. This was why they needed the briefing—but where to begin? He looked around the table, hoping that someone would let him off the hook and volunteer to fill them in. But the traitors all looked away (except Christy, but the laughter she was trying to hold in made it clear she wasn't going to be helpful). Chloe raised a brow at him, waiting for an explanation.

And with another sigh, DJ launched into the summary of the last few months. He started with what he knew they were aware of—the fight in the underground factory where José had given his life to save his daughters.

"They know all that already," Christy interrupted. "They were there, remember?"

"I was establishing a baseline," DJ muttered, "but whatever. It's fine. Let's fast forward." He skipped to explaining Manar's plan to take the fight to Helene by uploading his consciousness to the internet. "That's what the Virtual Realm is. Stupid name, right? But anyway..."

He explained how Ndidi's betrayal forced his brother to join Manar and how both were trapped there for months. "And you know what? She still thinks she did the right thing because she got Bethany back. Can you believe that shit? I mean, getting Bethany was a win, for sure. But do you know *how* we got Bethany? When we went to save Ndidi's ass because Helene manipulated her."

"They know that too." Christy sighed, rubbing the bridge of her nose. "They were there. That's how we found José."

"Oh yeah," DJ muttered, rubbing his chin. "I forgot about that."

"Can you please take this seriously?" Hermione muttered, her head on the table. "Some of us have better things to do. Like sleep."

"*Anyway,*" DJ said, glaring at Hermione, "the whole Virtual Realm stuff took a few months. CJ and Manar ended up defeating Helene. Except they didn't. Helene faked her death and used the chance to sneak into Manar's body. No, don't ask," he said when he saw Chloe about to speak. "No one knows how she did it. In fact, no one knew that she *had* done it until Ndidi found out and called us a couple of weeks ago that Helene, in Manar's body, had knocked her up and was pumping her child full of nanites and picospores in order to make some kind of super baby or something." DJ looked around the table. "Did I miss anything?"

"Tyra Chityothin," CJ said.

"Oh yeah," DJ snapped his fingers. He stared intensely at Chloe. "She's a bitch."

"*DJ...*" Olsen growled.

"I was gonna explain! God!" He blew out a breath. "Anyway, Tyra is Helene's henchwoman. Apparently, since Helene's cut off from her AI bullshit while in Manar's body, Tyra came out of the shadows to pick up the slack. She led a raid against us sometime back. Brought in a couple hundred drones and thralls, just to fuck with us."

"Just to fuck with you," Chloe repeated, smiling slightly. "No other reason."

"None that we can figure out anyway." DJ shrugged. "Like I said, she's a bitch. Now, any questions?"

Chloe wiggled her fingers. "Just one. Helene somehow trapped Manar Saleem's consciousness on the internet, took over his body, deceived you all, and impregnated Ndidi?"

"That's a... concise way to put it, but yeah."

"And now your brother is trying to rescue Manar's consciousness?" Chloe continued.

"Yes..."

"But if Helene is inhabiting Manar's body, where is his consciousness going to go if he succeeds?"

DJ started to reply, then paused with a frown. He turned to his brother. "CJ? You wanna take this one?"

CJ shook his head.

"Well..." DJ cleared his throat awkwardly. "I'm sure we'll cross the bridge when we get there. For now, let's continue with the briefing. CJ, you were filling us in on your progress?"

His brother sighed. "My...uh...my current theory is that Manar will be in a location that Helene visited frequently. And...um...I have figured out a way to find the places where Helene spent considerable time. The problem is that there are a dozen potential locations, and all of them are far away from each other. Helene could fly while in the Virtual Realm. I can't. Fifteen minutes ago, I discovered something that might help, but I was *rudely* yanked away before I could explore the option more." CJ was glaring at him again by the time he finished.

DJ rubbed the back of his neck. "Well, I'm sure that whoever interrupted you had a good reason for it."

He was about to continue, but Hermione lifted her head from the table, her eyes narrowing at CJ.

"Didn't you say you created something the last time you were there? Something that allowed you to go against Helene?"

CJ nodded sadly. "It...um...must have been destroyed when my previous avatar was deleted because I didn't spawn with it when I created this new one."

Hermione nodded as if what CJ had said made any lick of sense. "How long are you thinking?"

CJ frowned. "How long am I thinking about what?" DJ absently noted that his brother had become better with his facial expressions.

"How long do you estimate it would take you to make contact with Manar? We could use his brains around here."

CJ hesitated, thinking. Eventually, he shrugged. "I can't say. If my method is...uh...feasible, then it would be faster. If not, it might take months, if not years."

"*Years?*" DJ repeated in surprise.

CJ shrugged again. "The Virtual Realm is a big place, and right now I'm searching for a needle in a haystack."

DJ grimaced but nodded. He wouldn't pretend to understand half of what his brother spoke about when he explained the Virtual Realm and the things in it. But if nothing else, he trusted CJ, so if his brother said that it was complicated and he'd need some time, then DJ wasn't going to question it. "Just let us know if you need anything. Hermione, what about you?"

Hermione slowly raised her head from the table. "The usual. Bashing my head trying to figure out Helene's picospores. Recently, I've been experimenting with programming the spores to synthesize themselves from their host's biological material."

DJ blanched. "Why...why are you doing that?"

Hermione shrugged. "According to Ndidi, Helene has already figured out how to do it. I figured it would bite us in the ass later. But if I understand how to do it, I might be able to counter it. Don't hold your breath though."

"That's true," Christy said. "Where *is* Ndidi? Shouldn't she be here too?"

"She *should*," DJ agreed. "And she would have been, if I could get in touch with her or Pratima."

Christy leaned forward in her chair, and even Hermione straightened. "Wait, you can't reach her?" Christy asked. "Since when?"

"About a half hour ago? When I called the rest of you guys here."

"And you didn't think to say anything?" Hermione demanded.

"Don't do that." DJ's eyes narrowed, and his easygoing expression finally slipped off his face. He met Hermione's glare with one of his own. He didn't like the implication that he'd deliberately not said anything because of that. As much as he had issues with Ndidi, DJ would never do that.

"I informed Olsen before the meeting started because he's the only one with the connections to be able to actually *do* anything," DJ said. "And I didn't bother informing the rest of you because I knew it would cause this exact reaction." Hermione didn't apologize, but she *did* back down, which was what was important. DJ forced a smile back on his face. "Speaking of which…Olsen, any update?"

"That's Admiral Olsen, you disrespectful brat," Olsen said. *"And the answer's no. Tracking her cell gave us nothing. We're monitoring her social media right now even though I tried to tell the nerds that she's not going to have the opportunity or inclination to post her location. Her finances gave us nothing, but when we checked her bodyguards, we found that Pratima had made a series of small withdrawals over the last week. But the transactions were all made in different banks, equally spread out, so there's no way to narrow down a location from that."*

"Did you try what I suggested?"

Olsen sighed. *"Against my better judgment, I spoke with a few friends of mine, but they agreed that satellite imagery and surveillance was off the table unless we could get the Nigerian government to sign off on it. Which they will not do. And no, before you ask, we cannot just sneakily do it. If the Nigerian intelligence agencies notice, we'll have a diplomatic issue that no one wants to deal with."*

"So we got squat," DJ summarized.

"We have begun mobilizing some ground assets, but it's only been half an hour, so I wouldn't hold my breath on hearing anything soon."

"So that's it?" Hermione said. "We're just going to leave Ndidi in Helene's hands? Again?"

Both times, Ndidi was the one who willingly went to Helene, DJ thought, then immediately grimaced. That wasn't fair to her. The first time was hands down her fault, sure, but this time, they'd all been tricked. Plus…

"You're assuming that this has anything to do with Helene," he told Hermione.

"It's *Helene,*" Hermione said. "Of course it has to do with her. And Ndidi already told us the AI needs her baby for her big plan. Helene obviously captured her or something so she could do whatever she wanted to Ndidi."

"DJ has a point," CJ said, interrupting DJ before he could say anything. "E-even if Helene has had dealings with the Okafor Corporation before, this would be the first time that…um…that *Manar* has been there. In contrast, Ndidi owns the company and has lived there for most of her life. Helene would just be getting established in the new place, but Ndidi is already entrenched."

"Which means that it would be difficult for Helene to do anything to Ndidi there," DJ said. "So yeah, this could be related to something totally different."

"A coincidence?" Christy whispered, low enough so only he, and probably the Murder Twins, could hear. "Where Helene's involved? You don't really believe that, do you?"

Not even a little bit, DJ thought. It definitely had something to do with Helene. But there was very little they could do about it from halfway across the world. Whatever the problem was, Ndidi would have to figure it out by herself. *Or,* DJ snorted internally, *more like we'll figure it out and have to rescue her.*

"Olsen will give us updates once we get them," DJ continued, keeping his thoughts to himself, "and if she's in trouble, then we can all come up with a plan to help her together." It was obvious from her expression that Hermione didn't buy it one bit. But like DJ, she must have realized that there was nothing she could do about it. "In the meantime, Admiral? Wanna fill us in on your progress with the other stuff?"

"On that," Olsen said, *"we've had a little bit more progress, but not much. We haven't been able to find Tyra Chityothin's current location. We haven't even been able to narrow it down. Every avenue for tracking her down has failed. We aren't sure if it's the AI shutting us down or—"*

"It can't be Helene," CJ said, cutting Olsen off. He didn't even seem to realize that he'd done so. He was staring straight ahead, but his eyes showed that he wasn't all there. "She's limited herself while within Manar's body. All her skills should remain, but she no longer has the processing power to constantly and simultaneously monitor everything like she did before." He blinked, then looked around the table as if confused before he continued. "If...um...if she is interfering with your tracking, then she is doing it manually, and I... I do not think Helene would go through that effort for someone she probably considers a servant."

"She might, if Tyra is vital to whatever plans she has," DJ pointed out.

"Tyra has been in the shadows for years," Hermione said, "and she came out right now. We have to assume that whatever brought her out is important enough for Helene to want to protect it."

"Tyra doesn't need anyone's help to evade you guys," Chloe said, speaking up suddenly.

"I take it you are familiar with her?" Olsen asked.

"Professionally. Her name's come up a few times. Enough to know that if she doesn't want to be found, she's not going to be."

"Yes, it took us a while, but we realized that too. And when we did, we pivoted into searching for something that might force her out. Interestingly enough, when we finally found something promising, it was in another project that I was working on with DJ: the bomb that Helene seems to be developing."

Chloe raised a brow. "Bomb?"

DJ narrowed his eyes. He'd seen the bomb several months ago when they'd rescued Ndidi from the underground factory. It was a giant-ass thing, forty or fifty feet high. It hadn't been completed yet, but according to CJ, Manar had heard of a mysterious organization buying obscure and highly illegal materials off the dark web—the kind needed to make a bomb. Naturally, he'd immediately told Olsen about it, but they hadn't found a trace of it in months. Even going back to the underground factory only got them a cleared-out room and a bunch of wasted effort.

"You found something?" he asked.

"Something like that. When we couldn't find the thing itself, I remembered you said it wasn't complete. So we started looking into the materials. Some of the names I could get pretty easily, but most of them were locked up behind a clearance wall. After the president saw your report on it, however, the idiots finally coughed up the full list, and we've been tracking every known supplier since."

"And?" DJ pressed, leaning forward in his seat.

"And a couple of days ago, we finally got something. One of the suppliers was hit by—guess what? A swarm of weaponized drones. They lost all their products."

"It's obviously Tyra," DJ said.

"I know that, numbnuts," Olsen growled. *"The point is, the drones went underground before we could follow them, but—"*

"What do you mean underground?" DJ cut in. "They fly. They can't be that hard to track."

"*First of all,*" Olsen growled, "*none of the AI's drones can be tracked. They don't show up on any radar or sensor. Second of all, I meant that they literally went underground. They dug a goddamn tunnel and disappeared inside. And third of all, if you interrupt me one more time, you brat, I will come over there and break my foot off in your ass.*"

DJ winced. He might have gotten a bit too excited. "I'm sorry, I'm sorry. You were saying?"

Olsen took a deep breath. "*We were not able to follow the drones, but the nerds assure me that they have a pretty good idea where Tyra is going to strike next. And as the experts on all things related to Helene, the president has personally requested that your team be there.*"

DJ's grin was savage. "Well, if that's the president's orders..."

THE AIR INSIDE THE WAREHOUSE was cool and carried a faint smell of oil and metal. A bearded man in thick jeans and a jacket stood underneath the single bulb dangling from the ceiling. The light was too low to the ground, and most of the room was covered in shadow. Ndidi tensed instinctively but relaxed when she didn't see anyone else in the room. The man straightened when they entered.

"You're late," he said in a gruff voice.

This again? Ndidi thought. Pratima seemed to be tired of it as well because she didn't respond. The silence dragged on for a few tense seconds before the man continued, making his way toward them.

"Come on, let's go. The plane's waiting, but the pilot won't sit there forever."

Outside, he led them toward an old Jeep parked by the corner of the warehouse. The paint was chipped, and one of the doors didn't open from the outside, but it wasn't like they could afford to be picky. The man took the wheel, and Ndidi and Pratima climbed into the back seat.

"I'm Ayo, by the way," he said and then paused, probably expecting them to reply with their names. Ndidi covered up a yawn. She was far too exhausted for this. "We're going to move fast. Something has all the berets up in arms." He glanced at them in the rearview mirror. "You wouldn't know anything about that, would you?"

"Why would we?" Ndidi asked.

"Right," he muttered sarcastically. "Why would you indeed?"

The road to the airstrip was little more than a dirt path. The Jeep rattled with every bump, which was good because Ndidi would have dozed off otherwise. She'd been tense for most of the day, and the mental strain was catching up to her.

"Something's wrong," Ayo said sometime later.

Ndidi's eyes snapped open—When had she closed them?—and she leaned forward. "What is it?"

"Lights," he said, pointing to a distant glow. "There shouldn't be anyone here this late."

"Helene?" Ndidi whispered to Pratima.

"She can't have found us," Pratima said. "That wouldn't make sense. That was the entire reason we kept switching cars and stuck to the backroads. It could just be locals, or scavengers."

Neither of them said what they were thinking: Those methods might have been enough to fool a regular person, but this was Helene.

As they approached the lights, the outline of another car came into view—a pickup parked sideways across the road. Several figures stood around it, but Ndidi couldn't make out their faces through the glare of their headlights.

"Looks like a blockade," Ayo said. "We can't drive through."

"How far away are we from the airstrip?" Pratima asked, her hand resting on her gun.

"Not that far, a few minutes at most."

"Go around," Ndidi said.

Ayo hesitated. "We might miss the plane if we take much longer."

Ndidi didn't say anything. After a few seconds, Ayo put the car in reverse and turned off the road into the bush. The path was rough with thick undergrowth, but they managed to keep moving. The lights from the blockade grew distant, swallowed by the trees. But within a minute, another light grew in front of them and the outline of vehicles became visible again. The Jeep skidded to a halt.

"We're surrounded," Ayo said. "Now, this is probably a stupid question, but is there any chance the blockade is for someone else?"

Ndidi ignored him, peering through the back window. She couldn't make out more than vague shapes, outlines of people moving through the bushes around them. But that was enough. They were closing the net. It was possible that the blockade was completely unrelated and that they'd stepped into a trap by coincidence. But either way, it was already too late to back out. Still, no matter how unlikely, Ndidi would prefer to believe that than believe Helene was involved.

Because if it was Helene, how had she tracked them? They'd been so careful.

It was possible that Chinedu had set up similar traps at every airstrip in the Federal Capital Territory, Abuja. She and Pratima had planned for that, crossing two state borders to put enough distance between themselves and the city. Apparently it hadn't been enough.

Pratima handed Ndidi a pack. "We need to move."

Ndidi took it and checked the pistol by her side. Would she have to fire it? Would she choose her own survival over someone else's life? Was *that* the right choice? Her hands trembled. "What are our options?" she asked softly.

Pratima didn't answer immediately, her eyes on the windows and the road ahead. It was too dark to make out faces or details, but the people outside were close enough to see clearly as shapes moving together. They stayed a few yards out, as if waiting for a signal. "We cannot fight through this," Pratima said finally. "Not out in the open, with so little cover and so few of us."

"Then what?"

Pratima pulled something from her bag and tossed it to her. Ndidi had never seen dynamite outside of movies. She wondered where Pratima had acquired it—though that line of thought was mostly to distract her from the reality of what she was holding.

"We will run," Pratima said, "but we will need a distraction for us to succeed. Light it, then throw it into the trees where the most men are gathered. And then we will run that way, where there is a gap in their circle."

She pointed east. But the airstrip was to the north, and getting to that plane was the only way they were going to survive this without getting captured. Ndidi was sure Pratima knew that, too, which meant part of her plan was to take a wide arc and then double back in the right direction. But it would take too long to run far enough to evade pursuit, and it would take even longer if they had to sneak back. The plane would have left by then. And if it hadn't, the idiots surrounding them would obviously recognize the airstrip as their goal and simply wait for them there.

"It won't work," Ndidi said and then summarized her reasoning.

To her credit, Pratima didn't waste time arguing, even though she would have been justified, since she was the expert. Instead, she took a break from monitoring the figures to glance at Ndidi. "What do you suggest?"

Ayo shifted uncomfortably in the front seat. "Is there a plan? Because they're moving closer."

Ndidi ignored him. "We can't afford the time it would take to double back. We need to run straight to the airstrip. Ayo said we're only a few minutes away so we should be able to make it."

Pratima shook her head. "If we run straight, they will pick us off before we're halfway there.

"You're right. We'll need something to distract them," Ndidi said, holding up the stick of dynamite.

It took a few minutes to set it up, during which time the idiots had drawn close enough that Ndidi could start to make out a few faces. She figured that they were about fifty feet out. That was good; it would only take a few seconds for them to clear that distance. Beside her, Ayo stared at his gun with barely contained terror. Ndidi empathized with him, but the man didn't need empathy at that moment.

"For Christ's sake, it's not going to bite you," Ndidi whispered harshly. "You're a smuggler. There's no way this is your first gun fight."

"Of course I've never been in a gunfight," Ayo replied, looking affronted, "because I'm actually *good* at what I do. This is Nigeria. We own most of the authorities up to their second cousins. And when new ones are brought in with a conscience, we're warned days in advance so we can plan and work around the inconvenience."

Work around the inconvenience, Ndidi repeated in her mind. What the hell was wrong with this country? "Look, if it's too scary for you, then you can stay with the car."

Ayo gave her a flat look. But he was forced to swallow whatever he'd been going to say when Pratima crawled out from underneath the Jeep. She nodded at Ndidi's questioning look and held up a spool of rope that led under the car. "Where?"

Ndidi pointed directly in front of them and to the side, where, in the dark, the men surrounding them didn't realize they'd left a little too much space between each other. "We'll have to sprint if we're going to clear the distance in time," Ndidi said, more for Ayo's benefit.

Pratima took a second to recheck her gun. Ndidi did the same, though with far less ease. Pratima raised a small lighter and moved the fire toward the rope. An inch from it, she met Ndidi's eyes. *Are you ready?* Her gaze asked. Ndidi didn't know the answer, but she nodded all the same.

The fire licked the rope.

"*Go!*" Pratima hissed.

Ndidi ran. *Five,* she counted in her head.

Pratima passed her easily, though she stayed just a few feet in front of Ndidi, as if she intended to block any shots that came their way. Knowing her, she probably did. Ndidi could only hope that the men didn't have time to shoot, because Ndidi couldn't pump her legs any faster. She risked a glance behind her and found Ayo stumbling after them, his face frozen in an open-mouth scream.

Four.

Ndidi snapped her head forward as the sound of a gun being cocked pierced through the thrum of her heartbeat. It was too late, though, because Pratima was already tackling the man to the ground.

Three.

Ndidi tore through the underbrush a second later, ignoring the half a dozen men belatedly raising weapons. She gave a kick to the man on the ground, helped Pratima up, and continued running.

Two.

She could sense the men's eyes on her; she felt the guns trained on her back.

One.

The Jeep exploded.

Ndidi flinched, even though she'd expected it. The blast tore through the silence of the night like a knife through butter. It echoed in her ears and drowned out everything but her own ragged breathing. Heat blossomed all around them, searing her back. The shockwave crossed the distance faster than they had, and the force knocked some wind out of her. The ground bucked beneath her, and Ndidi stumbled but kept running. The air was quickly filled with smoke and the stench of scorched oil and burning rubber.

Ndidi didn't look back, but she imagined the chaos that the blast must have caused. The men had already been closing in on the Jeep before they'd run so several of them would have been in the blast radius. The ones who hadn't would hopefully have been caught by shrapnel. Either way, the fire and smoke should cover their tracks for a little bit, at least enough for them to get a head start to the airstrip. That was *if* Ndidi could make it to the airstrip. Her legs were burning, and she was panting, despite the adrenaline coursing through her.

Suddenly, Pratima appeared by her side. "Keep moving," she said. Ndidi jumped and swung her pistol without thinking. Pratima calmly ducked beneath it, not even losing her stride. "Your plan worked. The blast scattered their formation, and the light blinded most of them, leaving them scrambling in chaos. Allah willing, it lasts until we reach—"

"The driver?" Ndidi asked, her voice tight.

"He ran too slow," Pratima said, softly. "He was still within the blast radius when it went off. He was hit by shrapnel."

Ndidi's lips pulled into a line, but she didn't reply. They continued running, and Ndidi allowed the burn in her legs to distract her. It was easy. The excitement of the day had left her mentally exhausted, so her thoughts came slowly, and she focused all of them on putting one foot in front of the other.

At some point, Pratima nudged her, and Ndidi raised her head and finally noticed the airstrip a dozen feet away, dimly lit by the moon. The underbrush still covered them, so Pratima gestured for her to slow down, and they made their way toward it as silently as they could. Ndidi was focused on her feet—placing her steps deliberately to avoid giving their position away—so Pratima was the first to spot them. Four men stood around the plane: one near the nose, a rifle slung over his shoulder, another leaning against the wing, and two others holding the pilot between them, a pistol pressed to his temple.

All four were shouting at each other, and more than a few gestures were made in their direction. At first, Ndidi thought they'd been spotted. But no, the men had seen the explosion and were discussing what to do.

"Ndidi..." Pratima started softly. Ndidi nodded sharply, cutting her off. There were too many for Pratima to handle herself, especially with the pilot still being held hostage. If they were going to succeed, Ndidi would have to pull her weight. She'd have to choose her survival over the lives of the men.

"Take the left," she said, trying to keep her voice steady. She gripped her pistol, ignoring the sweat on it. Her heart thudded painfully in her chest. Was she ready for this?

Pratima didn't give Ndidi a chance to back out. She nodded once and immediately broke right. Ndidi exhaled, raising her gun. *Breathe. Aim. Don't overthink it.*

A shot broke through the silence, sharp, deafening. Ndidi barely realized that it was hers until the man by the wing dropped. There was a split-second pause while the others tried to process what'd happened. Pratima's shot dropped the one at the plane's nose in that instant.

The remaining two finally reacted, ducking under the plane. Ndidi had hoped they would forget about the pilot while trying to figure out where the shots had come from—but only one of them pulled away, while the other held the pilot closer, as if planning to use him as a shield.

Ndidi was sprinting before she'd consciously decided to. She ignored the way her stomach twisted, or how her heartbeat thudded in her ears. This wasn't sparring, and there were no second chances. The men had probably been asked to capture her alive but Ndidi doubted either of them would remember that in the moment.

As if to confirm it, bullets zipped past her, kicking up dirt where they landed. Ndidi flinched and then dropped flat as a burst of automatic fire sprayed the ground nearby. One of them must have found their teammate's rifle.

"Cover me!" Pratima yelled, darting toward the plane.

Ndidi forced herself to a knee, used two hands to steady her pistol, and aimed at where she could see the two men. One of the men went down, clutching his chest. The other fired wildly, rounds pinging off metal. Pratima reached the plane but cried out as a bullet tore through her thigh. She collapsed, clutching her leg.

Shit, Ndidi thought, charging forward. On the ground and probably bleeding out, Pratima continued shooting at the man, forcing him to take cover. That allowed Ndidi to cross the distance until she was close enough that her shaking hands didn't stop her from putting a round in the last man's shoulder. His gun went sprawling away and Ndidi put another round in his leg when he tried to dive for it. A kick to his head knocked him out for good.

"Get up!" Ndidi shouted to the pilot, who'd stayed on the ground, staring at one of the men with wide eyes. "We're leaving."

She scrambled to Pratima, grabbing her under the arms and helping her into the plane. Thankfully, the pilot was already inside shouting something Ndidi couldn't hear over the roar of the engine. Ndidi climbed in after Pratima and closed the door just as a group of men rushed onto the airstrip, guns raised.

Too late, Ndidi thought, as the plane lurched into the sky. For a moment, all Ndidi could hear was the thrum of the engine and Pratima's labored breathing.

"We made it," Pratima rasped, blood soaking her fingers.

Ndidi didn't reply. Her hands wouldn't stop shaking.

CHAPTER

9

DECEMBER 2043
VIRTUAL REALM

CJ MATERIALIZED UNDER BLUE SKIES and barren lands, exactly where he'd stood before his brother had yanked him out. He relaxed. He didn't know when, but at some point, he'd become more comfortable in the Virtual Realm than anywhere else. It could have been because during his first foray to the Realm, he had a taste of a side of himself that he hadn't known existed. That was certainly part of it.

But more likely, CJ thought, *it's because I don't have to pretend here.*

With Bethany's picospores running through his veins, and their commands blocking off his autism symptoms, CJ had finally achieved what he'd wanted since he was old enough to realize it: He was finally normal. He could speak without stuttering, smile without spending his full focus on it, and could remember the name of his favorite artist at the drop of a hat. CJ had expected to feel more excited about all that. And he would have…

If he didn't have to hide it.

DJ had locked him up in their room for days after he'd caught CJ trying to inject himself with the picospores. If he found out that he'd succeeded...CJ didn't know what he would do. *That's a lie.* He sighed to himself. CJ knew that DJ's issue wasn't with using the spores to cure his autism; it was using them while Helene was still active as a threat. He was afraid that she would turn CJ into one of her thralls.

But if DJ found out that CJ had already inoculated himself, his brother wasn't going to hold him down to extract them—which was only possible because Bethany's spores were an earlier version, from before Helene had made them impossible to extract without rendering their host comatose. As angry as DJ would be, he would never do that to CJ. Still, it wasn't a conversation that CJ was ready to have.

And so he pretended. But even that was harder than he'd thought. He'd slipped up several times during their meeting when he spoke without stuttering. *Maybe I just shouldn't talk at all? How frequently did I speak before?*

CJ grimaced and then shook the thought out of his head. He had better things to think about.

He stared at the wasteland, picturing what he'd done the last time. First, he had to replicate it, and then he'd try expanding on it. With some luck, he'd get somewhere before his brother pulled him out again.

He dropped to the ground, scanning the area of sand that he'd altered before. But after searching for a quarter of an hour without finding the specific line of code, he was forced to give up. CJ straightened, sitting on the back of his legs. Either he was searching in the wrong area, or the Virtual Realm had ways to repair itself. Both were possible—he was pretty sure that he'd searched the right place, but it wasn't like he couldn't be wrong, especially since everything looked like everything else. Still, CJ favored the repair theory. It was logical for an ecosystem, digital or otherwise, to have ways of correcting itself.

But it's not like it matters anyway, he thought. Finding the altered line of code would have given him a reference, but CJ had planned to repeat the same thing regardless. So, it was all the same.

Now that he'd discovered the trick, he could take in the ocean of codes that made up the wasteland. It stretched endlessly before him, a vast landscape of tapestries woven infinitely together. CJ focused on the ground in front of him. There was no noise and no wind, so it was easy to block out everything. This was different from when he lost himself in his mind. He was still conscious of everything around him, but it was in the way a person was conscious of the leaves on a tree they weren't actively studying; they knew the tree had leaves, but they didn't pay them any attention. It was all background.

All his focus was on the grains of sand and the codes that shaped them. He closed his eyes, but the codes were still vivid in his mind. He reached his hand out, palms wide open, and the lines jumped at him. He traced a section and could almost feel the flow of data, like a heartbeat pulsing under his touch.

It's familiar, he thought with a frown. He'd felt this before, months ago, when he'd bonded with the Sphere. With it, CJ had been able to manipulate small sections of the Virtual Realm. Each time he'd done so, he'd felt this pulse, but he hadn't realized it because it had been the Sphere handling the flow of data; CJ had just been directing it. He didn't have the Sphere now, so he had to do it all by himself. He spread out his awareness—

—and plunged into a tidal wave.

Data rushed into him like a flood. His mind crashed against the torrent of information, and he almost immediately lost himself. In a fraction of a second, he passed through dozens of websites and went through hundreds of files, thousands of transactions, and millions of conversations. He was bombarded by images, sounds, whispers of fragments of conversations, and the flickers of memories from billions of people across the world. CJ felt his mind splinter to try to make sense of it. In his mind's eye, his vision split into countless windows, each spilling out flashes of someone else's life—a boy chatting with the girlfriend who was cheating on him, a doctor typing out a report of consanguinity in a family, a hacker breaking into an organization's database. It was endless.

As CJ struggled not to lose himself in it, his avatar flickered, and an infinitesimally minute part of CJ wondered what would happen if he was pulled out now. Would the stream stop, or would it continue to burn out his brain?

The thought started small, but CJ latched on to it with the strength of a drowning man. Somehow, he'd tapped into the pulse of the Realm, and if he continued to let it flow through him, then there wasn't going to be *him* for much longer; just another stream of data, and a body trapped forever in a coma.

That might be what finally pushes DJ over the edge, a fragment of his mind thought. CJ rallied the remaining fragments, centering himself on that thought. DJ would never be able to move on, and CJ couldn't let his brother suffer like that. He *had* to survive this.

CJ had been right in that there was no such thing as distance in the Virtual Realm. So, the pieces of his mind were both close and a world apart. CJ strained against the tide, using the beacon that was his avatar to drag himself back together. He couldn't say how long it took, but eventually he was no longer bombarded by millions of pieces of information per second. He limited his consciousness to an area that stretched several yards around him. Even that threatened to overwhelm him, but CJ was better able to handle it after his ordeal. It also helped that there wasn't so much data passing through the wasteland. What little there was, CJ filtered out until it was nothing but background noise.

Once that was done, it was easier to search the tapestry for patterns, the points that he could change without unraveling the entire tapestry. There was a section a few feet from him that was denser than the others, with interwoven loops of codes that made mirrors of themselves, almost like a self-replicating pattern. CJ started to take a step toward it and then paused to reach out with his awareness instead. He was careful to continue filtering out the background noise, even as he reached out slowly with his mind. He studied the knot closely, then observed how it connected with the larger tapestry.

Finally, he slowly, *slowly*, reached out. He shifted one of the lines to the left, exchanged another one to replace it, and continued like that, as if he were rearranging the pieces of a puzzle. Eventually, the knot began to loosen, but CJ was more focused on the changes he could feel in the landscape. A flash of excitement and fear surged through the section of the void where his mind was, but CJ ruthlessly suppressed them both before they could threaten his focus. He continued his work on the knot until it fully unraveled, releasing a wave of data that spread out over the ocean of code. Finally, CJ opened his eyes.

And met a field of green. A field that wasn't just growing—it was waking up.

"DJ," OLSEN SAID, his voice gruffer than usual through his comm. *"Are you there? Come in."*

It had to be a desert, DJ thought, wiping the sweat from his eyes. It'd been less than five minutes since the helicopter dropped them off, but DJ was already baking. The air was still and thick, but it carried a faint metallic tang from God knows where. "I'm with you," he replied.

He squinted against the glare of the sun and stared at the endless expanse of hardened clay and cracked earth. It was just miles and miles of flat terrain with little to break the monotony except distant mountains and small patches of wiry desert brush.

But it wasn't always like that. He glanced to his left, where only a collection of trailers and rusted-out vehicles remained as a memory of a time when the area had seen a bit of life. From the rust, DJ figured that had been decades ago. Overhead the sky was a vast, piercing blue, clear and empty so the sun could better boil them. DJ turned his gaze eastward, where a narrow road cut across the desert toward the horizon. It was one of the few routes out and was probably one of Tyra's planned escape paths. DJ almost hoped she would take it. But if she did, that meant he'd failed his part.

"Our satellites cannot find any evidence that anyone has been here in several months. But we never planned on relying on that. You're to assume that Tyra beat us here and is waiting for us."

Duh, DJ thought. The entire team had moved shortly after Olsen had received the information, but it had still taken them nine hours to get there from New York. Tyra had probably started moving days before them, but she would have been slowed down by her need to avoid detection. Hopefully that meant that they'd arrived just hours after her, not days or more. Regardless, she'd have had more than enough time to plant a few surprises. With the unknowns, DJ would have preferred to recon first, but the helicopter meant any chance of that was shot.

They'd have to settle for what they had.

"I know this," DJ told Olsen. He switched the channel on his comm to the raid chat. "Everybody in position? Roll call. Christy."

"Locked in," she replied.

"Chloe?"

The sound of yawning came through the speakers. *"I'm already bored. Let's just get this started."*

DJ ignored her. "Karla?"

Silence.

DJ rubbed the bridge of his nose. "Liz?"

"We are ready," Liz replied. Both Karla and Liz had refused any plan where they were not together. It kind of sucked since they were their two best fighters, so splitting them up made the most sense. But they had refused to budge, even when Chloe had tried, so DJ had paired them up. He consoled himself with what Chloe had said about how they were unbalanced when split up.

"Good. Let's move in." The order was for everyone except Christy. As a sniper, she would be best suited to watch the area and guard the entrance. Everyone else would be trying to flush Tyra out from wherever she was hiding.

From the outside, the facility resembled a former military installation. Half-forgotten and remote, it blended seamlessly with the desert. DJ studied it for a moment, noting the squat, concrete structure that stretched into a series of interconnected buildings and bunkers. The exterior walls were weathered and cracked, sun-bleached to a dull gray that made the whole thing look like it'd risen straight from the earth. A low perimeter fence circled the compound, rusted in several spots, with coils of barbed wire sagging from years-long neglect. Near the main gate, faded signs in a blocky, military-style font warned of restricted access and high surveillance. The surveillance in question hung on the building's corners, many of them with lenses clouded with dust.

Put together, the facility was a story of abandonment and extreme neglect—*not* the repurposed high-security storage facility that it once was.

DJ made his way into the central building, where the interior was markedly different. It had a utilitarian design, with narrow corridors and reinforced doors. There were few windows, also reinforced, allowing only silvers of natural light to filter in. His nanites ensured he had no trouble seeing, but the average person would be stumbling around, nearly blind.

The section he was in must have been reconfigured into a storage wing at some point because the walls were lined with secure compartments and heavy-duty storage lockers. A few doors led to smaller rooms that had probably once been used for briefings or planning sessions. Now the rooms had been repurposed to store objects of interest. DJ noted faint markings along the floors—a network of lines and numbers stamped into the concrete, possibly remnants from when the facility coordinated troop or equipment movement. *The lines should converge at central points, where the larger and more fortified storage rooms are.*

As DJ moved from the section, he pulled up a mental map of the place, and slowly moved toward where Olsen had estimated their target was kept. Everywhere was silent, which said something, considering the new range of his hearing after his enhancement. His guns were out, and he kept his footfalls light as he crossed one hallway after another.

"Progress report," DJ whispered softly, after several minutes of silence. He wasn't far from the target now, which meant the others should be close as well, coming in from different directions.

"Nothing on my side except the smoke coming from my ass," Christy said. *"I should have found a better cover to set up in."*

"It's not as if you had a lot of options," DJ replied. "But maybe next time. Liz?

"My sister and I have seen nothing."

"Chloe?"

"Still bored," she yawned. *"Maybe the girl's a no-show."*

That was a possibility, but he doubted it. Granted, he had no evidence other than his gut, but DJ's gut hadn't led him wrong yet. He opened his mouth to reply but paused when he noticed a glint from the corner of a wall. DJ slowed even further and crouched when he was a foot away. It was a small metallic device, no bigger than his thumb, and rectangular. DJ would have thought it was something left over from before the facility was abandoned, but there was no rust on the device—or *dust*. It had obviously been placed there recently, but the way it was positioned gave the impression that it'd been carelessly tossed aside.

That doesn't necessarily mean it isn't a trap though, DJ thought, leaning over the device. It didn't look like an explosive, but DJ could have been missing something. He studied it for another minute before shrugging. *I'll let Olsen's nerds figure it out.* He reached down and picked it up. Immediately, his instincts started screaming at him. DJ threw the device away, but it was too late. A soft click echoed in the passage, and there was a subtle shift in the air as a hum picked up around him. A second later, metal plates slid out from the wall to block off the corridors. DJ had a second to react. "It's a trap!" he screamed into his comm. "Rendezvous at the target as fast as you can. She's trying to isolate us. Christy, anything?"

"It's still clear out here," Christy replied. *"No movement at all. Whatever this is, she set it up ahead of time."*

Yeah, and I set it off like a freaking idiot, DJ cursed. "Olsen, the building's gone into lockdown mode. Everywhere is cut off from everywhere else. How do we shut it off?"

"We can't," Olsen replied. *"The facility's systems are on a separate server. We'd have to be on site to control it."*

"Then that means Tyra has been here long enough to access the server and still go around the facility to set her traps," DJ realized. "In that time, she could have stolen what she came for and gone before we even got here. But she stayed just to fuck with us."

He felt the familiar rage build up within him as he continued moving through the narrow corridors toward the target. Metal walls cut off several passages in the middle, but DJ simply pivoted and tried another path, following the mental map in his head. He was a couple of passages away from the target when he rounded a corner and stopped short. In the middle of the hallway was a makeshift barricade blocking the way forward. Behind it, a familiar face smirked at him.

"Still no sign of Tyra, DJ," Christy said over the comm.

"That's understandable," DJ replied softly, "considering she's standing right in front of me."

DECEMBER 2043
BLACK ROCK DESERT, NEVADA

"HEYYYY, DJ," TYRA DRAWLED, a grin stretched across her face. She leaned against the barricade, still wearing her signature labcoat. "Funny seeing you here. What brings you?"

That's how she wants to play it? He pushed down the anger raging inside of him and forced a grin onto his face. He stopped a few feet in front of the barricade and gave his most casual shrug. "I heard Nevada was beautiful this time of the year, and I just *had* to check it out. Nothing says Christmas like endless sand and sun that'll roast you alive, y'know? What about you? Here for the sights as well?"

Tyra's grin grew. "Not me. I'm way too busy for that. I just came here to pick up something, embarrass a few old friends, and jet out. You know how it is. I played a prank I honestly didn't think anyone would be dumb enough to fall for. And what do you know? They actually *fell* for it." She barked a laugh, and the sound echoed through the corridor. "But I guess that's what I get for overestimating someone."

From somewhere close by, several deep, reverberating impacts echoed through the corridors. Each blow landed like a sledgehammer and sent heavy vibrations through the walls. DJ paused at the sound, then ignored it. He also ignored Tyra's obvious taunt, as hard as that was, and focused on keeping his smile in place. "Jet out?" he asked, raising a brow. "You don't really think that you're leaving here, do you?"

"You don't really think you can keep me, do you?" she countered, her eyes twinkling. She must have known that they had the place surrounded, but there wasn't even a hint of concern in her expression. Was she just bluffing? Or was there something he'd missed?

Tyra tapped a finger to her chin. "I wonder what makes you so confident. Is it maybe the brute currently trying to break down a five-inch reinforced steel wall?"

On cue, the impact came again, and the whole building shook with the force of it. DJ kept his eyes on Tyra, though he could sense the direction the sound had come from. The best option was to wait for Karla to break through to the wall and let the group go after Tyra together. But DJ couldn't count on that since he wasn't sure it was even possible. Karla was strong, but everything had limits. Plus, it wasn't like Tyra was going to wait around while he got reinforcements.

Right now, she was calm and unconcerned, but that was probably because she believed she could handle anything DJ threw at her. He was tempted to show her how wrong she was, but he knew better than to simply charge. So he stayed put and ignored the frustration boiling beneath his skin.

Suddenly, DJ frowned, glancing around. The pounding had stopped, and the building was eerily still. *Did she break through? Or did she give up?*

"Oh," Tyra purred, "don't look so confused. You didn't think I came alone, did you?"

DJ narrowed his eyes as he pressed a finger to his ear. "Anything I should know, Christy?"

"Still no movement around the building," Christy replied. *"Though the whole thing was shaking a few seconds ago, but from my vantage point, I can't see what's causing it. Tyra's up to something, that's for sure."*

"That's what I'm trying to figure out. Out." He switched the channel, and immediately, he was blasted with the sound of gunfire. "Liz!" he shouted so he was heard over the noise. "What the hell is happening over there?"

"Drones," Liz grunted back. The word had more annoyance to it than actual concern, which made DJ believe the twins weren't in any actual danger. *Of course they aren't,* DJ thought. *They've fought swarms of these things at once.*

But while the Murder Twins would be able to handle a few drones, others might not. "Hey, Chloe—still bored?"

"Not as much anymore," she replied immediately, not even sounding out of breath. *"But you know, DJ, there are better ways to entertain a lady. Not that the drones aren't fun, but they won't even bleed when I tear them apart. They're just a bunch of teases."*

DJ made a face. *What the hell is* wrong *with her?* "Get here in the next few minutes, and you should be able to get what you want."

"Promises, promises," Chloe tsked before she cut the channel off—just in time for DJ to notice Tyra slipping down the passage, away from him and toward the room that held what they'd come for.

"Where do you think you're going?" he snapped at her.

She smiled over her shoulder. "I wish I could stay, Darren, but playtime's over. Now, I gotta jet out before the place becomes noisy."

"All the more reason for you to stay," DJ said, leaping over the makeshift barricade. He started to kick off his back foot, then stopped. Everything in him wanted to charge over to her and deck her right in her smirking face. But that was the anger clouding his judgment. Their last fight had proven he couldn't beat her in close combat. His training with Karla meant he'd improved since then, but why risk it? His job was to hold her down until either Chloe or the Murder Twins made it to them.

He could hold her down. After all, their last fight in Sparta had proven that, unlike the twins, Tyra wasn't bulletproof.

His guns were already in his hands, and DJ squeezed out a shot a split second later. It should have been an easy shot, since Tyra had her back toward him. But evidently, Tyra wasn't as relaxed as she'd pretended because she turned the moment DJ lifted his gun and was moving out of the way a nanosecond before he squeezed the trigger. Her right hand flashed, and a *ding* echoed through the corridor. Tyra stood there for a moment, smirking with her fist raised.

Then, with far more drama than was strictly necessary, she splayed open her fingers, and a bullet fell to the floor. DJ squinted at her, and then he groaned.

"Do you like it?" Tyra asked, wriggling the fingers on her new prosthetic hand. "I loved the old one, but I was forced to upgrade, and I can't say I'm disappointed. You know what they say..." She grinned at him. "New is always better."

Tell that to scotch companies, DJ thought, raising the gun again. He squeezed off three shots, one after the other, aiming in different places each time. The Murder Twins had a full half of their body made of a bulletproof material, so for them shielding was as simple as turning to one side. But Tyra only had five fingers to use, and she'd barely had weeks to get used to them. Surely he should be able to find a weak—

Tyra's hand blurred, and with a thought, DJ stimulated his nanites until they came back into focus. Because of that, he could literally see Tyra pluck the bullets out of the air, one after the other.

DJ sighed. *This is bullshit. All of it.*

"Tingles," Tyra said, letting the bullets fall from between her fingers. DJ holstered his guns. At this point, he didn't even know why he still carried them. Maybe he was hoping that he'd eventually get lucky and the bad guy would be able to get shot like a regular person.

Until then, he thought, bringing out the new pair of daggers that he'd had made, *I'll do things the old-fashioned way.*

With a relieved sigh, he stopped holding back the part of himself that'd wanted this from the beginning, and launched himself at Tyra.

She met him with a crazy grin.

DJ struck out with a punch that Tyra easily countered, but then followed it up with a relentless barrage that finally let loose all the rage he'd been holding back in the weeks since the raid. There'd never been any safe outlet for it, so DJ had pushed it down, again and again.

All for this moment.

DJ had been training with Karla almost every day. And although he couldn't say that he'd mastered the new techniques, he'd absorbed enough to utilize his new attributes. His movements were fluid and precise, and every strike brought out the full force of his strength. But Tyra met him with her own rhythm, blocking, deflecting, or evading each strike with that infuriating grin on her face.

Their movements merged into a rage-filled frenzy, and their attacks sped up, each strike thudding with enough power to reverberate through the room. DJ swung a right hook with enough force to dent the metal wall, then smoothly transitioned into a mid-high kick that *would* have ruptured several organs. But Tyra pivoted and caught his ankle. She tried to pull him off-balance, but DJ's leg was like a steel beam. He spun out of her grip, and his heel grazed her shoulder before dropping to the floor and resetting the sequence.

For a moment, they stared at each other—DJ with hate-filled eyes, Tyra with a mocking smile—before they both darted in at the same time. For the next minute, the entire corridor was filled with a symphony of focused violence. DJ struggled not to lose himself in his overwhelming anger. He tried to read her moves—to adapt and then predict her. But she'd learned her lesson from the last time they'd clashed. Now her moves were completely random, with no reason to them except for the fact that they worked.

Still, their first fight had proven that DJ was the better fighter, and that hadn't changed. Slowly, the momentum of the fight was shifting in his favor. Tyra must have realized it, but her eyes never lost their challenge. DJ ignored the taunt and focused on tightening the web.

And then finally—there. DJ aimed a low kick to Tyra's heel, knocking her off-balance. She stumbled, and DJ lunged. His fist was halfway to her jaw when he noticed the glint of metal in her hand. DJ's fist blurred, but somehow—*somehow*—the bitch twisted out of way in the same moment that a sharp, stinging sensation cut across his side.

DJ tried to ignore the pain, to counter before she could create some distance. But a wave of fire washed over him, originating from his side. It stung far more than a simple cut should, especially since his nanites should have already been working on the wound. Tyra spun the knife in the air, and a droplet fell to the ground.

DJ's eyes widened. "Fucking poison?" he gasped as another wave of fire burned through him. He stumbled again, and his daggers slipped from his suddenly sweaty hands. "Seriously?"

DJ's vision was starting to blur, but he could see Tyra pull something familiar from her pocket and flick it into the air. "This was fun." She winked. "We'll have to do again sometime. Maybe by then, you'll learn to stop fainting at the end?"

HERMIONE'S FATHER had always told her that you never know a person until you've seen their lab. Of course, it had never occurred to him that not everybody had a lab, and Hermione hadn't had the heart to point it out. Especially since she'd understood his point: A person's workspace often revealed more about their true character than their words ever could. In the same way, a scientist's lab would reflect their curiosity, discipline, and work ethic.

Hermione stared blankly at hers.

When it had been assigned to her several years ago, it'd been average—just a spare room that had gone unused for years on end. It had sleek white counters and polished metal tables lining the walls. Bright bulbs lit the room evenly, leaving no room for shadows. Her workstations had been arranged precisely, with each area designated for a specific function.

That was several years ago. And it was still mostly the same. However, one of the counters held her coffee machine, so it was less white and more brown. The bright lights had started irritating her eyes at some point, so she'd turned them off entirely and made do with the luminescent liquid of the picospore tanks. Her workstations were still arranged precisely, but the arrangement was a scattered system of thrown journals, marked research papers, and half-written notes and ideas that only Hermione could understand.

It'd gone from an average lab to the kind that they showed in sci-fi movies, usually with a mad genius at a countertop, tinkering with budget-friendly tools of mayhem. What did that say about her?

Against a wall stood a row of transparent containment tanks filled with an incandescent orange liquid. Each tank contained an iteration of picospores, starting with the original that Hermione and her father had developed at the Okafor Corp, and continuing through every variation that Helene had created over the years. For security, the tanks themselves were constructed from rein-forced glass. Hermione had confirmed that when she'd taken an axe to one several months ago in a moment of unhinged rage and frustration. She didn't like thinking about that day—or the one earlier in the week when she'd done the same thing after hitting yet *another* dead end in understanding Helene's latest improvements.

She sighed. *Maybe it's time that I gave up on it*, she thought, not for the first time. But unlike the other times, Hermione allowed herself to seriously consider it. Yes, the picospores had originally been developed by Hermione and her father. And yes, she still believed that the technology had a lot of potential applications for good. But after years of studying every improvement that Helene had made, Hermione couldn't justify pushing out the original, less-advanced variations— assuming Helene got out of the picture anytime soon, making the spores safe, anyway. She'd also accepted that without the AI, or a couple more decades, she couldn't figure out what exactly Helene had changed.

The way Hermione saw it, she could either switch sides and work for Helene, learning her secrets while hoping that DJ and the others figured out how to defeat her, or she could give up on the whole thing and focus on something she might be able to help with.

Hermione sighed again. *I'm going to need a new lab. Maybe I can...* Her thoughts trailed off at the sound of the door opening.

"Why's it so dark in here?"

Hermione turned. She'd become so used to working in the light of the tanks that she'd never considered how it looked like to someone else. Even DJ had stopped complaining whenever he dropped by. She squinted at the door, trying to identify the silhouette with the familiar voice that was stumbling around with hands outstretched. It only took a second.

"Ndidi," Hermione breathed. A moment later, the light flickered on as Ndidi finally found the switch. Hermione winced at the brightness—and then promptly forgot about her pain as she crossed the distance and pulled her into a firm hug. Ndidi melted into it, resting her chin against Hermione's shoulder. Hermione ignored the wet feeling on her labcoat and pulled Ndidi even closer. They stayed like that for several moments before Ndidi pulled away.

Ndidi was chubbier than when she'd left, so much so her clothes—a long-sleeved top and a pair of jeans, both of which had seen better days—could barely fit her. She'd pulled her hair into a loose bun, but that just made it more obvious how haggard her face looked. There were bruises on her cheeks and neck, her knees had scuff marks, and her hands trembled by her sides.

Despite all that, her posture was straight and her eyes, though puffy from crying, burned with determination. Hermione had seen that look in her friend often. But it was different this time, in a way Hermione couldn't put her finger on.

"You look like shit," Hermione said finally. Ndidi's brows went up in surprise, but Hermione had already turned and led her by the hand over to the stools.

"Well, excuse me for not taking the time to freshen up before rushing down to see you," Ndidi said, plopping heavily on the stool.

"When did you get—You know what? Scratch that. What the hell happened?" Hermione said, her voice raised. "DJ said he couldn't reach you. And then Olsen got word that there were missing-person posters of you and Pratima going around the country. Nobody knew where you might have been, and I've been worried sick, thinking that Helene couldn't wait until you were due and decided to get the baby out ahead of time or something."

"I didn't even consider that," Ndidi said.

"You didn't think that we would be worried?"

"No, I didn't consider that Helene might want to get the baby out faster. It would be pointless. At the rate it's growing, I'll probably be due by my first trimester."

What? Hermione thought, trying to process that. She took a deep breath and then let it out. "Let's start from the beginning."

"Pratima had some contacts who helped smuggle us out of the country," Ndidi explained. "But we couldn't risk Helene finding out, so I couldn't say anything to anyone because she had my phone bugged, and I was watched constantly."

"But wait," Hermione interrupted. "When'd you find out that your phone was bugged? Because you had several calls with us where you basically spilled everything she told you. If she knew you were passing it on then, we'd have to—"

"She knew," Ndidi cut her off softly, "but she didn't care. She doesn't care if we know what she's doing. she doesn't even care if we know *how* she's doing it. She's confident that we won't be able to do anything to stop her regardless. And you can't blame her since, so far, she's been right."

Hermione drew her lips into a line, thinking over everything that'd happened over the last few years. Helene had always been one step ahead, and everything they'd done had just played right into her hands. Hermione had thought they'd have a better chance with the AI being more limited in Manar's body and distracted by Ndidi and her child—but even her *henchwoman* was kicking their asses. With a score sheet like that, it was no wonder Helene didn't care whether they knew her plans.

But Hermione didn't want to be depressed; she could do that any other day of the week. Ndidi didn't need that right now, not after she'd put herself through hell. So Hermione forced a smile onto her face and put a hand over her friend's. "We only need to win once, Ndidi."

Ndidi drew her hand away and placed them on her lap. "That's the thing: winning once isn't going to be enough. Because Helene always has a backup plan. It's just that so far, she hasn't needed to use it."

Despite her words, the determination in her eyes didn't waver. If anything, she looked even more resolute. She placed a hand on her stomach absentmindedly.

"But I refuse to let my child be born in a world where Helene has won. Even more, I refuse to let my child be an instrument to make that world a reality. So we're not just going to win once; we're going to win once and for all."

Hermione blinked, then blinked again. It was a rousing speech, even though it was somewhat wasted on her. Hermione didn't need to be motivated. Words were cheap; it was easy to say that they were going to wipe the floor with Helene, but the *how*? That was what Hermione was interested in. The movies always left that out: the part after the rousing speech. They always cut into a training montage. But this was real life, and clips of her sweating in the gym weren't going to help.

Still, Ndidi didn't need her skepticism right now, so Hermione forced the smile back onto her face and gave a little clap. "Well, that's what we're working on. I'm guessing you and Pratima ditched your phones when you left?"

Her question pulled Ndidi out of her thoughts. "Yeah," she said, "so Helene couldn't track us. We went through the back roads, switched drivers and routes several times. Despite that, because it's *Helene*, there were several groups of people waiting for us at the airstrip. There was a gunfight..." Ndidi trailed off, staring at her hands, her gaze growing distant.

She snapped back when Hermione placed a hand on her shoulder. It was meant to be comforting, but it made her flinch and lean back. Her eyes focused once more, and she plastered a smile onto her face. "Anyway, it was rough, but we made it out. Pratima was wounded in the fight, so I forced her to go to the clinic to get treated. Then I came here."

"You need to get looked at too," Hermione said. "And you *definitely* need to freshen up. And rest. You look dead on your feet."

"I will soon. But I had to give you this first." Ndidi reached into her pocket and pulled out a syringe filled with—

Is that blood? Hermione thought. *Why the hell would she...?* Her thoughts cut off as her brain kicked into gear.

It *was* blood. And judging by Ndidi's urgency, it had to be important. There were only two people whose blood Ndidi might risk everything to bring. And she wouldn't rush if it were her own, as they could always take a fresh sample. That left…

"Manar," Hermione breathed. "It's Manar's. Or Helene's, right?"

Ndidi nodded. "Manar already had nanites in his blood from when he went to the Virtual Realm. I think that's what Helene used to latch on to him and hijack his body. But apparently, it wasn't enough, because she synthesized more." She nodded toward the syringe that was now in Hermione's hands. "She took that sample to show me how the nanites and picospores interacted in her body."

"You want me to study it," Hermione said.

"With Dr. Martin Bryan's help, since he's the expert on the nanites. Hopefully whatever you find out will be able to help me." Ndidi rubbed a hand on her stomach. "Helene said that no doctor would know what to do with a pregnancy like mine. But I figured with you and Martin working together..."

"You want me as the pediatrician to what's probably the most important baby in the world," Hermione summarized. "And I have less than two months to learn and understand an entirely new technology before the child is ready to pop."

Ndidi gave a soft smile. "No pressure, right?"

Shit, Hermione thought, sending back a thin smile.

CJ KNELT IN THE CENTER of a lush green field that stretched several yards around him. The grass was vibrant, the blades tickling his legs as they swayed to a wind that shouldn't exist. Around him, the very air seemed transformed; the light above was brighter somehow, suffused with soft golden hues.

But the field only lasted for a few yards before giving way to the wasteland once more. The boundary between the two was stark: Right now, CJ was immersed in life, with hints of wildflowers scattered in purples and yellows. But if he took a few steps forward, he'd be in the wasteland again, where the light was dull, the air stagnant, and nothing seemed to grow.

Until now, CJ thought, grinning like a Cheshire cat. He didn't even know what to feel. Waves of residual anxiety, exhilaration, and pride sloshed around within him and threatened to overwhelm him.

And for a moment, CJ let them. He knew he didn't, or couldn't, fully understand the implications of what he'd just done.

Everything he saw in the Virtual Realm was simply a representation of other things in the real world. And for that reason, until now, all his experiences in the Virtual Realm had had a logical explanation and connection to the real world. His avatar was simply a physical representation of his online presence, so when he'd manipulated programs and websites, all he'd done was hack into those specific systems and alter them in the way he wanted. His actions could probably have been tracked in the real world, though it would be virtually impossible for someone to home in on his avatar.

Still, the premise remained: He'd done something in the Virtual Realm, and it'd resonated in the reality because the Realm was simply a mirror.

But what he'd just done had broken that premise because he hadn't manipulated something *in* the Virtual Realm, like a program or a website. To create the field of grass, he'd manipulated the Virtual Realm itself. He could still see the new patterns that he'd created when he rearranged the code—the code of the world.

And he'd done it without the Sphere. It was right there. Why was there no one here to see this? Manar might have actually cracked a smile.

That thought helped ground CJ back into the present. He slapped both cheeks. It didn't get rid of his smile, but it did help him focus. Manar would definitely be impressed, maybe even enough to smile. But CJ would never know for sure if he didn't find him and bust him out of whatever hell that Helene was keeping him in.

Fortunately, with the field of grass, he'd proven his theory was sound. But changing the landscape wasn't what CJ needed. He could still feel the tug from a dozen different directions. CJ needed a way to get to each of those places without physically crossing the distance. That was teleportation, something that he hadn't been able to do even with a cheat code like the Sphere. CJ was sure that he'd be able to figure it out. Eventually, at least.

Hopefully, they had enough time.

DJ WOKE UP SLOWLY. Then his memories came back to him, and he woke up all at once. "That mother*fuc*—" DJ let loose every string of curses he'd learned as a marine, and a few vaguely remembered ones he'd learned as a kid. He strung them together in a tirade that went on for well over a minute. Out of the corner of his eye, he saw Chloe taking notes.

"Are you done?" Christy asked when he finally ran out of breath. DJ shook his head and opened his mouth to continue, but Christy slapped a hand over his mouth with a growl. "It wasn't a real question, D. Either you're done, or I'll knock you back out and give you time to cool off. Take your pick."

DJ took a moment to seriously consider it before waving her off and glancing around the room. He'd recognized the hospital room the moment he'd woken up since it was the same one he'd been brought to the last time he fought with Tyra and fainted. Either it was a huge coincidence, or someone somewhere was messing with him. DJ knew which one he'd put his money on.

Karla and Liz stood by the wall beside the bed, both idly sharpening their daggers in perfect synchronization. Without the snarl, Karla almost looked content. DJ quickly looked away before she noticed. On the other side of the bed, Chloe put away her notepad and smirked down at him. "You couldn't hold her back long enough for me to get there?"

"The bitch fucking poisoned me!" DJ exclaimed. "I was literally *this* close to having her, and she pulled a knife out of freaking nowhere and stabbed me." His side still throbbed. It was less than before, but it was still surprising since, for him to be in Sparta, he must have been on a nine-hour helicopter ride. What the hell had Tyra used? His nanites should have been able to fix him in that time.

More importantly, DJ thought, *when the hell did I start depending on my nanites so much?*

"You got beat up by a girl, and now you're making excuses," Chloe tutted. "What's happening to men these days?"

DJ sighed. "She got away then?" he asked no one in particular.

"She was gone by the time Chloe and the twins got to you," Christy answered. "The QECS was also missing."

The quantum entanglement communication system functioned as a high-tech walkie-talkie. But instead of connecting people, it connected systems, allowing them to "talk" with each other in real time, anywhere in the world. On a bomb, it would ensure that the explosives could be monitored, adjusted, and triggered from anywhere in the world, almost instantaneously.

If Helene had been the one controlling the bomb, then the QECS wouldn't have been necessary since she could have just communicated with it directly. However, in Manar's body, Helene didn't have that ability—and Tyra had even less chance of doing so—which was why they needed it. In DJ's hands, they could have potentially disabled the bomb or overridden its commands from a distance.

Theoretically, at least. In reality, it was more likely that Tyra would have found an alternative that they couldn't interfere with. But it would have bought them some time—if they hadn't lost it.

"I'm pretty sure she'd already taken the module before we got there at all," DJ said. "I saw her take something out of her pocket before I fainted. She wanted me to know that she'd won before we even fought. She could have left before we got there, but she'd stayed back just to fuck with us. To fuck with *me*." DJ felt another surge of anger bubbling up, but he pushed it aside with a sigh. "How did she escape?"

"*She flew,*" Olsen said, his voice coming through a computer that'd been placed on a chair. "*After her last stunt, we were watching the ground for tunneling and were prepared for that. But she rode out on one of her drones like she was the freaking Khaleesi.*"

DJ and Christy looked at each other, confused. Chloe cocked her head. "Who?" DJ asked.

"*Khaleesi?*" Olsen repeated. "*Daenerys Targaryen? The Mother of Dragons?*" When their expressions didn't change, he snorted in disappointment. "*Kids these days. Anyway, we didn't have any anti-air missiles, so we couldn't do anything but sit on our thumbs.*"

DJ nodded. "How badly does this hurt us?"

"*Hard to say,*" Olsen said. "*Even if we had acquired the QECS, our aim would still have been to get close enough to the bomb to make it a nonthreat. We went for it this time simply to keep it out of Helene's hands. We failed, but in the grand scheme of things, nothing has changed. There are still several items on Miss Chityothin's shopping list, and we have that many chances to nab her. Or at least, stop her from getting what she wants. The boys are already trying to predict her next target.*"

Christy spoke up. "All we have to do is win once."

DJ knew she was trying to be comforting, but she was wrong. He shook his head. "Winning once isn't going to cut it," he said. "It's just going to delay them until they find another method. This is Helene we're talking about. Even if we stop Tyra at every point from now on, all we're doing is buying time. And that's not a winning strategy."

"*Your tirade better be leading up to a plan, son,*" Olsen grunted. DJ wished that it was, but all he saw were traps on every side. No matter what they did, he only saw Tyra toying with them, using their plans against them. She'd done it during the raid, and she'd done it again back in Nevada.

DJ gritted his teeth. "How's the progress on tracing the bomb?"

"*It's a dead end. However they're making that thing, it's as undetectable as the drones.*"

"Radiation? Thermal imaging? Nothing?"

"*I do not enjoy being doubted, son,*" Olsen growled. "*All the arms of the government are working together on this. We have several methods at our disposal to trace a normal warhead. However, none of those work here. None of our usual informants have any information about where it might be or who might be tracking it. Our efforts with Miss Chityothin have already proven the futility of trying to track it through signal monitoring or satellite surveillance.*

"*We have radiation and chemical sensors mounted on drones, planes and ground vehicles roaming about the entire country, but none of the hundreds have picked up anything. Thermal, infrared imaging, and seismic monitoring gives us the same result: nothing. But despite the massive failure, everything is still being run round the clock around the country just in case we get lucky and Miss Chityothin slips up, an event that is highly unlikely.*"

The room was silent for a minute. The Murder Twins were as disinterested as always. Christy seemed embarrassed, and Chloe looked like she was barely holding back laughter. DJ felt sick to his stomach. Usually, DJ went to the admiral with a problem, and it either got fixed or started getting fixed. The old man never gave details of what he had to do or the amount to work that he had to put in. The only hints DJ got were if the admiral looked more tired than usual, or if he'd added more wrinkles or something.

But none of that was an excuse for why DJ had started taking it for granted. Olsen had had his back since their first meeting. The man didn't believe in half measures. And DJ knew that he had burned a lot of bridges and used up a lot of favors helping DJ over the years. So, why the hell had DJ pressed him?

DJ sighed. "I don't know what to say. I'm sorry, Olsen. I know you're doing everything you can."

"*That's Admiral Olsen, you brat. Show some respect.*" The words were harsh, but there wasn't any heat in them. "*And I understand your frustration, son. But you have to be patient. These things take time. It's only been a few months, after all. I remember, back when I was a captain, there was a perp that took us over two years to track down. He was hiding in the dark..."*

Olsen's voice faded into the background after a while. DJ's gut told him it was the wrong move to try to use the materials to get Tyra. It felt too much like they were just being led around. But Olsen was also right. The materials were their best bet at tracking her down. DJ certainly didn't have any other ideas, and he didn't know what he could come up with that every other intelligence agency hadn't already thought of. So even though it felt off, their best bet was to follow the materials and find a way to box Tyra in. Everything would end if they managed to capture her. Still, he tried not to dwell on the feeling of a noose tightening around his neck.

He interrupted Olsen after a few minutes. Somehow, the old man had hooked Chloe and the Murder Twins to his story. Liz was staring at the computer with interest, while Karla was actually leaning over it. She snarled at him when he interrupted, but DJ was in no mood for her nonsense.

He asked Olsen for more specifics about what had happened back in the desert. The one silver lining was that the trap DJ had triggered hadn't been the only one Tyra had placed in the facility—which meant she'd been working against them longer and more deliberately than they'd realized. That confirmed DJ's theory that she'd stayed behind to sabotage their efforts, and while it didn't reveal much else, it at least gave them proof they were on the right trail. The team had dismantled and collected every device they'd found, handing them over to Olsen for analysis, just in case. DJ doubted they'd get anything useful, but he kept that to himself. Everyone probably knew they were grasping at straws by now.

"What's the estimate before the next one?" he asked.

"We're not sure. We have a pretty good idea of what she's going to hit next, but everyone agrees that Tyra would probably go to ground for a few days first. It's red alert, though, so as soon as we get the word, we can be out almost immediately. We being you and your team, of course. Assuming you're rested enough by then." Olsen hesitated. *"Will you be rested enough by then? Christy told me the docs were able to flush the poison from your system and patch you up. But you were still hit pretty badly."*

DJ started to wave the statement away, but Karla interjected before he could, snarling at the computer. "Do not insult my student. He might be weak still, but he is steel compared to the rest of you."

DJ raised his brows at that, not sure whether to blush or feel insulted. *Where the hell did that come from?* It was nice that she'd finally acknowledged him as a student though; maybe she would stop beating on him so hard. *Who am I kidding?* he groaned internally. *She'll probably go harder on me now.*

Still, disregarding the weirdness, Karla wasn't wrong. DJ felt fine. He wouldn't say he was back in top shape, but whatever cuts and bruises he'd received in the fight were gone. He'd have to see how standing up felt, but he could probably fight right then if there was an emergency or something. Hundred percent was probably just a few hours away. And that was just from the passive enhancements of the nanites; if he actively engaged them, that time would be drastically cut short.

DJ cleared his throat, ignoring the look Christy gave him. "I'll be ready."

After that, Olsen updated DJ on a few minor details and hung up. Chloe and the Murder Twins left immediately, with Karla leaving a very unsubtle threat about what she would do to him if he wasn't at the gym by the end of the day. Christy wanted to stay longer, but DJ persuaded her to leave. He could see the exhaustion on her face, which meant she hadn't rested much, if at all, since they'd returned from Nevada. With his nanites, DJ had enough stamina to last for days without rest. But Christy didn't have that to fall back on, and everyone needed to be in top shape when Olsen's call came.

Surprisingly, she listened after only a few minutes of argument, and DJ was finally left alone with his thoughts. He leaned back against the bed and closed his eyes.

A knock sounded on the door.

Oh, what fresh hell is this? DJ groaned internally. He opened his eyes to see Hermione, of all people, striding into the room.

"Poison, DJ?" she asked, stopping a foot away from the bed. "Seriously?"

"You say that like I wanted to get poisoned," he mumbled, sitting up. Hermione was similar to Tyra in that she always wore a lab coat, even when she wasn't in a lab. At this point, DJ wasn't even sure if she knew she was wearing it again.

Does she take showers with it? The thought popped into his head before he could stop it, and he shook it away. *Well, she doesn't look like she's about to fall over from exhaustion.*

That was always a fear with Hermione. The woman worked herself until she crashed, then continued working when she woke up. Ndidi was the only one who could convince her to get some sunlight. The most DJ had succeeded in doing was forcing her out of her lab for a conference every few weeks. Now, though, it looked like Hermione had taken some time off to rest.

"Tyra didn't really ask for permission," he finished.

"Do you know what kind of poison it was?"

"I didn't ask." He shrugged. "I survived, and what doesn't kill you—"

"—has the chance to try again if you don't learn your lesson and take measures to prevent it," Hermione finished for him.

DJ closed one eye and tilted his head to the side. "Yours seems different. It doesn't roll off the tongue. Maybe try adding a rhyme at the end."

She huffed out a breath. "At least you're well enough to still be a pain in the ass." DJ gave a sitting bow. "Now, will you listen to me?"

DJ sighed, then gave her an exhausted grin. "I might as well since it's not like I'm going anywhere. Lay it on me."

"Ndidi is back."

DJ blinked. Of all the things he'd expected... "That's fucking awesome!" he exclaimed, grinning. "Where is she?"

"She's freshening up now, and then I assume she's going to sleep until New Years. Wait until she's up before you start interrogating her, okay?"

DJ leaned back on the bed, his expression slightly sheepish. "You can't blame me for being curious about how she escaped Helene."

"She said Pratima had some contacts in a smuggling ring. They went to a deserted airstrip two states from where Manar was, and they *still* had to fight through several groups to get to the plane. She's pretty shaken up about it. So, be nice." She glared at him, which made DJ feel a bit guilty.

"All right, all right, I will," DJ said.

"Good. And that leads me to the second thing." Hermione took a deep breath. "I'm giving up on the picospores." She stared at DJ intensely while waiting for his reaction.

For his part, DJ didn't say anything immediately. There was a lot to unpack there, especially since Hermione considered the picospores to be her family's legacy. Helene's perversion of the technology had hurt her deeply, and so she'd spent years barely getting enough sleep, trying to understand what the AI did so she could counter it. She could have given up at any point, but she didn't. For her to do it now...she must have hit the mother of all dead ends. That didn't bode well for them since her discoveries were the only thing that gave them the slightest, most minuscule chance against Helene's spores. But it wasn't as if DJ could force her to continue her research. He wouldn't even try to persuade her; that shit had made her miserable. They'd just have to figure it out.

"All right," he said finally. "What do you want to work on now?"

"Look, I know that's not what you want to hear, but it's my choice, and I'm the one to decide—" Hermione stopped, confused and a bit deflated.

"I know," DJ said. "I agree with you. So what do you want to work on now?"

"You're not gonna..." She trailed off, stared at him a moment longer, and then seemed to collect herself. "Nanites. I want to work on nanites."

DJ blinked. Now it was his turn to be confused. He understood the logic behind her decision to pivot from the picospores, but the new direction didn't make sense to him. The nanites had originally been invented by Dr. Martin Bryan, on Helene's orders, to be used on the Murder Twins. Since then, only José had received a fresh batch from Helene. DJ had received his from Martin, who'd extracted them from the twins to keep Helene from controlling them. But with the Murder Twins on their side and José out of the picture, the nanites were no longer a threat.

"Why?"

"Partly because I need a break from the spores before I go mad," Hermione admitted. "Partly because of Ndidi, and partly because of you." She gave him a look that was part disappointed and part concerned.

"Me? What'd I do?"

"Your brother told me what happened in the White House."

"Oh." DJ grimaced. "He was exaggerating."

"He also showed me the video he pulled from the surveillance cameras. And I was there when you beat on him so much that his face was too swollen to speak."

"Oh, come on," he protested. "He was about to inject himself with the pico-spores. You can't blame me for being pissed off."

"I'm not. But your response was disproportionate, and you know it."

DJ wanted to protest again, but Hermione just gave him that look, and he swallowed his words. It was bullshit anyway. He knew what she was getting at, and he knew that it was a problem. He'd even spoken to Karla about it, though he didn't think that her advice was going to work for him. DJ had been trying to figure it out by himself, but he hadn't made much progress.

"How'd you know it was the nanites?" he asked. He had his suspicions but hadn't been sure until he'd asked Karla. Since he couldn't picture Hermione and Karla having a conversation, he was curious how she'd figured it out.

"Simple deduction." Hermione shrugged. "Your behavior changed after you got the nanites, and there was nothing else that could have affected you the same way. Plus, you've mentioned several times that your nanites enhance every part of your body. I figured that extended to your hormones."

DJ's lips made a flat line, but he once again swallowed what he wanted to say. "So you think you can help?"

"I could try. It would be a lot easier with Martin's help though."

DJ snorted. "He's with José. And unless you wanna go rescue him from the freaking Terminator, that's where he's going to stay until I can figure out a way to pull him out without risking my tongue or my balls." Hermione gave him a confused look, so he added, "He'd cut off my tongue for lying to him."

"And your balls?"

DJ shrugged. "Jealousy, I'd imagine."

Hermione shook her head. "Moving on...I'm going to need Martin's help. I still have some of the old man's notes from when we worked together, but he needs to be here."

DJ rubbed his chin. He needed to shave soon. "Honestly, I don't know if I can help you there, Hermione. Martin's with José, who'll never let him go. And I don't see him walking out on his own anytime soon."

"Well, you're going to need to figure it out," Hermione said. "Because he's important if any of this is going to work."

DJ groaned. "Fine. Anything else?"

"I'm also going to need a blood sample from you."

"Knock yourself out. But you might want to talk with Chloe and the twins. For some reason, they get touchy whenever someone else starts playing with the nanites."

Her face paled, and she looked behind her as if one of them were sneaking up on her. "I'll uh, I'll leave you to handle that, if you think it's important."

"Not so important," DJ said immediately. "Anything *else*?"

"Only one," she said in a tone that DJ immediately did not like. "Since I'm changing my research, I'm going to need some new equipment. And since the research benefits *you*, I figured you'd want to help me."

DJ crossed his arms. "And how did you think I could help you?"

Hermione smiled. "Well, your brother told me that you have some pull with the board of directors here."

Fuck, DJ thought. *This must be his revenge for pulling him out. Why couldn't he just have punched me like a normal person?*

15

AS HE'D SUSPECTED, DJ was back in top shape after a few days. Christy came into his room to find him doing push-ups with his shirt off. DJ pretended not to notice her and gave her a full minute to stare before standing, slowly enough that she had time to look away. It was the kind of courtesy he would have appreciated a woman giving him. And it wasn't like he didn't understand why she stared.

He was *ripped.* Like, goddamn ripped. But not in the disgusting bodybuilder way. It was Henry-Cavill-meets-modern-Adonis ripped. He'd checked *himself* out, for God's sake.

DJ had always been in good shape. Even after leaving the Marines, he'd worked out regularly enough that nothing much had changed. The first few months after getting the nanites had enhanced that, but the poisoning seemed to have forced the little bots to kick it up a notch once again because *goddamn.*

DJ shook the thought out of his head and picked up the towel he'd kept by the foot of the bed. He cleared his throat to snap Christy out of her trance and tried his best not to grin when her ears turned red. Instead, he stood in the center of the room and spread his arms, still shirtless. "As you can see, I am still alive."

"Too bad." She scowled at him. "We had bets going. Now, put on a goddamn shirt, D. Olsen sent a message." That was enough to get him moving. He'd expected to sit on his ass for another few days before Olsen got back.

He and Christy made their way back to the conference room, and DJ tried to ignore the stares that followed him all the way. He would have loved to believe it was because of his good looks, but the stories of his "feats" during the raid still hadn't died down. If anything, they'd become more exaggerated, if that was even possible. DJ could barely go two floors or enter a room without everyone staring. He couldn't even have a beer with the guards anymore, not when most of them looked at him like he was a god or something. The whole thing sucked. And it was something else he was going to pay Tyra back for.

"So," he said, "what'd Olsen say?"

"Nothing," Christy replied. "I was supposed to check if you were combat ready and then report back."

DJ smirked. "Oh, you didn't say anything. I don't really think that I'm up for combat—"

"I saw the weights by the side of your bed, D," Christy said through gritted teeth. "How'd you even get them anyway?"

"I brought them down from the execs' gym after training with Karla yesterday."

"And the nurses let you?"

DJ rubbed the back of his head. "Well...I was still sweaty from the workout, so I took my shirt off on the way down. They didn't exactly stop me."

Christy huffed out a breath. "I didn't take you for an exhibitionist."

"I'm not. I was just really sweaty, and the water pressure upstairs sucks. Plus, y'know...if you got it, flaunt it and all that."

"Slut," Christy muttered under her breath.

DJ laughed but then steered the topic to safer waters before he got punched. "Is the Murder Team there?"

"Karla wanted to be the one to come get you, but I figured I should go in case you weren't combat ready. Now I'm wishing I'd let her."

"They slept here then." DJ nodded to himself. "How'd they get rooms?"

DJ had a permanent room in the building, but that was because Manar—the real Manar—was part of the board of directors. He'd had all of them assigned rooms, and Hermione a lab, when it became obvious that dealing with Helene was going to be a little more involved than everyone was expecting. By the time he'd gotten trapped in the Virtual Realm, the team members were already well known in the building, although DJ didn't think that any of the staff knew why they were there or what their duties were.

Still, DJ had befriended the guards, their superiors, and as many of the staff as he could. That connection had come in handy twice: once when they'd needed a place to stash the hostages they'd rescued from Helene, then again when DJ had needed to take command during the raid. He was pretty sure he could have acquired rooms for the Murder Team, but he hadn't even been asked, so naturally, he was curious how they'd done it.

"Karla broke down one of the doors," Christy replied.

Ah, DJ thought, nodding to himself. "And no one tried to stop her?" That was unexpected. Sparta's security detail had been decimated after Tyra's raid, so while it made sense that their defenses were weakened, it was still surprising that nobody intervened.

"She beat up the first few that did. But then we just told one of the captains that you'd added her, Liz, and Chloe to your team, and what do you know? They left us alone."

DJ groaned internally. He couldn't complain too much though. He hated the attention that he was getting, but it'd saved a few people some broken bones and maybe even a disembowelment. He just didn't like the smile that Christy gave him as she said it. But DJ accepted the payback for what it was and left it at that. Fortunately, he was pushing open the doors to the conference room moments later.

The first thing he noticed was Olsen up on the projector screen glaring at him. No, DJ realized a moment later: not glaring at *him*. Olsen was just glaring in general, so intensely that he didn't seem to notice when DJ and Christy entered. That didn't bode well for the meeting. Chloe gave him a little wave as he took his seat while Karla and Liz ignored him completely. Hermione was noticeably absent, as was CJ. However, DJ hadn't expected either of them to show up. CJ had been spending increasing amounts of time in the Virtual Realm over the last few days, and DJ was beginning to worry that his brother was using it as a way to escape reality. He was trying to decide whether it'd be the right move to talk to him about it or to just let it be. After all, it was his time in the Virtual Realm that had started the whole bullshit about CJ wanting to inject himself with picospores.

"I'm glad to see that you're feeling better, son," Olsen said.

DJ nodded. "We got something on Tyra?"

"The boys seem to think so, but we're not sure. Regardless, we believe we know where she's going to hit next, and whether or not she's ready to make her move, it'll be in our best interest to secure this so she can't get her hands on it."

"Fair enough. What's the thing?"

Olsen picked up a piece of paper from his desk and squinted at it. *"According to the boys in the lab, it's a high-purity isotopic stabilizer. They have all read your report on how large the bomb is, and there have been fights and bets about what the payload for such a thing could be. Most of them agree, however, that regardless of the payload, the stabilizer would be critical for the dispersal mechanism of a bomb that large. Without it, the bomb would be rendered ineffective—which, naturally, is a win for us. Fortunately, the isotope thing is relatively rare, and it has a lot of other uses—so much so isn't even sold on the black market. Anyone that has it, keeps it."*

DJ raised a brow at that. He'd thought anything could be bought on the black market. However, from what Olsen was saying, it wasn't that the stabilizer *couldn't* be sold, but that no one who had it wanted to sell, probably because they had illegal uses for it.

"There is an oil rig located off the coast of Louisiana," Olsen continued. *"Very remote, only accessible by boat or helicopter. Our intel says there's an abandoned shipment there. We believe that the shipment is one of the last known places where someone can get the isotope."*

"And you think Tyra is going to go after it," DJ said.

"Yes."

"When do we leave?"

"We have just received confirmation from Sparta. The chopper is landing on the helipad right now. Gear up and meet it. ETA at the location is six hours."

SEVEN HOURS LATER, the helicopter blades slowed to a steady hum as it touched down on the oil rig's corroded platform. Karla and Liz were the first ones out, bolting through the open door like the chopper was on fire. DJ would have laughed, but he wasn't sure it wouldn't cost him a finger. As it was, the rig was made of solid metal and isolated in the middle of rough waters. That meant Tyra couldn't dig through it, and her drones would be visible for miles. Olsen had a team by the coast with anti-air weapons, ready to shoot down any drones before they became a threat.

The oil rig itself was a massive structure. DJ estimated it was about three times the size of a typical rig, but it showed the wear of years of being exposed to the elements. The metal framework was streaked with rust, and the grated walkways were slick with a mixture of seawater and oil residue, making movement potentially dangerous. Several parts of the platform were corroded and had jagged edges that threatened anyone who got too close. It also didn't help that the wind seemed particularly vicious. It howled through the rig, rattling loose cables and sending debris clattering against the steel. DJ could picture one of those knocking someone into the water before they could react.

Several large, dormant machines were parked across the deck. Each was coated in rust and grime, so much so DJ could barely make out their original coloring. Pipes ran through the whole thing like a maze, many of them leaking oil or emitting the faint hiss of escaping gas. DJ didn't even know how that was possible, considering how long the setup had been abandoned. The waves churned around them, and the entire structure swayed under its own weight.

Lovely, DJ thought, shifting his balance. He tapped his comm. "All right, where's this thing located?"

"The storage bay is the most secure place," Olsen said. *"Our boys believe that's where it would be."*

"Then that's where we'll start," DJ replied, raising his voice to be heard over the wind and crashing waves. "Spread out! Shout if you find the entrance or any sign of Tyra. If she got here ahead of us, she's probably set some traps. We can't let her gain the upper hand."

Immediately after he said that, the faint groaning of the rig suddenly intensified into a sharp, grinding screech. DJ's head whipped instinctively to the helicopter, and he saw the platform beneath it started to shift.

"Take off!" he shouted to the driver, sprinting back. He waved his hand to get the idiot's attention. "Take the fuck off!"

The helicopter blades started spinning, but it was far too late. The screeching grew louder, and the supports below the platform let out a final, tortured wail before they finally collapsed. The helicopter followed it a second later, despite its struggles, and the entire craft plunged into the water. DJ ran and reached the edge in less than a second. He dove, and the wind stole Christy's yell and what he assumed was Chloe's laughter.

DJ had heard that diving into choppy waters was like hitting a wall of needles. But when he hit the surface, he was surprised: It didn't hurt as much as he expected. The chill pierced through his layers, but instead of overwhelming him, it felt distant, almost insignificant. Adrenaline surged through him, and for the first time, he realized the nanites were doing more than he'd thought: They were making him tougher, stronger. The chaos of the water's surface didn't scare him; it barely registered.

The waves roared around him, trying to fill his lungs and making it impossible to take a clear breath. The currents pulled at DJ, who was weighed down by his soaked clothes. Every stroke felt like wrestling a fierce rottweiler, claws and teeth thrashing, twisting against him with relentless force. DJ's stamina held though; he knew he could keep it up for hours before fatigue became a real threat. Once he stopped being disoriented, he let the current force him beneath the surface. The water stung his eyes, but DJ forced them open. His enhanced sight sliced through the darkness, and within seconds, he spotted the wreckage of the helicopter—and the pilot trapped under a piece of metal, bubbles streaming from his open mouth.

DJ surged toward him, ignoring the debris bobbing past. He reached the man and yanked at the metal trapping him. There wasn't much leverage underwater, but DJ's strength was still formidable. The metal bent and then was ripped away. DJ grabbed onto the man before he could float away and then started kicking toward the surface.

It took another minute for DJ to swim close enough to the rig to grab the rope that Christy had sent down. Christy and Liz pulled them up while Karla watched with a sneer on her face, Chloe with an amused smile. Resuscitating the man once they were safe on the platform would have been another problem, but fortunately, Christy had experience with it, so DJ let her take over while he lay down a distance away.

Chloe came to stand beside him. "What was it you were saying about traps and not allowing her to take the initiative?"

"Seriously?" DJ said. "Now's not the fucking time, Chloe."

She shrugged. "Okay, what're we going to do about the fact that she obviously knew that we'd be coming?"

"We already figured that, and we planned around it."

"What part of your plan had her cutting off our escape route?"

"The helicopter was never our exit," DJ said. "We'd have basically been begging Tyra to steal it from us. Sure, she's setting the stage, but we're not trapped yet. And now we've confirmed that she's here somewhere. We just have to smoke her out."

Christy walked up to them. "I bet she's thinking the same thing about us right now."

The moment she said that, the sound of unhinged laughter drifted with the wind. At the same time, the rig came alive around them. DJ spun around and watched as the machinery whirred and began to move. The pipes gurgled and the doors screeched on their hinges as they struggled to slam shut.

"How the hell is she doing this?" he asked no one. "Most of this shit is a stiff kick away from falling apart."

"She's on the catwalk," Chloe said, angling her gun.

DJ's head whipped upward, just in time to catch a shadow darting across one of the crisscrossing walkways. His hand inched toward his gun, but he knew better. "Don't bother. She's too fast, and she has the high ground."

"Then we force her to come down to us," Christy said. She was carrying her pack over her shoulder, though DJ doubted she would be using it much during the mission. A sniper would be nearly useless with the wind and all the obstructions. More likely, Christy would have to get close and personal, though DJ knew she didn't like it.

She did have a point though. Tyra had proven several times that she loved to show how smart she was. Even in the first minutes they'd been there, she'd shown that by waiting for the perfect moment before activating her traps. They could probably use her need to gloat—to toy with them, to toy with *him*—to force her to come to them.

"All right, let's make her think that her traps are getting to us, that it's working. Let her play her games. And then, we flip the board."

Chloe smiled at him. "You better hope that we don't run out of moves before we get there."

DJ ignored her. "Let's move."

THE METAL WALKWAY GROANED dangerously beneath DJ as he moved deeper into what he was quickly starting to believe was a labyrinth. The rig was far larger than he'd originally estimated, and having to use the catwalks only made it seem larger.

"Why do you keep stopping?" Christy asked.

Against his better judgment, the team had split into different groups to cover more ground. Karla and Liz had been an easy pair, and Chloe had insisted that she didn't need a babysitter or someone to babysit, so she'd gone off on her own, which left DJ and Christy as another pair.

"Because I'm freezing my balls off, Christy," DJ replied and then continued moving down the rickety path. He tapped his comm. "All right—stay sharp, guys. If you see her, don't engage. Just call it in so the rest of us can make our way to you." DJ didn't know why he said that—he knew none of them were going to listen. That didn't matter much if it was Karla and Liz that found Tyra; if those two couldn't handle her in a straight-up fight, then they should all just quit now. It was Chloe he was worried about, partly because she was the only one without a partner, and partly because she and Christy were the only ones on the combat team without any nanites. Sure, Chloe was an excellent combatant in her own right, but Tyra had nanites, and that would give her an edge that—

DJ frowned. What was he thinking? Just because Tyra had nanites, she'd automatically beat Chloe? From what he'd picked up, Chloe had been whupping both Karla and Liz in their training sessions. Shit, DJ and Tyra were about the same level combat-wise, and DJ had no illusions that Chloe could whup him up and down the street like he was a child.

Since when did I start thinking nanites made a person invulnerable? DJ wondered. It was a dangerous mentality, especially since it could make him underestimate most people. Karla could afford that kind of thinking because even without the nanites, she and her sister were still peak-level fighters in any bracket. Before his enhancements, DJ had been slightly above average at best. But that didn't really matter when you could move faster than most people could even begin to react to.

Ah, DJ thought, grimacing. *I'm getting addicted to it. Fuck.* How hadn't he noticed this sooner? Maybe because he hadn't wanted to notice it. Because unlike with his anger, this wasn't something he could blame on his nanites. No, DJ was simply getting addicted to the power he felt when the nanites were active. Honestly, it was somewhat inevitable. What person wouldn't like being able to punch through concrete, hear a conversation several rooms away, or jump off a five-story building and land without a scratch? But what was even crazier was the fact that DJ knew that he could get even stronger. Karla and Liz were obviously further along with the enhancements than he was—and that meant he still had room to grow.

"D, look at this," Christy said, pulling him out of his thoughts. The rig was a maze of narrow catwalks, rusted stairwells, and towering tanks that plunged most parts into shadows. Christy was crouched close to the railing, brushing her hand against a smudge of grease in the shape of a footprint. "This is fresh, which means she came this way."

DJ nodded, but before he could say anything, his comm buzzed. *"There's something here,"* Chloe said to DJ's surprise. He hadn't thought any of them would actually buzz in if they found anything. *"I'm on the lower deck. Looks like recently moved equipment."*

"Hold your position," DJ said. "Liz, you and your sister rendezvous with Chloe. Christy and I will clear this level and come meet you guys." Liz would know how to corral her sister. Karla would have ignored him just to spite him if he'd asked her directly.

"Understood," Liz replied.

DJ and Christy continued as silently as they could, which wasn't very quiet since the rig creaked with every step. They found more and more footprints the deeper they went, and the tension rose until it was almost physical. DJ's hands were tight on his daggers, and he squinted at every shadow before moving on.

"She's close," Christy muttered.

A loud crash followed her words, coming from the direction that the Murder Twins had taken. "Liz, report! What's happening over there?"

Static filled the line for a second before Liz's voice came through. *"We are fine. It was just a distraction. She knocked over a stack of crates to throw us off. My sister wanted to chase but I stopped her."*

"She is playing with us," Karla growled over the comms.

"Let her," DJ said, forcing himself to be calm. "The more games she plays, the more time we have to corner her."

The comms went dead, and DJ and Christy continued toward the tanks. After a few minutes, Christy signaled a stop. DJ came up beside her, and she pointed at a faint shimmer that stretched across the walkway. A tripwire.

"She's definitely close," Christy said, disarming the trap.

The comm crackled again, this time with Chloe's voice, low but tense. Still, somehow, DJ could hear the grin in her voice. *"She's here. Lower deck, moving fast. I'm staying on her, but if you don't want me to engage, then you need to hurry up. I don't know how long I can hold myself back."*

"Well, control yourself for five minutes," he said as adrenaline flooded his system. He picked Christy up and started running. "We're heading to you now."

CHAPTER

17

JANUARY 2044
VIRTUAL REALM

CJ LOVED NUMBERS. He always had. Words—words were difficult. There were so many of them, and it was so hard to remember the right ones to use and how to pronounce them. But numbers were easy. They were logical, consistent, and they didn't require him to talk. It was surprising that CJ hadn't picked up programming until after Mayday. And even then, he'd started only because it'd been necessary to find out who'd been responsible for the death of his parents. Still, his love of numbers had translated easily into a love of code, and it had only grown the more he learned.

Until now. Now, CJ was frustrated.

He struggled to keep the emotion off his face. He was the only one around for miles, but he needed the practice. For most of his life, he'd put in effort to be more expressive, not less. But acting on his frustration and throwing a tantrum felt like he'd be moving backward somehow. CJ limited himself to simply gritting his teeth, even though he *really* wanted to throw a tantrum.

CJ glared at the lines of code hovering in front of him. It was just a small fraction of the tapestry, and it was still connected to the rest, but now it floated at eye-level. It hadn't taken him long to figure out how to do that, once he got tired of kneeling. They glowed slightly in his mind, and even without touching, CJ got a vague impression of the infinity that they were connected to. A part of him wanted to experience that endlessness again, but it was a part that CJ was used to ignoring. It was easier now, since he was pissed.

He studied the mini tapestry again. He couldn't read binary. No one could. There were some myths that people had, decades or centuries ago, during the first era of programming. But if that was true, the existence of programming languages made that skill obsolete. In most cases, at least. However, since the Virtual Realm was pure binary, being able to read it instead of relying on the impressions he got would make his life easier.

In CJ's defense, he'd tried to learn it after his last trip, but well, programming languages existed for a reason. He could decode small snippets of binary, which was why he'd isolated the mini tapestry. But trying to read anything larger was overwhelming. It was like reading a novel written entirely in ones and zeros, without spaces or punctuation—it was theoretically possible, but highly impractical.

Focus, CJ scolded himself, glaring at the code. He'd never thought that teleportation would be straightforward. But he *had* thought it would be easier once he'd learned to change the environment at will. It should have been; everything else had come quickly once he'd figured it out. Constant practice had allowed him to slowly expand the range of his effect, and after that, it'd just been a step to recreating his Zone—his area of influence. It was one of the abilities the Sphere had given him, and now, CJ had created a version of it by himself. Naturally though, there were slight differences.

For one, his Zone was much smaller than it had been with the Sphere, but CJ was confident that would change the more he practiced. The second difference was that it tired him out much more quickly. With the Sphere, he could have kept his Zone active indefinitely. The flip side to that was that he was much more sensitive to stimuli while the Zone was active, even more than he had been with the Sphere. He could sense not only everything within his influence but also its underlying code.

So far, it'd only made it easier to manipulate the environment from a distance—which was why he was surrounded by several pockets of grass that contrasted greatly with the desolate land—but it should also be incredibly helpful when he started teleporting.

If he ever did.

His first attempt had been a tether system. He'd created two knots in the tapestry, one that would mark his current position and another for his destination. His theory was that a simple command would collapse the distance between the two points, moving him instantly. The reality was that something about the two points meeting had created an explosion of data that had sent CJ screaming on the ground as he tried not to lose himself.

He'd made several attempts after that, but the results either saw him on the ground or staring in confusion, wondering what had gone wrong. Now CJ glowered at his latest attempt. It wasn't going to work; he could *see* that it wasn't.

"But why?" CJ muttered to himself. He let the tapestry fall and instead sat on the soft grass. His mind whispered that his efforts were pointless, that he was wasting time. Every minute he spent failing here was a minute Helene was using to further her plans; it was a minute that Manar remained trapped in his prison. But CJ didn't see another way. He'd spent hours trying to think of what he was missing.

He'd even briefly considered pausing his search for Manar to try to help somewhere else. But how? What other project would he work on that the dozens of programmers provided by Mary Pastore couldn't? This, however, was something only he could do. And it was necessary. Once Manar was freed, he would know what to do. He always did. CJ just had to figure out what he was missing.

He exhaled slowly. He needed to start from the beginning, from the basics. The world could be bent to his will. CJ had experienced this months ago, when he'd used the Sphere to practically merge with a website, controlling every part of the building as easily as he controlled his limbs. *Well,* CJ considered, *as easily as I control my limbs now.*

Still, the fact that he'd now managed to replicate a fraction of that confirmed that the Sphere had just been a tool. The world could be bent to his will, as long as he manipulated it the right way, according to its rules. The fact that teleportation wasn't working didn't mean it wasn't possible, just that he hadn't yet figured out the right combinations.

CJ sat like that for a long moment, his breathing slow and deliberate, until the frustration bled out of him. Only then did he pull up the mini tapestry again. And then he pulled up another one right beside it, and then a third. He wove one of them into a facsimile of his first attempt but stopped short at the last step. With another, he re-created what he'd done for his second attempt. Last, he followed the steps he took whenever he altered a part of the environment. He stared at the two failed approaches and the one successful one, comparing them, line by line, searching for patterns. It was tedious and frustrating.

But CJ loved numbers. And he wasn't leaving this spot until one of them bent the world to his will.

18

"I LOST HER," CHLOE'S VOICE SOUNDED in DJ's ear, low and annoyed. *"She ducked into something and just vanished."*

DJ let loose a stream of curses that had Christy looking impressed. "Hold your position. She couldn't have gone far, and she might have left tracks. Christy and I are almost there. We should be able to corner her."

Chloe gave a grunt that DJ took as acceptance, and then the line went dead. They were less than a minute from Chloe when a crackling static sounded around them. DJ paused, looking around for the source of the noise.

"Heyyyy, guys," Tyra's voice filled the space a moment later, echoing from all directions. "For a second, I was worried that you didn't figure out all those hints I dropped. But I'm so glad you guys could make it. The game's about to start."

Hints? DJ questioned internally. Olsen had said the analysts felt pretty confident that this was the place Tyra was going to go next. *And now we know why,* DJ thought, rubbing the bridge of his nose. He put Christy down and guided her toward where Chloe was supposed to be. He was clenching his daggers so hard his fist was white, and his head was on a swivel, trying to keep everything in his line of sight at the same time.

"Hey," Christy said, almost making him jump. "Superhero or not, you're going to snap your damn neck if you don't calm down." She had her pistol raised and was slotting armor-piercing rounds into it. She'd strapped the scope from her sniper rifle onto its barrel and was using its thermal setting to counter the shadows that covered everything on the damn rig.

DJ forced himself to calm down. He let out a breath and, very deliberately, loosened his shoulders. Christy was right; it was all well and good to be alert, but letting his paranoia get to him would only dampen his reaction time when it counted.

"Thank you, guys, so much for splitting up," Tyra said. "The result wouldn't have changed regardless, but it does make my job easier."

DJ scowled. She was obviously trying to manipulate them. A part of him wanted to order a rendezvous immediately, but that was the stupid part, the one that had Tyra living in his head, rent free.

"She's stalling," Christy muttered.

DJ nodded. Tyra liked to gloat, but so far she'd preferred to do it face-to-face. Shouting about how smart she was over the intercom was too obvious, especially since it meant she remained in one place and gave them more time to search her out. It smelled like a trap.

As if on cue, a deafening clang echoed through the rig, followed by a hiss of steam bursting from a nearby pipe. DJ spun toward the sound and squinted, trying to see through the steam. It could have been a coincidence—the place was so old that it was surprising more systems hadn't broken down—but DJ didn't think so. And Tyra's voice confirmed it a second later.

"Careful now." She laughed. "You wouldn't want to lose your way, would you? Not when you're so close."

DJ growled and waved his hand in front of him. Was that movement? He turned toward it, but there was nothing there. He could see through the steam, but it was difficult. He grabbed hold of Christy, who had—wisely—tucked away her gun and instead brandished a belt knife. That was good. If someone came close enough for her to use that, then vision wouldn't really be a problem.

Hand in hand, DJ led them slowly down the walkway. The steam curled around them, blurring the edges of the railing and obscuring the floor beneath their feet. It slowed them down and forced DJ to pause occasionally, squinting to make out the path ahead. Not that it mattered—by now, they'd taken too long, and Chloe had undoubtedly moved on.

"What's your location, Chloe?" DJ asked. "Send up a flare."

"Can't," Chloe responded. *"I lost it."*

"How could you lose it?! It was attached to your pack."

She mumbled something inaudible.

"What?"

"She snuck up on me," Chloe snapped. *"We fought for a few seconds, and she somehow managed to cut the strap to the pack. It fell off when I chased her, and it'll take too long to go and retrieve it. She's close. I can almost taste her."*

DJ blinked, too shocked to even say anything. Tyra had snuck up on Chloe. Fucking *Chloe.* The woman still managed to sneak up on DJ, and he could hear conversations through walls. And yet Tyra had snuck up on her. And more than that, the crazy bitch had managed to hold her own against Chloe and then escape unscathed. From *Chloe.*

Fuck.

Fortunately, he was distracted from the implications of that by the whirr of machinery somewhere in the distance. The steam had cleared by now, and DJ was high enough that he could estimate where it came from. Northeast, where the Murder Twins had gone.

"Liz, report."

The response came after a few seconds. *"My sister and I are pinned down by the automated loaders. The robotic arms activate when we get close and start throwing things at us."*

DJ rubbed his forehead. *What the hell is happening right now?* "Can't you... dodge them or something?"

Liz started to reply, but a thunderous crash drowned out her words. DJ jumped, despite himself, and his head snapped toward the source of the noise. Unsurprisingly, it was the same direction the twins were.

"I'm guessing the loaders are no longer a problem?" DJ asked.

"*Yes,*" Liz replied, and was that pride in her voice? "*My sister seems to have reached the end of her patience.*"

"Good, you guys should keep moving. You must be close to her if she's trying to slow both of you down. Chloe, you're basically on the other side of the rig, so make your way to the twins. Keep your ears out. Tyra should be somewhere in the middle of you guys." He waited for their confirmation before switching off the channel.

"And what are *we* going to do?" Christy asked.

"She's obviously in the system somehow, even though that shouldn't be possible. So far she's been baiting us to chase her while she clears the path to her own goal, slowing us down at the same time. So let's stop chasing. Corner her and bag her."

"And how do we do that?"

DJ pointed toward the far end of the bay, where he'd noticed a terminal blinking several minutes ago. He'd ignored it then, but that was before Tyra had started taking control of things. If the rig's systems were still operational, then DJ would bet that terminal was the key to shutting them down. "We take away her control."

INTERLUDE

JANUARY 2044
NEW YORK CITY

JOSÉ OLVERA did not cry.

The last time he had allowed such weakness was after his wife's murder. That was years ago, in another life. And after Helene's modifications, José did not think that it was physically possible to cry. He had no memories of those days, just a mesh of colors and vague impressions. What he could remember, in extremely vivid detail, was pushing his daughter from the path of that light, and the searing pain as every part, every inch of his flesh was burned.

José had never known such pain as that before. He had been sure he would die once the pain was done with him. He had been prepared to die. He had *welcomed* it. But then he'd woken up on a metal bench in a darkened room and found God staring down at him with eyes of molten gold.

In hindsight, that was the day he'd started to hate his daughters.

It was natural. Every parent grew to hate their children eventually. The seed of it was planted early on: They watched their offspring grow up and hated how fast the time flew. And then they hated how often the child disobeyed. José had skipped that stage, as he'd never allowed such weakness in his girls. He had trained them to be obedient. Karla had her bursts of independence, but it was always within limits, always within what José could control, because he would never allow it to get out of hand.

Until, of course, he did.

His time with Helene had separated him from his daughters for too long. And without him to guide them, they'd grown wings. His own daughter had accused him of caging them. But how could she not see that José had never caged them? He had guided them, he had protected them—because he couldn't bear to see them taken from him like his wife had been. Everything he had done—it had been to protect them or at least give them the ability to protect themselves. He had been prepared to die for that. Yet Karla had spat in his face.

José admitted that he had let his anger get the better of him when he'd sent her away. But it was still a good decision. She'd wanted freedom, so José would let her explore the world without him. And when it humbled her, he would welcome her back with open arms—and provide a fitting punishment for her disrespect.

Instead, she'd gone and managed to get herself captured by Tyra Chityothin.

If it had been anybody else, in any other organization on the planet, José would have destroyed anything in his way as he went to rescue her. But José had memories of Tyra Chityothin from his time in Helene's care. And fighting against her would be hopeless—almost as hopeless as fighting against God herself.

That was what his family did not understand. Chloe and Liz had gone rushing off, but they had already lost and did not even know it. One did not fight God.

And José...José would not squander his second chance on a fool's errand. Not for anyone. Not even for his family.

CHAPTER

19

JANUARY 2044
COAST OF LOUISIANA

DJ WAS PISSED. He always seemed to be when Tyra was involved. And it was because of that that he was able to control himself, even though his nanites raged in his veins, pushing him to move, to do something—anything—against the person who had annoyed him. DJ shoved down the instinct and controlled his expression; his lips pulled back into a snarl when he wasn't actively focusing on it.

It had taken them half an hour—a full *thirty minutes*—to shut down the terminal, due to Tyra's interference. Forklifts had suddenly come alive and either tried to ram them or block their paths and force them to waste time finding another way. Several times, crates filled with random machine parts had dropped on them from conveyor systems that should have been too rusted to move. Fortunately, Chloe and the twins had used the time to corner Tyra inside the storage bay, so DJ and Christy headed there when they were done. Without control of the systems, Tyra couldn't delay their return, and it only took a few minutes before they got there.

The storage bay was a cavernous, shadow-filled expanse. Its walls were lined with rusted scaffolding, and dust covered heavy-duty machines. There was a large, reinforced container near the edge of a raised platform, and its protective casing gleamed even in the poor lighting.

DJ scanned the area, Christy close beside him. The others were already there, weaving through the scattered equipment and the tangle of cables to try to find Tyra's hiding place. Why couldn't she just make this easy and give herself up?

Well, if they couldn't find her, they'd just have to force her out.

"Anyone got eyes on the target?"

"North side," Chloe responded, *"in the container. Tyra was messing with it when we got here. We've searched the place twice in case it's a trap, but there's no other place it could be."*

"Chloe, you and Liz work to open it. The rest of us will flush the rat out. We don't have to beat her—we just have to keep the device out of her hands." It was almost physically painful to say that, but obviously he didn't think straight when Tyra was involved, and she'd already proven adept at manipulating his hatred of her. DJ decided to take the easy win when he could get it and use the extra time it bought to figure out how to beat her. The fact that she'd singled him out during their last fight implied that she was confident in coming out ahead in any one-on-one fight they had—and that fact grated on his nerves.

A flicker of movement above him had DJ jumping backward. Nothing attacked him, but he caught the faintest glimpse of Tyra before she vanished back into the maze of pipes and walkways crisscrossing the rig's ceiling.

Found you, DJ thought, hiding a smile. He had deliberately whispered over the comm, knowing the silence in the room would make it easy for Tyra to overhear—and react. Now just to wait for her to...

A sharp clang rang out as a large pipe crashed to the ground, mere feet from where DJ stood. DJ spun toward where it had come from, but Tyra was already gone. His back bumped into a pipe, and it released a hiss of steam that forced DJ back, distracting him for an instant. Apparently, this was too tempting for Tyra, and she lunged out of the darkness.

"Got her!" DJ yelled, jumping back and narrowly dodging the attack.

"Chloe, you and Liz keep working on the container. Christy, I'm going to need some support. Karla..." DJ hesitated. He couldn't order her, and pleading wasn't going to work either. "She said your daggers are blunt. You gonna stand for that?"

Tyra laughed, straightening. Her lab coat fluttered behind her like a cape, somehow still pristine despite everything. "Finally admitted you can't handle me alone?" Her tone was as mocking as ever, but she moved like a coiled spring, waiting for an opening. DJ didn't bother responding. He shifted into a fighting stance, his hands steady, eyes locked on hers. Tyra grinned, and the low light cast sharp shadows across her face.

She lunged—and immediately twisted out of the air to avoid Karla's dagger. "You," Karla growled, "are going to pay for this." But she glanced-glared at DJ, leaving him wondering who the statement had been meant for. He took several steps back so he wasn't in the way as the two began their battle. What could he do?

He had his gun, but this fight was out of his league. At their speed, any shot risked hitting Karla—or just distracting her—and Christy wouldn't be able to see more than a blur anyway.

Still, DJ kept his gun raised just in case he saw an opening. Several feet away, Karla pressed her attack. In the darkness, her daggers looked like the claws of a beast, swiping at its prey. The growling didn't help. Unfortunately, Tyra was smart enough to know that she couldn't match Karla head-on. So she didn't. She darted between rusted pipes, ducked under thick cables, and generally did everything she could to avoid taking Karla's attacks.

It barely worked. For the first time, DJ saw Tyra panic. There was no fear on her face, of course, but she'd lost her mad grin, and her eyes showed her focus— and that passed the same message. Each time Karla's dagger came close, Tyra twisted just out of reach. But it was a near thing every time.

She and Karla were matched for speed, which was surprising enough, since Tyra and DJ were supposed to be matched—*When and how had she become faster?*—but Karla had far more skill and experience.

DJ was surprised that the bitch was lasting so long. Every time he and Tyra had fought, she'd won by outsmarting him in some way, never by overpowering him. So, he'd figured that the gap between her and Karla meant that the fight would be over instantly.

It took him a moment to understand the problem though.

Karla had Tyra beat in skill, but her fighting style was overly aggressive, full of furious swipes designed to break through her opponents' techniques. Tyra wasn't fighting back, though, so there was no technique to break. She just had to keep ahead of Karla. Usually Karla's enhanced attributes would make that impossible—it was hard to run and evade when she was several times faster than you, and when even a single strike meant death. But Tyra matched her in speed, and with the same enhancements, she could stay just out of reach, making Karla's attacks ineffective.

DJ almost face-palmed. Karla's fighting style would be enough to defeat most opponents, but it had gaps. DJ would bet good money that Liz's fighting style would cover those flaws, but since she wasn't here, Tyra was free to exploit them as she wished.

And she did.

Karla snarled as the blade scraped metal instead of flesh, throwing out sparks. She adjusted, baiting Tyra with a feint to the midsection, then immediately striking at her neck. But Tyra was already gone, sliding across the slick grating to take cover behind a broken piece of machinery. She blended into the mesh of pipes and almost disappeared into the shadows. Karla followed her without missing a beat.

"She's stalling," DJ muttered, running after them. He couldn't keep up with either of them, but he didn't have to. He couldn't anticipate and cover for Karla like her sister could, but he could still provide support. In this case, that meant controlling the battlefield, stopping Tyra from using the terrain to her advantage. His eyes darted across the platform, taking it all in.

Pipes thick with rust crisscrossed overhead, while broken machine parts cluttered the floor. Steam hissed intermittently from the joints, forming a thin veil that obscured vision the deeper one went into them. Tyra moved among all this like a monkey in the trees, darting across the pipes. She stopped at one and grinned at him, eyes wide and lips pulled back.

DJ recoiled and then cursed at himself as Karla passed him. He rushed to follow, but then paused, following Tyra's path with his eyes. There was a valve near one of the larger pipes, and DJ veered toward it. A second later, his fingers gripped the wheel and forced it open with a sharp twist. A plume of steam erupted in Tyra's path, cutting it off. She hesitated for a split second, glancing at him. DJ gave a small wave as Karla took advantage of the moment to close the distance. And suddenly, Tyra was too busy staying ahead of Karla's attacks to glare at him.

DJ moved again, weaving between the clutter to stay parallel to the fight. He fired a shot at the base of a stack of crates Tyra was heading for, and it collapsed in a cascade of wood and metal that forced Tyra to pivot away or risk getting blinded by the dust. She darted toward another section of the platform, but DJ was already there, grinning at the look of annoyance on the bitch's face. Another burst of steam hissed as he twisted a second valve that forced her away.

Karla growled at his interference, but she didn't hesitate to press the advantage. She adjusted instinctively, and her attacks grew sharper, more focused, pressing Tyra to take more and more hits as she tried to stay ahead.

We're doing it, DJ thought. *We're actually fucking doing it.*

Tyra's movements grew sharper as well, but less fluid, her evasion more desperate than deliberate. DJ's pulse hammered in his ears as he shifted again, stepping into her line of retreat. He leveled his gun—not to fire but to force her to recalculate. And truly, she started to raise her right hand—with the titanium prosthetic that would allow her to deflect his bullet. But all DJ had been after was to give Karla the split-second distraction she needed to ram her dagger into Tyra's back.

Tyra twisted immediately and stepped back toward the dagger to stop it from doing more damage. She threw her elbow back, forcing Karla to lean away and loosen her grip—giving Tyra enough space to leap several feet to a pipe overhead. With the dagger still stuck in her back, the move must have been excruciating. Surprisingly, Karla didn't press her advantage.

Above them, Tyra crouched. She tilted her head slightly, as if processing the audacity of what had just happened. The dagger came out with a spurt of blood that stood out starkly against her white lab coat. She stared at it.

And then she laughed.

DJ froze, and even Karla paused. The whole world seemed to be suspended in that single frame where Tyra's laughter was the only thing that existed. It was sharp, uneven, like something broken trying to piece itself together. It echoed off the steel walls, hollow and jagged. DJ could almost feel it crawling under his skin, and he recoiled instinctively. It wasn't the laugh of someone unhinged. Just the opposite: It was the laugh of someone in extreme control, someone who had already decided what came next.

The sound lingered, stretching the moment, until Chloe's voice broke it.

"It's open!" she shouted in his ear. Her voice carried far more urgency than usual, as if she weren't sure he'd hear her through the comms. Tyra's head snapped toward it.

And then the world snapped back into focus.

Tyra shifted her stance slightly, making DJ tense. Karla lunged at her instantly, but with a sharp flick of her wrist, Tyra sent Karla's dagger spinning back toward her. In the same heartbeat, Tyra vaulted through the air—not at Karla but straight toward DJ. Karla snatched the dagger just inches from her eye, ready to retaliate, but Tyra was already moving past her, faster than he could track.

DJ gritted his teeth, squeezed off two shots—which she deflected—and braced for the impact. Despite that, he staggered when her shoulder slammed into his. DJ recovered immediately and tried to grab hold of her, but she was still somehow faster, twisting around him like a snake. One moment she was in front of him, and the next she was hooking an arm around his neck from behind.

She turned him around, just in time to evade a strike from Karla, and then brandished him like a shield. "Well?"

The implication was obvious. Karla could attempt to continue her attack, but she'd risk hurting him. DJ would have laughed if he had the air for it. Karla was the most bloodthirsty person he knew. She didn't care about hitting him. She could gut him and think of it as a fair price if it got Tyra too. It shouldn't have been a question.

And yet, she hesitated.

It was only for a split second, but that was more than enough for Tyra. She lunged toward Karla—who sidestepped to avoid her—then launched off a crate, propelling herself to the other side of the room.

Toward Chloe and Liz.

"She's coming toward you," DJ yelled into his comm. He pressed his finger to his ear to change the channel and repeat the message—and felt nothing. His earpiece was gone. "That bitch."

The ground had too many obstacles that would slow him down, so DJ jumped up to one of the pipes overhead. He leaped from pipe to pipe as fast as he could, but even though he could move easier after Karla's training, he wouldn't be fast enough to make it in time.

From this high up, he could see across the room as Tyra got close to the container. Liz rushed out to meet her, and Tyra responded by pulling a device from her lab coat pocket. With a savage grin, she activated it, and all the pipes around the container exploded. Several jets of steam filled the area, and within a second, everything was covered with a thick haze.

DJ crouched on a pipe. He could hear furious fighting within the cloud, but he couldn't make out anything. Should he go in? Or would that just risk Tyra using him as a shield again? Especially since he wouldn't be able to see anything. DJ gritted his teeth but stayed where he was.

The cloud dissipated in only a minute, but by the time it did, Tyra was gone.

And so was the stabilizer.

20

DJ LAY ON HIS BED, staring blankly at the ceiling of his room. Tyra had somehow escaped the oil rig with the stabilizer, a feat that no one had been able to explain. Karla and Liz had been the fastest ones out of the storage area, but they'd only seen her dive off the edge. While Liz had restrained her sister from jumping after Tyra, DJ had contacted the ground team that Olsen had posted at the shore. Their job had been to watch for drones or shoot down any craft Tyra used—which they couldn't do, as there'd been no sight of her. Even the satellites Olsen had covering the area hadn't caught her. Somehow she'd disappeared the moment she hit the water.

It'd taken the admiral an hour to rustle up a chopper, since the one they'd arrived in was at the bottom of the Gulf of Mexico, and then they'd endured the six-hour trip back to New York, just in time for DJ to collapse on the bed. He was the only one in the room, which meant CJ still had his consciousness uploaded to the Virtual Realm.

That was another thing that DJ had to worry about: whether his brother was getting addicted to that place. CJ was probably the only one who could rescue Manar's consciousness from there—which made his mission important and the time spent there valid. And it wouldn't have been a problem if DJ didn't know that his brother was also using the mission as an escape from the "problems" of his real body.

The question was, What should he do about it? Could he even do anything about it? DJ already felt like a dick from spore-blocking CJ.

One at a time, DJ groaned, shifting onto his side, cuddling one pillow while resting his head on another. *Tyra. Let's figure out how to deal with Tyra.*

He replayed their last few confrontations in his head and released another groan. Where did he even start?

Their first fight against her in Nevada had shown that numbers meant nothing. DJ had chalked it up to the fact that she'd separated their heavy hitters—Chloe, Karla and Liz—and focused on him, who she had proven to be a match for, and who she seemed determined to keep humiliating. But they'd all been together at the oil rig, or at least close enough to cover one another. Yet she'd treated them like children. She'd even been able to match Karla, something DJ hadn't even thought was possible when she wasn't holding back. She'd somehow become faster in the twenty-four hours between Nevada and the oil rig.

How though? DJ couldn't figure that out. Obviously it had something to do with the nanites, but DJ had the same nanites, and his improvements had come with weeks in between, usually after something—usually Tyra—pissed him off to a new level. It was never within a day, and something about the whole thing bugged him.

But it didn't really matter. Even if he figured it out, it wouldn't help him deal with her. Tyra had proven that their numbers didn't matter and that even the Murder Family working against her wasn't enough to slow her down. And that meant running after her whenever she surfaced was pointless—though that didn't mean they'd stop.

DJ hugged the pillow closer. He needed to come up with a better plan. But what?

His thoughts were interrupted by someone barging into the room. DJ turned to look and met Christy's eyes as she stood at the threshold, staring at him as he hugged a pillow in a fetal position. DJ sighed and lay back. *I don't even give a fuck anymore.*

"Get your ass up," Christy said, slamming the door shut. She smacked his shins, which he barely felt.

DJ hugged the pillow tighter. "Honestly, Christy, I just got back from having my ass handed to me, so I'm not really in the mood right now."

"Yeah, well, you and me both," Christy replied, smacking him again, hard enough that she probably hurt herself too. "But unfortunately we don't have a choice. Sit up. Tyra is back to work."

DJ sighed again, this time more deeply. He straightened so he was sitting at the edge of the bed. "Honestly, we can just let her have this one. Facing her again right after that fiasco..."

"It's not that." She grabbed the remote from the nightstand and switched on the TV, surfing through the channels before stopping at a news station. "Watch."

The two anchors stared at the screen, their expressions uncharacteristically serious. DJ barely noticed that. His gaze was instead fixed on the headline below them: Breaking News: Ex-SEAL Rampages Across White House, Displays Superhuman Abilities.

"What the hell?" DJ said, his eyes wide.

A video hovering at the edge expanded to take up the whole screen, and suddenly, DJ was staring at himself rampaging through a hallway with a portrait of Jefferson on the wall. The White House. Fuck.

By the angle, the footage had been taken from a surveillance camera. Although the video was blurry, DJ's face was crystal clear. *Suspiciously* crystal clear. It showed him punching a Secret Service dude so hard in the chest that it sent the man flying into a pillar. DJ remembered that. It was after they'd started shooting at him and he'd gone ballistic. The video switched, showing another hallway and another altercation with the guards. Debris rained down as he tore through them, his punches cracking ribs and sending the men flying like they'd been shot out of a cannon. In another one, he stood at the opposite end of the hallway from the guards, dodging bullets.

"This is bullshit," DJ said.

"I know," Christy replied.

"No, I mean it's actually bullshit. I couldn't dodge bullets then. Shit, I can't dodge bullets *now*. No one can. Even the Murder Twins have to use their prosthetics to tank them. It's bullshit."

"How about that one?"

The next video was a closer shot clearly capturing DJ's face. His expression was a mask of fury, and his eyes glowed red. Like he was the Terminator or some shit. The camera panned out to show a visible distortion around him, as if his raw power was warping the air. On the screen, DJ grabbed an agent's rifle mid-swing—*Bullshit,* DJ thought. *They didn't use rifles; they used batons.* He snapped the rifle over his knee like a twig before hurling the agent against the wall. The force left a crater in the plaster, and DJ stepped back, effortlessly dodging another agent's tackle with supernatural grace. The video provided no sound. If it had, they would have heard DJ loudly explaining that he just needed to see someone in charge and that he had information that would clear everything up.

"Some of it, yeah," he said, answering Christy.

The anchor's voice returned, dripping with accusation. *"These shocking videos were released earlier today by an anonymous patriot. And as you saw, they show someone who might be familiar to some of our viewers. That's right, the video shows the ex-SEAL Darren Kojak engaging in what can only be described as a violent rampage in the White House using what seems to be superhuman abilities.*

While the circumstances of the event remain unclear, this isn't the first superhuman controversy that Mr. Kojak has been involved in. A few months ago, during the raid on the headquarters of the worldwide conglomerate Sparta, Mr. Kojak was observed—"

DJ smashed down the mute button hard enough to break the remote.

"Jesus, D," Christy said, snatching it from him. "You gotta get that under control."

DJ barely heard her over the ringing in his ears. All he could see was the image of himself on the screen—angry, destructive, and terrifying. The video had shifted again, this time showing DJ at Sparta during the raid. Fires raged in the background, and civilians—scientists, technicians and regular staff—were shown fleeing in terror, though all of them had been safely secured inside bunkers and nowhere near the fight that day. It showed DJ tackling a drone, his fists slamming into the machine and sending shock waves through the area. To anyone watching, the sheer force of the impact made him look like an unhinged person destroying whatever was in his path.

Another clip showed Liz and Chloe—who, again, had been nowhere near the fight that day—fighting another group of drones. But the angles made it seem like they were taking potshots at civilians whenever they got the chance.

This was what he'd been afraid of when the rumors about him had started, of his image being distorted and weaponized against him. The stuff in the White House had been an accident. It was around the time that the nanites had started affecting his emotions, but DJ hadn't realized it, and it'd taken him a while to learn to control it. But the world didn't have that context. All they saw was a monster running around in their nation's fucking seat of power, with no one being able to stop him.

It was the worst kind of nightmare for DJ: He was going to be a hashtag.

CHAPTER

21

JANUARY 2044
SPARTA HEADQUARTERS, NEW YORK

THE AIR INSIDE SPARTA felt thick, almost suffocating, as DJ and Christy made their way toward the elevator. His room was in the residential part of the building, the part reserved for guests or staff high enough on the ladder to merit on-site quarters. During a normal day, DJ could pass one or two of his neighbors while making his way down. Today, all of them—about half a dozen— were standing outside of their rooms for no discernible reason.

DJ nodded at Max, who stayed a few rooms down. "How's Martha?" he asked. Martha was either Max's wife or lover. DJ had never been able to get a straight answer, but asking about her was their ritual. Usually, Max would make a somewhat sexist joke and ask about CJ. He would laugh, DJ would laugh, and then they'd move on.

Today, Max gave him a strained smile and an awkward wave with the hand holding a coffee mug. "She's fine. Thanks for asking."

After two more interactions like that, DJ got the hint and stopped. Christy kept pace beside him, her lips pulled into a grimace. Her cherry-blonde hair was pulled into its characteristic bun, but it just hung limply down her neck, as if matching her mood. The elevator ride was silent, but it only lasted a minute before the doors opened into the hallway that led to the conference room.

This time, DJ knew to keep his eyes forward and ignore the fact that people gave him a wide berth, or that conversations faltered as he approached. Unfortunately, DJ could still hear the hushed whispers, no matter how low their voice was or how far away they were. An intern turned the corner and jumped when he saw DJ and Christy. He raised the stack of papers he was carrying to avoid eye contact and adjusted his path until he was basically hugging the wall. Others weren't as subtle. A technician stopped in the middle of the hallway, staring openly as DJ passed. At the end of the passage, two security guards watched him with barely concealed unease.

"This is ridiculous," DJ said when they passed them. "A few weeks ago, I was these people's hero. I mean, I hated the attention, but that was still better than this shit. From their expression, you'd think I'll randomly start smashing heads into walls."

"In their defense," Christy said dryly, "they just watched you doing exactly that."

DJ groaned but pushed open the door to the conference room without a word.

"There you are," Hermione said. "Where the hell have you been?"

"Trying to take a nap," DJ replied, pulling up a chair at the end of the table so he faced the others. "I understand now that was a mistake." He gave a nod of acknowledgment to Ndidi, which she returned. He'd have to find some time to talk to her soon. Hermione was pacing the length of the table, running her hands through her hair. DJ raised a brow at that. Why did she have her panties in a twist? None of the videos had shown her.

DJ had expected the Murder Family to be up in arms—the fact that they'd shown up in the videos at all was heavy proof that the leak was planned and Tyra wanted their faces out there. But surprisingly, all three of them sat calmly at their usual spots. Chloe had made herself a cup of coffee and was smiling softly as she sipped it. Even Karla looked relatively mellow. At least, she wasn't proclaiming that her daggers thirsted for blood or anything. Liz—well, Liz was being Liz: completely unreadable. As was CJ, though that was expected.

Fortunately, the TV was turned on but muted. The videos played on a loop in a corner of the screen while the anchors discussed. Below them, headlines flashed in bold, sensationalist fonts.

Footage Leak: A New Era of Fear?

Can the Berserker Virus Grant Superhuman Abilities?

**Superhumans Are Real—What Other Legends
Might Be Walking Among Us?**

DJ sighed. "Can we please turn that off?"

"I think it's fun," Chloe chuckled. "They got my good side."

"No joking, please," Hermione groaned. "This is serious stuff. Tyra didn't just release the videos—she weaponized it. She didn't just send it to the media but to all the social media platforms, private networks, and even some encrypted channels. She wasn't taking any chances."

"Yeah, we can see that." Christy sighed. "But what I want to know is, why now? The stuff with the White House happened ages ago, and even the raid was several weeks ago—"

"That's another thing," DJ said, cutting her off without meaning to. "How the hell did she get the White House footage? It was supposed to be locked up tighter than a nun's asshole." Chloe chuckled into her cup, but Ndidi, Christy, and Hermione glared at him. "You can crucify me later, ladies."

"Um, I was able to break into the White House's security," CJ said. "It was only periphery access, and I was only piggybacking on the cameras, but it's not a stretch to imagine that Tyra could do the same thing, especially if she wasn't afraid of being caught."

"Either that," Ndidi added, "or she has a thrall in the government who had the necessary clearance to access it."

That was a scary thought. Helene had several thralls within the government. Olsen's boss and the man who'd forced DJ from the SEALs—Admiral

Austin—had been one of them until DJ had used the pulse on him, deactivating the picospores in his body long enough to extract them. In fact, the situation at the White House had occurred because DJ had learned that Helene planned on dousing the entire Cabinet, including the president, with picospores. DJ had managed to stop the attempt, but everybody knew Helene had several others already embedded. The problem was identifying them.

Mary Pastore, the president, had assured DJ that everything involving the incident would be subject to a lot of red tape. If someone could access it, they were pretty high up in the government.

"However she got it," Christy said, glaring at DJ, "she obviously released it for a reason."

"Christy's right," Hermione said. "She's stoked a fire and turned the public against us. We need to figure out the next move before it gets worse."

A part of DJ wanted to believe she'd done this as retaliation. Even though she'd escaped from the oil rig, they'd still managed to grievously injure her. He wanted to believe that she was just angry and therefore was trying to ruin their lives—but Hermione was right. That was too simple an answer. It could have been part of it, but it definitely wasn't her entire plan.

He leaned forward, resting his elbows on the table. "Let's focus on what she gains. The footage obviously wants to make us out to be the bag guy, a monster with superhuman abilities that even the White House can't control. I'd assume that's to destabilize our position, make us lose credibility, or something."

"But we had no credibility in the first place," Christy said. "We've never needed it. The whole thing with Helene was in the background."

"But now it's not," Ndidi pointed out. "Helene had already started making public moves, but now Tyra's brought the whole thing out into the open. Now that the public is involved, their opinion is going to matter a lot. And with the video, we're already on the back foot."

Chloe slurped loudly from her cup. "Plus, it distracts us," she said. "While we're dealing with this, she can move virtually unobstructed toward whatever goal she and Helene have planned."

"Classic misdirection," said Christy with a groan. "She keeps us tied up managing public fallout while she gets closer to her objective. And with the public watching now, we can't afford a misstep."

"We can't let the public dictate our mission," DJ said firmly. "If we focus too much on damage control, Tyra wins."

"But we can't ignore it either," Hermione said, running her hand through her hair again. "This was designed to create pressure on all sides—public, political, and, hell, even internal. And it's working. Social media is going crazy with this. Half the world thinks that you're a monster that needs to be jailed."

"They can shout all they want," DJ snapped. "This isn't a popularity contest, Hermione, and if they're stupid enough to believe videos that are so obviously doctored, then let them. But I'm not going to start bending over backward to please a bunch of idiots who haven't been able to see the shit going on under their noses for the last couple of years—even with drones flying over their heads. They want to jail me? Let them fucking try."

The entire room fell silent, everyone staring at him. And then Karla grunted, speaking up for the first time since DJ had entered the room. "That is a good response. Why does the opinion of sheep matter? Kill anyone who puts themselves against you and prove to them that they were wrong to consider you prey. That is the mindset of a predator."

"Predator?" DJ repeated, surprised. "The hell? I'm not going to kill anybody."

"Yes," Karla agreed, twirling her dagger between her knuckles. "I'm sure when you punch them in the chest with fists strong enough to dent steel, you would only hurt them a little. Or maybe you would just give them a firm warning while their guns are pointed at you?"

"You're not helping," Hermione snapped—quite bravely, considering who she was talking to. She must have been more worked up than he'd thought. "And DJ, this isn't just noise. People are scared, and fear is a powerful motivator. It makes people do stupid things."

"Then someone needs to explain to them what's really happening," DJ said.

Hermione stopped pacing and raised a brow. "What, you're going to hold a press conference? Tell the world about Helene, Tyra, everything? DJ, if you think the video is bad now, imagine how they'll react when they actually find out the truth."

"They'd find out the truth eventually. The problem is that it might be when there's a missile headed straight for a populated city, carrying a payload that could kill us all. Helene obviously doesn't care if the public knows, and Tyra has already opened the can of worms. We're just kicking it over. And at least, this way, we're the ones controlling the narrative. If we wait, Tyra is going to do it for us."

"That's a big risk, DJ," Hermione said. "Humans are dumb. They don't want to hear the truth. Especially, if the truth is that they've been blind and lied to for the last few years." Ndidi, CJ, and Christy nodded in agreement, but the Murder Family didn't say anything, as if they didn't care either way.

DJ sighed. Sure, some people would take it badly, but there was no way the majority of them would side with Helene. If public opinion was important, then this was the way to get it. His gut was telling him this was the right move. But his gut was pretty pissed off at the whole thing. "Fine, we'll put a pin in it. But we can at least release a statement, right? Denouncing the bullshit?"

"Yeah, staying silent is worse," Hermione agreed. "But what're we going to do about Tyra herself?"

DJ shrugged. He had no idea.

It was Ndidi that spoke up. "We could beat her at her own game," she suggested. "Regardless of her overarching plan, part of her goal with the videos had to be to distract us, to split our focus. So we do the same thing for her. DJ, Admiral Olsen mentioned that he has a list of the components that Tyra needs and where she's most likely to find them, right?"

"Right..."

"Well, so far, we've been waiting for her to strike so we can catch her. Since that hasn't worked so far, it's pointless to keep trying. What we *can* do is take advantage of the fact that Tyra works alone and, thus, can't be everywhere at once. We use Olsen's list and some agents and target all the components that Tyra needs simultaneously. That'll force her to divide her attention, and it'll tell us which piece she considers the most important, because that's the one she'd go after."

DJ rubbed his chin. "That's actually not a bad idea. And I'm not gonna lie, I'm tired of getting my ass kicked. As much as I hate the bitch, I could do with never seeing her again. I'll talk to Olsen and see how many agents we can round up. Thanks for that."

Ndidi looked surprised, and she gave him a small smile. It was a really good idea, though Karla looked like she wanted to stab Ndidi. She probably thought it was cowardly or something. Fortunately, Liz placed a hand on Karla's shoulder before the redhead could say anything—or leap across the table.

"Anything else?" DJ asked, looking around the room. "No? Well, I'm going back to my nap."

IN FACT, DJ DID NOT GO back to his nap. He signaled for Ndidi to wait behind while the rest of the team trouped out. Hermione noticed the gesture and gave him a stern look as she left. CJ cocked his head, asking a question with his eyes, but DJ waved him off. DJ would have to talk to him later as well.

Eventually, the room was empty except for him and Ndidi at opposite ends of the table. DJ rummaged through his brain for what to say. His plan, originally, had been to ask for more details about Ndidi's escape, but Hermione had already summarized it, and she'd warned him not to poke further in case it triggered her. DJ hadn't taken her seriously initially—since when could anything trigger Ndidi?—but looking at her now…

DJ didn't know if it was exhaustion or something deeper, but the Ndidi who sat in front of him wasn't the same person who'd left for Nigeria. She looked smaller somehow—despite showing noticeable signs of pregnancy. She'd freshened up, but the cuts on her face and arms would take a while to heal. The only thing that convinced him she was still the same person was the stubborn resolve in how she met his eyes. That resolve had made her betray the team for Bethany and justify it to herself. But that determination was somehow different—familiar yet new at the same time.

"How's Pratima doing?" DJ asked finally. "Hermione said she was wounded during your escape."

Ndidi nodded. "She's been patched up at the clinic. Now she just needs to rest so she doesn't aggravate the injury."

"I can't imagine she's taking that well." Pratima was like a mountain—except it could move, and it always did. Being forced to sit still would have been torture for her, especially since her charge, Ndidi, was up and about.

"I threatened to tie her to the bed," Ndidi admitted. "When that didn't work, I had to guilt-trip her. Pointed out that she wouldn't be able to protect me if she opened up her wounds again and extended her recovery period."

"Devious." DJ smirked. "But smart. I'm glad you're both okay. I can't imagine what it must have been like for you over there."

Ndidi clasped her hands tightly, and DJ noticed a faint tremble in her fingers. "It was a nightmare, DJ. At first, I didn't even realize—she imitated him so well. Same pride, same quirks. Everything. There were flaws, of course. Little things she said—or didn't say. But I brushed them all off, and I probably would have kept brushing them off, deluding myself, if I hadn't caught her that night."

DJ stayed silent. Ndidi had already told them the story of how she'd found Manar-Helene in what was supposed to be an abandoned lab within the Corporation, fabricating new nanites for herself. Helene had caught her peeping, and since the jig was up, the AI no longer bothered to pretend. From then on, Ndidi had been a captive in her own company.

"But you made it back," DJ said comfortingly.

"I did. And I owe you an apology."

DJ frowned. "For what?"

She took a deep breath as if to prepare herself. "I've been...thinking. A lot. About everything, every decision that I've made and justified, thinking I was right. Ignoring Helene's flaws was one, and so was allowing her to convince me to restart the picospore project. I've been reconsidering everything, and I realize how wrong I was, about what I did to save Bethany."

DJ's eyes narrowed slightly. He didn't say anything, didn't blink, and didn't give her an inch. Several years ago, during the chaos of Mayday, Helene had kidnapped several people—including Bethany, who was Ndidi's ward—held them captive, dowsed them with picospores, and controlled them as thralls to be her eyes and ears without anyone even realizing.

However, more than a year ago, the AI had deliberately revealed Bethany to Ndidi in order to convince Ndidi to betray the team and sabotage Manar's plan to upload his consciousness to the Virtual Realm. In return, Helene was supposed to release Bethany. Ndidi fulfilled her end of the deal—and her betrayal placed Manar and CJ in a coma for months while their consciousnesses were trapped on the Virtual Realm.

However, Helene hadn't released Bethany. Instead she'd captured Ndidi and held her for a couple of months until DJ, the rest of the team, and the Murder Family had finally tracked down the place and raided it. They rescued Ndidi, Bethany, and several hundred other people that Helene had been holding captive.

However, that incident caused a rift between him and Ndidi, especially since she never apologized. Until now, at least. DJ didn't know what to think.

Ndidi took another deep breath. "I know that my actions hurt you—hurt all of us. But I wasn't thinking about the consequences. And I wasn't thinking about the team every time I convinced myself that what I did was right. I'm sorry that it took me so long to see that.

"I'm not going to pretend that I regret saving Bethany," Ndidi continued, her voice steady. "But I *do* regret how I went about it, and I regret the cost. I regret that your brother and Manar suffered because of my decision. I regret that I betrayed your trust. And I'm sorry for that. Truly."

DJ let out a slow breath, running his hand over his face. He didn't know what to think. "It's hard, y'know? I get why you did it—I do. But it doesn't make it easier to accept. It wasn't just selfish—it was reckless. I'm mostly pissed at what it did to my brother, but your betrayal is what led to where we are right now. You know that, right?"

Ndidi flinched but then steadied herself. "I know," she said, her voice shaken but resolute. "And I doubt I'll ever stop regretting that. I don't expect forgiveness overnight or even at all. I just...I want you to know that I'm committed to making things right. To stopping Helene and protecting my child. Whatever it takes."

DJ studied her for a long moment. "You sound determined."

"I am. Helene used me, manipulated me, and I fell for it. But never again. I won't let her get her hands on my child or anyone else I care about."

DJ nodded, unable to stop the flicker of respect he felt. He wasn't sure if he believed her yet, but he could see she believed herself. For now, that would have to be enough. "All right then. We're going to need everyone on board for what's coming. Tyra and Helene are not done with whatever they have planned."

Ndidi gave a small, tentative nod. The air between them wasn't clear—not yet—but it was a start. And sometimes, that was all that was needed. "Tell me again how you guys escaped," DJ said. "Hermione is shitty at giving reports."

CJ DIDN'T TURN AROUND when the door opened and his brother walked in. He adjusted the towel around his waist and used another to dry off his hair. He'd hoped he would already be gone by the time DJ finished talking with Ndidi, but he'd started puzzling out some problems he'd encountered in the Virtual Realm and had lost track of time.

"Hey, bro," DJ said, deceptively upbeat. CJ was probably the only person who would have been able to notice the forced cheerfulness in his tone. "Whatchu you up to?"

CJ turned around, glanced down at the towel around his waist, at the shirt he'd laid on the bed, and then raised a brow at his brother, who smiled awkwardly.

"I meant, whatchu up to *after* you're done dressing?"

CJ nodded slowly, as if he were processing the question. A few weeks ago, he wouldn't have had to pretend. "Work," he said simply. Would he have said more before?

"Work, huh?" DJ said, crossing the room to sit on the swivel chair next to the table. "You've been on that for days now. When was the last time you took a break?"

"Half an hour ago," CJ replied, "when I came for the meeting."

"Come on, you know that's not what I meant."

"I'm fine," CJ said.

"You always say that."

"Because it's true."

Their eyes met, and for a moment, CJ felt a flash of guilt. His brother worried about him. He knew DJ thought the Virtual Realm was consuming him, but how could he explain that it wasn't the work that was pulling him in—it was the freedom?

When he was there, he didn't have to worry about endless societal accommodations or watch for facial expressions, worried that he missed something behind their measured smiles and side glances.

But most importantly, he didn't have to pretend to still have a neurological disorder. That was the worst. It was stressful, frustrating, and annoying, to the point that he was afraid to speak so his brother wouldn't notice when he slipped up. Because he *always* slipped up. Because he no longer had to spend several minutes processing questions and searching for the right word. It was just... there. It was natural to respond immediately. The life he'd lived before, that was the unnatural one.

And CJ hated pretending that he was still living it.

But his brother wouldn't understand that. Things hadn't been the same since that night DJ had caught him about to inject the spores into himself. CJ couldn't forget the look in DJ's eyes—half anger, half desperation. He understood why DJ was worried, why he was afraid. But more and more, CJ was tired of understanding. Couldn't he be allowed to make his own decisions just once without everyone treating him like he was made of glass?

They'd barely spoken since that night. DJ would never say it, but CJ knew he didn't trust him anymore. And that was fine. Because CJ didn't exactly trust DJ to understand why he'd done what he did—or why the Virtual Realm had become a sanctuary for him.

DJ shifted in the chair, and his posture softened slightly. "Look, I get it. You want to save Manar. I'm not saying stop. All I'm saying is maybe take a step back for a few hours. Take a walk, put some food in your stomach, and sleep for more than an hour at a time. You're wearing yourself thin, bro."

CJ let out a shaky breath. "It's not that simple, DJ. This isn't something that I can just step back from. Manar doesn't have time."

"And neither do you," DJ shot back. "Not if you keep going like this."

CJ yanked the shirt over his head. "You don't get it, okay? This isn't just about Manar. It's about fixing everything. It's about…" He trailed off, searching for the right words.

DJ frowned. "About what?"

CJ shook his head, running a hand through his hair before putting on his pants. "Nothing. Forget about it." But he knew it was pointless. DJ would sometimes let things go, but that was back when there had still been trust between them.

This time, he lasted a little over five seconds before he spoke. "What aren't you telling me, bro?"

A lot, CJ thought. But there was no point telling him when he wouldn't understand. So CJ deflected. It was something new he'd learned, when all his focus wasn't solely about answering the question. "I'm stuck, all right? There are too many places Manar could be, and they're too far apart. I've been trying to figure out how to teleport to each place."

DJ's expression softened, just a little. "And how's that going?"

CJ hesitated. "It's a work in progress. But I'm close."

"Right." DJ exhaled, and the tension eased slightly with that. "Look, I'm not here to tell you how to do your job. I just…I don't want to lose you to this place. You've been spending so much time there, and—"

"And what?" CJ said, his voice sharper than he intended.

"And I'm worried, all right?" DJ admitted with a shrug. "I'm worried you're getting too comfortable in there. Like maybe you don't want to come back."

CJ's chest tightened, but he forced himself to laugh it off. "That's ridiculous."

"Is it?"

CJ didn't answer.

DJ stood from the chair and walked closer. He licked his lips and squared his shoulders, as if bracing himself for what he was about to say. "I'm not saying stop. I'm just saying...let me in. Let me see what's got you so hooked on this place."

CJ blinked, caught off guard. "*You* want to come into the Virtual Realm?"

"I mean, I figure it's possible since you jumped in after Manar." DJ shrugged. "Show me what's so great about it."

CJ hesitated. He'd expected an argument the moment his brother had entered the room—and they'd done that. He'd considered a compromise, but he hadn't expected *this*. DJ hated the Virtual Realm—more specifically, tech flew over his head, and he hated that. But now? Now he was offering to give it a try, even though he hated it, and was probably a little terrified of the thought. And he was doing it because he was worried about CJ.

"All right," CJ said finally. "But don't say I didn't warn you."

DJ smirked, though CJ was the only person who could notice the nervousness he tried to hide. "I can handle it."

CJ nodded, though his mind was already racing. This wasn't just about showing his brother around. It was about showing him why the Virtual Realm mattered so much to him—getting him to, if not understand, then at least accept.

CJ STOOD IN THE MIDDLE of an almost-desolate wasteland, which had been ruined by patches of grass he'd created when practicing. Behind him, DJ shifted uncomfortably, clenching his fists with an unreadable expression.

He won't be able to use his nanites here, CJ thought. His brother's abilities would probably manifest in another way, like how Manar's had. Except DJ had several times more nanites than Manar had, so his abilities would probably be orders of magnitudes stronger. *Unfortunately, it's wasted on him.*

CJ flinched. Where had that come from? His brother probably wouldn't be able to use his abilities to their full potential while in the Virtual Realm, but he was able to back in the real world, and he used them for good. To be a hero.

CJ's lips pulled into a flat line. Obviously, there was a part of him that resented his brother for how their lives had turned out. Logically, he knew it wasn't DJ's fault—his brother had always looked out for him, even when it might have been easier not to. But CJ couldn't help his emotions. What he could do was fight those thoughts whenever they popped up. Because he would *not* let that bitterness grow.

He turned to see that DJ had stopped staring at his fists and started looking around. He wasn't used to the Virtual Realm, and it showed in the tenseness around his shoulders and the way he glanced around like he expected something to leap out at any moment. It must have been worse for him, since he knew he couldn't count on his nanites here.

CJ made his way over to him. "This is it," he said, making a sweeping gesture.

"So I see," DJ replied, nodding. "Why'd you choose this place?"

"I didn't. Not really. Each person is generated into a random place when their avatar is created. You would have been too, but since your neural uplink is connected to mine, I was able to modify it so the world would consider us as one."

DJ glanced at him. "You're doing that thing you do—shrugging it off and pretending it was easy. I take it it wasn't?"

CJ blushed. It hadn't actually been easy. The modifications had taken him half an hour, and the only reason it'd worked was because CJ had arrived a few minutes before his brother and set up his Zone as an anchor point.

"Here's a crash course," CJ said, ignoring the question. "Everything here"—he gestured to the sand, the sky, the faint patches of the grass—"is made up of binary. Ones and zeros. The ones in the sky are easy to see, but you'd have to squint, and sort of...sort of uncross your eyes to make out the ones on the ground. It's all just lines of code."

DJ glanced up. "And you're...rewriting it?"

CJ nodded. "Exactly. I tap into the stream of data that makes up this very small space—that's important because there's an infinite amount of data flowing through here, and connecting to it could overwhelm you."

"Sounds like you're talking from experience."

"That's because I am."

"And by *overwhelm*, you mean..."

"Short-circuit your brain like a fuse during a power surge."

DJ nodded and glanced around again, this time with a new appreciation for the place. CJ tried to hide his grin.

"Anyway," CJ said, "I've learned how to connect to it, and I can manipulate the codes to some extent. That's how I made the pockets of grass around us. And it's how I'll learn how to teleport."

"And that's important because the Virtual Realm is too large for you to search each place for Manar," DJ surmised, lips pursed. "It's much easier to understand what you mean when I'm actually seeing it in person."

"Wait until you see the cities," CJ chuckled.

"Cities," his brother said, folding his arms. "Are those the places you think Manar is being held?"

"Not exactly." CJ waved his hand, and a holographic map appeared in front of them. To his credit, his brother didn't flinch, though he tensed for a moment. The map was something CJ had stumbled on during his practice. But since he didn't know where he was in relation to the city, it didn't show actual places, only a dozen dots glowing in different directions.

"Each of those dots is a potential location for Manar." CJ explained. "I thought that being able to see the resonance that I felt would help me better visualize it. So far, all it's helped is help me panic."

"Why are some of them glowing more than others?"

"I'm tracking Manar by dowsing the locations that Helene has spent the most time in over the last few months. But since I've taken so long, I'm losing the connection to some of those places. That's represented by the lights going dim. If I don't figure this out soon, they'll disappear altogether, and it'll be like finding a needle in a haystack the size of a city."

"I see why you're fixed on the teleporting thing. You need to get to each of those places before the light disappears," DJ said, frowning at the map. He seemed lost in thought for a minute before he snapped out of it and glanced at CJ from the corner of his eyes. "I'd be stressed too if I was in your shoes."

"That's what I've been trying to tell you," CJ said, relieved. A part of him had been worried that his brother had only suggested coming to the Virtual Realm to find a reason to tell CJ that he was getting addicted or obsessed, and he shouldn't spend so much time there. But now CJ realized that he'd been unfair: DJ seemed like he understood.

And CJ had let his bitterness taint his impression of DJ, something he'd promised himself he wouldn't do. CJ tried not to let the guilt show too obviously on his face. Fortunately, DJ was still staring at the map.

DJ rubbed the back of his head. "I'm not gonna lie, bro. I'm having trouble wrapping my head around the whole teleportation thing. Don't get me wrong, I get why it's necessary, but everything I know about it comes from movies. How would it even work?"

"If I knew that, I wouldn't be having so much trouble. But I figure that it's about shifting the patterns of the codes in a specific way to create a bridge between two points. That's what I've been trying to do, anyway."

"Sounds like coding."

"Because it is. But it's also somewhat intuitive. There's syntax involved, but also...feeling." CJ hesitated, trying to find the right words. "The places I'm trying to reach—I don't know them. I've never been there. Or at least, I don't know if I've ever been there. I can't visualize them. I just have their direction, and that's vague, imprecise. That's part of the problem."

"What's the other part?" DJ asked, and CJ detected a note of genuine curiosity in his tone.

CJ turned away from him, letting his gaze wander over the wasteland. The silence stretched while CJ tried to organize his thoughts. And to his credit, his brother didn't push, which CJ appreciated.

"A few days ago, I figured out how to create a connection between two places," he started after a minute. "But it requires an anchor, which I don't have. I can alter the codes, but I can't anchor them long enough to make the jump. It's like..." He paused and let the mounting frustration bleed out of him before continuing. "It's like trying to write a program without knowing the language. I can guess, but I can't guarantee it'll work."

DJ hummed. CJ glanced at him, but his expressions were frustratingly difficult to read sometimes. "What if you're overthinking it?" he asked finally.

"What do you mean?"

"You're trying to stick yourself to one of the dots, yeah? But you don't know them, you can't picture them, so the connection can't stabilize, right?"

"Yeah…"

"But you can feel them?"

"What're you getting at, DJ?"

"What I'm trying to say is, you *already* have a connection to each of those places, so you probably don't have to picture the place at all. You could probably just use the connection you already have and, y'know, let it yank you where you need to be."

CJ hesitated. "Let it yank me?"

"Like a big ol' string," DJ replied, completely straight faced.

At first, CJ couldn't tell if he was joking or not. *Let it yank me… What does that even mean?* Soon enough, however, he realized it was his brother's way of saying he shouldn't think too much about it. He should just go with the flow. But of course DJ would suggest that; going with the flow was his forte. He'd been following his gut since he'd been old enough to say the word. He probably thought it was easy. But CJ was more logical. He preferred having solid explanations and reasons for doing anything. With just a bit of thought, CJ could come up with half a dozen for why DJ's advice wasn't feasible. He took a breath, about to list them, but paused.

It wasn't like any of his logically sound ideas had led him anywhere.

"Let it yank me," CJ muttered, then closed his eyes. Unlike what he'd been doing before, he didn't reach out to the tapestries that appeared in his mind. Instead he focused on the tugs he'd felt since the first day he'd created this avatar. Some of them were strong and insistent, which CJ took to mean that the locations were closer or that Helene had visited them more recently.

CJ focused on one of them until it filled his mind, until it was the only thing in his world. The tug grew stronger, more insistent. It pulsed with a vibration that matched his heartbeat. CJ struggled not to analyze the feeling. Instead he did as his brother suggested and surrendered, allowing it to guide him. CJ didn't know how long he stayed that way, basking in that feeling. But eventually he realized he wasn't being pulled anywhere. He'd lowered all his resistances, and he could feel the tug trying to carry him somewhere—but there was something stopping it, one last step he needed for it to work. Fortunately, as soon as he realized it, he figured out what he needed to do.

CJ spread out his awareness. The bulk of it was still focused on the tug, but a small part extended toward the tapestry of data around him. He didn't try to manipulate it as he would if he wanted to alter the environment. Instead he just touched it—and data rushed into him like a flood. His mind splintered, but CJ had felt this before, dozens of times, whenever he created his Zone. He didn't struggle. He didn't have to. His mind blended seamlessly with the data, and the codes flowed around him, pulsing to a rhythm that slowly matched his own until there was *resonance*.

CJ gasped and almost lost the feeling, but he held onto it like a drowning man to a raft. CJ had felt this before, months ago, when he and Manar had battled against Helene in front of a website they'd modified for the purpose. When Helene defeated Manar, he and CJ had retreated into the building, and CJ had used the Sphere to merge with the website. CJ doubted he would ever forget that feeling.

And now, he was living it again. It wasn't as intense as it'd been that day, but that didn't lessen the feeling. There was no struggle, no chaos. He could sense everything within the radius of his consciousness, but further and to an even deeper level than he'd been able to achieve with his Zone.

It was *perfect*.

The tug grew stronger, more insistent, and this time there was nothing stopping it. It filled him, not just in his mind, but his entire being. It pulled at him, like a string. CJ let it yank him.

And he disassembled

He felt it. He *felt* it. But it wasn't painful—not in the traditional sense. It was more like being unraveled—every atom, every bit of code that made up his avatar peeling away. It was similar to when he returned back to the real world, but only in the way a candle was similar to a bonfire. This was much deeper than anything he'd ever felt. The tug became a force, dragging him through the stream of data. CJ didn't fight it. For what was probably the first time in his life, he surrendered completely.

His awareness shifted, and he was no longer a singular entity. Instead, he was a collection of fragments scattered around. Each piece of him was still connected, held together by the same resonance that pulsed through him. Time lost meaning. There was only the sensation of movement, of being carried forward by something far greater than himself. He was weightless, untethered, yet somehow completely grounded. Slowly, the tug began to weaken. The pull that had dragged him forward started to release him, and the fragments of himself came back together like pieces of a puzzle.

Eventually, CJ opened his eyes. He hadn't gone far—not yet. He was only a few feet away from where he'd started. But the experience had left its mark. He exhaled, steadying himself. He wiped at his eyes, and his fingers came away wet. *Am I crying?* CJ chuckled. *How's that even possible in an avatar?*

That was how DJ met him, wiping his eyes and giggling to himself. "Not bad, little bro. I told you you were overthinking it."

The words hit CJ like a breath of fresh air and loosened the invisible knot that'd been in his chest for weeks. He grinned back. "Thank you, DJ. I mean it." He tried to impress as much sincerity as he could into the words. He hadn't gone far, sure, but it'd worked. After weeks of trying, he finally had a proof of concept, and CJ already had ideas about how he could improve his range the next time out.

"No problem," his brother said. "As long as you remember that although this place might feel like home to you, your real home is still waiting out there. Don't get lost here."

CJ's grin faltered and turned into a wry smile. "I know. It's just...it's easier here. There's no noise, no expectations."

"No younger brother nagging you?" DJ said. CJ started to deny it, but DJ just waved a hand, chuckling dismissively. "Nah, I'm not angry. I know how I can get. And for what it's worth, I *am* sorry for what happened at Hermione's lab. I was trying to protect you. But more importantly, I was trying to protect myself. Because I don't know what I'd do if I had to put you in the chamber with the rest of Helene's other victims."

"DJ..." CJ swallowed. What should he even say to that?

"Don't sweat it. I trust you to make your own choices. But a word of advice..." DJ met his eyes squarely. Did he even know how intense his gaze was? CJ had to force himself not to look away like a rebellious child. "I get it. It's a mess out there, and unfortunately, you were born with a condition that made you less equipped to deal with it than the rest of us. But the mess is part of life—it's part of being human. And you *did* deal with it, so makes you stronger.

"I've only been here for a few minutes, but it's obvious that this world brings out that part of you, which is why you prefer it. But nothing stops you from being that same person out in the real world, too, CJ. The condition you hate so much? That's what made you the person you are right now, the person you love so much when you're in the Virtual Realm. There aren't two of you. There's just *you*. It doesn't matter what world you're in. All that matters is whether you decide to stop hiding."

Finally, CJ couldn't hold the gaze anymore. He looked down, but he could still feel his brother's stare burning into his head. There was no judgment there, no critique, which was what he'd been afraid of. There wasn't even concern, which he would have expected. None of that. There was just confidence and pride.

Confidence and pride.

"Did you practice that?" CJ asked.

"I've been working on it on and off." DJ shrugged, grinning. "It doesn't mean it isn't true though. I know I've been a dick lately, and I know I joke around a lot. But I'm serious about this."

"You don't actually."

"I don't what?"

"Joke around a lot. Not anymore, at least. Not in a while."

DJ started to reply and then stopped, cocking his head. "Huh. I guess you're right. There isn't much to joke around about with Tyra holding a fucking bomb over our heads."

"You know your hatred of her is unhealthy, right?"

DJ raised a brow. "Am I supposed to be happy that she's screwing up my life? Or that she's responsible for the deaths of hundreds of people?"

"So are the Murder Twins," CJ said calmly. "Yet you don't hate them. Not like you hate Tyra."

"That's because it's different."

"Because the people Karla and Liz killed are people you don't know? Or because they are more straightforward when they kill, without any mind games?"

DJ narrowed his eyes. His expression told CJ that he felt trapped by the question. If he answered no, then he knew that CJ would force him to clarify how Tyra was different from the Murder Twins. And he couldn't answer yes because it would make him an asshole, even though it was the truth. It was just one that he didn't want to admit, even to himself.

CJ didn't blame him. Tyra had attacked because of the team, so it made sense that DJ felt guilty and enraged about all those deaths more than he did about the people Karla and Liz had killed. It was made worse by the fact that DJ had befriended several of the guards and all their commanders, and Tyra had made it obvious that she was toying with them throughout the battle.

So, CJ understood his brother's anger. He was just pointing out that it wasn't necessarily healthy.

"Look," DJ said finally, "let's solve one of our problems at a time, okay?"

CJ nodded. "Fair enough."

"Good," DJ exhaled. "Now, it's been one round of bullshit after another since I got back, and I haven't eaten. Let's go get some lunch."

"But..." CJ stared at the horizon. He could still feel the tug in his chest, and it felt stronger now. He could finally teleport; he should be focused on mastering it as fast as he could. CJ met his brother's eyes and sighed dramatically. "It's been a while since I got a hamburger."

DJ grinned. "Same, but I heard of this great place a few blocks down." He started grabbing at the air, then put his hands around his head as if he was trying to take off a helmet. "Now how do we get out of here? The place is giving me the creeps."

CJ chuckled and reached out to help him, but the tug pressed harder now, insisting that lunch could only delay the inevitable.

CHAPTER

24

JANUARY 2044

SPARTA HEADQUARTERS, NEW YORK

IT DIDN'T TAKE LONG for DJ to realize he couldn't step outside without being swarmed by a crowd—people who clearly had nothing better to do in the middle of January than loiter outside a building. DJ was pissed enough to try to push through the crowd, but his brother talked him out of it. They ended up having lunch delivered to their rooms. A full stomach after several weeks went further to convince CJ to take a nap than DJ ever had, and both brothers crashed on their beds minutes after finishing their meal.

DJ woke up sometime later to someone dragging him off his bed by his ankles. DJ jerked up and threw a punch that bounced off Karla's titanium arm. She didn't even react to it. A moment later, DJ fell to the floor with a heavy thump. He tried pulling on his leg, but Karla's fingers were like steel clamps.

No, that's not right, DJ thought. He could probably pull away from clamps. The redhead crossed the room and pulled him into the hallway in the direction of the elevator. DJ tried several times to get free, including raising himself up and trying to pry her fingers apart. She didn't turn around. Hell, it didn't even seem like she noticed.

Finally, DJ gave up and slumped back down with a sigh. "Is this really necessary?"

"Yes, you are too weak."

DJ gritted his teeth at that, but it was hard to argue when he was sprawled on the ground and being dragged by the ankle. They passed several people in the hallway, including Max and his wife. DJ gave them a chin nod and tried to pretend that everything was perfectly normal. Maybe it was good for people to see him like this. Everyone had been scared by the videos, imagining him untouchable and unstoppable—but seeing him manhandled by a woman who looked like she'd struggle to lift a heavy grocery bag might make them realize he wasn't invincible, that even he could be caught off guard.

DJ frowned. As small as she was, nobody would ever think of Karla as weak. It was in the way she snarled at everyone, the way she prowled instead of walking, the way she effortlessly hauled a man twice her size without any visible strain. *Yeah,* DJ thought, grimacing, *this will probably just add to the fire.*

They reached the elevator a minute later, and Karla dragged him in. There was barely enough room with DJ lying down, and he was forced to lean against one of the walls so his spine didn't break. Karla slammed a button.

"Where are you taking me?" he asked.

Karla ignored him, along with every other question he asked. Eventually DJ stopped when he saw her reaching for her dagger. He sighed. He didn't like being manhandled and hated being ignored even more. But at this point, he knew that Karla wasn't going to hurt him. At least, she wouldn't go through such a convoluted method to do it.

A part of DJ realized he trusted the homicidal maniac. There was something refreshingly honest about her. She hated everybody, sure, but she hated them equally. You always knew where you stood. Piss her off, and she'd kill you. But as long as you didn't, she didn't give a shit about you.

For the most part at least. For some reason, she'd decided DJ was her student, and although the experience was mostly frustrating, painful, and edged on being downright fatal, it was effective.

They reached the gym a few minutes later. Once he resigned himself to the fact that he was going to get a few bruises, he was surprised to realize that he was a little excited. It annoyed him that Tyra had supposedly become stronger than him. Hopefully, he'd learn enough to close that gap.

Liz was already in the room, sitting calmly. She turned when they entered and met DJ's eyes as he sprawled on the floor. Surprisingly, she looked at her sister with what seemed like reproach. Karla bristled at the look as well but finally let go of DJ's leg. She glanced at him before crossing over to her sister and muttering something in Russian. Liz said something back, and DJ—on his feet now—watched as they went across the gym and systematically started dismantling all the equipment, and even some parts of the walls.

DJ started to say something a couple of times, but eventually he shrugged. *I was going to have to talk to the board at some point anyway.*

A few minutes later, the twins stood before DJ. Their fists were clenched, which made him tense for a moment. But then they opened their hands, revealing a collection of listening devices and surveillance gear.

DJ sighed. He knew the board had had the place bugged, and whenever he and Karla sparred, he took a few minutes to disable the cameras—which the girls had simply pulled out of the walls this time. Usually that was enough, but apparently Tyra's videos had made them more invested in finding out his secrets. He'd probably have to do a sweep of his own room now.

Stress, DJ thought, and then pushed it out of his mind. "So, what now?"

The twins crushed the bugs like they were pretzels and then dusted off their hands. Liz met his eyes. "My sister and I are going to train you on how to use your nanites."

DJ ran his hand through his hair. "I mean, that's awesome, I guess, but I thought we'd already started when you forced me to jump off a roof."

Karla tensed her mouth, like she was about to spit on the floor. But a glance from her sister stopped her. She swallowed it, which was more disgusting some-how. "That was *not* training. It was me desperately trying to get you to stop fumbling with your nanites like a brainless toddler still figuring out how to move its own limbs."

"Wow." That hurt a little bit. "Brainless toddler, really?"

Karla bared her teeth at that. "Are you about to cry, little baby? Are you so afraid to hear the truth? Should I coddle you and soften my words so your feelings are not hurt?"

Well, yeah, DJ thought, *that's basic human decency.* Out loud, he said, "Just tell me what I've been doing wrong so we can get on with it."

"Your nanites are not toys for you to play with," Karla said, pointing her dagger at him. When had she even unsheathe it? "They are as much a part of you as the eyes you use to see, the nose you use to breathe, and the balls you use to fuck."

Jesus, DJ thought. *There* had *to have been a better analogy for that.* "They have been a part of you from the moment the old man injected you with them. They have merged with your system, with your organs, with your blood, and have made them *more.*

"They enhance them," DJ said.

"Yes." Karla nodded sharply. "Immediately after injection, the nanites begin to adapt to your system, and then they improve your bones and muscles, your skin and blood, until your strength, speed, stamina, and reflexes are better than that of a cow."

"A cow?" DJ frowned.

"An average person," Liz explained. DJ drew his lips into a flat line.

"You will hit harder," Karla continued, "move faster, have more endurance, and enjoy accelerated healing for minor injuries. But you will *not* be superhuman." She poked him with her dagger then. A few months ago that would have drawn blood, but now, he barely felt it. That definitely seemed superhuman.

"So I'm guessing I've passed that?" DJ asked.

Karla tensed her mouth again, then glanced at her sister and stopped, grimacing. "It was inevitable. The first level enhances you passively, without your input—"

"Wait, first level? What's that mean? Are there actually levels?"

Karla's dagger stopped an inch from his eye; her wrist was held in place by her sister's grip. DJ could see the struggle as Karla tried to push the weapon farther. Just one more inch and it'd pierce his retinas and find his skull. DJ jumped back—too late, far too late. Adrenaline flooded his veins in reaction to the danger. But he hadn't even *seen* the dagger. There'd been no sign, twitch, *nothing*. If Liz hadn't been there…

DJ tried to tell himself that Karla had known her sister would stop her, or that she would have stopped herself at just making a threat, that she wouldn't have killed him—but the glare she sent his way shattered his confidence. She would have. She absolutely would have.

Once he was out of range, Karla stopped struggling and lowered her hand. Liz stared at her, and though she glared back, Karla sheathed her dagger. But Liz continued staring. Karla snarled, but her sister remained unfazed. Eventually, Karla unclipped her weapons and gave them to Liz, who put them away.

Only then did Liz meet DJ's eyes. "My sister dislikes being interrupted." That was it. No apology. Nothing.

DJ straightened. Rage burned through him like a wildfire—mixing with his adrenaline and compelling him to move, to do *something*. But what? Every scenario DJ imagined ended with him either dead for real or close to it. He couldn't defeat Karla. Not the way he was.

DJ took a breath and pushed down the anger—pushed it *way* down—until not a bit of it showed anywhere in his expression or his bearing. Only then did he return to his original position, a foot away from Karla. Somehow, at some point, after interacting with them for so long, DJ had briefly forgotten why he called them the Murder Twins. That was his mistake. And it was probably one he was going to make several times more. At least, until he became stronger than them.

After that, it wouldn't matter.

"The first level enhances you passively," Karla continued, as if nothing had happened—which, to her, might've been the case. "It does this without your input until you reach a threshold of strength that pushes you into the next level. The process can take weeks or months, depending on the host—and how weak or cowardly they are." She sneered at him when she said this, but DJ didn't react. He simply looked to Liz for an explanation.

"The nanites grow and evolve with use, with the amount of stress you put on them, and with how well you can handle their power," Liz said. "The more stressful the situation, the more they are forced to work, the more you are enhanced, and the faster the process. It took you several months to pass the first threshold."

"How long did it take you two?"

"Days," Liz said simply. There was no pride in her voice. Instead, it was reflected in Karla, who gave him a smug look. DJ ignored it. In hindsight, it was very obvious when he'd broken through from the first level to the second. The raid on Sparta definitely counted as a stressful event, and DJ had leaned heavily on his nanites throughout the entire thing. But he remembered a specific moment close to the end when he had been fighting with Tyra: Something had seemed to click in his head. DJ had never been able to explain the feeling, and he'd lost consciousness shortly after—but the feeling remained whenever he engaged his nanites.

"What's the second level do?" he asked.

Karla looked at him like he was an idiot, and he realized he was, once he put a little bit of thought into answering his own question. When he was in the White House, his nanites had only reacted to his anger; DJ had never actually had any conscious control of it. But after his battle with Tyra, it was like he had a switch in his brain that he could flip on and off.

"It gives me active control over the nanites, right?" DJ said. "Like, I can decide when to turn them on and off."

"It is impossible to completely turn off the nanites," Liz said. "They are always active in the background, working to improve you even further. The difference is that, on the second level, you can draw more of their power and temporarily exceed your normal strength or speed. However, nanites enhance *everything* in the body. And at the second level, they begin to target your hormones."

"Yeah, that's been a real pain in the ass," DJ said, his lips pulled into a line.

Karla snorted in contempt. "This is a problem for the weak. You will learn control."

That's rich coming from you, DJ thought but kept that to himself. "I'm guessing the second level also comes with more healing?"

Liz gave a sharp nod. "It's the reason you recovered so fast from Tyra Chityothin's poison. The toxin was lethal—enough to put you on the brink of death—but your healing nanites kicked in before it could finish the job. Without them, you'd have been bedridden for days, exactly what she was counting on. She must have thought you were still on the first level."

"Gotcha," DJ said. "Now let's talk about this boost. Tyra used it the first time we fought, during the raid."

He'd been matching her speed for speed, and then suddenly she'd become so fast that his eyes had no longer been able to follow her. Although he'd easily tanked her punches before, suddenly he was flying several feet from each attack. DJ hadn't given it much thought since then—which, in hindsight, he realized was pretty stupid—but if the bitch had just been at a higher level than him, then the technique was something he could learn as well.

"I have seen this fight," Karla said. "Then, she required the boost in order to match your skill. It was the only way she stood a chance to win. However, she has improved greatly since then, and she is still faster and stronger than you, so you are no longer her match."

Karla stared at him with a hint of mockery. "It is why she toys with you like a child and discards you as she desires. If you no longer wish to be at her mercy, you must do better. You must become stronger than her, until she is forced to resort to tricks to match you. And then you will crush her still. *That* is what will make her fear you."

What a weird way to motivate someone, DJ thought. "Well," he said, "that's why I have you guys."

NDIDI STOOD AT THE ENTRANCE of the chamber. This was the room where the team kept the captives they'd rescued from Helene. Most of them had already been reunited with their families. Dozens of them didn't have families to return to or had been rejected by their families. A few more dozen of them, however, had been messed up by the procedure to extract their spores and so had to be isolated.

Those people ended up there, in the isolation chamber.

To his credit, DJ had tried his best to help. Ndidi didn't know where he'd acquired the couches, vending machine, or the pool table from, but it did little to make the place look anything other than the common room of an asylum. The image was cemented by the fact that most of the residents sat on the floor, clutching their knees, staring blankly at a wall, or muttering to themselves.

Bethany was kneeling beside a man, soothing him until his episode finished. She spoke softly to a woman gazing into the distance and drew her attention to the food by her side. Then she pushed the bowl into her hand and stayed there while the woman fed herself, prompting her each time she spaced out. Only when the bowl was empty did Bethany move on to another person. Through it all, her expression never shifted once—not to frustration, anger, or even pity. It might have been because Bethany was autistic and found it difficult to express her emotions. However, Ndidi knew her ward's tells, and all she could make out was a patience that would have made saints ashamed of themselves.

Eventually, Ndidi forced herself to enter the room. Bethany looked up, and her eyebrows twitched, which was her tell for a frown. Ndidi forced a smile and signaled to one of the couches at the side of the room. Bethany joined her several minutes later, sitting opposite Ndidi and watching her warily. Her eyes asked the obvious question.

"I wanted to talk to you," Ndidi said, speaking slowly while she arranged the words in her head, "about everything that's happened recently. Your decision to extract your spores, and my part in it."

Bethany tensed for a long moment. And then she stood. "I...um...do not have time for another lecture."

"No!" Ndidi blurted. She reached out instinctively but pulled back before actually touching her. Fortunately, Bethany stopped, though she didn't turn around. "This isn't a lecture. It's an apology. Or at least, it's supposed to be. I probably could have started it better."

Bethany sat back down and stared at something over Ndidi's shoulder.

Ndidi drew in a careful breath, willing her pulse to settle. "I'm sorry about everything," she said quietly. "After Helene...did what she did, and I was finally reunited with you—after DJ and the others broke us out—you were in such a vulnerable state. I can't even begin to imagine what you went through. I knew Helene's use of the spores affected your mind, but part of me thought that might've been...good, in a twisted way."

Ndidi paused, waiting for the backlash. But there was no sign of anger or frustration on Bethany's face—just a guarded neutrality. She continued, her voice steadying. "Not the horror you lived through, but the fact that the spores neutralized the symptoms of your condition. I believed it would be one less hardship for you. But that was selfish. Your sister and I—we were wrong to think we knew best. We pushed you away when you needed us most. And I'm so, so sorry for that."

Bethany didn't say anything, and Ndidi allowed her to process it. She steadied her breathing while she waited and wiped at her eyes. Somehow this was harder than it'd been with DJ. But it was *Bethany*. Ndidi had practically raised her, and whenever Ndidi thought about what she and Hermione had done—how had they not realized what they were pushing her to? How had they been so stupid?

Finally, Bethany spoke. "You...uh...were selfish." Ndidi flinched even though she expected it—deserved it, even. Still, the bluntness made her throat tighten. "Y-you thought I would be better off with the picospores. You thought I would... um...that I would *want* to keep the thing that controlled me for years, the thing that trapped me in my own body. You believed I'd be...uh...happier with it because it 'fixed' me.

"B-But all of that was for you, not me. Because if you had...um...really thought about me, you would have understood that I have never hated being on the autism spectrum. It...uh...wasn't easy to be stigmatized since I was a child. But I never felt like I was less than anyone else, that there was something...um... wrong with me. Because there is nothing wrong with me. You were the one that helped me understand that." Bethany exhaled softly. "So it hurt, when...uh...I found out that was just something you said. Because if you truly believed that, you would have understood."

"Bethany..."

"You don't have...um...any idea what it felt like. You and Hermione—treating me like I wasn't capable of understanding myself, telling me how I should exist. It is *my* life. *My* mind. *My* identity. I get to...uh...choose. Not you."

Ndidi lowered her gaze. Bethany hadn't looked at her through it all, but Ndidi wasn't sure she could face the hurt she saw in her eyes any longer. "I'm sorry," she said. "And I know that's too simple a thing to say. But you're right. I've been a hypocrite. I've always seen autism as something to be treated, to be cured, and I was so wrapped up in protecting you from it that I forgot your own autonomy. But you're no longer the little girl that would barf on me and then laugh.

"I'm not asking for instant forgiveness. I just wanted you to know I respect your decision. You have the right to make your own choices. I'm sorry I violated that. And I'm sorry it took me so long to see it."

Bethany's gaze flicked to her for a moment. "H-how do I know you will not keep trying to 'fix' me the next time...um...you think I'm broken?"

"You're not broken," Ndidi murmured, voice tight with remorse. "I've never thought you were broken, Bethany. And if you never want my help, I'll respect that. But if you need me, I'll be here. That's all I'm saying."

Bethany's arms stayed crossed, but her posture relaxed by an inch. "I know... um...that you and my sister meant well. But it still hurt like hell. I...I am not sure I can forgive you, Ndidi, but it helps that you at least...um...understand now. I...I will need time."

Ndidi released a breath she hadn't realized she was holding. She hadn't been forgiven, but a part of her was happy about that. She'd have to work to prove to Bethany that she could trust her again. And that was good. She was just grateful for the chance to have been heard at all.

"Thank you," Ndidi said, trying to infuse as much sincerity into the two words as she could. Bethany nodded but didn't reply. She rose with measured calm and turned away, heading back toward the people who needed her.

Ndidi stood as well. She had one more apology to make.

HERMIONE STRAIGHTENED.

The nanoscope had the same design and size as a traditional microscope, but it blended AI programming and high-resolution imaging to view elements on the nanoscale. More to the point, it came with a monitor that hung about a foot above the equipment, which meant Hermione didn't have to lean in to view anything.

But old habits die hard, Hermione thought, cracking her neck. She rubbed her eyes. *I knew I shouldn't have taken a break.* She used to be able to go hours staring through the lens without flinching. A few days off and now she couldn't even go half a day without her eyes hurting.

She adjusted the setting on the nanoscope, and the image on the monitor glitched for a moment. She already had it magnified to the maximum, as that was the only way she'd be able to see the nanites and picospores within the blood sample. Even then, it wasn't as clear as she'd like, but it was the closest she would get without the specialized extensions that Eze Okafor had had made when Hermione and her father were developing the original iteration of the spores. She'd made Manar build her a similar one early on when they realized Helene was using the spores.

Maybe I could get CJ down here at some point to write a better AI program, Hermione thought. The nanoscope and its in-built program were nearly a decade old, which made them practically relics at the rate technology was developing. It spoke to the decline of the field that someone hadn't developed a better program already.

Though, Hermione considered, *maybe that's for the best. Better AI is the reason we're in this mess, after all. Plus, I doubt a different program is going to help much here.*

She stared at the image on the monitor as it stabilized. The issue wasn't the nanites or the picospores—she could see them clearly, in great detail. The issue was her own state: She was tired, confused, and irritable, which made it hard to process what she was seeing.

Hermione ignored the suspended cells and platelets and focused on the swarm of tiny sphere-like objects swimming though the blood like a school of microscopic fish. Each of the nanites had several delicate limbs that extended from a central sphere and propelled them around the cells and organelles. A group of them clustered around specific cells...and did nothing since the blood was an old sample and the cells within were long dead. Hermione had an idea of what they should be doing, however, from the sample she'd collected from DJ.

Her eyes moved to another part of the screen, where the picospores were grouped together. Each one was spherical, with thin lines etched across its surface that glowed with alternating hues of silver and an almost ethereal blue. The entire swarm pulsed in rhythm, which made them seem almost alive. Hermione nearly hadn't recognized them the first time she'd seen them— because they looked completely different from the originals she and her father had developed. And it was that fact that made her suspect that the third group of microscopic nonbiological elements she saw was just another iteration of either the picospores or nanites.

However, the fact that it looked so very different from either of them made her hesitant. It had the same basic spherical shape as the others, as well as the nanite's delicate limbs. However, instead of plates, the rest of its surface was covered in layers of folds etched with pulsing lines and little bud-like nodes—similar to what the spores had. The most noticeable difference, however, was its central core, which pulsed with a faint golden light.

Hermione winced and rubbed her eyes. Something about that light gave her a headache whenever she stared at it too long. Fortunately, the door to the laboratory opened, and Ndidi entered, giving her a reason to take a break.

"Keep leaving the lights off," Ndidi said, "and one of these days someone's going to trip and fall."

"I'm hoping the same thing," Hermione replied, chuckling. "I can move through this place blind, but anyone who tries to attack me is in for a rough time."

She looks better than before, Hermione noted as Ndidi took a seat beside her. The bags under her eyes were less defined after several hours of dedicated rest, and the injuries on her face looked several days old already. She still had the look of someone who'd been through the emotional wringer, but it was better than it'd been just a day before.

"You got a minute?" Ndidi asked.

Hermione glanced at the nanoscope and immediately felt her headache flare up. She grimaced and turned back to Ndidi. "Take all the time you want."

Ndidi took a deep breath, which created a flicker of apprehension in Hermione. *I thought that we dealt with all the heavy stuff yesterday? What could possibly have happened within a day that required a deep breath?*

Ndidi started to say something and then hesitated before asking, "Do you have any idea where CJ is? I swear I've looked everywhere, but I can't find him."

Hermione released a small breath. "He really only goes to three places, so if he's not in his room or the conference room, then he's definitely up in Manar's office."

Ndidi frowned. "Why would he be up there?"

"That's where all the equipment is set up. He's been trying to rescue Manar from the Virtual Realm, so he's been going by himself. He figured out a way to track Manar, but he's been having problems crossing the distance, so he's been spending most of his time there. At this rate, he'll become more of a workaholic than I am." She chuckled. "Why were you looking for him?"

"I wanted to apologize to him," Ndidi replied softly, "for what I did. I never apologized before because I thought I was justified."

"And now you've rethought that," Hermione said, nodding. That was probably long overdue. She had never been angry at Ndidi because her decision had ultimately saved Bethany—but the whole thing had caused a rift within the group, which had ultimately led to Ndidi and Manar going to Nigeria. "I don't think CJ was angry though. If you're trying to mend the rift, the person you should start with is—"

"DJ," Ndidi said, nodding. "He was the first one I spoke with. And I know CJ didn't hold it against me, but he still deserves an apology, more than anyone else, apart from Manar. I also spoke with Bethany."

Hermione tensed.

"I had to apologize to her," Ndidi continued, speaking softly. "About the decisions we made for her, about what we pushed her to do, about pushing her away when she needed us. Everything." Ndidi took a deep breath. "I *had* to apologize, and she listened. She's still angry, understandably so. But she's your sister, Hermione, and this has dragged on for too long. So...so, I think you should do the same."

Hermione could still remember the resentment on her sister's face the last time they spoke. That memory alone was enough to make her stomach twist. How would she handle seeing it again? "I don't think she wants to hear from me," Hermione said, measuring each word. "Not yet, anyway."

"She's hurt, but she's not closed off."

Hermione ran a hand through her hair, tugging at the ends. "I can agree that the picospores are a bad idea since Helene is still hovering around. But how about after? This bullshit has to end at *some* point, right? How about then? Would she agree to use the spores then?"

"No, but—"

"That's my point though," Hermione continued. "The picospores are already being mass-produced, Ndidi. Yes, they are tainted now, but people already know about them. After Helene's gone, the spores are going to go global, and mental conditions are going to be a thing of the past. Except with Bethany. It's going to be a worldwide stigmatization, Ndidi. Can you blame me for wanting to protect my sister from that?"

"It's her choice, Hermione," Ndidi said.

Hermione shook her head, smiling wryly. Where would she even begin to explain? "Look, let's just drop this for now. I'm willing to apologize for pushing her away. But not yet. I'm not ready to talk to her, or talk about her. So, let's just... leave it, okay?"

There was a long moment before Ndidi nodded. She was clearly disappointed, and Hermione knew they weren't done talking about it—but at least she wouldn't keep pressing today. Hermione turned her attention back to the monitor, and Ndidi followed her gaze.

"Is that my blood sample?" Ndidi asked.

"I haven't looked at yours yet," Hermione replied. "This is the sample you gave me of Manar. Or Helene, I suppose. The picospores and nanites are easy to identify, even though Helene seems to have upgraded them again. But *this...*" Hermione highlighted the third cluster and let it fill the screen. "This is something else entirely. It has parts of both the spores and the nanites, but...I don't know."

Ndidi leaned forward even though it wasn't necessary. "Could it be a mutated form of one of them?"

Hermione shook her head. "I mean, we can only hope Helene has given herself some sort of cancer. But it's doubtful—and also not a good thing, considering it's actually Manar's body." She grimaced. "But no, a mutation wouldn't explain why it has features of both the nanites and the spores."

Suddenly, Ndidi tensed and placed a hand on her stomach. "You don't think that they're inside me, do you?"

That thought had occurred to Hermione, and she planned on confirming with the blood sample she had of Ndidi. Hermione would have preferred Ndidi not be present when she analyzed the sample, but based on the look Ndidi was giving her, she didn't think she had a choice.

Hermione sighed and started switching the slides. Ndidi stopped her with an outstretched hand. "Take a fresh sample."

A minute later, the image stabilized on the monitor. Hermione zoomed in on the picospores and nanites, both of which were clustered around cells. A third cluster was at the side, propelling itself through the medium, but if it was doing anything, Hermione couldn't tell. Beside her, Ndidi exhaled. "Do you think it's related to the baby's sped-up development?"

"I can't say, not until I extract it and run some more tests. But Helene told you that your pregnancy was progressing faster because of the nanites, and that's more likely because, for one, we already know that the nanites work to enhance everything in their host. And for another, if this new thing had to do with your baby, then why was it in Manar's blood sample as well?" Hermione turned to her. "You're not feeling anything, are you? Sick? Nauseous?"

"I'm always nauseous." Ndidi chuckled humorlessly. "But no, I don't feel anything strange. The baby's...active. More active than you'd expect this early in a pregnancy. But otherwise, I'm okay."

"Okay physically, sure. But we have to figure out what the hell that thing is."

Ndidi's hand drifted protectively over her stomach. "What's the next step?"

Hermione pressed her lips together. "We need Martin. I've reached the mother of all dead ends with the spores, and I have no idea what the hell I'm doing with the nanites. Now we have a problem that involves both, and he's the only one I can think of who can help. I'm sure if we put our heads together, we can figure out this new bullshit too."

"Where is he now?"

"I have no idea." Hermione shrugged. "He was with the Murder Team, but then Karla was kicked out, and Chloe and Liz ditched José to come here. Martin is wherever José is, I guess."

Ndidi grimaced. "Taking him from José...that's not going to be easy."

"Yeah, I've spoken to DJ about it, but I figure that's why he's dragging his feet about it."

"He's had a lot on his plate, Hermione."

"I understand that, but this is important too. It's *critical*, in fact, because if we don't figure this out soon, it might endanger you and the baby."

Ndidi looked worried, but she gave a firm nod. "All right. Let's talk to him. And in the meantime—" She hesitated for a moment, then softened her tone. "Think about what I said regarding Bethany. That's critical as well."

Hermione forced a smile. "I'll consider it."

"Good," Ndidi smiled. An actual genuine smile. She stood up to leave but turned back when she got to the door. "As for DJ...some of the staff were talking about a redhead dragging him through the hall by his ankles."

Hermione raised a brow. *Kinky.*

Though the flicker of humor didn't last; DJ being hauled through the hall by anyone usually meant the next crisis had already begun.

DJ WAS SPRAWLED ON THE FLOOR of the gym. Above him, Karla sneered.

"Get up," she said.

It was the only thing she'd said since they'd started the "training." DJ had come up with a good retort—something about what he would do if he got it up—but unfortunately for him, he was too busy sucking in air to speak. With the nanites, it took a lot for him to be exhausted, and that range had only grown as he'd adapted to them. During the Sparta raid, DJ had gone about half a day constantly moving without getting tired. After leveling up, he'd gone days without sleeping or even feeling tired.

So it was kind of pathetic that the twins could get him to that state within just a couple of hours.

Both of them stood over him, speaking softly in Russian. Neither of them had broken a sweat. Shit, neither of them had even moved from their starting positions. DJ didn't know how spoiled he'd been by Karla matching his speed during their previous training session, until Liz had suggested that they take off the training wheels. He hadn't been able to land a hit on either of them once in two fucking hours.

It hadn't even been that bad during the first SEAL training session.

DJ tried to sit up and winced as every nerve in his body protested at the same time. It felt like a concrete truck had run him over and then backed up over every bone. *It's probably worse than that,* DJ thought, *considering I might be able to tank being run over by a truck by now.*

He felt the weight of someone's gaze and opened his eyes to meet Liz's stare. "You need to learn how to fight," she said.

DJ got his breathing under control enough to reply. "I already know how to fight."

"As a normal human, and with their limits. However, your technique wastes a lot of what the nanites grant you. We will break you out of your patterns."

"Well, you've done a pretty great job of that so far." DJ took a deep breath and then sat up in one quick motion. Several of his bones cracked, and all his bruises flared up. DJ gritted his teeth through the pain and waited until his breathing was back under control before he continued. "But like I said, I already know how to fight. I realized what you said a while back and devised another fighting style that takes my nanites into consideration."

Several feet away, Karla barked a laugh. She was spinning one of the weights on her finger like it was a freaking basketball.

Liz's reaction was more muted in that it was nonexistent. She simply continued staring at DJ. "My sister and I noticed your new 'technique' during the spar. It is an improvement"—Karla barked another laugh—"but it was developed with your abilities at the first level. Therefore, your abilities then are not your abilities now, and so your 'technique' becomes part of the things limiting your strength."

"First off, can you stop saying *technique* like that? I worked really hard on it," DJ said. "Second of all, what's wrong with it?"

Liz's reply was interrupted by the gym door being pushed open. DJ turned to see Hermione marching in with her mouth set in a hard line. DJ sighed mentally, already feeling the stress. She glanced at him, on the ground, sweating like a turkey the day before Thanksgiving, then at Liz, standing over him in a tight leather jumpsuit, and then at Karla, who was at the other end of the room bench pressing the bench press bench. DJ could almost see her brain glitch before she very deliberately chose to ignore it and focus on him.

"Can you stand?" she asked.

DJ countered, "Can *you* come around so I don't have to twist my neck to look at you?"

Hermione sighed, but she crossed the room to stand beside Liz. "Do you want the long version or the short version?"

"Short, please," DJ groaned, trying to stand up.

"I need Martin," Hermione said, holding out a hand to help him. Liz pushed it away without even looking at her.

"We've spoken about this, Hermione," DJ replied, steading himself. His entire body protested, but DJ was already used to ignoring it. "Martin's with José, and unless you want to be the one to take the Terminator's charge away from him, there's nothing we can do."

"And like *I* told *you*," Hermione retorted, "you're going to have to figure it out. Because we need him if we're going to make any progress studying the nanites he invented. There's only so much I can do with his notes, and it would take years to reach the level he's at right now."

"Hermione—"

"That's not all," she said, speaking fast. "I've been analyzing the blood sample from Manar—I mean, Helene—that Ndidi brought back with her. Now, there are a lot of things there that I don't understand, but there's one specific thing that makes no sense to me whatsoever. And that's what scares me, DJ. Whatever it is, it's also in Ndidi's bloodstream."

"You're afraid that it's affecting the baby somehow?"

"Yes," Hermione said softly. "I have no idea how. But I don't think that any of us want to risk waiting too long to find out."

DJ wiped sweat from his brow. "So you want us to somehow rescue Martin," he said, his voice grim. "Or at least convince José to let him go."

"I'm stuck, DJ," Hermione said, blowing out a breath heavy with frustration. "I need a second set of eyes, and Martin's the only option I can think of."

DJ blew out a breath of his own. He did *not* want anything to do with José. It was a good bet that the guy would kill DJ on sight for tricking him, and a better bet that he'd torture DJ first because his family had abandoned him. Honestly, DJ didn't see a way of coming out of that interaction alive and with all his limbs.

But it wasn't as if he had a choice. It was one thing when Hermione had just been stuck, but it was a different ball game if there was even a slight chance that whatever Hermione had found was affecting Ndidi's child.

Fuck, DJ groaned mentally, then he turned to Liz. "Well, he's *your* father. How do you figure we play this?"

There was a loud bang, and then Karla was by her sister's side, her lips spread in a manic smile. "We fight."

"We are *not* fighting," DJ said immediately. Best to shut down that hard and fast. "No," he said, cutting Karla off before she could reply. "I'm not calling you guys weak, I'm not calling you cowards, or any other word that you could use to psych yourself up into doing something monumentally stupid. But we are *not* fighting him."

"I am not your slave that you give ord—"

"Have you guys ever defeated him?" DJ asked, cutting her off again. He realized what he'd done only when Karla's eyes flashed. But Liz was already holding her, looking at him without expression. DJ gulped but continued. "Have you guys ever won a fight against him? Even once?"

"We are stronger—"

"No," Liz replied. Karla looked at her sister like she'd betrayed her. "He is right, sister. Our father is a monster. He was a monster before, and the nanites would only enhance his worst traits. We are not strong enough to win against him, not as we are. And trying will only lead to our deaths. Would you want to see me killed?"

The last line shut Karla up completely. She stopped struggling, so Liz finally released her. Karla brought her dagger up—which made DJ tense for a moment—but she just started stroking its blade. "He will kill me first," she said finally, "for insulting him."

"No, Chloe and I abandoned him to save you, but he will see it as a betrayal, which is a greater sin. He will kill us first, then try to control you."

Jesus Christ, DJ thought, struggling to hide his revulsion. *What sort of childhood did they have?* It was the way they calmly analyzed who their father would murder first. They didn't doubt that José would kill them, just in what order. *Fuck.*

DJ cleared his throat softly. "Any chance he'll hear us out if we approach him directly?"

Liz shook her head. "Our father...José is not one to listen. He has always been convinced that everyone is against him. It would be even worse now."

"I insulted him," Karla added. "He will never forgive that, especially since he knows I spoke the truth."

"We don't need him to forgive you. We will just ask him to release Martin."

"He will see that as weakness," Karla said, tightening her grip on her dagger, "and he will reject us because he is a bastard."

"Then we'll remind him of all the times he wasn't a bastard," DJ said. "He'll remember the time we were on the same side, when he had enough compassion to cut a deal with Helene to save both of you, and when he gave his own life in exchange for yours. I mean, those aren't the things a bastard does. So, we'll appeal to that side and hope Helene left a shred of honor that we can anchor to."

Liz started to say something but turned as Chloe strode in, closing the door behind her. She took one look at DJ's disheveled state and then turned to Karla and Liz, amusement twinkling in her eyes. "Did you at least leave some bones intact?"

"No," DJ replied for them. "They didn't. But it's good that you're here because we need your input." He waved her over. "Hermione's found something in Manar's and Ndidi's blood that she believes might be dangerous. And since it relates to the nanites, she needs Martin's help to figure it out. It's urgent, so we need to figure out how to get Martin from José pronto."

Chloe crossed her arms over her chest and thought for a moment. "I'll go," she said finally. "I know how to handle José. And if anything happens, I can handle myself."

"Who would have thought the entire family was so self-sacrificing," DJ tsked. "You're not going alone, Chloe, and we're not going to fight him—"

"Let me guess, she's the one who suggested fighting him?" Chloe asked, pointing at Karla. The redhead growled at her but left it at that, fortunately.

"Look," DJ said, letting some of his anger bleed into his voice, "José is basically unstoppable right now, so if any of us are going to walk in there, then we're all going to walk in there. At least then we can cover each other's backs if shit hits the fan."

"And if he attacks us?" Karla asked.

"Then we'll cross that bridge when we get there," DJ replied, then narrowed his eyes at her as something occurred to him. "But don't provoke him on purpose. Martin's useless to him anyway, so there's no reason he'll refuse."

"Except that he's a bastard," Chloe said.

Hermione cleared her throat, and DJ turned. He'd forgotten she was still there. "So you're all going?"

DJ nodded. "Yeah, we're probably going to leave soon. Just keep doing your stuff and see what you can figure out. If we manage to bring Martin back, you can compare notes or something."

Chloe stared at him until DJ met her gaze. She bit her lip. "I gotta say that I'm loving this new bossy DJ. If I'd known that all we had to do was break every bone in your body, I'd have done so a long time ago."

From the corner of his eyes, DJ saw Hermione bite back a smile. He sighed. "Let's just get this over with. I didn't get nearly enough sleep."

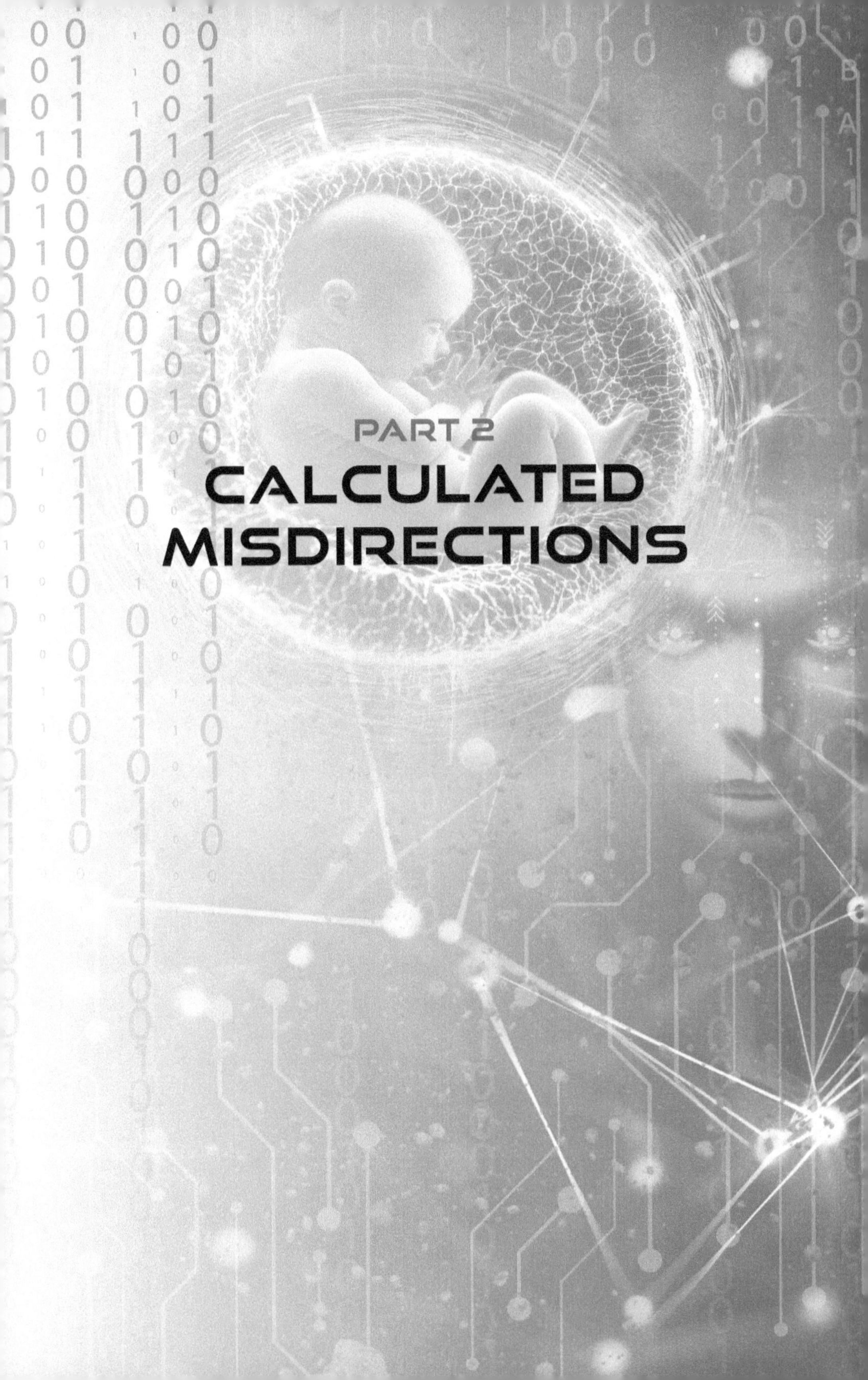

PART 2
CALCULATED
MISDIRECTIONS

DJ WIPED HIS BROW with a towel as he stepped back into the gym, his hair still wet from his shower. The cold water had helped him feel human again. His body was still one giant bruise, but he felt far better than he had just a few minutes ago. Some of his bruises had even started fading. A few months ago, that would have been miraculous. Now DJ barely gave it a glance.

Hermione had returned to her lab, and the Murder Family had gone to prep. Neither Karla nor Liz had needed to freshen up, considering they hadn't broken a sweat while beating him to a pulp. DJ hung the towel around his neck and closed the door behind him when he left the gym. He made a mental note to talk to someone about the damage the twins had done to the place. Upper management undoubtedly already knew about it, but with some luck he'd be able to get everything fixed before they decided to press the issue.

DJ pulled out his phone and drafted a text to Olsen. He was halfway to the elevator when the sound of footsteps made him slow down. A moment later, a man turned the corner into the passage. DJ didn't recognize him, but his dark-blue blazer identified him as one of the staff—someone pretty high up, if he was working on the upper floors. He stopped in front of DJ, staring at him with a look of both awe and fear that made DJ deeply uncomfortable.

"Mr. Kojak," the man said. "Mr. Flynn would like to see you."

DJ's lips pressed into a thin line, but it wasn't like he hadn't expected this. He'd hoped, however, that he would be able to speak to Olsen beforehand. Unfortunately, it seemed like the board of directors were impatient. "Top floor, right? Lead the way."

Both of them continued to the elevator in silence. DJ sent off another text and then tucked away his phone. He'd been staying at the Sparta Headquarters for over a year, but it was only a couple of months ago that he'd been invited to the executives' floor.

And it was vastly different from the lower floors. Generally, the upper layers of Sparta Headquarters were reserved for those in the highest echelon of the organization, or for extremely high-profile guests, like senators or presidents. And it showed. His feet sank into the plush carpet, almost disappearing completely. Paintings hung a few feet apart on every wall. Some of them DJ recognized as past presidents or dignitaries, and he assumed they were sponsors or stakeholders in the organization. Most of them, however, were unknown. He *did* see a painting of Manar, though, which was weird. It shouldn't have been. Before Helene had shut down and the world had turned against Sparta, Manar had been the company's golden goose.

But it was still weird.

The man led them to a set of end-game-boss-type double doors that opened to reveal half a dozen pairs of eyes staring at him. DJ grinned back at them, as if he didn't have a care in the world. He closed the door behind him and deliberately glanced around.

The hundredth-floor conference room was different from the one the team had commandeered. The most interesting thing about that one was the television that descended from the ceiling when they needed to do a presentation or something. This room reminded him of the Oval Office—comfortable but intimidating in how everything within it was more expensive than most people could afford. Sunlight bathed the room through windows that were probably bulletproof, and the only obvious exit was the door that DJ had just entered. He'd bet good money on there being another door hidden somewhere though.

There were six chairs around the table, and in each of them, a different type of old person lounged. Behind each of those old people was a pair of men in black. DJ had expected the private security—even though they hadn't been there in the last meeting—but twelve men for just him seemed a little excessive. Clearly, the board had taken the rumors after the Sparta raid seriously. Whether or not they believed Tyra's videos, they weren't willing to take any chances.

DJ didn't know what they'd expected; killing them wouldn't solve anything, and it wasn't like he could kidnap them in the middle of their own headquarters. He stopped a foot away from the table. Naturally, there wasn't a chair for him, which was a power play that DJ had expected, since they'd done the same thing the last time.

Strangely, DJ felt himself getting annoyed. He should have been nervous—Sparta was widely considered to be the most powerful company in the world, after all. Despite the hit they'd taken with Helene shutting down, in most countries, their branches were regarded as national assets. Their headquarters was officially recognized as the largest, tallest, and most expensive single structure in the world—and the half dozen people currently staring at him owned it. Any single one of them could make his life a living hell. And yet, DJ was more concerned with the fact that this was yet another problem he had to deal with, yet another hoop he had to jump through.

Deep breaths, DJ.

"Look," he said as calmly as he could. "I didn't get to say it the last time we met, but I appreciate everything you've done for me and mine over the past year. You've tolerated, looked the other way, or indirectly supported us through some weird shit. Most of that, I understand, is because of Manar's influence. Even so, I appreciate you. And because of that, I'm going to level with you."

DJ panned his gaze across the room, making sure he had everyone's attention. He did. "The last time I was here, I gave some vague hints about how true the rumors flying around about me were. Now I'm going to be clearer: Most of them are, in fact, true. The videos are also true, although they've been heavily doctored and edited to make me look like a homicidal maniac. They were released by a woman called Tyra—"

"Wait, please," one of the men said. Harrison Flynn looked to be in his late fifties, though he carried it well. He had salt-and-pepper hair and clear eyes, and he wore a suit that probably cost more than everything DJ owned combined. "While I am loath to interrupt you, Mr. Kojak, you said something that is rather difficult to believe without further proof."

"You want me to prove that the rumors and videos are true?"

"Do you expect us to just take your word for it?" asked another man, Ethan Sawyer.

"If none of you believed them, then I doubt I'd be here right now," DJ said.

"Quite right," Flynn said, nodding calmly. "But rumors can be exaggerated, and videos, as you mentioned earlier, can be edited. However, it is difficult to deny what one sees with their own eyes, wouldn't you say?"

I'd say that you'd be surprised how deeply a person can delude themself in order to avoid a truth they don't want to face, thought DJ. Out loud, though, he asked, "How would you suggest I prove it then?"

Ethan glanced at the men standing behind him and then met DJ's eyes. He raised his brows in a silent question.

Despite himself, DJ chuckled. "Nah, that's not a good idea at all."

"Why?" Ethan challenged. "My men are the best in their field, granted, but if your feats in the videos are even halfway accurate, you should have no problem."

"That's not—"

"Or are your so-called powers conditional? We know you just destroyed our gym during your recent session with the Polova twins. Are your powers on cooldown? Do you need some time to—"

The world slowed as DJ activated his nanites. Ethan froze as one second stretched almost indefinitely. Energy coursed through DJ, washing away most of his exhaustion. It pushed him to move, and a vindictive part of him wanted to listen to it, to appear behind Ethan, knock out his guards and set one of their guns in front of the exec—all at a speed faster than Ethan could process.

But that was what Ethan wanted. That was what he was trying to push DJ to do. The idiot probably thought his guards would be able to contain DJ if he got out of control. DJ was sorely tempted to show him how wrong he was. And he was close enough to the edge that he might have—if he had been able to see a way that it wouldn't end badly for him.

So DJ deactivated his nanites.

"—recharge? Or maybe you need to be exposed to the Earth's yellow sun?" Ethan finished, chuckling at his own joke. He leaned back in his chair, looking quite proud of himself as he waited for a flare-up.

DJ gave him his best grin. "I didn't take you for a fan of Superman, Ethan. I didn't think he was created until long after you were a kid." Ethan's smug look was immediately replaced by a scowl, but DJ continued before the man could say anything. "But the reason why I can't take you up on your offer is that if I did, I'd be proving I'm the brutish savage the videos are trying to portray."

"Are you claiming you can defeat everybody in here?" Flynn said, raising a brow in skepticism.

DJ considered it for a moment and then disappeared—to them, at least. He wasn't as fast as Karla and Liz, but at the first level, he'd already been pushing the peak of what a human being was capable of. At the second level, he could move more than fast enough to appear as a blur to the average person. That being said, wherever the board had acquired their security, each person in the group was a professional. They couldn't see him, but by the time DJ went around the table and got to the last two, they were already reacting, reaching into their holsters for their guns.

A moment later, DJ stopped exactly where he'd stood originally, cradling twelve pistols in the crook of his arm like they were loose oranges. He then placed the guns on the table, one after the other. He very deliberately didn't make eye contact with any of them. He'd just done something very threat-like to prove a point, but he couldn't afford to make them think he was truly threatening them.

So when he was done, he took a very obvious step away from the table and waved for the guards to come pick up their weapons. Naturally, they hesitated, staring at him with expressions ranging from anger to fear to curiosity. DJ ignored their looks and waved them on more insistently. Eventually, one of the closest ones stepped forward, and the rest followed. DJ noted, however, that none of them holstered their guns. They didn't point them at him, fortunately, but they weren't taking chances anymore.

It didn't really change anything, but it would probably be better if they thought it did.

"Thank you, Mr. Kojak," Flynn said finally. "I doubt any of us need another demonstration. However, this leaves us with another problem, specifically the angry mob of people currently surrounding this building, as well as several of our other branches across the country. Right now, most of the outcry is aimed at you and your team. However, it is inevitable that eventually some of that backlash will come back to Sparta. And the organization cannot afford that. I'm sure you understand."

Annoyingly, DJ did understand. The world had finally moved on after Helene's crash, and Sparta couldn't afford another media outcry so soon. So, they wanted to cut ties with DJ before the public turned their attention to the organization. They'd probably release a statement saying they disavowed DJ's actions or some other bullshit, and he and his team would have to find somewhere else to operate from.

DJ might have considered bowing out and leaving if he knew where the government stood with the videos—especially since he still felt guilty about the lives that'd been lost during the raid. But he and Olsen hadn't had the chance to talk, and he couldn't risk the government hanging them out to dry like Sparta was trying to do. That would leave the team without a place to stay, lose them all their resources, and play right into Tyra's hands.

So to hell with that.

DJ met Flynn's eyes. "With all due respect, Mr. Flynn, you're gonna have to afford it. Because this is going to bite you regardless."

"How so?"

"All of this..." DJ swirled a finger in the air. "Everything that's happening right now started several years ago when Helene hijacked Gaius and triggered Mayday."

None of the members reacted to his statement. No surprise, anger at his accusation, or apprehension. Nothing. Not even from the security detail, who still looked one order away from firing at him. That, more than anything, confirmed something for DJ: The board had already known that their AI had caused the biggest human tragedy since the World Wars.

"Manar?" DJ guessed, raising a brow at Flynn.

Flynn stared at him for a beat, and DJ could almost hear his brain churning out options. At that moment, DJ was glad they'd asked for proof of his abilities. His demonstration was probably the reason he wasn't already being attacked right then.

"Yes," Flynn answered finally. "Mr. Saleem is a member of this board, and he revealed the role he—and by extension, Sparta—played in Mayday when he approached us several years ago to shut down the AI."

"Which you refused," DJ stated. He could have continued to say that they were in the mess they were in right now because the board had turned Manar down then—but that would cross a line, for one. For another, it wouldn't be true. Because DJ knew Manar did try to shut down Helene from her source code, but by then she had grown too powerful for him. Sparta wasn't really to blame.

Flynn didn't say anything.

So DJ continued. "Despite what you might be thinking, I'm not trying to threaten you guys by bringing this up. I'm trying to say that the information is going to get out regardless. Not because of anything that I'm going to do, directly or indirectly. But because Helene no longer cares about working from the shadows. Her drones have been flying everywhere for the last few months. The government is leading everyone to believe it's some kind of terrorist-preparedness drill, but I'm sure you guys are more informed.

"The raid that happened here a couple of months ago is another example. It's a better example because it was led by Helene's henchwoman, Tyra Chityothin. She's the one who leaked the videos, and we believe she did it partly in retaliation for something that happened the last time she crossed paths with my team. She has abilities similar to mine, but she obviously didn't care about letting the world know. And considering she chose to attack us here instead of somewhere else, she obviously has a vendetta against Sparta."

Ethan Sawyer leaned forward. "Are you implying this woman might expose things about Sparta as well?"

"I'm saying that too many people already know about it," DJ replied, shrugging. "It's almost inevitable that the secret gets out. And if it does, either Helene or Tyra is your best bet for who'd be responsible."

The board reacted with a jumble of expressions—some frowning in concern, others raising skeptical brows, a few glancing nervously at one another—before immediately breaking into hushed whispers. Snippets reached DJ:

"Is he exaggerating?"

"…we can't afford exposure…"

"…if this Helene is real, then…"

The murmurs overlapped until they blurred into noise. Flynn didn't join in. He stared at DJ with an unreadable expression. DJ returned it with his best poker face. He probably knew what DJ was trying to do. DJ could have tried telling them that Helene was dangerous and was a threat to the whole world. But since she wasn't an immediate threat that affected them directly, the board would almost definitely have brushed it off with a stupid justification. So DJ had made it into one. If they were afraid of backlash from their relationship with DJ, what sort of outcry would fall on them if the public found out they were in any way responsible for Mayday? Sparta was one of the most powerful organizations globally—but even they might not survive that backlash.

Eventually, Flynn made a gesture that cut off the whispering. "If I understand you well, Mr. Kojak, you are indirectly suggesting that not only should Sparta not cut ties with you, as you have undoubtedly guessed was the reason for this meeting, but we should support you in dealing with Helene and Tyra Chityothin in order to preserve our reputation."

DJ struggled not to smile. "I'm saying that you would be best served in supporting us, yes, for your sake, and for the fact that Helene is a global threat. But if you can't actively support us, then at least let us return to the status quo."

"Which is what?"

DJ shrugged. "It's what you've been doing so far: tolerating, ignoring, or otherwise turning a blind eye to whatever weird shit we get up to in your building."

28

JANUARY 2044
SPARTA HEADQUARTERS, NEW YORK

DJ LEFT THE CONFERENCE ROOM while the board was still deliberating over his statement, but he was confident they'd agree with him. It was the best thing for them, and it wasn't like they were losing anything. The claim that Sparta feared another uprising was bullshit—a ploy to put DJ under their thumb and make him a pawn that they had control over.

Going in, he'd been prepared to spill the beans about the nanites and the spores—being who they were, they undoubtedly already knew a lot about both— but it was probably best that he kept some things close to his chest. And this way, he had some ammo for the next time he was summoned and indirectly threatened.

In the elevator, he brought out his phone and replied to a text from Olsen while the carriage descended. A minute later, the doors opened into the lobby. The sun had set sometime between being beaten up at the gym and getting grilled by the board, so the lobby was relatively empty, except for Mark, the receptionist.

Chloe and Liz sat on one of the lounge chairs, while Karla paced impatiently in front of the door. Christy stood to the side, her strawberry-blonde hair pulled into a bun. She was tapping her foot and trying to look bored and disinterested, but her eyes flicked to Karla whenever she came anywhere near her. DJ held back a sigh. He'd very deliberately not informed Christy about their outing, so he didn't know how she'd found out.

Karla glared at him the moment he came into view. DJ raised both hands up. "Yeah, I'm sorry. But the board called me up. They didn't like what you did to their gym, by the way."

Christy came up to him. "What'd they say?"

"They wanted to kick us out, but my charming personality won them over in the end, and they agreed to leave us alone. Y'know, same old, same old. More importantly, though, you should get some rest. You still have bags under your eyes."

Christy's eyes hardened, which just made the bags more distinct. "I'm coming with you."

"No, you're not. Go rest."

Christy glared at him, and DJ met her eyes, even though his stomach was twisting into knots. On one hand, there shouldn't be any fighting, since they were just going to talk to José. But if shit hit the fan, any fighting would be done at speeds she wouldn't even be able to process. Christy had been by his side since day one, so it hurt to leave her behind. But he was doing this for her sake. If something went wrong, he couldn't bear it if she got hurt. She wasn't going to see it like that, though, so DJ had to be the bad guy.

"Look," DJ said, softening his voice. "I understand that you want to have my back, and I appreciate that. But we're just going to talk to José. There isn't going to be a fight, which means there's no need for backup."

Christy snorted.

"I'm serious," DJ insisted, giving her a grin. "We already have it planned out. Chloe, Liz, and Karla are going to get José to let Martin go. We'll grab the old man and be back in a few hours."

"Why are *you* going then?" Christy asked. "The Murder Family, I get. But doesn't José hate you?"

DJ froze. That was a good point. His mind churned, and then he jerked his thumb at Chloe. "I'm her ride. This is urgent, so we're going to be moving fast.

Without nanites, Chloe isn't going to be able to keep up. And since neither of the twins is willing to carry her, I have to do it."

Karla burst out laughing immediately, clutching her side and pointing a dagger at Chloe. Liz didn't even crack a smile, but there was an unmistakable glint of amusement in her eyes. Chloe just stared at DJ with an unreadable expression. *Yeah, I might have fucked up,* DJ thought, meeting her eyes.

"You'll carry her?" Christy asked, drawing his attention back. She was smirking now, which was better, at least. "Like, cradle-style or on your back?"

There was a thump as Karla fell, laughing harder than ever. DJ grimaced at Christy. She obviously knew he was bullshitting and was getting her revenge by helping him dig as deep a grave as possible. "We, uh, we haven't really talked about it yet."

"So you'll just go with what feels right?"

DJ sighed. "We'll see. But hey, you should be getting off to bed now, and I'll fill you in once we're back."

Christy shook her head. "No way. I gotta see this. Y'know, in case you have to carry me too."

"I'm sure that's not necessary. I can just tell you if—"

"She is right," Karla wheezed from the ground. She pushed herself up but didn't even try to hide her grin. "If this is the reason why she cannot come along, then it is only right that she witnesses it."

"Look, that's not at all necess—"

"We have to hurry," Liz interjected. "You said this was urgent, yes?"

DJ gaped at her and then flinched when Chloe placed a hand on his shoulder. She leaned up so her lips were next to his ear. "That's two favors you owe."

DJ felt a chill go down his spine. A while back, to prevent Helene from controlling the Murder Twins through their nanites, Dr. Martin Bryan had extracted some nanites from each of them, leaving only the amount they needed for their prosthetics to work. For some reason, the old man had then given those nanites to DJ. Karla had almost killed him when she'd found out. Chloe had stopped her but insisted that DJ owed her the favor. She hadn't called it in yet, but it had always been at the back of DJ's mind, keeping him on edge.

And now, he'd earned himself another one. *Fuck me,* he groaned mentally. DJ rubbed the bridge of his nose and straightened. "Let's just get this over with."

29

JANUARY 2044
NEW YORK CITY

NIGHT HAD FALLEN, but this was New York City, so just meant there were slightly fewer people on the street. Fortunately, the mob that had surrounded the building earlier had found better things to do. Their group—two redheads in skintight leather jumpsuits, and Chloe—drew some attention, but people were used to seeing weird shit in this city. A breeze blew past, and DJ drew his jacket tighter around him, more out of habit than anything else.

"So where are we going exactly?" DJ asked.

"Several miles south of here is the warehouse where we left José," Chloe said. "We'll start by checking there. If he's moved on, we'll check the other safe houses."

"How many safe houses are there?"

Chloe gave him a blank stare.

"Fine, keep your secrets. But we have to get moving," he said, moving closer to her. "Now, how do you want to do this?"

Chloe muttered something under her breath but forced him into a crouch and climbed onto his back. Chloe was just as psychopathic as the twins, but *goddamn* was she hot as hell. She leaned forward and wrapped her arms around his shoulders to secure her grip. DJ barely felt her weight, but there was no way he was going to forget she was there. He focused on keeping his breathing steady, trying to ignore the two nubs he felt rubbing against his back. It didn't help when she shifted to get into a comfortable position.

Christy stood aside. She didn't look so smug anymore, though DJ was sure that was going to come back to bite him somehow. "Get some rest," he told her. "I'll brief you once we're back."

Liz nudged her sister, and once Karla had composed herself, the three of them took off down the street. The asphalt blurred beneath his feet, and the city's glow smeared into elongated streaks. The wind whipped across his cheeks, making his eyes water. He'd have to get a pair of glasses for next time.

Initially they'd run on the sidewalk, but it didn't take long for Karla to get annoyed at having to constantly dodge people. When her hand started inching toward her side, Liz directed them to the street. At first, DJ was worried, but they were running with the flow of traffic, so there was little risk of causing an accident when they raced past a car from behind. At the speed they were moving, most people wouldn't be able to make out anything more than a blur. Even with closed-circuit television cameras, it would take a dedicated effort to pull out any usable footage. And even if someone *did* see them, what was the worst that could happen? Thanks to Tyra, the world already knew about his abilities. At most, he would be confirming it.

Honestly, DJ couldn't bring himself to care anymore. *I'm basically the Flash right now,* he thought, unable to stop the grin on his face. *Does anything else really matter?*

The twins raced beside him, in perfect sync as always. He knew they were holding back so he wouldn't be left behind, yet even at that pace, the sheer speed they were moving at was beyond anything he'd ever thought possible. They left the road eventually and wove through wide avenues and narrow side streets. Chloe tightened her grip whenever he took a sharp turn but otherwise didn't say anything. At some point, they ran past rows of shuttered businesses and dimly lit apartments with graffiti scrawled across the walls. DJ made out the words Beware the Berserker as he flashed past.

The berserker virus was a nationwide plague that pushed people into random acts of violence. A man could randomly attack another person on the street. A wife could come home from work, prepare dinner for her family, and then try to murder her husband while they were doing dishes together. There was no rhyme or reason to it, and there was no way to tell who was infected with the virus until they attacked.

At least, that's what the public thought. Hermione had discovered a while ago, however, that the berserkers were victims of picospores whose minds had been warped. No one had been able to figure out why Helene—or Tyra now—was doing it. But there was little they could do to stop it, apart from what they were already doing. Almost immediately the virus was popularized, groups started forming, and people learned not to leave their homes without weapons.

DJ heard raised voices just as they ran past an alley. A gang of people were hunched over a guy, raining down punches. There was another guy deeper in the alley, lying still. DJ couldn't tell whether he was dead or simply unconscious.

"He's got the virus!" one of the idiots shouted. "You saw what he did to Jake! Take him down before he kills us all!"

A split second later, DJ was within the crowd, flinging bodies away. He had enough presence of mind to tone down his strength so no one went into the street, but he hoped there would be a few broken bones from landing. When he was done, he stood in front of the beat-up man, staring down the mob as they shouted in confusion and tried to pick themselves up.

"This isn't going to work out how you think it will," Chloe said, climbing down. She sounded amused. "You should have kept running."

DJ ignored her. He knew that this probably hadn't been the best idea. They were on a time crunch, and this was going to eat up some time. But what sort of person would have seen this and kept running?

"Who the hell are you?" one of the fools asked, clutching a baseball bat. There were six of them, and most of the others had risen to their feet. They were warily eyeing him, fingers tense on their bats, hockey sticks, or in one case, broken bottles.

"Who the fuck are *you*?" DJ shot back. Fortunately, it was dark enough that they couldn't make out his face. Being recognized would add a layer that DJ couldn't afford. "A little more and you'll kill him."

"He's got the virus," the lead idiot said, pointing. "He jumped our friend."

"And you've beaten him into unconsciousness, so I'm sure he's learned his lesson. Now, instead of wasting your time trying to commit murder, take your friend to the hospital, then move on with your lives."

The lead idiot looked at his friends and seemed to get courage when he saw them slowly closing in on DJ. "He's going to infect us if we just leave him."

DJ sighed, trying to keep his annoyance out of his voice. "How do you think he's gonna infect you? By sneezing on you? Biting? What the fuck do you think this is, the zombie apocalypse? The virus cannot be transmitted. Either you have it or you don't."

"How do you know that?" the idiot asked, hesitating.

"Because I take the time to find out shit instead of just eating up whatever I hear on TV," DJ replied. In truth, he knew it because Hermione had told him, but technically he hadn't lied. The group was still hesitating, so he made the choice easier for them. "Look, either you take your friend and move the fuck on, or I move all of you, and your friend bleeds out because you numb nuts were such pieces of shit that you chose to beat up an unconscious person instead of saving his life."

He met each of their eyes, activating his nanites for a split second to give his gaze an extra punch for an added oomph. They wouldn't be able to explain what about DJ made them feel ready to shit their pants—but that only added to the effect. "So, what's it going to be?"

Fortunately, they made the right decision. DJ would have felt bad about leaving their unconscious bodies on the street. Chloe stepped up beside him when they were gone, and both of them stared at the beaten-up form of the berserker victim. "Now," she whispered, "what're you going to do about him?"

It took ten minutes for DJ to run the victim to the nearest hospital because he had to moderate his speed to not jostle the dude too much. He left Chloe by the sidewalk, and by the time he returned, Karla and Liz were with her. Karla looked on the edge of murdering someone, which would have been normal, except she turned the look at him.

"No, you can't kill him, Karla," Chloe said. "We all went through the hero phase. He'll grow out of it eventually. Or y'know," she shrugged, "be killed first. But I'm sure you don't want to miss that either way."

Karla stalked up to him. "While you were playing," she snarled, jabbing her dagger against his chest, "my sister and I returned to the hideout where we left our father."

"And?" DJ asked, his expression carefully neutral. He'd wasted time by stopping, but he didn't regret it. He was never going to "grow out" of doing the right thing.

"It was cleared out, unfortunately," Chloe said, answering for Karla. "He might have moved out of paranoia, or he knew we were coming."

"He couldn't have known we were coming," DJ said. "*We* didn't even know we were coming until a few hours ago. But it doesn't change anything. Where would he go next?"

Chloe gestured for him to come closer, stretching her arms out like she wanted a hug. "Come on. I'll show you."

JOSÉ WASN'T AT THE NEXT hideout Chloe directed them to, or the one after that. Eventually they crossed over to New Jersey, running across the Lincoln Bridge in a blur. DJ started flagging toward the end. At that point, they'd been running full sprint for well over an hour, and even with the nanites, he had his limits. Fortunately, they stayed on the outskirts of the city, and Chloe led them to a dimly lit storage facility.

It was a large industrial space with a low ceiling, exposed ductwork, and fluorescent lights so old they couldn't have been made that century. Most of them were broken, and the few that worked cast a yellowish glow that illuminated only the center, leaving shadows that stretched to the corners. Rows of metal shelving units lined the walls, and all around were stacked wooden crates halfway eaten by termites. The air was stale with dust, cardboard, and mildew. The place felt abandoned—forgotten.

But it was even sadder when the four of them walked into the room and found José lying in the middle of it, clutching a canteen. He raised his head at their approach, and his features immediately twisted into anger. He pushed himself up to his feet, and DJ appreciated, not for the first time, what a monster José was. Not in any hypothetical or philosophical way—though that was valid too. José was an actual monster.

He'd once been human, but that was before most of his body had been obliterated by one of Helene's drones when he sacrificed himself to save his daughters. Unfortunately, Helene hadn't been willing to let him go, and she'd somehow fused what remained of him with a ten-foot-tall titanium exoskeleton, inadvertently creating the best Robocop cosplay ever.

DJ still couldn't figure out how she'd done it, but knowing what he knew now about the nanites, combined with Tyra's skillset, he was starting to get an idea. If he was right, it would explain why José was such a bitch when it came to Tyra.

None of them spoke as José stared at each of them in turn, getting more furious as he moved down the line. DJ tried not to flinch when it was his turn. He couldn't say he was used to being on edge after interacting with Chloe and Karla for so long, but he was more inured to it than he would have been otherwise. Still, there was just something about José that made his hackles rise. José looked at a person the way a lion stared at a pregnant deer that wobbled up to it and showed its belly: like it was prey just *begging* to be consumed.

A muscle in DJ's jaw ticked. His hands were itching to reach for his gun, but instead he casually took out his phone, as if he didn't give a shit that the Terminator remake was currently contemplating whether to take off his head.

"So," José said at last, voice rumbling, "you have come crawling back."

DJ put his phone back. "I don't know if you noticed, man, but none of us were the ones just lying on their backs in the cliché anime I-was-defeated pose."

Karla barked a laugh, Liz turned to stare at him, and Chloe face-palmed. DJ winced, wishing he could take the words back as soon as he said them. What was wrong with him? Did some part of him *want* to fight?

Understandably, José took a step toward him, his fist clenched.

DJ raised his hands in a show of peace. "I apologize for that. My mouth tends to run away from me sometimes, but that was uncalled for." *True though,* he added mentally. "We're not here to fight. We just need to pick up Martin, and then we'll be out of your hair."

"No," José replied coldly.

DJ's lips pressed into a thin line. "Not even going to consider it, huh? Look, I understand that you're in a bad place. You've been dealt a shitty hand. But this isn't the way to lash out. Martin's useless to you. Less than useless, actually, considering you have to lug him around every time you move. You might not need to eat—"

DJ cut himself off, frowning. He glanced at Chloe, who sighed but then nodded. DJ's brows went up, and he turned back to José. "I'm sorry about that. I was going to exaggerate to make a point, but apparently you *don't* need to eat anymore, which is halfway cool but also kinda sad. But anyway, it must be annoying having to feed the old man every few hours and stuff, right? So he's worse than useless; he's a burden. Let *us* take him off your hands so you don't have to go through that anymore."

José stared at him like he was an idiot. "You must enjoy hearing yourself talk."

"Well, I wouldn't say that, but I do have a pretty nice voice, wouldn't you say?" DJ replied, forcing a grin on his face. "On a more serious note, though, Martin really is useless to you. However, we have a very pressing need for him."

"Need?" José asked rhetorically. "You seek to force him to your cause, into your pointless war with the AI and Tyra Chityothin."

DJ's expression hardened. "Is it pointless to fight against something that's killed millions of people and is trying to destroy the rest?"

"It is *pointless*," the cyborg sneered, "when you are doomed to fail regardless. What difference has your defiance made? How many times has the AI outsmarted you and trapped you? How many times have your actions not only been fruitless but indirectly helped to further her cause? Do you know? Do you *want* to know?"

The words reverberated in DJ's mind. After Ndidi had confirmed that Helene was in Manar's body, it hadn't taken DJ long to realize that everything that had happened in the Virtual Realm had been part of her plan. DJ didn't like thinking about that. If his thoughts spiraled too much, he'd end up just as apathetic as José.

A part of him understood. José was right that the team hadn't been more than a minor annoyance to Helene since they'd started, and the whole thing with Tyra was just pathetic. But DJ couldn't afford to give up. He couldn't afford to become so depressed that he'd lie around, hoping the storm would miss him. Someone had to take the fight to Helene. And although DJ wouldn't have been his own first pick either, he'd do the best with the hand he'd been dealt.

But it was pointless to start explaining that to someone who'd so obviously hit rock bottom. So he turned to the others and raised a brow. "Anyone wanna give it a go?"

Liz spoke up. "We did not come here to fight, father, or argue our philosophies. We only came to collect Martin and leave."

"Father..." José said as if tasting the word. A dangerous edge crept into his tone. "You no longer have the right to call me that. Not when you abandoned me the moment I refused to die a second time for a worthless cause. You left me, the one who raised you, for *him*." He leveled a glare at DJ. "And now you return to me with demands?"

Liz narrowed her eyes, and for the first time, her expression shifted into something that wasn't guarded neutrality. "I left because you banished my sister, your *daughter*," she snarled, "and you were going to abandon her when she was in trouble."

"Your sister was out of control—"

"My sister," Liz hissed, her voice rising above his, "is as she has always been— what you raised her to be. You are the one who has changed. After you returned from Helene, you became a coward, paranoid at everything, seeing shadows in every corner and running away like a dog with its tails between its legs. You became pathetic. My sister saw that and rightly refused to follow you into your self-destruction. I was slower, blinded by the memory of the man you used to be."

Liz's voice dropped until it was barely above a whisper. "I convinced myself that I had to follow your orders because the last time I chose for myself, I watched you give your life to save mine. So I stopped choosing for myself and just did what I was told, no matter how I felt. And it was so familiar—because I'd done the same for years, as you took my childhood from me. But then I watched you give my sister up for death because you were too afraid to leave the prison you built for yourself...and I realized something."

José narrowed his eyes. "What did you realize?"

Liz's lips pulled back into a sneer. "That I would rather watch you die a second time than abandon my sister."

That, DJ thought, whistling mentally, *is cold as ice.*

José stared at Liz. DJ couldn't even begin to imagine what the guy must be feeling. For all his scars and rage, José had shown that he cared deeply for his daughters. To hear one of them reject him like that—it was hard not to feel guilty for the guy.

After a long moment, José turned to Chloe. "And you? Are your thoughts the same?" he asked softly.

Chloe had lost her ever-present smirk at some point and met José's eyes with the most solemn look that DJ had ever seen on her. It only lasted for a second though. "Of course not, you idiot. I'm old enough to know not to blame my parents for how fucked up I turned out. Now, I might not agree with your choices lately, but for the last couple of decades, the three of you idiots have been my family, and I didn't put all that effort into stopping you from killing each other just to watch one of you die. Once was hard enough, and I am not going to put myself through that again. I left when DJ told me that Karla was in trouble because, as often as I want to bash her head in, she's my daughter too. I'd do the same thing for Liz. And I'd do the same for you, even if Helene forgot to weld some fucking balls on you. Now, for the love of God, get your head out of your ass and hand over Martin."

The tension in the room became so thick that DJ could have cut it with a knife. The twins leaned forward, preparing to intervene if José lunged, but José just stood there, staring at Chloe with narrowed eyes. "You dare speak to me like that?"

"Yeah." She chuckled in reply. "Because I knew you before you became a piece of shit. I knew you when you were the kind of man who would do anything for his daughters, face any threat, no matter how 'pointless' it might be. You might have lost most of your organs, José, but I know you still have a heart in there."

DJ nodded slowly, impressed. "That was deep," he whispered to her.

"You're a bad influence on my wife, Darren Kojak," José said, turning his gaze on him.

Well, we finally have a title, DJ thought. He shrugged in response. "Unfortunately, you're not around to counter it."

Chloe face-palmed again, but José didn't seem angry. He stared at each of them in turn, deep in thought. Karla looked like she wanted to say something, but Chloe stomped on her foot—and surprisingly, she stayed quiet without a fuss. Finally, José exhaled. "Fine. You can have him."

DJ let out a breath he hadn't known he'd been holding. Karla blinked, looking almost disappointed.

"Just like that?" Chloe asked warily.

José scowled. "Do not mistake me for a fool. Releasing Martin gets you out of here faster. I will not be dragged into your war."

José strode to a side door and typed a code into the digital lock. It clicked, and he swung the door open. Inside, Martin lay on a makeshift cot, pale as death, various tubes trailing from his wrists. The faint beep of a heart monitor filled the silence.

"He is just sedated," José said.

DJ stepped into the room cautiously, kneeling at Martin's side to check his pulse. It was weak, though that was probably due to his age. DJ carefully removed each tube and checked again. "His breathing's steady."

José lingered in the doorway, arms crossed. Karla stared him down, her dagger still clutched in one hand. Chloe studied José as if trying to figure him out.

"Thank you," DJ said firmly, straightening up and facing him. "I mean it."

José's expression was unreadable. "Leave. Do not find me again."

That was all DJ needed. He pulled Martin's limp arm over his shoulder and cradled him. Martin mumbled something unintelligible under his breath, his eyelids fluttering. Karla hovered close to her sister. She'd unsheathed her dagger but had the blade pointed downward. She brushed past José, making no effort to hide the hostility in her eyes. Liz followed behind, so expressionless that DJ almost doubted whether he'd seen her outburst just a few minutes ago. DJ and Chloe brought up the rear and returned to the main storage facility. Chloe stopped beside José, placed a hand on his cheek, and whispered something that DJ deliberately tuned out. Instead, he focused on how the hell they were going to return to the headquarters. With Martin in tow, they couldn't afford to return the same way they came. That meant that they had to find a ride and drive back.

Ugh, DJ thought, *Christy's going to kill me.*

A hollow metallic clang echoed through the room as Karla shouldered the heavy door open. A gust of cold air rushed in, pushing away the stale air. The twins stepped through first, followed by Chloe. DJ turned sideways so Martin's head didn't bang on the way out. He was halfway across the parking lot when something in his gut twisted, like his sixth sense was firing off a warning shot.

DJ frowned. Was all of that too easy? He'd expected a fight—planned for one, even—which was why he hadn't wanted Christy to come. But they'd come and insulted José nine ways to Sunday, and the man had just let them go. Just like that.

The others had gone ahead, but DJ turned back to the warehouse—just in time to see José stagger out. DJ let out a breath, almost relieved. With deliberate care, he dropped Martin at the side just as José's face contorted. His eyes were wide and unfocused, and veins bulged out the side of his neck, like a gym bro who'd overestimated his max bench. He slammed a fist against the metal door, squishing it like it was made of cheese.

"Hey, guys?" DJ yelled, without taking his eyes off the man. "Time for the boss fight."

Karla was already by his side, her eyes narrowed. "Something is wrong with him."

Yeah, no shit, Sherlock, DJ thought. José looked like a man fighting off his demons, which probably wasn't far off from the truth. DJ panned his gaze around, focusing on the shadows, looking for a figure he knew was there. The first time DJ had seen José after his "death," he was being controlled by Helene, forced to fight against his family. But Helene was currently possessing Manar's body in Nigeria, so there was no way she could be responsible for this.

That left one option.

"Fight it!" Liz shouted. "You are stronger than it is. Do not let it take control. Fight!"

To his credit, José *was* fighting it. His expression was a mixture of pain and defiance, his muscles straining. His lips were curled into a snarl, and his growls echoed in the silence of the night. But it was a losing battle. His movements were more erratic, and he was moving toward them, despite very clear efforts not to.

"Chloe," DJ said as she stopped beside him, "we need a car. We can't run with Martin, so the twins and I will hold him back as long as we can. You get us a ride out of here."

"He'll kill you," Chloe said, without taking her eyes off José.

"Eventually, yeah," DJ agreed. "You better be back before then, or you're the one that'll have to break the news to Christy. And *she'll* kill *you.*"

"I'd like to see her try—"

José let out a guttural roar that reverberated through the open air like a crack of thunder. He lunged—DJ saw it in slow motion as he activated his nanites. There were about twenty feet of space that separated them, but one leap cleared it like nothing. DJ didn't know if it was because of what Liz had said earlier, but José rocketed toward her first.

To her credit, Liz reacted immediately, unsheathing her daggers to meet his charge. But Karla knocked her aside and countered with a punch that made the air scream. José blocked with a titanium forearm, grabbed her fist with his other hand, pulled her closer, and—still midair—headbutted her so hard that *DJ* was left seeing stars.

"Go!" he shouted to Chloe, then jumped into the fray the same moment Liz did. After that, he couldn't pay attention to anything except staying alive.

IT ONLY TOOK DJ a few minutes to die—of embarrassment.

He had only fought José once before, a couple of months back when he'd tried to convince the Murder Family to join the team against Helene. José had given him a condition: he and his family would join if DJ managed to land a single punch on him. Needless to say, after less than half an hour of José toying with him, DJ had limped back to Sparta covered with bruises.

But that was ages ago, and DJ had improved a lot since then. Not to the point where he'd be able to join the twins in a direct fight against their father, but at least enough to support them—like he'd done when Karla had fought against Tyra at the oil rig: intercepting, cutting off escape routes, that sort of thing.

The difference, and what DJ had failed to consider, was that the difference between himself and Tyra was slight. She was stronger and faster, but it was a gap that his skills and experience were able to bridge to some extent.

José, on the other hand, was orders of magnitude faster, stronger, more skilled, and more experienced than DJ. He was also made of solid titanium below the neck. That meant nothing DJ did had even the slightest, most minuscule effect on him.

It was honestly pathetic.

DJ snatched a chunk of broken concrete off the ground and hurled it with all his strength. But the debris disintegrated the moment it hit the cyborg. José glanced at him for a moment, then simply ignored him. Undeterred, DJ dropped down for a low kick, but he might as well have kicked a steel pillar for all the response he got. He tried a punch to the ribs, and his knuckles exploded with enough pain to send him reeling back. That saved his life from a backhand that would have taken his head off like a bottle cap. In a final burst of desperation, DJ pulled out his gun and took aim. The first few bullets clanged off the man's back, but José ducked a punch from Karla, dropping low enough to put his head—his sole fleshy part—in line with DJ's last shot, just as the bullet left the chamber.

DJ yelled, lunging to catch the bullet—which was stupid for a number of reasons. But they didn't actually want to kill José.

However, whether by accident or by some sixth sense or other bullshit, José turned just as the bullet was about to reach him. He blurred, becoming so fast that DJ couldn't see him, and then stopped in exactly the same position—with the bullet between his fingers. He glared at DJ with eyes full of rage.

DJ backed up immediately. "Unfortunate mistake, man."

Fortunately, Karla exploited her father's moment of distraction to land a punch that launched him several feet. And then she glared at DJ herself. "Are you so tired of life?"

"Yeah, yeah, that was my bad," DJ replied, tucking away his gun.

She wasn't talking about what would happen if José considered DJ a threat. She was talking about what would have happened if the bullet had hit. Because regardless of what the twins said about him, José was still their father. That was part of what made the fight so dangerous. José could try to kill them all he wanted, but their goal was only to incapacitate him.

The last time Helene had controlled him, DJ had knocked José out with one of Hermione's synaptic pulses, which had broken the connection between the picospores and Helene. But the device didn't work on the newer iteration of the spores, so DJ had stopped carrying it around.

DJ was about to jump back into the fray when he caught movement out of the corner of his eye. He glanced up and met Tyra's eyes. She was perched on the roof of the building, her lips pulled into a wide smile, her lab coat billowing out behind her. She gave DJ a small wave.

Fuck, DJ thought. He'd figured she was here the moment José had lost control, but no. They couldn't deal with José and Tyra at the same time. The twins were already struggling to hold down their father, and DJ had accepted that he couldn't deal with Tyra directly. Maybe if Chloe had been around, but definitely not in a one-on-one.

The bitch leaped from the roof and landed deftly. She tapped something on her wrist, and several feet away, José blurred. He sent a kick that launched Karla away. Liz tried to take advantage of the opening, but José was already behind her with his fist clenched.

A second later, José made his way to Tyra. His expression wasn't strained like it had been before. As he crouched beside Tyra so she could place a hand on his shoulder, his eyes just showed resignation.

"Family reunions are always fun, aren't they?" she asked DJ. "And here I thought this was just going to be a simple retrieval."

"He's a *person*, Tyra," DJ said, not bothering to hide his disgust. "And you're controlling him like a puppet. What the hell is wrong with you?"

Tyra raised a finger. "That's the thing about the picospores, DJ. They can't control someone's mind. They interact with the brain, sure, but the best they can do is tinker with the hormones, controlling which ones get released and which are withheld. Right now, for example, the spores are suppressing his oxytocin, cutting off that warm, fuzzy connection he has with his daughters. In his eyes, they're basically a bunch of strangers.

"At the same time, they're ramping up both testosterone and cortisol so he's more prone to violence, jumpier, more irritable, and less rational. Considering that and the way you came to his house—insulting him and guilt-tripping him into releasing a prisoner he'd kept as leverage—can you really blame him for attacking you?"

"How the fuck isn't that mind control?" DJ exclaimed.

"Because he's still the one who chooses how he reacts to those feelings," Tyra said, her grin widening. "After all, it's still your decision whether or not to punch someone who's pissing you off, isn't it? Usually what stops you is your personality, past experience, and all that. But José's past basically demands that he lash out. I'm just giving him a little nudge."

Anger boiled in DJ's gut. "Let him go, Tyra."

Tyra gave him an insane grin. "I'll trade him for Martin."

DJ frowned. Helene had initially used Martin to design the original iteration of the nanites. However, by Martin's own admission, the AI had long since moved past his design and upgraded the nanites to a level that Martin had barely been able to recognize, as the AI had done with Hermione's picospores. Considering that, why would Tyra still need Martin?

It was possible that, like Hermione, she had a problem and needed Martin's expertise. If nothing else, he was the creator of the nanites. But it was also possible that she didn't need him at all and just wanted to mess with DJ by convincing him that she did.

This, DJ thought, seething. *This is why I hate dealing with this bitch. These mind games. You can never tell what the hell she's planning. Fuck.*

Fortunately, this decision was relatively simple: Whether she needed Martin or not, refusing the trade would spoil her plan. It was a shitty deal anyway because even if she did release José now, she could just control him again later. Extracting the nanites wouldn't work like it had for the twins because he was basically a full cyborg; the nanites were the only reason he was still alive.

"No—" DJ started to say. But then Karla and Liz appeared in front of him, twin glares drilling into his head. DJ sighed. "Look, I know. He's your father, and it sucks, but do you really think she's going to let him go?"

"Then we kill her," Karla said.

DJ pinched the bridge of his nose. "With your father by her side, she's basically unstoppable right now. We can't change that, not as we are, and you know it." Karla snarled at him, so DJ ignored her and faced Liz. She was obviously trying to mask her emotions, but her lips were pressed into a thin line, and her knuckles were white around her daggers. DJ felt terrible, but he couldn't allow them to fall into Tyra's trap. "And even on the off chance that we *do* manage to kill her, Helene can still do the same thing."

"We could—"

Whatever Liz had been about to say was drowned out by the sound of helicopter rotors slicing through the air. A spotlight raked the lot and bathed everyone in harsh white. DJ squinted against the glare and immediately noted the US insignia on the body of the chopper.

About damn time, he thought. He'd sent Olsen the location as a fail-safe in case shit hit the fan. Now that decision might be what saved their asses. Sirens blared, and multiple armored vans screeched to a halt along the edges of the storage facility. Half a dozen people in black tactical gear piled out from each of them and formed a perimeter around the lot.

DJ was surprised to see that two of them wore mechanical exoskeletons. Dark composite plates hugged their limbs, with neon lines pulsing along the seams. Their movements were surprisingly graceful despite how much the suit must have weighed. They had been made to be as lightweight as possible, based on the design, but that was only to a point. DJ was impressed—until they stood opposite José. Compared to that, they just looked like a couple of kids playing dress-up. Tyra stared at them with undisguised glee, like a kid who just found out what they'd be getting for Christmas. DJ didn't like that look at all.

Olsen stepped up to DJ's side. "Seems like we got here just in time."

"Yeah, a few minutes later, and you might have met a me-shaped bloodstain on the ground," DJ replied. "What took you so long?"

"Ungrateful brat," Olsen growled, smacking the back of his head. DJ exaggerated a wince, and the admiral glared at him. Instead of his usual suit that showed his rank, Olsen wore a khaki uniform with a command ball cap and standard-issue US Navy coat. DJ didn't see his rank insignia anywhere, which was basically the admiral's way of going incognito—not that anyone would have confused Olsen for a normal grunt. The man must have been pushing eighty, but he had the physique of an ogre. "What's the situation?"

"José let us go with Martin," DJ said, nodding toward the scientist's unconscious form. "But then Tyra showed up and started controlling him. We've been trying to stall while Chloe gets us a ride out of here. What's with the suits?" He nodded toward the exoskeletons.

"The president ordered more funding for their research after your meeting with her several months ago. Apparently one man tearing through her security team made quite an impression on her. The suits are an upgraded version of a model that's been around for decades. They're supposed to pack quite a punch, but that depends on tonight."

"You're using my rescue mission to test-run new tech?"

Olsen shrugged. "I saw an opportunity. And we needed an edge. José Olvera would have torn through our normal troops like tissue."

"He's going to tear through these ones too."

Olsen grunted. "I didn't expect him to be so big."

"That's a relatively new development."

The admiral stepped closer, and his tone grew serious. "We needed an edge, yes, but I was also ordered to take the suits along. I suspect their drivers have orders to bring you in if they have the chance."

DJ's lips pressed into a thin line. "I'm guessing the people upstairs aren't too happy about the videos."

"Most of them were already aware of what you could do, and they know the video was heavily tampered with. But seeing it like that..."

Yeah, DJ understood. Humans weren't creatures of logic. You could know something was fake, but what mattered was how it made you feel. And that video had been made to invoke fear. And unfortunately, it did its job well. "I'll keep an eye out," he said. "What's your play here?"

"What else?" Olsen grunted. He gave a signal, and one of the lead operatives stepped forward.

"José Olvera, Tyra Chityothin!" the operative shouted over the din of the helicopter. "We have you surrounded. Stand down! By the authority of the—"

They never got to hear whose authority. Tyra tapped something on her wrist, and José launched himself at the man just slowly enough for the operative to fire a burst of shots that ricocheted harmlessly off José's chest. José's fist crashed into the soldier's sternum, ignored the Kevlar, and sent the man flying into one of the vans with a metallic crunch. There was a moment of silence.

And then everything went to hell.

Shots rang out from all sides, centered on the hulking behemoth at the center of the lot. Tyra blurred, and then disappeared, while José just stood there, hands raised over his head. DJ picked up Olsen and dropped him behind one of the vans. He took a wide turn to where he'd placed Martin and carried the old man away. He was barely lucid, muttering unintelligible words. DJ dropped him beside Olsen—who'd turned the back of the van into a makeshift command center. One of the suits was beside him while the other was getting his ass kicked by José.

DJ cursed under his breath. This was not how he wanted this to go down. Bullets pelted the ground nearby, ricocheting off the asphalt. He got glimpses of Tyra as she weaved between the operatives and systematically took them down. All the while, the chopper hovered overhead, flooding the area with bright light. DJ's ears rang from the gunfire and shouted commands.

Naturally, Karla and Liz weren't idle. Karla snarled with rage and barreled after José, daggers at the ready. Without hesitation, Liz sprinted after her, although DJ couldn't tell whether it was to stop her or join her. Tyra tried to attack from behind but immediately twisted and jabbed at the woman. Her dagger sparked against Tyra's titanium arm, and the bitch's grin widened, but she withdrew, knowing better than to force a fight.

Karla had already reached José and attempted a tackle, hooking an arm around his waist. José's foot shifted, and for a second, DJ thought the pin would work. But José's arm slammed back, catching Karla in the ribs. It wasn't enough to make her let go, but DJ didn't think she could handle much more of that. One of the exoskeleton-wearing agents tried to take advantage of the opening, but a backhand sent the guy flying into a nearby van.

DJ clenched his jaw. He couldn't leave Karla and Liz in the middle of that. But he also couldn't leave Olsen and Martin by themselves. Tyra had disappeared again, so she was likely skulking around somewhere, looking for an opportunity to screw him over. DJ wouldn't give her one.

DJ caught movement out of the corner of his eye a moment before Chloe stopped beside him, scowling. "I can't even leave you alone for five minutes?" she hissed. "What the hell is this?"

"I only caused half of this," DJ replied absently, his eyes scanning for Tyra. "The rest fucked itself up all on its own. Where's our ride?" Chloe pointed at a beat-up old truck on the other side of the street. "Seriously?" DJ asked before his mind could catch up with his mouth.

Chloe narrowed her eyes.

"Sorry. Look, we're going to make a break for it. Take Martin to the ride and hold there while I go get Karla and Liz."

"You've been giving me a lot of orders lately," Chloe said, a dangerous edge to her voice.

Normally DJ would've been worried, but the only thing on his mind right then was getting the hell out of dodge, and he did not have the patience for bullshit. His head snapped to her. "Do you have a better plan?"

Chloe raised a brow in surprise. "Testy, testy," she said in her usual tone. With one last glance, she picked up Martin and carried him away. In case Tyra tried anything, DJ watched her until she reached the truck. But Chloe laid the man in the back seat without any trouble.

With that taken care of, DJ turned his attention back to the battle.

BULLETS TORE THROUGH THE AIR as the idiots continued their futile efforts. Karla crouched low behind a car that had been destroyed, ignoring the fools for the moment. Her sister wheezed beside her, clutching her side where José had struck her. Karla's own body hurt, but it was a burn she was used to.

"We cannot stop him," Liz said. "Not like this."

Karla's face twisted in fury. She knew her sister was right. It was a struggle to defeat their father in a direct fight; it was impossible when they were constantly distracted by flies. At their level, bullets were not enough to kill them, but they could not afford to ignore them the way their father could. That split their focus, which José took advantage of. Still...

"We cannot let these people take him," Karla said.

"Do you think they can?"

Several feet away, José hammered his fists into the asphalt, causing tremors that made the nearest soldiers stumble. One particular idiot tried to club him with the butt of a rifle, but José simply grabbed the gun and beat the man with it. The savagery of the attack bought him a few seconds of peace while the others backed up in fear—but a shouted command resumed the battle.

These ones were not enough to defeat José. Eventually, though, Karla said, "They will call more—and more after that. Our father cannot fight forever."

"Neither can we," Liz said. "What do you suggest we do?"

"Make a break for it," DJ said, appearing beside them. "Chloe got us a truck. It's on the other side of the lot, and she and Martin are already there."

"We will not abandon our father," Karla said, baring her teeth.

"Well, if we wait here any longer, we're gonna get caught in the crossfire. José's unstoppable right now, and Tyra is slipperier than a buttered eel. We don't have time to play hero, especially since, once they're done with him, they'll probably come after us as well. So what's it going to be: Go, or end up in a government black site ourselves?"

Karla ground her teeth. She hated her father—she *hated* him—but he did not deserve to be controlled like another's puppet, and he did not deserve to be cut open in a lab. Karla wanted to save him from that fate, if only for the possibility of seeing gratitude in his eyes for the first time. But her student was right. She was too weak, and staying would only lead to her doom. The thought sent fresh flames of anger coursing through her, but Karla channeled it, using it as fuel. She panned her gaze across the battlefield just as her father flung yet another operative aside like a rag doll. Tyra—the bitch—somersaulted over a cluster of agents, cracking one's spine as she landed and grinning all the while.

"Fine," Karla spat, helping her sister up. "Let us leave."

CHAPTER

32

JANUARY 2044
NEW JERSEY

DJ SIGHED WITH RELIEF and led them toward the truck at a jog. Smoke from the smoldering van drifted across the asphalt, and the stench of burning rubber and fuel clogged DJ's nostrils. Overhead, the helicopter circled. Fortunately, its spotlight was centered on José, so the three of them could slip out relatively easily, giving the chaos a wide berth.

Eventually they reached the truck. Karla and Liz got into the back seat where Martin lay. DJ jogged around to the passenger side, but an operative suddenly lunged in front of him, rifle aimed.

"Freeze!" the soldier yelled, louder than was called for. The dude was no doubt spooked from seeing superhumans tearing through the place. "Hands in the air!"

DJ respected the man's bravery, but he did not have time for it. A brief activation of his nanites, and he was behind the man, holding him so he didn't hit his head when he dropped. DJ dragged his unconscious body off to one side and then entered the truck.

Chloe thundered away immediately. DJ leaned his head back against the seat as Chloe navigated the abandoned streets. "Well," he said, releasing a shaky breath, "that was...intense."

"Intense?" Chloe echoed with a hollow laugh. "That's what you're calling it?"

"It's a good enough word," DJ said. "I'm sticking to it."

"And what would you call the fact that you leaked our location to Olsen without warning the rest of us?" she asked, glancing at him.

"What are you talking about, Chloe?" Liz asked from the back seat.

"Whether he was there for us or José, I find it very coincidental that Olsen knew where to find us. I mean, *I* didn't know where José was, but Olsen had enough time to form a task force and still meet up with us? Weird, don't you think?"

DJ felt something cold and sharp on his neck. He glanced down to see Karla's dagger. "Explain," she said.

DJ sighed. He was far too tired for this. "What's there to explain? Chloe basically hit the nail on the head. I figured it was probably inevitable that shit hit the fan with José, so I sent our location to Olsen the moment we got there. Granted, I didn't expect Tyra to be there, and the whole thing escalated more than I planned, but yeah, I'm the reason the government showed up. You can kill me now."

"So your speech about not fighting?" Chloe asked without taking her eyes off the road. So far, her tone had been casual, but a dangerous note was creeping into it. And DJ didn't give a shit about it.

"I didn't want us to go in there *looking* for a fight," he replied. "But if talking to him didn't work, then I wanted us to have backup. Tyra showing up derailed that, but Olsen and his taskforce are probably the only reason we were able to get out of there. We wouldn't have been able to take on both Tyra and José."

"And if Tyra Chityothin had not shown up," Liz said softly, "your plan was to give our father up to the government."

DJ didn't respond immediately. That *had* been the plan. His reasoning had been that there was practically no chance José would let them walk away with Martin, so when the inevitable fight started, Olsen's task force would help skew the ensuing fight in their favor and then take José into custody. It was killing two birds with one stone: They got Martin, and José was removed as a possible threat. Against all odds, though, José had actually released Martin without a fight.

"No," DJ said, "I would have called it off." And he meant that. If José was serious about not involving himself, then he was no threat to them.

"We're supposed to take your word on that?" Chloe asked.

"If you can't, you can kill me right now. I'm sorry for not telling you guys, but I'm tired of defending myself. You all obviously have the same blind spot when it comes to José. And that's understandable—I'm the same way as my brother. But even though any of you can kill me at any time, I'm not your slave. For better or worse, we're teammates now, which means it's my job to watch your blind spots."

"Look at you, all grown up," Chloe said. She was smirking, but it was forced. DJ didn't know how he knew that—he'd never been able to read Chloe. But somehow, at that moment, it was obvious that she was forcing herself to be light-hearted. Hopefully, it was because she knew he was right and not because she wanted him to lower his guard so she could knife him in the back later. "What's going to happen to José?"

"Olsen will keep him safe, though I'm not sure there's a prison that'll be able to hold him. Regardless, he's not going to be tortured, experimented on, or anything like that. He'll just be kept out of the way until either Helene and Tyra are stopped for good, or we figure out a way to stop them from using him like Tyra did tonight."

Chloe nodded, and they rode in tense silence for the next few blocks. The truck rumbled over a pothole, jostling everyone inside. In the back, Karla cursed softly. Eventually, they crossed back over to New York and started making their way back to Sparta.

DJ glanced over his shoulder. There was enough room in the back for Martin to lie flat, but not with the twins there. His head was on Liz's lap, and Karla got his legs. The old man's mutterings had become progressively louder, so DJ switched with Liz so he could check on him. DJ didn't know much about first aid, but Martin's pulse was stronger than it had been before, which had to be a good sign.

Martin stirred as DJ leaned over to check his breathing. He blinked, and DJ paused two inches away the man's face. "Wh-Where am I?" he asked, his voice groggy and dry. "Why're you trying to kiss me?"

"You're safe with us," DJ replied, leaning back. Martin started to fidget, attempting to sit up. But DJ gently stopped him. "Don't push yourself. You've been sedated for God knows how long. Just rest until we get to Sparta, where hot nurses can take care of you."

"Sedated?" Martin pressed his eyes closed, as if trying to process. "José. Yes, he sedated me when I wouldn't stop talking about how he was treating his family..."

"Well, it seemed like he listened to you. Or he finally got tired of your yapping, because he released you to us when we asked. I mean, we had to insult him a few times first, but..."

Martin licked his lips. "Wh-Where is he? He really shouldn't be left on his own. He's balancing on the edge as it is."

DJ looked up, meeting Chloe's eyes in the rearview mirror. *Well, too late for that.* He forced a casual smile onto his face. "We'll fill you in on everything later. Right now, just focus on getting back to a hundred percent, okay?"

Martin nodded groggily and drifted back to sleep. DJ checked his breathing, then leaned against the headrest as the truck settled into a restless hush. Martin stirred occasionally, and DJ calmed him when he could, but his mind wouldn't stop replaying the night.

He knew exactly where things had gone wrong. He hadn't expected José to surrender Martin so easily; that wasn't in his nature. Tyra's influence was the only explanation—and proof that calling Olsen in had been the right move. Facing both Tyra and José would've been impossible.

At least they'd gotten Martin out. That was something. With luck, he and Hermione could uncover what Helene had done to Ndidi and get a clearer picture of the AI's plan. For now, though, they were still fighting blind.

DJ closed his eyes, listening to the wind whistling, the late-hour traffic, and the sirens in the distance. He was pulled out of his light sleep when the engine of the truck cut off. DJ blinked out the window, recognizing the towering shape of Sparta.

Finally, he thought. He jumped out, gently lifting Martin with him. He tried not to wake him, but the old man let out a soft groan and his eyes fluttered open. "Where...?"

"Sparta Headquarters," DJ told him, trying for a reassuring tone. "I'll take you to the clinic for a checkup."

The Murder Family went off to their rooms immediately after they entered the building, while DJ hustled Martin to the in-house medical center. Despite the late hour, there were still several staff members idling around. Most of them recognized DJ—their conversations suddenly ended as soon as they noticed him—but by this time, ignoring the stares and tuning out the whispering was old hat for him.

DJ had been to the med center enough times not to be surprised at the smell: a faint blend of antiseptic and metal. The overhead lights were harsh and reflected off the steel walls. A pair of nurses took one look at Martin cradled in DJ's arms and rushed forward to help. DJ waved them off but followed their directions to an empty room and dropped the old man on a bed. Immediately, one of the nurses began a flurry of checks while the other hurried off somewhere.

The other nurse was speaking rapidly, and DJ struggled to push through his exhaustion long enough to focus on what she was saying. "His vitals are stable. He's weak, but there are no signs of internal trauma. What happened to him?"

"He was held against his will for a few months," DJ said. "We're not sure what happened there, but at some point he was sedated, probably multiple times."

The nurse nodded and then shooed him away from the room. DJ happily found a quiet corner near a vending machine and spent a few minutes trying to collect himself before he remembered to send Hermione and Christy a text. Both responded that they were on their way, but DJ texted Christy not to bother. He didn't have the energy for two conversations. He could bring Christy up to speed tomorrow, but dealing with Hermione was more pressing.

Ten minutes later, Hermione turned a corner and spotted him. The bags under her eyes told him she was coming from her lab. "Where is he?" she asked the moment she was close enough.

"Upstairs," DJ replied, gesturing vaguely with a tired wave of his hand. "They wheeled him to do a scan or something, check for internal injuries, and stuff like that. But he's all right. He's fine. He regained consciousness on the drive back."

Hermione blew out a breath and slumped down beside him. "Tell me everything. José just let Martin go?"

"Surprising, right? But he did. Granted, we had to insult him a little bit, but Chloe got through to him in the end. We were about to leave when José staggered out of the storage facility—there was a storage facility, by the way—with the crazy eyes."

"He was being controlled," Hermione said. "How's that possible though? Helene's in Nigeria."

"Apparently she passed the tech on to Tyra," DJ replied, unable to keep the bitterness from his voice. "Anyway, after that, it got messy real quick. Tyra appeared, José lost it, and then Olsen arrived with a chopper and some troops. It was a whole thing, but we escaped."

Then something occurred to him. "Tyra said something about the picospores though. She claimed that they don't directly control people, only manipulate hormones to create urges. That the host can choose whether or not to act—like how any random person can choose whether or not to punch someone who bumps into them."

Hermione frowned. "Well, that's a convenient oversimplification."

"How so?"

She lowered her voice. "The spores mess with the hormonal pathways, yes. That's partly what makes them so insidious. They heighten aggression, paranoia, basically any emotion the controller wants. But that's only part of what they're capable of."

"What's the other half?"

Hermione took a moment to choose her words. "They block specific memory sites in the hippocampus and the amygdala—those are the areas of the brain tied to emotional regulation and personal associations. They also partially suppress the prefrontal cortex, which handles impulse control." She must have seen DJ's eyes begin to cross, because she quickened her explanation. "Basically, if Tyra or Helene wants someone to attack their own family—like what happened with José, for example—the spores temporarily dampen the memories of those loved ones, reduce the internal checks that stops that person from committing violence, and increase aggression through their hormones."

DJ's stomach twisted. "So you're saying that Tyra literally erased José's recollection of Karla and Liz as his daughters?"

"In a sense," Hermione said. "It's not a total erasure; it's more like pushing those memories behind a locked door so José's raw aggression overrides any familial bond."

A surge of guilt and anger flared in DJ's chest as he thought of Karla and Liz risking their lives to hold back their father. Their father who basically didn't even recognize them at that moment. "That's—" He tried to find words, but all he managed was a shaky exhalation. "That's fucking sick. And Tyra knows that's what she's doing?"

"She might not, but is that an excuse?"

No. No, it was not. DJ forced himself to push down the anger and disgust coursing through his veins. "I assume that's the same method Helene—or Tyra—is using for the victims of the berserker virus. Is there a way to help?"

"I've been trying to help," Hermione said, throwing her hands up in exasperation. "Anyone who had the older iterations of the spores, we could knock out with the Synaptic Pulse and extract them. But if it's used on someone with the upgraded versions, removing the spores just sends them into a coma, like Albert's wife."

DJ grimaced. Albert was one of the hostages Helene had taken during Mayday. He'd been rescued alongside many others when the team had raided one of Helene's facilities to rescue Ndidi. He'd been brought to Sparta, and his spores had been extracted, leaving him free of Helene's influence. Unfortunately, his wife, Debi Willingham, who worked as one of the aides to the president, had also been one of Helene's thralls, and the AI had been using her for a plan to take control of the entire Cabinet. Albert had noticed his wife's strange behavior when he reunited with her. He'd called DJ in, but after DJ had used the Synaptic Pulse to subdue her, and Hermione had attempted to extract the spores, she'd fallen into a coma.

"Yeah, I understand," DJ said. "Hopefully, once Martin's stable, you can pick his brain about it. We don't have a lot of time."

"You've said that before," Hermione noted, glancing at him. "But how do you know?"

"I don't really," DJ replied. "It's just a hunch, but I've learned to trust my gut. And it says we gotta pick up the pace."

Hermione started to respond, but DJ's phone buzzed. He pulled it out, held out a finger to Hermione, and accepted Olsen's call. "You never call. Should I be worried?"

"*Probably,*" Olsen replied through a wave of static, "*considering that—after decimating my team, the surroundings, and my helicopter—Tyra Chityothin got away with José.*"

DJ closed his eyes, dread pooling in his stomach as his mind raced with the implications. Tyra had already been running circles around them when she was working by herself. Now she had a nearly unstoppable José under her control. DJ glanced at Hermione, who arched a brow at his expression.

Do I tell her? Shit, do I tell Chloe and the twins? He knew he *should* tell them immediately, but it was like he'd already said: They had a blind spot when it came to José. DJ didn't want to risk them going on a rampage and getting themselves killed or turned into thralls as well.

Is it up to me to make that decision for them though? a voice whispered at the back of his mind. Another voice whispered the answer. No, it wasn't up to him. No matter how DJ had justified it earlier, he'd already broken their trust when he'd leaked José's location to Olsen without telling them. He couldn't do the same thing again.

Actually, he thought, *this would be worse.* If it were about his brother, DJ didn't know what he would do if he found out that someone had hidden something like this from him. Unfortunately, it was easy to guess what the Murder Family would do.

"Well, that sucks," he said, replying to Olsen. "I'll let the girls know."

Olsen was silent for a moment. "*If you think it's best,*" he grunted finally.

He doesn't think I should tell them either, DJ thought, grinning despite himself. He wasn't going to change his mind though. He couldn't make their decision for them.

"*We need to talk about the videos that Tyra leaked earlier today,*" Olsen continued.

DJ's grin fell off his face. "Yeah?"

Olsen blew out a breath. "*It's a mess. I've been in more meetings today than I have in the last twenty years. Everybody's got their panties in a twist, but fortunately for you, you have Mary Pastore, the president of the United States, on your side. She kept the worst ones under control, and right now, the government's leaning toward releasing a statement recognizing you as an 'enhanced consultant' who acted under extenuating circumstances. They won't confirm the existence of the spores or nanites—only that we're dealing with an undisclosed threat. They're also disclaiming official sanction of your actions."*

DJ frowned. "Disclaiming official sanction...what? What the hell is that?"

"It means they're hedging their bets. They're saying that they do not officially approve or endorse your actions. But that's just to cover their asses."

DJ leaned back, letting out a breath. At least that was one headache gone. "So basically a middle ground type thing."

"You'll still have your enemies in the press, and among the government," Olsen warned him. *"But at least you won't be labeled a rogue vigilante. For now, at least."*

"Well, I'll take that," he replied, closing his eyes. "Do you think that'll take care of the angry mob outside Sparta?"

"You could always go and whine at them," Olsen said dryly. *"No one likes a whiner."*

"Oh yeah? Well, no one likes a... hello? Hello?" The line had gone dead. DJ stared at it. "That mother—"

"What happened?" Hermione asked, cutting him off.

DJ pocketed his phone. "Tyra escaped with José. Olsen just confirmed it."

Hermione nodded, her gaze thoughtful. "That's basically worse-case scenario, isn't it?"

"By far. But the good news is the government isn't branding me as a public menace, at least not officially. So, small blessings."

"Well, that's something," she said, giving a mirthless smile. "One less fire to fight."

"Yeah..." DJ leaned back. "I feel like that battle's not yet over. But for now, let's focus on Martin. Once the doctors give him the all-clear, we'll see if he has any insights. The man has been with José for the last few months; he must have learned something. But that's on you to pry it out. I need to fill Chloe and the twins in on the situation, and until there's another fire to put out, I'll probably be stuck with them for the next while. I need to get stronger, quick."

Hermione patted his arm and stood. "Do what you have to. I'll catch up with you later, after I'm done talking to the medical staff. I think I've given them enough time." Without another word, Hermione strode down the corridor, her lab coat swishing behind her. Absently, DJ watched her go. He'd give himself a few minutes before heading to meet Chloe.

That, he thought, drawing in a deep breath, *is probably going to be a shitshow. But one crisis at a time. Hopefully CJ is having a better time than this.*

CHAPTER

33

JANUARY 2044

VIRTUAL REALM

CJ STOOD IN THE MIDDLE of the street in a city made out of ones and zeros.

He was surrounded by buildings that each represented a website in the real world, and as such, they were each unique in their own ways. One was completely round and hovered several feet off the ground. Another was shaped like a pyramid stretched until its point almost touched the clouds. Yet another was built just like a giant cardboard box, with a swarm of drones orbiting it.

Like their shapes, each building had its own color scheme. Some were muted and elegant, others were professional and classy, while others still screamed for attention with clashing colors and style. The sheer individuality had been difficult to take in the first time CJ was there. But he'd long since learned to ignore it, especially since, with a slight mental flex, he could shift his vision so he only saw the tapestry of binary that made each of them.

Avatars streamed around him in a constant flow, hundreds of them representing a person currently logged into the internet. Most disappeared around the corner, on their way to different sections, while some entered the buildings on the street. CJ had created a small Zone around him, several feet wide. It acted as his own mini-world, where he had total awareness, and almost complete control of everything within. That gave him several advantages, as long as he could keep up with the drain on his stamina. Its most basic form acted as a barrier of sorts that physically stopped avatars—and others—from passing through without his permission. And since it was just a few feet in diameter, its drain was almost negligible.

Right now, he was using it to give himself some space so he didn't feel crowded.

CJ massaged the side of his head as he made his way through the stream. The Virtual Realm might not have taxed him physically, but it was a strain on his mind, one that became worse the longer he stayed in. Maybe he should have taken his brother's advice and taken a break for a few hours. CJ didn't know how long ago this session had started. He'd spent some time after his brother's visit getting comfortable with teleportation. And while CJ couldn't say that he'd mastered it, he'd at least made some headway, so much so that he'd visited over a dozen possible locations over several days, slowly narrowing down his search.

And it was taking a toll, especially since each time he teleported, his awareness shifted and fragmented into hundreds of different pieces that drifted along the stream of data that made up the Realm. He was still himself, but in several parts that were held together by a resonance CJ found difficult to explain.

CJ could admit to himself that the feeling was slightly addictive, but without that process—and the understanding he'd gained over the last few days—CJ doubted that he would have gone as far as he had right then.

Suddenly, CJ's head snapped up. He stopped in front of a building shaped like a giant swirl of ice cream. His eyes glazed over as he focused on the tugging sensation. After so long, CJ had learned to ignore the pull, unless he wanted to travel to that location. That was probably why it'd taken him so long to notice that one of them was guttering, like a candle about to go down. This had happened to several other locations; the tugs had become weaker and then faded entirely. CJ figured those were the most dated locations that Helene had visited, and they'd been the ones he'd checked out first once he mastered teleporting.

This tug, however, had always been one of the strongest, so CJ had left it for last. It didn't make sense that it was suddenly about to fade. *Unless the site's about to crash,* he thought. Usually that happened if something forced the site to shut itself down, the owner themselves was shutting it down, or if it'd been abandoned for too long. The fact that Helene had been there recently meant it couldn't be the latter. That meant that someone, or something, was shutting it down.

It also meant CJ had to get there before it crashed completely.

With a brief flex of will, CJ activated his Data Sight, and the world bled into a tapestry of ones and zeros. CJ extended his Zone further and watched as the curtain expanded several feet. Several light-blue threads snaked off into the horizon, each one representing one of the tugs connecting him to distant locations. There were fewer of those than there had been at the beginning, and CJ had already visited most of those that were left. He focused on the one that glowed erratically, like a light bulb about to die.

And then let go.

His mind splintered as it blended with the data stream around him. The tug grew stronger, filling him, pulling him. CJ felt himself unravel and then drift. The first few times he'd done this, he'd lost all sense of time, distance, and everything happening around him. After a few tries, though, he'd learned how to retain enough of himself to remain aware. When he traveled, he had no "eyes" to see the landscape change around him. But in many ways, at that moment, he *was* the landscape, and the clouds and the buildings. As long as he was aware, he always knew where exactly he was and how far he traveled.

And this time, he traveled far. Farther than ever before. Eventually, there was a short, familiar sensation of passing through a veil, then the clouds disappeared and were replaced by a darkness that pressed in on him on every side. CJ reformed a short while later, in front of a cluster of buildings. Most looked decrepit, as if they had been constructed in a rush and were meant to be temporary. A few were better made, big and blocky, with a steady flow of avatars—each with hoods up—streaming in. One in particular was taller than the rest, imposing with spires that rode up in odd angles. Not only was there no traffic, the few avatars that appeared seemed to give it a wide berth as they passed.

Naturally, his tug pulled him toward it.

CJ ignored it for the moment and immediately set up his Zone again. He extended it half a mile and closed his eyes as his mind expanded to fill up his space. His first impression was the darkness. Everything was dark as if there was a blanket covering the whole world beyond. It made it difficult to see and gave everything a darker edge. Half a mile away was a familiar collection of dilapidated stalls arranged haphazardly along a deserted street.

CJ retracted his Zone and sighed. He was in the dark web.

He'd known that there was a chance that one of the tugs would lead there, but he hadn't wanted to consider it for long. He'd gotten familiar enough with the dark web during his and Manar's last foray—and the market stalls confirmed that he was basically in the same location as last time. But that wasn't necessarily a good thing, since he and Manar had made some waves the last time they'd been here.

CJ glanced back at the building. The tug still led to it, and it still flickered but not as urgently as it had before. CJ figured the distance or something else had exaggerated it. It was annoying, but at least he had more time now, which was good because he'd rather not go into what was obviously a Helene stronghold without some information.

CJ set his Zone to cover a few feet around him, turned, and walked down the path to the market stalls. Each of them was like something he'd expect to see in a farmers' market, and most had the same rickety construction and signboard with their letters missing. These were obviously built to be temporary, even more so than the buildings had. In the days before they'd fought Helene, Manar had shown CJ the stall where he'd picked a fight with the owner. CJ passed it as he walked down the street and gave it a wide berth.

Several pairs of eyes followed him, which made him uncomfortable. CJ tried his best to ignore them, comparing each stall until he decided that one looked less run-down than the others. Hopefully that meant the owner had spent more time on his site than every other. CJ hesitated for a moment before walking up to the counter.

The attendant wore a hood and stared at him as he approached. "Can I help you, friend?"

CJ was still using his Data Sight, so he saw a dome made of code rise from the stall over the area around them. The tapestry expanded and the space warped. It lasted for a moment, and when it settled, he was in a McDonald's. It was painted bright yellow and red and had plastic tables and chairs arranged around the room, just like the actual restaurant. The attendant stood behind a counter with cash registers and menu boards. The attendant wore an apron and held a notepad that it didn't seem to notice. Its hood remained, however, hiding everything except its eyes.

CJ took a seat on one of the barstools and ignored the way his legs dangled off the side like a child's. Immediately, there was a can of Coke in front of him. CJ jiggled it for a moment and then opened it out of curiosity. He tried to take a sip, but the liquid inside didn't move. *Cheap instance,* he thought.

Instances were subspaces integrated into websites to deal with a massive amount of traffic. It was why billions of people could use the Gaius search engine at the same time without having to wait for one another. In the Virtual Realm, that was represented by each person entering an instance the moment they stepped into the company's website. Since only AIs had the processing power to handle billions of users simultaneously, they were put in charge of instances until a problem forced the owner—or an employee—to take over.

Most artificial intelligences became prohibitively more expensive the larger the workload—meaning they were easy to afford for a household with relatively simple needs, but the price rose to exorbitant rates for companies. When a business couldn't afford an AI, they used bots. The bots were given a bit of autonomy to make their interactions with potential customers more relatable and lifelike. However, since they weren't true AIs, they couldn't be completely self-aware. If the programming was done well, most people wouldn't even realize they were talking to bits of code.

"You can," CJ said, replying to the bot. "I'd like some information"

The attendant wrote something on its notepad. "What can you trade for it?"

CJ hesitated for a moment. "I have some information as well about the enhanced humans in the video that's been going around."

Suddenly, the attendant stopped scribbling, its eyes boring into his own. They were the same eyes, but something about them had shifted. CJ noticed a line of code stretching somewhere beyond the boundaries of the interface itself. That definitely hadn't been there before, which meant…

The owner's taken control, CJ realized, holding back a grimace. Something in his statement had probably been a trigger word, and that'd alerted the owner. CJ hadn't considered that, and he would have rephrased it if he'd known because, honestly, he'd have preferred to deal with the bot.

"What do you know?" the owner asked gruffly.

CJ started to tell him but stopped himself in time. "I *want* to know," he said instead, "everything you know about Helene."

There was a pause, and it stretched for so long that CJ began to worry he'd said the wrong thing. When the attendant suddenly lashed out to grab his arm, he was sure of it. Fortunately, CJ had never taken down his Zone, so the bot's arms just bounced against its invisible surface, unable to make contact.

"What the hell?" the owner muttered in surprise. "Who the hell are you? Is this some kind of test?"

"Did you just try to hack me?" CJ asked. It was something he recognized from one of Manar's stories. Manar had been saved because of the inherent protections built into his avatar, whereas the attendant hadn't been able to touch CJ because of his Zone. But what if CJ hadn't had the ability, or didn't have the habit of always keeping it activated?

The thought was annoying, and a part of CJ wanted to simply leave; he'd obviously messed up with the attendant, so he doubted he would get more information out of him. He could try a different stall. But something told CJ that he was going to get the same response regardless. And he didn't have so much time to waste going from stall to stall hoping to get lucky.

No, he thought, squaring his shoulders. He was already here, and the attendant obviously knew something. There was no reason why CJ couldn't get the information. He just had to be careful about what and how he asked. CJ decided to try something that Manar had told him. He straightened and stopped swinging his feet.

"Test?" he repeated, turning his nervousness into a tone of annoyance. "I don't know what you mean, and honestly, I don't care. I'm just here for some answers, and I don't like wasting my time."

The attendant withdrew slowly, a flicker of caution crossing his features. CJ could almost feel him thinking. He might have dismissed CJ out of hand, but the fact that he couldn't even *begin* to hack CJ's avatar gave him pause, because it meant that CJ had powerful protections, which usually meant a powerful backing.

At least, CJ thought, *I hope that's what he's thinking. He could also be considering how to throw me out.*

"You come in here and ask about Helene out of nowhere, what's a guy to think?" the attendant said finally. "Most people don't even know that name, and the ones who do don't dare to say it out loud." He shrugged. "I thought you might be one of them, or working for her. Can you blame me?"

CJ forced himself not to show his concern. To most people, Helene had simply been a highly advanced virtual assistant before she'd crashed, but this attendant knew more. From what Manar had passed on, Helene had been making waves on the dark web for a while, but the fact that her name had already started becoming commonplace confirmed that the AI was done hiding in the shadows.

"If I was working for her, why would I be standing here, asking you for information about her?" CJ asked after a moment. "And if this was a test, you'd be dead by now for trying to hack me."

The attendant weighed CJ's words for a long minute before conceding with a grunt. "Fine, but your information better be worth it."

"It is," CJ assured him, not missing his eyes.

The avatar leaned closer, and his voice dropped as if he was worried someone might be eavesdropping. "Businesses like mine used to run independently, you know? We offered whatever was available, no restrictions. But now there are all these new rules. No one talks about them openly, but they're there, slowly choking the market."

"Choking it how?"

"Like, now there are fewer items on display, fewer suppliers willing to deal on the side. It's all been consolidated, and either you comply or you vanish. If you want to move anything high level, you have to know the right person, and it has to be the *right* person. Because if you go through the wrong one, you're gone. It's like we're working in a company."

"So it's about control," CJ mused thoughtfully.

"Not control. Enforcement," the attendant clarified, tapping a finger on the counter. "Break the rules, and suddenly your supply lines dry up, and your customers disappear."

"It's like someone's nudging the entire market toward a single point," CJ muttered. "She's gathering all the resources. But why?"

"That's the question, isn't it? And rumor has it they're snapping up every bit of high-grade material. Oxidizers and propellants used in rocket fuel, alloys used in building rocket frames and engines—all gone as soon as they're listed."

"And no one knows why?"

"Everybody has theories, of course, but anyone who proved theirs has probably vanished." He gave a humorless chuckle. "Some people agree that it's some sort of power grab though—because why else would someone go through this trouble, right? Me, I don't know what to think."

"What does this have to do with the website up the street?"

It was only after that he realized his mistake. He saw Helene's stronghold as a large building literally up the street from the stall. But reality was obviously going to be different. He waited in tense silence while the attendant processed his words.

"I don't know what you're talking about, man," the bot said finally. "But a few of us have noticed that it's always one specific business that snatches up the new listing. No one knows where the goods go, but the business itself is no joke, completely impenetrable."

"You've tried to break into it?" he asked, surprised.

The attendant shrugged. "Not me specifically, but where do you think you are? Testing another person's defenses is like giving a firm handshake around here. But it doesn't really matter. Rumor has it that the business is shutting down soon. No one knows why, but I mean, it's obvious, right? The owner doesn't need it anymore. The person running the show? They're almost done with what they came for, and they're packing up. I'd say it's good news for all of us."

That was probably why the signal was starting to fade. "But it isn't just one business, right? They control multiple places?" It was a backup plan in case he didn't find Manar at the site or the last location. He'd have to visit every other business that Helene held; one of them must have been holding Manar.

"Yeah," the attendant said, "but a guy can hope, can't he? It could be a rolling-stone-type thing. When one packs up, the rest start to pack up. Anyway, that's all I know. Now it's your turn. What do you have on enhanced humans?"

CJ's gaze was distant. "Hmm?"

"You said you had information to trade about the metahumans," the attendant prompted. "Well, I've told you everything I know. Now it's your turn."

CJ immediately became nervous. He'd made that promise to get information, but now that the moment was upon him, he realized he wasn't comfortable telling anything he knew to a random vendor on the dark web.

I could lie, he thought. The video had only been released a few days ago, so there was very little information. That meant there would be no way for him to catch CJ in a lie. It was a good plan. Solid, likely to work. But the thought of doing that made CJ deeply uncomfortable. Lying wasn't a skill that someone on the autism spectrum picked up. Between trying to process the question, find the answer in his mind, and actually get the words out, there had never been any space in his mind to lie.

"What's the holdup?"

"The video's fake," CJ blurted the first thing that came to his mind.

"Well, no shit, Sherlock. Everyone knows that. But the White House has already released a statement saying one of the people in it is like a meta-consultant or some shit. That means either the part about the powers is real, the government wants us to think it is, or both are full of crap. Which is it?"

CJ hadn't heard about the government's press release, but that wasn't surprising, considering he hadn't returned to the real world in a few days. And it wasn't like he was browsing through forums while he was in the Virtual Realm. Maybe he should start? He couldn't afford to be totally out of the loop whenever he was in the Virtual Realm. *That'd be ironic,* CJ chuckled to himself.

"Hello?" the attendant called again, a note of annoyance creeping into his tone.

"The powers are definitely real," CJ said. That was a safe response, right? Everyone knew about it, so confirming it shouldn't do any harm.

"Now we're getting somewhere. What else?"

CJ searched his brain for something else that was safe to say. He came up empty. "That's it."

The attendant slowly leaned forward until his eyes were level with CJ's. CJ didn't know how the Virtual Realm decided on that motion, considering he was speaking to a guy on a monitor. "You think this is a joke? I could get killed for the things I told you."

Now CJ felt guilty, but not enough to give the attendant information that might hurt his brother. He told himself that this was the dark web: The attendant was definitely not a good person. It didn't help. CJ came down from the stool. "I'm sorry."

"I don't know who you are, but I'm going to find you. You think you can shortchange me? I'll kill you." His avatar lashed out and struck CJ's barrier again, but this time he didn't back down. He pressed his palms flat against the bubble, and bright-red tendrils sparked out from the point of contact like crimson snakes seeking a place to latch onto.

It burned wherever they touched, and CJ felt a higher drain on his energy as the barrier fought off the intrusion. It was noticeable, but not so much that it was a problem. CJ stared curiously at the tendrils and didn't even realize when he stretched a finger to touch the closest one. It was slowly burning its way through it. And when CJ's finger touched the spot, he apparently fulfilled some sort of condition. CJ could see it with his Data Sight as the code that made up his avatar connected with that of the hack, clashed—and lost.

His finger grew colder, even though that shouldn't be possible in an avatar. But suddenly, CJ felt exposed, like a part of him was being uncovered. It was deeply uncomfortable, and CJ instinctively pushed out his awareness to fight against it.

Immediately, his mind split into two.

In one of them, he saw the world as it was: in an instance designed to look like a McDonalds. In another, he saw the world in ones and zeros, as if he'd activated his Data Sight. With the latter, he saw blue tendrils clashing with the red—and winning. With a brief mental flex, CJ extended his awareness further, and watched as the lines of blue pushed the red back into the attendant's fingers and merged with the avatar.

Immediately, images flashed within CJ's mind. They moved too fast for an average person to process. But dealing with fast-moving information had become second nature to him by this point. He absorbed what he could, focusing on the impressions rather than any specific thing. Within a split second, he saw glimpses of past transactions, heard snippets of conversations with customers, scanned through hidden folders, and buried conversations in dark forums.

When he felt he'd learned enough, CJ withdrew his awareness. Freed from CJ's mental grip, the attendant snatched his hand and took a step back for extra measure. He stared at CJ with abject horror, which didn't make CJ feel less guilty. Yes, the man had threatened and tried to hack him, but CJ had provoked him. And it wasn't like the attendant had ever stood a chance against CJ's barrier.

"I'm sorry, once again, Zaid Resendiz," CJ said. The attendant's eyes widened. "I don't plan on telling anyone what you told me, but I wouldn't recommend trying to find me. For your sake."

CJ turned and left. The instance dissolved around him, leaving him standing once more in the middle of a nearly deserted street. He felt Zaid's eyes from his stall, but CJ pushed down his guilt and started making his way back to the stronghold. He could probably try to get more information from other vendors, but CJ doubted he would learn much more than he had.

Plus, he'd already taken too much time. He needed to find out what Helene was keeping in that building before it disappeared.

CJ STOOD OUTSIDE one of Helene's strongholds and tried to ignore the part of him that said this was basically suicide. The structure looked even larger up close. It was built like a block, with spires that rode up in odd angles and a deceptively simple gate that sat open. Like Helene, the building's presence radiated a palpable weight that pressed against CJ's barrier. He instinctively expanded his Zone to rebuff the influence—but the fact that he had to didn't bode well at all.

The Zone was a manifestation of CJ's influence on the Virtual Realm. He'd created it by merging with and manipulating the world itself to carve out a piece that was distinctly his. So, when his barrier pushed away the building's influence, CJ should not have had the impression he was clashing against another Zone. But what else had he expected? Helene was the most powerful artificial intelligence in the world; it was natural for her to be so powerful in the Virtual Realm. The building was one aspect of it, and CJ would probably meet the others once he was inside.

Once again, he ignored the voice in his mind that told him he was walking to his death. *It's not like I have a choice,* he told the voice. *Manar might be in there. And even if he's not, I have to find out what she's spending so much effort to hide.*

CJ stepped through the gate, not allowing himself to stall further. Space warped around him as he was brought into the website's instance. When it settled, CJ was inside a lobby reminiscent of a grand hotel's entrance, complete with polished floors, marble columns, and plush red carpet that stretched deeper into the building.

CJ took a step forward, and the space resisted him. It was as if he were walking through an invisible sludge. He grimaced. He'd experienced the suppression of websites before, but none had been this strong, and it seemed to be growing. He took another step and felt an awareness lock in on him, a physical presence that pressed against his barrier, looking for a weakness. CJ expanded his Zone just to be safe. If it worked the same way as the attendant's hack, it might require actual contact with his avatar, and CJ didn't want to risk it.

Suddenly, alarms blared around him, startling him enough to make him jump. CJ grimaced but did his best to ignore them while he studied the room. The place looked like a lavish atrium, with a circular desk in the middle and broad hallways branching off in multiple directions. One corridor displayed moving posters like LCD screens—images of something CJ couldn't make out because they flickered too fast. Another glowed with a golden hue and led into another room.

CJ toggled on his Sight, and the world bled into binary. It was blurry, indecipherable, like something was blocking him. That'd never happened before, and CJ was torn between concern and curiosity that urged him to find out how it was possible.

Before he could decide which emotion to focus on, a figure emerged from one of the hallways. It was about seven feet tall, with metallic plating running along its arms and a helmet shaped like a knight's visor. It held a large rectangular shield in one hand.

That armor's going to be annoying to deal with, CJ thought. He glanced behind the figure, half expecting another knight. The website gave off the feeling that it should have entire squads of these.

After a few seconds of staring at each other, the antivirus started marching toward him. CJ tensed and realized with more than a little bit of surprise that he wasn't afraid. More than that, a part of him was actually excited. Him! For most of his life, he had hated confrontation—and he still did. He'd go out of his way to avoid it. But somehow it was different when he was in the Virtual Realm. It was as if he were a different person, one who was bolder, more comfortable with taking risks, and not afraid to get into a fight against something bigger than himself. This might have been because he'd found himself in several similar situations just a few months ago.

But it might also have been because he knew he wasn't as powerless as he'd been then.

One of the initial things CJ had done when he began learning to manipulate the Virtual Realm was attempt to recreate the abilities he'd once had with the Sphere. His Zone had been the starting point—and the easiest. But recreating his Nullification Aura had been an exercise in frustration because with that ability, the Sphere had done most of the work. CJ had only needed to connect to activate it. Without the Sphere, he had to figure out every step of the process on his own. It had taken him weeks and dozens of failed attempts.

But he'd figured it out eventually.

CJ expanded his Zone once more, and didn't stop until it covered the room so the knight was within its confines. Within his own world, the knight became the intruder, one that CJ could reject. That rejection manifested as a force within the Zone that pressed in on the knight. CJ could leave it like that, but diffused as it was, the pressure wasn't as effective. Instead he compressed it around him and shaped it into a Nullification Aura.

The knight lunged. Its shield came up to bash him—and CJ rolled away. The Sphere's aura had also worked as a shield, allowing him to tank a few hits at the expense of energy. CJ's variation, however, was exclusively offensive. Usually, his Zone worked as his shield, but his powers only functioned within its confines; if he retracted it, he'd have a shield but nothing else.

So he couldn't meet the knight's charge head-on, but he *could* slam an Aura-coated forearm into its back as it ran past him. Sparks flew, and the knight staggered. It recovered a second later and turned to face him, but it didn't try for another charge. Instead, its shield morphed into a broad-bladed sword. CJ didn't have time to do more than grimace before the sword was coming down on him. He couldn't block it, his Aura wouldn't do much against an attack like that, and he *definitely* wouldn't survive taking it head-on.

So CJ teleported.

He barely felt his mind splinter before he reformed ten feet away, his eyes wide as he stumbled over the plush carpet. Short-range teleportation had been a necessary step before CJ learned how to travel over long distances. His mind kept reforming before he'd gone more than a dozen feet out. At first, CJ found it annoying, until he'd realized the potential.

Without a shield, CJ would have been forced to dodge every attack. But as the knight had just proven, CJ wasn't fast enough for that. Fortunately, in some ways, teleportation was even better because it allowed him to simply remove himself from danger. The only problem was the energy requirement.

But it was better to be exhausted and forced to log out than to be dead.

The knight paused for a moment, as if considering this new variable. And then it began advancing methodically, forcing CJ to keep darting away. But CJ wasn't a fighter, so it was inevitable that he would slip up at some point. The knight was obviously waiting for that. But CJ knew that. He baited it into a wide swing, then teleported behind it at the last instant. He spread his Aura to cover his entire body, then wrapped his arms around the guardian, hugging it from behind.

It jolted immediately, nearly flinging him off. But CJ held on, gritting his teeth as he powered waves of energy into the construct. It tried to stab him with the sword but couldn't reach him. The sword morphed back into a shield, but that was even worse. After a few seconds, it stumbled and collapsed to one knee. That was when CJ knew that he'd won, but he held on until it toppled sideways. CJ gave it a few seconds more before he sprang back, panting. He recalled his Aura to save energy. The entire exchange couldn't have taken more than a minute, but it had felt far longer.

He was exhausted. But he was also grinning.

He knelt beside the construct. It wasn't destroyed—CJ didn't know if these kinds of programs *could* be destroyed. And if they could, he didn't have anything in his arsenal capable of doing so. His nullification only weakened it and blocked its connection to the rest of the site, temporarily incapacitating it.

Steadying his breath, CJ placed a palm on the knight's chest. When he'd tried this against the attendant, he'd used the man's own hack as a connection. He couldn't do the same thing here, but his Data Sight already gave him a point of entry. CJ leaned over the knight's visor and pushed his awareness through the armor, focusing on a specific line of code. Immediately, he felt a chill race through him as blue tendrils extended from his palm and pierced through the knight.

CJ's mind split into two, but this time he was ready for it. He pushed his mind further, deeper, following each tendril as they tasted their way through each line of code. A rush of images poured into his head. Most were in hard binary and even more incomprehensible than the attendant's code. But CJ still caught broad impressions—snapshots of code logs, bits of incoming data, half-finished routines referencing a meltdown script and a "merge sequence." The context wasn't clear, but CJ could feel the urgency that the program felt. He tried to push deeper, but an awareness locked on to him and stopped him short, as if he'd run into a wall. Each tendril was caught, trapped, and ejected, while the mind—cold, emotionless, and unmovable—clashed against CJ's own and won. CJ lashed out to absorb as much information as he could before, and he latched onto two things that rang an alarm bell in his mind. The first was an image of Manar slowly being chipped away. The second was a countdown script that read, Time Left: 72 hours.

CJ jerked his hand away, staggering backward. His ass landed on the carpet, but that didn't even register with him. Seventy-two hours. That was all the time Manar had. Or maybe less, if Helene sped up the process. CJ closed his eyes, trying to get rid of the image of Manar slowly being chipped away. Was that what he'd been going through? For the last few months while CJ had been wasting time, Manar was slowly being destroyed piece by piece. And the process was going to be completed in three days,

CJ jerked to the side, heaving. Nothing came out, of course, but he could feel his stomach churning.

Eventually, he straightened, pushed the dizziness aside, and forced himself to analyze. There was no question now: Manar was here somewhere, trapped and slowly being erased. And CJ had less than three days to stop it. Fear and guilt warred in his chest, but CJ pushed them aside. He didn't have time for the pity party. The website was huge, and since he didn't know where exactly Manar was, he'd have to search everywhere—which meant he had to move immediately.

CJ pushed himself to his feet, shaking off the last threads of vertigo. The knight spasmed, but CJ ignored it, scanning the three hallways in front of him. The knight had come from the leftmost one, but CJ imagined that each of them would have their own brand of security waiting. His heart pounded at the thought of facing another knight—the battle had been too close—but it was better than risking his life on an entirely new threat; at least he knew the abilities of the knight. That would give him an edge, and CJ told himself that it'd be enough.

CJ drew in a steadying breath and retracted his Zone so it was only a foot around him. With his shield back, he crept down the left passageway. Artwork hung from the walls, but when CJ glanced at them with his Sight, he only saw swirls of meaningless data. He followed the passage a dozen feet before it branched in two directions. A dull rumble echoed from the right—a mechanical thud, like giant pistons crashing down on something. A faint shimmer of blue light flickered across the ground to the left.

CJ glanced in both directions, biting his lip. His Sight revealed a stream of code converging in the right, while the left just glowed with the same bluish glow. At any other point, CJ would have opted for the left hallway, simply because something was obviously happening in the other direction and he wanted to avoid it. But everything happening in the building was a point of interest for him because it might lead him to Manar.

Without allowing himself time to second-guess his decision, he took the right hallway. Somehow the site's suppression grew with each step, until CJ was forced to add more energy to his Zone. CJ had to be careful of that. His Nullification Aura required a lot, and each teleport took even more. CJ had gained some since the fight, but it was far from enough to replace what he'd spent. He couldn't afford to run out—it was a resource he had to manage carefully.

The passage opened into a large high-ceilinged chamber. Giant mechanical arms protruded from the walls, smashing down in timed sequences. Each strike created a thunderous boom that shook the floor and created the rumble that CJ had heard earlier. At the far end, a firewall formed a barrier to the path leading deeper into the site. CJ squinted at the fire. He could vaguely make out silhouettes moving on the other side, likely more defense programs waiting to attack anyone that got through the firewall.

CJ sighed. *She really isn't leaving anything to chance, is she?*

CHAPTER

35

MARTIN STAYED AT THE CLINIC for a few days. From what Hermione understood, he wasn't sick, and he hadn't been mistreated or abused. But he was severely malnourished, which was harder to deal with due to age. Hermione was there when he was finally released, and after a quick stop for lunch—since they'd probably forget once they began—she led him back to her lab.

Once they entered, Hermione filled him in on everything he'd missed over the last few months: CJ and Manar's battle against Helene in the Virtual Realm, Helene taking over Manar's body and impregnating Ndidi, Ndidi's escape, and then finally Tyra and all the bullshit she'd put the team through.

"Y'know," Hermione said. "Now that I'm saying it out loud like this, it sounds pretty unbelievable. Do...*do* you believe me?"

Martin chuckled, leaning back in his wheelchair. "Unfortunately, I saw just as many unbelievable things while I was captured by Helene. And then again by José. There's little I'm not open to considering right now."

Hermione let out a breath. "Well, that's a relief at least. But that brings us to where we are right now." She paused while she placed the culture sample on the nanoscope and adjusted the settings. The monitor flickered to life and magnified the sample until they had a clear picture. Martin adjusted his glasses and leaned forward. "I isolated the hybrid from Ndidi's blood sample, but I don't even know where to begin with the tests."

"I don't like the look of that golden gleam," Martin mumbled.

Hermione grimaced. The hybrid had the same basic spherical shapes as the picospores and nanites, as well as different parts from both of them. But the one thing that differentiated it was a core in its center that pulsed with a golden aura. Like Helene's eyes. "Yeah, it's creepy."

"The stability's weird too," Martin said, frowning and staring intently at the screen.

"I noticed that too. Without a host, the picospores would have shown signs of degrading at least partially by now, even with preservatives. The nanites would have gone completely dormant. But this..." She gestured at the screen, where the hybrid remained unchanged, as if completely unaffected by anything. "It's like it was designed to survive, regardless of its environment."

"We should start with a stimulus test," Martin suggested. "If we find out what it reacts to, we might be able to infer something from it. I was thinking we use Pastul's theorem to design—"

Hermione sighed in relief, as Martin described the test he had in mind. Usually, she preferred working alone—but she couldn't deny that having the old man beside her felt like a weight off her shoulders. Together, they had a chance of succeeding. And if they failed, at least it wouldn't be on her alone.

HERMIONE HADN'T BEEN PRESENT during the initial phase of her father's work on the picospores. She'd just been a teenager, and the project was supposed to have been a secret. But after several weeks of her father locking himself in their home lab, Hermione's mother got angry enough to force him out, and Hermione became curious enough to sneak in to try to figure out what had her father hooked.

She'd been caught almost immediately. The lab's security had notified her father the moment she'd entered—but not before she'd gotten a good look at her father's research papers and the original blueprint of the spores. She hadn't understood a word of it, so her father had sat her down and calmly explained exactly what he was trying to accomplish. Looking back, Hermione figured her father had just needed someone to whom he could gush about his work.

But for the next several years, Hermione had joined her father in the lab almost every day. At first, she'd just handled the drudge work—cleaning beakers, petri dishes, and stuff like that. But when she got into college, her father began to trust her enough to delegate some research.

Hermione had taken to that like a fish to water. That was the part she loved: the research. Immersing herself in the thoughts of other scientists, finding the patterns in results that were sometimes generations apart, Hermione could spend hours surrounded by books and not feeling it.

She should have felt the same way about experimentation—after all, most people considered it as the "fun" part of science. She would have, too, if it wasn't total bullshit. What did people like about it anyway? It was basically doing the same thing over and over again in slightly different ways.

The experiments she ran with Martin were no different. Hermione had started feeling sleepy after a few hours, but as the day dragged on, exhaustion weighed heavily on her.

"Hermione," Martin called, startling her awake.

Hermione slapped her cheeks. "I wasn't sleeping."

"I'm sure you weren't," Martin replied, giving her a grandfatherly smile. Hermione noticed he didn't look tired at all, which wasn't fair. "Maybe we should take a break."

Hermione adjusted her glasses. "How long have we been at this? Eighteen hours?"

"Nineteen," Martin said, flipping a page in his notebook.

"Nineteen..." Hermione covered a yawn. That was nineteen hours spent performing different tests on the hybrids. Hermione told herself that each test brought them closer to understanding them, that even the lack of results was a result by itself. It was still frustrating though.

They'd tried leaving a small extract of the hybrids inside a petri dish and doing nothing else. No reaction. They'd subjected it to a change in temperature, first mild and then extreme levels. That provoked some movement, but nothing beyond what they'd already known from the spores and nanites. They'd subjected it to a controlled dose of radiation, and the extract stabilized itself within minutes, once again confirming how resilient it was—but little else. There were numerous other tests, but none of them had given them anything concrete. And Hermione was about to start breaking stuff.

She exhaled through her nose. "We need to try something disruptive. Something that's guaranteed to force a reaction. At least that'll give us a baseline to extrapolate from."

Martin tapped his notebook with a pen. "Like what?"

"I don't know," Hermione said, pinching the bridge of her nose. She stood and started pacing. "We've done standard stimulus tests: mechanical, temp, and radiation. But it's too stable. What if we hit it with something external? Something it doesn't have to passively endure but actively responds to? Or that it should respond to, at least."

"You obviously have something in mind. What?"

"A year or so ago, I designed the Synaptic Pulse," Hermione explained as she crossed the room toward the cupboards where she kept one of the devices. "It's basically a Taser, except it was designed to direct a very small electrical current straight to the brain and disable the spores there, breaking their connection to Helene or whatever mechanism she was using to send commands to them."

Martin adjusted his glasses, his eyes glinting curiously. "Did it work?"

Hermione returned, holding the Pulse in one hand. "It did," she replied, unable to stop the bitterness from creeping into her voice. "For about a month, before Helene created a new iteration of the spores that fixed the flaw."

"But it still affects the spores," Martin guessed, catching her point immediately.

"Exactly. The current the Pulse generates is no longer enough to shut them down, and we can't increase it without killing the host. But the spores still react to it. I've never tried it on nanites. But it should at least give us something."

Martin nodded slowly. "The theory is sound, and at worst, we finally find something that can destroy them."

Hermione didn't like the way the thought of destroying them excited her. She raised the Pulse and aimed at the sample. The Pulse only had one setting, but it could be sustained for several seconds. "Start the watch," she said.

Martin activated the stopwatch the same moment Hermione fired the Pulse. She knew the second the ray hit the sample because it convulsed once on the monitor. Then it pulsed again. Hermione leaned in. "Did you see that?"

Martin didn't reply, his eyes fixed on the screen—where the image of the hybrid *jumped*. That wasn't the right word, but it was the only way Hermione could describe it. The hybrid jumped, and the monitor flickered and scrambled before correcting itself.

She gripped Martin's arm. "Tell me you saw that."

The old man was, in turn, gripping the edge of the table. His face was pale. "It just...adapted."

That's another word, Hermione thought absently.

"It—it took the signal and synchronized with it. Almost immediately. How is that even possible?"

Hermione's mind was racing. If the hybrid could interpret and adapt to electrical signals without being in a host, then... What did that even mean? What was the point? Hermione had never tested whether the spores could receive commands outside of a host. But even if it could, so what? Both the spores and the nanites worked by making use of their host. Without a victim, they were useless. What was Helene planning? Was it a deliberate design or just some side effect of whatever messed-up method she'd used to merge the spores and the nanites?

Hermione was so confused that she wanted to pull her hair out.

"We need to run more tests," she said finally. "A *lot* more tests."

SIX HOURS LATER, the lab smelled like burned circuitry and sterilized metal. Hermione and Martin had pulsed the sample with different electromagnetic frequencies, introduced it to organic tissue samples, and simulated external interference. Each time, the hybrid hadn't just reacted—it'd learned. It adapted faster than they could track, mostly because the nanoscope couldn't zoom in enough to view the molecular structures.

But no matter what they threw at it, the hybrid had absorbed it effortlessly.

Hermione collapsed back into her chair, rubbing her face. "This isn't about control anymore." That had been her first thought: the hybrids were meant to control people without needing to be inside them. It was still a possibility, but it'd become more and more secondary the more tests they'd performed. "It's integration."

"The compatibility analysis is done," Martin said from across the room, taking a petri dish out of a machine. Above it, a monitor showed the results of the test. Hermione couldn't make out the words from where she was, but she saw the effect they had on Martin. He slumped in his chair, as if he didn't have the strength to hold himself up. Hermione started to stand to help him, but he composed himself a moment later. Still, his voice was shaky when he spoke, and he didn't move his eyes away from the result. "It doesn't just bind to human DNA, Hermione. It can attach to anything."

Hermione's breath hitched. "Anything?"

Martin swiveled his chair until it faced her. His expression was grim. "Any living organism. Any biological matter or semi-biological matter. It doesn't just override—it merges. Seamlessly. It's not selective, and it can't be resisted." He hesitated and licked his lips as if he didn't know how to say the next part. "Hermione, it can rewrite an entire ecosystem."

Hermione crossed the room, needing to see it for herself. She stared at the results on the monitor, then at the petri dish containing the hybrid extract. Her mind went to Helene.

And then, for some reason, to the bomb.

The one DJ had seen in the underground complex where they'd rescued Ndidi. The one for which Tyra Chityothin had been sourcing materials over the last few months. The one they were all certain Helene would use to cause another Mayday—or something worse.

But that had never made sense to Hermione. What did Helene gain from blowing up the country? How did that serve her? Helene's core directive was to obtain power at all costs. How did destruction fulfill that?

Sure, the bomb could serve as a deterrent—a threat to force the world into submission. But deterrence relied on fear—on self-preservation. That might work for a while, but humans were notoriously self-sabotaging, and fear always faded. It was unsustainable. And Helene would know that.

So what was the point of the bomb?

A conversation with Ndidi resurfaced in Hermione's mind. It had been shortly after they'd rescued her. Ndidi had told her how, during captivity, Helene had spoken at length about humanity's flaws—about how they needed to evolve before they destroyed themselves. It had been the only conversation the AI seemed interested in having.

And now it fit.

Helene had improved the picospores until they could cure mental disorders. The nanites had been enhanced far beyond what Martin had originally envisioned, granting superhuman strength, speed, and durability. The hybrids were a fusion of both and—as they'd just learned—were designed to survive anything and integrate seamlessly with any living organism. If they functioned like the picospores and nanites, then anyone exposed to them wouldn't just be enhanced—they'd be changed. No disorders. No weaknesses. Smarter, stronger, faster, more durable.

They would have evolved.

But Helene wouldn't create something she couldn't control, which meant every person infected would still be under her command.

She didn't need destruction. She needed dispersal.

Hermione groaned, long and deep. "Oh, we're so fucked."

CJ KEPT A WARY EYE on the giant mechanical arms slamming into the ground, each blow creating tremors that rattled his teeth. The arms didn't move in sync either; some hit twice in rapid succession, while others paused intermittently before smashing down.

"Okay," CJ whispered to himself. "I can do this." He took a breath, condensing his Zone to a few feet around him and strengthening it as much as possible. If he got hit, the barrier was the only way he would survive, and it was doubtful that would even be enough. He could have spread his Zone to cover the arms and then tried nullifying it from a distance, but that would have drained him in seconds, and it probably wouldn't have made a dent considering how dense each arm was. For a similar reason, he didn't have enough energy to teleport to the other side.

He was going to have to run the gauntlet to get to the other side. But it was almost suspicious how completely the seemingly simple obstacle course countered his abilities. Helene couldn't have adapted to them that fast, could she? After just one battle?

CJ shook the thought out of his head. One step. Two steps, and he was directly under. The first arm lowered, moving faster than he'd anticipated. It crashed down, and CJ flinched, scrambling back instinctively. Less than a foot away, the arm landed with a force that lifted him slightly off the ground.

That would have killed me, he thought, wide-eyed and panting. If he had been slower, he would have died. CJ wasn't exactly sure what that meant in the Virtual Realm, but his best guess was that his mind would have broken, leaving him as little more than a vegetable. CJ could picture it vividly, and the thought terrified him. Why had he thought he could do this?

Because I have to, he answered himself, slowly standing. It didn't matter what he was risking—he had to do it still. He had to save Manar. CJ straightened, and his expression smoothed out. *It's better this way anyway.*

It was good that he was scared. It was a feeling he was used to. He'd grown up scared of bullies and even interacting with normal people, scared of confrontation and being pressured. Scared of being abandoned as a burden, scared of his incompetence, his codependence and the thought of being that way for the rest of his life.

The Virtual Realm had helped resolve a lot of those fears, but it'd also brought its own. When CJ had infiltrated his first few websites, before he'd acquired the Sphere, he'd been scared of the conflict and getting hurt. He'd been scared when he faced Helene, and then he'd been scared of returning to his own body after they thought they defeated her. Most recently, a part of him was terrified of the kind of person he was turning into and the bitterness he felt toward his brother.

Fear was as much a part of him as his fingers and eyes. He was used to it, and he'd learned to live despite it. Being squashed by the arms was a new type of fear, but it was a relatively minor one, all things considered. And he'd deal with it the same way that he dealt with every other problem.

Step by step, with logic.

The arm crashed into the ground again, and CJ flinched despite himself. He clenched his teeth. *First things first.* He pulled the Zone tighter around him, until it was a few inches away from his skin. It was the most it could constrict, and at that level, the cost in energy was negligible, even as condensed as it was. He toggled on his Sight with a mental flick, and the world bled into binary. The giant arms were replaced by contrastingly small bits. They still retained their shapes, but it was less real, like an outline haphazardly filled in with ones and zeros. As the arms smashed on the ground, a smaller wave of bits—so minute they were barely visible—spread out to fill the room faster than he could react. CJ tensed. This was the part he wasn't sure of.

The wave reached and passed through him, but that was fine. He simply nullified it within his Zone—and the thud that had started reverberating in his ears died immediately. CJ allowed himself a small grin. The wave was the rush of sound caused by the arms hitting the ground; it was the loud crash that made him flinch no matter how hard he tried not to. CJ eliminated the sound in the vicinity of his Zone, which stopped him from hearing it. It wasn't perfect though. The wave still reverberated in the room, so it wasn't that CJ didn't hear it at all—it just wasn't as startlingly loud and deafening.

And so, it wasn't as scary.

Combined with the fact that with his Sight he could focus more on the arm's codes rather than the scary pistons trying to crush him, he'd basically eliminated the fear factor. The danger was still real, of course, but now CJ could push past his anxiety and focus. That was important for the next part.

There were ten metal arms, each as large as a wagon and moving at different speeds. Generally, they maintained a set speed, but occasionally they would speed up suddenly for no reason. It made them harder to predict, but not impossible. And CJ had always loved puzzles.

It took him over ten minutes to figure out the sequence for the first three arms, and only because he could see their codes shift a second before they sped up. It took him half an hour to figure out the sequence for the next two sets of three arms, and that was because he had to keep the sequence for the first part in his mind as well. After staring at the last arm for another fifteen minutes without figuring out its pattern, CJ gave up. There was only so much he could hold in his head without mixing them up.

CJ spent another few minutes composing himself before stepping up to the arms. He held the sequence firmly in his mind as he ducked under the first arm.

It crashed down behind him, but the sound was muted, as if it'd come from far away. Almost instantly the second arm hammered down. CJ threw himself into a roll. It was far from graceful, and it hurt when he landed, but it worked. The next arm was already halfway down, and CJ felt a gust as it tore through the air toward him. CJ hadn't yet picked himself up from his roll, which meant he couldn't dodge.

Forcing down his panic, he extended his Zone a foot and immediately teleported away. Just because he couldn't teleport to the other side didn't mean that he couldn't use the ability within the gauntlet. He scrambled to his feet as he reassembled and threw himself sideways in time to dodge a horizontal swing that would have taken his head.

There were six other arms, and all of them sped up simultaneously, as if reacting to his presence. With his Sight, each was nothing more than a barely outlined pack of code, which helped CJ push past his fear.

The next few minutes were a dance of steel and thunder, as CJ made his way through the arms. Several times, he was forced to chain short teleports whenever an attack got too close or he wasn't in a position to dodge. Reducing their range helped with the cost, but his energy still bled away faster than he'd planned. He didn't know how long it took before he eventually stumbled past the final arm, his heart pounding.

The firewall blazed in front of him. It wasn't real heat, and even when he stared at it directly, the light wasn't blinding. It was more like the memory of a flame than the real thing. But that didn't mean it wasn't dangerous. CJ learned that when his curiosity got the better of him: He poked it with a finger, and something immediately started corroding his Zone around that point.

CJ grimaced. The corrosion worked like his Nullification Aura, which eliminated one of his options. And unfurling his Zone confirmed that it couldn't pass beyond the firewall without being corroded. That meant he couldn't just teleport behind it. Not that that had been an option either way. This close, it was easier to see the guardians on the other side, waiting for him. He couldn't afford to drain his energy if he was going to survive them.

With his Sight, CJ stared at the firewall for several minutes, and his frown became deeper. But eventually, he found what he was looking for and followed the thread to a cluster of lines near the floor. Every security type in a website had anchor points that connected them to the site itself. On entities like the knights, which actively moved and attacked, that point was difficult to find and even harder to manipulate. On a stationary defense system like the firewall, however...

CJ crouched near the wall, focusing on the cluster. He raised a finger, sheathed it with his Nullification Aura and slowly brought it down on the node. The firewall flared in response, raging like a bonfire that had just had fuel thrown on it. CJ pushed down, and a force pushed back. Although he had learned to ignore the constant pressure around him, it now doubled, trying to press him to the ground. CJ gritted his teeth and kept pushing.

A minute later, the firewall parted, and CJ scrambled through the gap just before it closed up again. Two knights turned toward him, one brandishing a shield and the other a spear.

CJ sighed.

37

SOMETIME LATER, CJ CRASHED to the floor, too drained to move. The constructs were in a heap behind him, disabled. He'd cut their connection to the website, so there wasn't any risk that they would recover anytime soon, at least until a maintenance program came to fix them. That possibility should have been enough to prompt CJ to get going—and it would have been if CJ had any energy left to move.

This was the first time he'd been drained so completely. Even when he fought Helene, the Sphere had reduced the cost of his abilities enough that he'd never completely run out. It was a new experience, and CJ wasn't sure how to feel about it. On one hand, he was glad that he wasn't completely brain-dead, but on the other hand, it was nerve racking to realize how vulnerable he was. If a knight or any other security construct stumbled on him right now, CJ wouldn't be able to lift a finger to defend himself. Mostly because he *literally* couldn't lift a finger.

It took a quarter of an hour before he regained enough energy to sit up against the wall, and double that before he could afford to activate his Zone once more. He breathed out a sigh of relief once the barrier billowed out from him. He condensed it as much as possible, which helped to resist the pressure of the site.

It also helped block out the presence he sensed watching him. CJ couldn't tell whether it was a security program or Helene herself, but it made him wonder why they hadn't taken advantage of his moment of vulnerability to attack. That thought kept him from moving until he recovered his entire pool of energy. That took him an hour, which meant that he'd spent around two hours on the gauntlet alone. Normally that would have counted as an achievement, considering that Helene had probably designed the security systems herself, but CJ couldn't count it as such. How much of Manar had been lost in that time?

The unease pushed him to his feet. His Zone spread out a few feet around him, its boundaries clearly visible to his Sight. CJ pushed it out to its maximum range. Usually, that would be around a mile. This time, it was stopped by the walls and didn't extend past the end of the hallway.

The website resisted the intrusion, and CJ had to push for every foot. It was easy when the Zone was close to him, but the farther away it got, the more he had to strain. His newly recovered energy drained by the second, but CJ finally managed to extend the Zone through the walls and into the surrounding passages. His success only lasted a few seconds before the strain became too much and his Zone snapped back, but that was all he needed to get a map of what awaited him.

He frowned. There were a lot of traps. Every path was littered with them. Some were similar to the gauntlet, but others were more complicated than CJ could parse in his brief glimpse. All were guarded by security constructs. Going by how long it'd taken him to complete the gauntlet, passing through each one was going to take up a lot of time.

CJ didn't have a lot of time.

"I'm going to need help," he muttered reluctantly. The words tasted bitter in his mouth, but CJ prided himself on being logical.

So, with a brief mental effort, CJ returned to the real world.

CJ BLINKED, TWISTING his face against the rays of sunlight streaming into Manar's office from the open window. He pulled off the neural uplink and his gas mask and then carefully removed the tubes that connected him to the life-support system. It'd gone mostly unused since he and Manar had woken up from their comas, but CJ had set it up again after he'd become tired of having to pointlessly break off his practice in the Virtual Realm in order to eat or go to the toilet. As long as he was connected to life support, he could go a week without having to return. The stiff limbs and throbbing ache behind his eyes were a small price to pay for that.

His clothes were wrinkled from lying on them for so long, his hair was messed up, and his breath smelled, but CJ didn't notice any of that as he left Manar's office in search of his brother. As he walked, his mind drifted to the gauntlet. Was there a way that he could have passed it faster? The entire course seemed to have been made to counter his abilities, but there had to be some tactic that wouldn't have cost him several hours of time. What had he missed?

CJ only passed two people on his way to the elevator, and both of them gave him a wide berth, holding their hands to their noses. One of them had been waiting for the elevator but simply waved CJ in when it arrived, unwilling to enter an enclosed space with him. CJ would have been embarrassed if he'd noticed, but his mind was firmly fixed on solving the puzzle.

Eventually he found his brother in the executive's gym, after searching for a quarter of an hour and crossing all of Sparta. Surprisingly, it was Hermione who had given him the idea to check there. He hadn't even known there was an executive's gym.

At first, CJ didn't see his brother. But a small explosion of sound drew his eyes to the ceiling just in time to see DJ plummeting to the ground. CJ felt a spike of alarm before his brain caught up to him. His brother crashed into the floor with the force of a small boulder. Thin cracks spread from the point of impact in every direction, and when CJ followed some of them with his eyes, he noticed that similar cracks were scattered around the room. Most of the room had them, in fact, across the floor, walls, and even the ceiling. The gym equipment had been pushed to a corner, and it was the only place that had been left reasonably untouched. The rest of the room looked like several hurricanes had blown through at the same time and clashed for dominance.

When Karla and Liz dropped down to land beside his brother, CJ realized hurricanes might not be far from the truth. He crossed the room until he stood beside DJ's prone form, on the other side of the Murder Twins. He acknowledged them with a nod, which they didn't respond to. Karla looked at him like he'd been dipped in mud.

"Hey, bro." DJ groaned, sitting up slowly. "Do you mind taking a few steps back? I mean, I'm happy to see you out and about, of course, but you smell like you lost a fight with a garbage truck."

CJ blinked and then slowly raised his shirt to his nose. He recoiled immediately, his face twisting to disgust, then embarrassment as he realized why exactly he hadn't had a problem with crowds while he'd been looking for his brother.

CJ forcefully squashed his embarrassment. "I need to talk to you."

DJ stared at him for a moment. CJ met his gaze steadily, trying to convey the importance. DJ sighed after a few seconds and pushed himself to his feet. He turned to the Murder Twins, ignoring the looks they gave him. "Don't get your panties in a twist. It's just gonna be a minute."

CJ didn't think that was likely, but he didn't say that, at least not until he and his brother were on the other side of the room. That wasn't far enough to stop the twins from hearing them, of course, but they'd begun sparring with each other almost immediately after he and DJ had left. Hopefully that would be enough distraction for them. "I need help."

DJ's brows rose in surprise. "Must be serious."

If it hadn't been—if there hadn't been a deadline—CJ would have spent as much time as he needed within Helene's website, overcoming each obstacle. Even as he explained everything to DJ, he had to force out each word, as it felt like he was giving away his secrets. It was ridiculous, of course, and CJ tried his best to suppress the feeling. It helped that DJ became noticeably more serious when he heard about Manar's timeline.

"Helene's designed the whole thing to counter my abilities," CJ said. "I can get through them, but…"

"It'll be faster with someone else," DJ finished for him. "I'm in. We can go now."

CJ blinked, closing his mouth. He'd expected to convince DJ to go, but only after several minutes of arguing. DJ was juggling so many things, and CJ was asking him to drop everything for several days. Plus his brother had made it very clear that he hated the Virtual Realm. CJ had expected more of a protest.

"Don't you need some time to…put some things in order, or something?" CJ asked, glancing at the twins, who were glaring at them—no, at DJ. Karla had a hand on the hilt of her dagger.

DJ ignored them. "I can continue my training with them after I'm back, and they know it. I doubt Ndidi and Hermione will notice I'm gone. I'll send a text to Christy so she won't be worried, and another to Olsen to let him know I'll be unreachable for a few days. It doesn't really matter. You need me, right?"

CJ did need him. He didn't have many people he could call for help, but he hadn't thought further than DJ because his brother had always been there for him. CJ felt his throat tighten, and he pushed down the sudden wave of guilt that washed through him. He nodded and forced his voice to remain steady when he spoke. "Thank you."

DJ waved it off. "Two things. You know I'm not going to have my abilities over there, right? You could run your ideas by me, and I could help you strategize and all, but apart from that, I'm probably going to be worse than useless."

"I've thought about that," CJ said. He had an idea of what was going to happen, but he couldn't test it until they actually got there.

DJ easily accepted the statement. "Second," he said, taking a step back, holding a hand to his nose. "We're not doing anything until you take a shower."

39

GENERALLY, WHENEVER CJ RETURNED to the Virtual Realm, he appeared in the same location he'd left from. But then again, he'd never left while still inside of a website before. So when his avatar materialized outside of Helene's fortress, he wasn't surprised. He'd felt the site reject him when his avatar had tried to spawn there, and without being fully formed, CJ hadn't been able to do anything except allow himself to be pushed away.

He expanded his Zone as far as it could go, and a moment later, DJ materialized beside him. His avatar didn't have the bruises his real body had, and it was dressed in a combat suit instead of his usual clothing.

"The suit doesn't give you more protection," CJ said. "You understand that, right?"

DJ ran his fingers over the body armor and knocked on his helmet. It made a hollow sound. "It might be made up of ones and zeros, bro, but it's still a second layer. It'll give them something to bang on while I finish them up."

"No, it won't." CJ sighed. He'd explained this four times already. "Because you're not under the armor. You forced me to design your avatar *as* the armor. When the constructs are hitting the amour, they'll be hitting *you*."

"Then it still works," DJ insisted, "because my new skin is armor thick. It'll soak up more damage than yours."

"No, it…" CJ paused as his brother glanced at him. He had a helmet as a face, so it was impossible to read any expression from him. But CJ could easily picture his brother's mischievous grin. He shook his head but couldn't stop a smile from pulling at his lips.

"Don't stress about it, bro. I'll keep them off you." DJ faced the fortress. "Now…what're we looking at?"

"Our target. Manar's in there somewhere, and we have slightly less than three days to find him before the site crashes and he's lost forever."

"What're we waiting for then? Shouldn't we be rushing in?"

That was a good question. CJ didn't know why, but in the half hour it'd taken for the brothers to get ready, he'd lost the pressure that had been on his shoulders. It could have simply been because he wasn't doing it alone anymore, but CJ was sure he'd still have felt the pressure if it'd been anyone else beside him. But it was his brother, so he knew it was going to be all right.

That's cringe, CJ grimaced. Fortunately, there was a better answer to DJ's question—one that was more relevant. "We need to determine what form your abilities take."

"What're you talking about? I don't have any abilities. We talked about this. My nanites enhance my physical body, but I'm not in my physical body right now, so—"

"So your nanites will manifest differently," CJ finished. "When Manar and I came here the first time, he also had nanites in his blood, and he designed the neural uplink to take that into consideration. His nanites were connected to Helene and allowed him to track her. But with some practice, he also unlocked some other abilities."

"You're thinking I'm going to have the same abilities?" DJ asked, and once again, even though he couldn't see his expression, CJ got the impression he was smiling.

"No." His brother's smile disappeared, so CJ hurried to explain. "Manar's powers allowed him to manipulate aspects of the world to some extent. But they were based on his understanding of codes and programming. If you get the same abilities, they'll be worse than useless in your hands."

"Oh yeah, no. I'd have to learn code and stuff? I'll pass. But if it's a bad idea for me to get Manar's powers, then what're you thinking?"

Explaining might affect the result, so CJ waved off the question. Instead, he tried to remember how Manar had explained the way he'd accessed his abilities. He wasn't sure if it was going to work the same way, so his voice came out shaky when he spoke. "Are you...you should be feeling something in your chest. Maybe like a lump?"

DJ looked at him oddly but patted his chest armor. "I don't feel anything."

"It's not physical," CJ said. "You have to sense it, like you sense your nanites."

"I don't really sense my nanites though. They're just *there*."

"How do you activate them then?"

"I don't know," he shrugged. "I just can. It's like a switch. Or a button. I just think of switching them on, and they're—" DJ cut himself off, staring down at his stomach. "Huh."

CJ started to reply but paused as he sensed a pressure coming from DJ. Though nothing about him changed physically, he seemed more solid, somehow, more present, and he gave off a feeling of steady strength.

Suddenly, DJ jumped a half a dozen feet into the air before landing with ease. He didn't even need to bend his knees. "Gimme a sec."

CJ started to say something in reply, but his brother had already disappeared—

No, that wasn't right. CJ spun around. DJ was moving too fast for CJ to follow him with his eyes, but CJ didn't need to follow him. As long as DJ stayed within CJ's Zone, he would always know where he was, without needing to look. But he couldn't see his brother in this way. He sensed him, as well as the subtle pressure radiating from him, and from those he got impressions, like images, about the specifics. But since CJ mostly used his Zone as a barrier and a conduit to manipulate areas in the Virtual Realm, his senses were mostly intuitive, barebones.

So, CJ expanded his Zone to its full size of about a mile, closed his eyes, and focused on his senses, trying to follow his brother as he ran around. It was easy to do whenever DJ stopped and stared down at himself, as if trying to figure something out. But it took him several minutes and most of his focus to match his brother while he was running.

At some point, DJ started scanning the sky, clearly searching for something. CJ had a hunch about what it might be, and that suspicion was confirmed a moment later when DJ's head pivoted, his gaze locking on the exact spot CJ was watching him from. CJ could almost feel the mischievous smile on DJ's face beneath the helmet.

CJ learned why when, a moment later, his brother disappeared again. CJ locked in on him almost immediately, but it took all his focus, and even then DJ constantly moved faster than he could track. CJ narrowed his focus until he was practically next to his brother and DJ was the only thing in CJ's vision, the only thing he could sense. That continued for a minute, until CJ felt something snap into place, like pieces of a puzzle fitting together. His brother must have felt it as well because he stopped for a moment and glanced back at where CJ's avatar stood with his eyes closed. When he saw that nothing was wrong, he started running again.

He was slightly faster this time, but CJ found it easier to stick with him. Far easier. It was like a switch had flipped in CJ's mind. He could feel his brother better, more vividly, as if he were running alongside him.

As an experiment, CJ activated his Sight and sent part of his awareness into the ground, which now appeared as rigid blocks of code. With a mental effort, he rearranged a section—and a wall appeared out of nowhere, directly in front of DJ.

To his credit, DJ reacted immediately. He tried to kick off the wall and use it to change his direction. But CJ hadn't made the wall thick, and DJ had underestimated the force his momentum carried. He crashed through, legs first, shattering it completely. Instinctively, DJ covered his face—forgetting he was wearing a helmet—and turned what could have been a bad fall into a roll that ended with him back on his feet.

For a moment DJ stared at him incredulously. Then he burst into laughter. CJ opened his eyes, unable to stop a small smile. When was the last time he'd been so mischievous? Usually, he was the serious one. *Like Manar.*

The thought sliced through his mirth like a knife.

A moment later, DJ arrived at his side, still chuckling. He started to say something, but CJ's expression must have made him reconsider, because he sobered up. "I guess playtime's over."

CJ nodded, glancing back at the fortress. "I think we've determined your powers manifested the same as they were..." He trailed off when his brother started shaking his head,

"What's the range of this thing?" he asked, gesturing to the Zone.

"About a mile," CJ replied, frowning.

"I ran half of it," DJ said, "which means I just covered half a mile in a few seconds. I can't do that in the real world. The twins, maybe. But I'm far from that."

"So you're faster here."

Once again, DJ shook his head. "Not necessarily. I think it depends on how much I tap into that lump stuff you were talking about. I felt it when I was running, like there was a lump of fire sitting in my stomach. It was draining steadily as I ran, and it drained even faster when I pushed myself trying to lose you. Not a lot though. I should be about three-quarters full right now, if I'm sensing the stuff right."

CJ nodded, thinking. Manar had spoken about a ball of energy as well, so it was understandable that DJ's source had manifested in the same way. It was actually better. CJ's abilities came from his understanding of programming and his mastery of the Realm, and each use cost him energy, which was basically a combination of physical and mental stamina. That had its benefits, but it meant that CJ was basically useless once he ran out of energy.

However, DJ drained directly from his nanites. That meant that even if he used them all up, he wouldn't necessarily be as vulnerable as CJ. More importantly, he could drain them faster if he needed a temporary boost. Manar hadn't been able to do that, but that could have been because DJ had more experience with the nanites.

"How much time do you need to recharge?" CJ asked.

"Hard to tell. About five minutes?"

CJ hid a grimace. It was hard not to feel jealous.

40

JANUARY 2044
VIRTUAL REALM

SIX MINUTES LATER, CJ and his brother crossed the threshold into the fortress. CJ's Zone deactivated automatically as he entered. In the second it took him to expand it once more, DJ was on his hands and knees, wheezing.

"What the..." he rasped. "What the hell is that?"

CJ would have liked to know the answer as well. He was by DJ's side immediately, trying desperately to force down his panic. He hadn't felt an attack, and CJ didn't think it was possible for one to have passed through his Zone without alerting him. The website could have taken advantage of the split second where his Zone hadn't been activated. But why had it just targeted DJ? Did the site identify him as the bigger threat? Had it just been testing them?

"Tell me what's happening."

"What do you mean what's happening?" DJ asked, surprised. "You don't feel that?"

Now CJ was more confused. He still couldn't feel an attack, but he retracted his Zone and directed more energy into it, condensing it as much as he could. In the same moment, DJ drew in a shuddering breath, like a drowning man getting his first gulp of air. His back was still arched, but his wheezing slowed and was replaced by labored breathing. His arms trembled beneath him, hands splayed on the ground, as if still bracing for impact.

CJ gave him a minute, but eventually he couldn't hold back his curiosity. "Feel what?"

"That pressure. How did you not feel that?"

"Oh," CJ said, straightening. As soon as they'd entered the building, the website had marked them as intruders and rejected them. That rejection had manifested as a pressure that'd tried to incapacitate them and force them out. CJ had felt it as soon as they'd crossed the threshold, and although it was far more intense than other websites, CJ had already adapted to it the first time around. Besides, he had faced far worse, such as when he'd pitted his will against the site's to stretch his Zone through the firewalls.

Now, since they were just at the entrance, and with his Zone repelling the bulk of it, it was more manageable.

"What the hell do you mean, 'Oh'?" DJ asked. He'd recovered enough to stand, though his knees were slightly bent, like he was carrying something heavy.

"The pressure is the website rejecting us."

DJ eyed him. "I don't like how casually you said that. Being rejected sounds like a bad thing."

"We're technically viruses right now," CJ said. "But my Zone cuts out a section of the site that belongs to me, and that counters the pressure to some extent."

"There was a second where your thing wasn't active, but I didn't see you gasping on the floor."

"I was here for several hours before I came to get you. I already adapted to it." That said, his brother's statement did raise a question. CJ was surprised by the pressure the first time he'd entered the site, but it still hadn't affected him as much as it had DJ. Why?

"So it'll get better, huh?" DJ asked, cracking his neck. "Hopefully fast. I can't bring out my full strength like this." CJ frowned at that and started to reply. But his brother had already moved on, glancing around the room. "So, what's all this then?"

For the first time, CJ looked around the room—and his heart dropped to his stomach. "It's different," he muttered. The entrance to the website was supposed to be a lobby with polished floors, marble columns, and hallways that led deeper into the building. That was what he'd seen the first time. Now, however, the room was a vast, cavernous hall that stretched in every direction. The ceiling soared so high that the light didn't even reach it, and lining each wall were elaborate archways that CJ couldn't see through.

He toggled on his Sight. The code for static objects like buildings, walls, streets, and the ground were generally rigid blocks that connected into tapestries that spanned the length of the object. But here, the tapestries moved: Floor tiles slid or rotated under them, and parts of the walls rippled in his Sight.

CJ expanded his Zone and immediately felt a presence lock on to him. The pressure of the site condensed, focused on the barrier, and tripled the strain for every inch that it grew. Waves of energy gushed out of CJ to power the Zone, and his knees buckled. He could have kept pushing, but the drain wasn't sustainable, especially if the force was going to keep increasing, so he retracted his Zone to a dozen feet around himself and his brother. That should have placed the area under his control and stopped the tiles from moving, but the floor kept shifting. CJ frowned as he met the same resistance while trying to push his Zone into the floor.

"What do you mean it's different?" DJ asked.

"It was a lobby before," CJ replied absently, still scanning the hall. "Helene must have redesigned it while I went to get you."

"Why'd she do that, do you think?"

That was the question, wasn't it? If they had been dealing with a normal person, CJ could have assumed they were threatened. But Helene had repeatedly shown that she didn't consider any of them a threat—and she'd also proven that she was right not to. Despite that, Helene had taken his abilities into consideration and designed the previous layout to waste as much of his time as possible. That was why he'd gone to DJ for help.

And now, in response, Helene had changed the layout, which meant the new design was meant to slow them down.

"She's underestimating us," CJ said. She was looking at CJ and his brother as two people working together. But they'd always been more than the sum of their parts.

DJ took a step forward, and CJ saw the codes beneath his foot cut off a split second before the tiles disappeared. DJ pulled back just in time to avoid falling into a gaping pit. He whistled. "It doesn't look like she's underestimating anything, bro, if we're already setting off traps before we've gone anywhere."

CJ knelt beside the pit. The hole itself was completely devoid of code, which he hadn't thought was possible. Everything in the Virtual Realm was made of code. But with a simple trap, Helene had proven that he didn't know as much as he'd thought.

"What do you think would have happened if we fell in?" DJ asked.

CJ would've liked to know the answer to that question as well. But his attention was drawn away as several sections of the floor reconfigured themselves, sliding away from each other. The hall changed—corridors split off into multiple passages, some leading behind pillars, others converging near arches that hadn't been there a moment ago.

"How's she even doing this?" DJ asked. "This isn't normal, is it?"

"No," CJ said, watching the changes. The only time he'd ever seen a website change this fast was when he and Manar had fought with Helene. CJ had used the sphere to merge with the website, making the entire building an extension of himself. It wasn't something he could replicate, and Helene couldn't have been using the same method. So how was she doing it?

"Well, it seems like we have options," DJ said. He gestured toward the half dozen passages. "Which one are you thinking?"

"She probably doesn't want us to pick one. More likely she wants us stumbling around while the clock ticks down." Absently, he sidestepped one of the moving tiles, moving onto a stable-looking section near the center. His gaze flicked around the room, scanning for something he knew was there: the anchor point that connected whatever program was running this, to the rest of—

There. CJ narrowed his eyes at a node in the corner.

"I'm guessing you have a plan?" DJ asked. "Because the columns are moving too." The tall pillars slid sideways and cut off potential routes as they drifted. If he or CJ stood too close, they might get pinned between one of the columns and a wall. The tile they stood on jerked and started sliding away, nearly tossing them off.

CJ gritted his teeth. "We have to head there." He pointed in the direction of the node. "I'll lock down the sections as we go, but I'll be pitting my will against the site's. That means I won't be able to pay attention to anything else."

"I'll cover you. No problem. Just do your thing. I'm getting dizzy just being here."

CJ knelt without another word and forced his Zone below the tiles. This time, he was ready for the resistance and immediately pushed back once the pressure started mounting. For a moment, the floor under him stilled as they came under his control. Then they started sliding once more, but in the direction of the node. He couldn't control the sections outside his Zone, so the website had to rearrange the layout so the codes weren't damaged as CJ bulldozed his way through.

I don't think it likes that, CJ thought, suppressing a grin when the pressure doubled once more. CJ gritted his teeth against the strain but held on to his control. He closed his eyes for better focus, but through his Zone, CJ felt his brother tense and lowered himself into a stance with a muttered curse. A moment later, DJ leaped out of the barrier's boundary. "Keep going," he yelled back.

CJ felt a flash of panic and started to turn, but he was forced to abandon the thought when the website chose that moment to redouble its attack. All his focus went into resisting the pressure, and he no longer had any thoughts to spare for his brother. His Zone kept the ground beneath him under his control, and CJ held on until he sensed the node within its boundary.

Immediately, he split off part of his mind and wrapped the node in his Aura while the rest of him focused on defense. Energy drained from him like a leaky faucet, and black spots soon began to flicker at the edges of his vision. But he held on. He sensed when his brother returned, noticing the reduced state of DJ's core, but he pushed the thought way. He pushed everything away—until he felt something give way in the node.

"Time to go," CJ said, springing to his feet. Behind them, on the other side of the hall, the walls slid inward and formed a new corridor that extended deeper into the site. DJ matched his pace as they jumped from sliding section to sliding section and stepped past columns that threatened to close in on them. CJ glanced at his brother, noticing the residual distortions in the air around him—the flickers and ripples left by defensive maneuvers and rapid energy bursts. That made him scan the room, and he finally noticed the hulking form of a knight lying in the middle of the hall. It didn't take much to understand what had happened.

"Thanks," CJ said.

His brother glanced at him. "Don't make this weird, dude."

There were fewer stable sections the closer they got to the exit, and CJ was forced to spend energy to take control of them as they passed. When they were several feet away, the entire wall holding the exit *glitched*, like static. It was only for a moment, but when it settled, there were two identical exits side by side.

"Man, she really doesn't want us to go, does she?" DJ muttered.

CJ didn't respond. Most of his focus was spent fighting against the resistance until his Zone expanded to reach the exits. Immediately he knew which of the two were real and headed toward it. The ground quaked, and the section between them and the passage fell away, revealing a gaping void. DJ stumbled, but CJ continued running, seeing the illusion for what it was. A second later, he passed through the archway, followed closely by his brother.

Behind them, the archway morphed into a solid but transparent wall. The foyer beyond had rearranged itself again, as if nothing had happened. CJ retracted his Zone and slumped against the wall, a hand massaging his temple.

"You okay?" DJ asked, looking at him with concern.

CJ nodded, not trusting himself to speak. His head felt like it was about to split from the strain it had gone through. CJ hadn't had to form and hold so many workings since he'd fought with Helene. He barely had enough energy to hold himself up. And all of this was with his brother protecting him. If he had been by himself...

More importantly, if the entrance had been that bad, how much worse would the deeper layers be? CJ had to imagine that Helene would save the best security for wherever she'd trapped Manar. If they'd had so much trouble at the first threshold, how would they—

CJ shook his head, cutting off the thought before he went into a spiral. Instead, he glanced at DJ. The hint of tension in his brother's stance reminded CJ that was new territory for him. CJ had had some time to explore the Virtual Realm before putting himself in danger. But DJ had been thrown into the thick of things almost immediately, and he hadn't said a word of complaint. He was tense but didn't seem worried. CJ could still read the confidence in his stance, the same confidence that CJ himself had had before they'd entered the fortress. The one that was possible because they were together.

"I'm good," CJ replied. "But I need a few minutes to regenerate some energy."

DJ cocked his head to one side. "That's what Helene wants, isn't it?" He gestured toward the transparent wall and the entryway beyond that they'd just escaped. "She wants to stall us, force us to waste our time on her bullshit, and then waste even more time recovering our resources."

"Well, yeah," CJ agreed. "If we try to bulldoze our way through the traps, that'll increase the time we spend recuperating. We'll have to find a balance. But apart from that, there isn't really much we can do."

"Well, for one," DJ said, stepping up beside CJ, "we can try this." He placed a hand on CJ's shoulders, and a warmth spread through him from the point of contact. His headache receded, and strength filled his body. But he could feel his brother's core draining for every second his hand remained on CJ's shoulder, so CJ stepped away.

"How'd you do that?" he asked.

DJ scratched the back of his head. "The twins have been training me on how to direct the nanites to specific parts of my body. Obviously, I can't transfer them to someone else, but I figured if they manifested as energy over here, then it might be possible."

"How'd you know it was going to work though?"

"My gut," DJ replied, shrugging. He seemed to think that was enough of an answer, but it just made CJ want to pull out his hair. Several months ago, while battling Helene, CJ and Manar had transferred energy in a similar manner. But CJ had never told DJ—mostly because he hadn't considered it important; the transfer had only helped when one of them needed a boost in the middle of a fight.

The problem was now DJ would need time to recharge—or so CJ thought. Already CJ could feel DJ's core surging back to full, far faster than he could recover his own energy. His jaw dropped.

Maybe this would work after all.

41

NDIDI GLANCED AT THE SAMPLE trays stacked on a nearby counter, then shifted her gaze to Hermione, who was staring at her with an uncomfortable intensity. Ndidi was already used to how harried and exhausted Hermione looked when she hadn't slept for several days—which was becoming the norm unfortunately—but this time it was different in the way it set Ndidi's teeth on edge.

It didn't help that Martin, sitting beside Hermione, looked like he had aged several decades since she'd last seen him shortly after he'd regained consciousness. *He shouldn't be stressing himself,* Ndidi thought, frowning. *He should be recovering after what he's been through.*

Ideally Ndidi would have insisted that Martin be allowed to recuperate properly for a few days, but they'd needed his help immediately. According to Olsen, the government was still working on stopping Tyra from gathering the parts she needed for the bomb. But from the admiral's tone, Ndidi doubted they were even slowing the maniac down. It could take a year for the bomb to be completed, but it could also be finished in six months, or even a week. There was no way for anyone to know. And in the meantime, there were daily protests outside of Sparta, calling out DJ and the Murder Twins. The whole thing was a mess.

Ndidi had hoped, when she saw Hermione's text, that Martin's presence had helped discover a breakthrough that would lead to some good news. Judging from the other woman's expression, though, Ndidi bet that only part of her hope was true.

She sighed. Best to get it over with. "You said I should come as fast as I could. What's up?"

Hermione must have been deep in her thoughts because Ndidi's words made her jump slightly. She opened her mouth to respond and then stopped as if she wasn't sure where to start. Ndidi turned to Martin, hoping for an explanation, but he just shook his head.

That was when Ndidi started to worry. "Just start from the beginning," she told Hermione.

"The beginning. Yes, I can do that. The beginning. You already know that we've been running tests on the new compound we discovered in your blood, and in the sample that you got from Helene. You also already know that the compound is a fusion of the picospores and the nanites."

Ndidi nodded slowly, absently putting a hand on her stomach. It'd grown bigger during the last week, and now she could have passed for someone in her third trimester. She'd need to have Hermione and Martin do a scan soon.

"Good," Hermione said. "Martin and I ran some tests—well...we ran *all* the tests. Every test that we could think to run, we did, and we did this to try to figure out what the hybrid is. Y'know, the characteristics that shape it. Helene's modifications to the picospores are geared toward mental enhancement and correction, for example, while the nanites are physical. We wanted to know what the hybrid was designed for."

"And did you find it out?"

"Yes. Its defining attributes are adaptability, resilience, and integration."

Ndidi frowned. "Okay...what does that mean?"

"I'm getting to that. We already know the hybrid has properties of both the spores and the nanites. But we haven't yet been able to determine whether it can functionally replace the two others or if all three need to be present to work." Hermione raised a finger. "That distinction matters for understanding how it operates, even if it doesn't change what we would do next."

"Where are you going with this, Hermione?"

"It is important because, as far as we can tell, the hybrid was designed to survive indefinitely and integrate with any living organism. Even if it doesn't work exactly like the spores or the nanites, that doesn't matter. All Helene has to do is disperse all three across a wide area. The hybrid can stay dormant indefinitely until it encounters a host already infected with the other two."

"Are you saying that—"

"But," Hermione continued, speaking over Ndidi, "if the hybrid *does* act like a combination of the spores and nanites, it will forcibly bind with and evolve every organism it touches. Enhanced strength, speed, durability, mental clarity—no disorders. And since Helene already has ways to control anyone affected by the spores or nanites, it's logical to assume she can control anyone infected with the hybrid too. Essentially, she could create a whole new race under her command. And all she has to do is figure out a way to disperse it. Martin and I think we already know how she'll do that."

"How?"

"Think World War II," Hermione said, and Ndidi's breath caught in her throat.

The bomb. Ndidi's mind almost exploded as she made the connection. It made sense. It made so much *sense.*

"It's the perfect method for spreading it," Hermione continued, pacing now. "She wouldn't need to rely on a slow infection by kidnapping people or gassing buildings. All she'd have to do is just wait for people to breathe, and she'd win. The wind will carry her brood around, and there'll be no way to stop it."

Ndidi gritted her teeth. What could they do? The obvious thing was to try to stop Tyra before she could complete the bomb. But the government was already trying that. And DJ and the team had also tried. Several times. Every time, Tyra had played them like fools and run circles around them. Unless a miracle happened, going after Tyra directly wasn't the way to go. They could go after Helene in Nigeria, but Ndidi's blood ran cold at the thought. Helene might be somewhat limited while in Manar's body, but Ndidi couldn't think of a way that attacking her directly would be effective. From experience, more than likely, they'd just be playing into her hands.

So what could they do? Ndidi could only think of one other thing.

"We can't keep this to ourselves," she said finally. "People need to know what's coming for them."

Hermione looked away. "I considered that. But you realize what would happen, right? This is bigger than the stuff with DJ, and the world's already going mad with that. People are going to panic, and then they're going to do stupid stuff. There's no going back from that."

"If you have a better idea, I'm all ears," Ndidi said, not unkindly. "As it is, we're going to need more support. Olsen says the government is on board, but he also admitted that most of them think everything's been fabricated. Even among the ones that believe, some are calling for our heads. We need to give them something they can't ignore, something they can't sweep under the rug. We've handled the burden of Helene for the last few years. Now it's time to make it everyone else's problem."

Silence settled on the room. Martin had his eyes closed, but he wasn't sleeping. Finally, Hermione let out a small breath. "Martin and I will compile our results. You can reach out to Olsen and run it by him. And... we'll need a press release. Or maybe go the Tyra route and leak it directly to major outlets..." Her voice wavered. "God, I can't believe we're doing this. I haven't given a presentation in years."

"You don't have time to waste," Ndidi said, her lips pulled into a thin line. "Every day counts—we need to be ready before the bomb goes off."

CHAPTER

42

JANUARY 2044
VIRTUAL REALM

CJ AND DJ MADE THEIR WAY deeper into the building. The archway led into a wider hallway, one where the floor didn't shift underneath them and there were no drifting columns threatening to crush them. Instead there were rows of reflective panels that ran along each side, floor to ceiling. CJ shifted, and the panels caught his reflection, doubling it in a disconcerting ripple before smoothing over.

"What is this, a mirror house?" DJ asked, poking one of the panels. It shivered at his touch, as if deciding whether to stay solid. "Is a clown going to jump out at us?"

"They're all illusions," CJ said, scanning the room with his Sight. "I can see the triggers, but barely. They're subtle, and they shift constantly. But they'll activate if we stray too close to the panels."

"So we keep our distance. Sounds simple enough."

That was the part that bothered CJ. Helene wouldn't have designed something that was so simple to pass, not if her goal was to delay them as much as possible.

They took a few cautious steps forward, and their reflections followed them, but moving in a slightly delayed fashion, as if they were half a second late. CJ tried to expand his Zone, bracing himself for the resistance. Surprisingly, his Zone easily stretched to cover the entire passage. CJ could make out the path between the mirrors, but his senses warped strangely when he tried to study the panels themselves. At some point, he stopped and stared directly at one with his Sight—and shivered when his reflection smirked at him, out of his sync with his actual movement.

"I think she's trying to unnerve us," CJ said.

"Good thing we don't scare easily, isn't it?"

That might not be the point. Helene had given them something to focus on. The reflections were new, creepy, and obviously hiding a trap. That would naturally draw his and DJ's attention, causing them to miss something else. But then again, CJ couldn't suggest they stopped focusing on the suspicious mirrors. That would just be stupid and might be Helene's plan in the first place—

You're spiraling, CJ warned himself, shaking the thoughts away. He'd go mad if he tried to figure out Helene's way of thinking. A little further in, the passage forked into three paths. All were identical, with the same polished surface and flickering lights. They stopped, and CJ tried to scan the paths.

"I don't know which is real," he said, his voice tight. "The site's warping my vision somehow."

DJ took a step, leaning forward to peer at each of them. "What if we pick one at random and see what happens?"

"That'll probably send us on a loop that we can't break out of," CJ replied. To one side, his brother's reflection smirked at them. CJ grimaced, suppressing a shiver. But then he straightened, his jaw set. He couldn't be unnerved by an illusion. He expanded his Zone again until it enveloped all three paths.

And then he flooded the area with his Nullification Aura.

CJ marked his brother so it didn't affect him, but everything else immediately started degrading. DJ went to lean against a panel but then thought better of it when the reflection reached for him. CJ simply sat on the floor while he waited for the Aura to do its work. He could have directed more energy into making the Aura thicker, but there was no point. They'd only spent a few minutes in the room; they could afford to wait a few more. And this way, CJ would still be close to topped off for the next room.

"Maybe she didn't expect us to do this," DJ wondered out loud. "Maybe she miscalculated. I mean, it had to happen at some point, right? Statistically."

Five minutes in, the website started to fight back, pushing against the Zone. But CJ wasn't trying to expand the area, and it was far less stressful to simply defend his spot. At the ten-minute mark, their reflections, over a dozen of them, peeled themselves off the panels and lunged at them. In response, CJ sent more power to the barrier, condensing it as much as possible.

The reflections beat their fists against its surface—and though none of them were individually dangerous, there were soon hundreds of them spread out across the barrier, banging on it. After five minutes, CJ felt the strain building up and massaged his temples. Fortunately, the first two paths shattered at that moment, revealing their illusory nature. He and DJ stared at the last one, the rightmost.

"It could be an illusion too," DJ said. "They could've all been traps to make us waste our time."

"We planned on waiting anyway. If it is an illusion, then there would have been no reason for her to have the reflections attack us. Plus..." CJ glanced at the swarm of reflections. "I don't think we have a choice. We can't take on that many at once."

DJ looked back as well, and his stance told CJ just how worried he was. He tried to hide it, of course, but CJ didn't see the point. It was understandable. There were hundreds of reflections waiting for them beyond the barrier—and CJ was quickly running out of energy to hold them back.

DJ glanced at him. "That's what I'm saying, they're forcing us to go in." But he sounded resigned, so CJ didn't bother to argue.

They moved to the sole remaining hallway. There was a mirror beside it, within his Zone, and CJ noticed a flicker of something in its depths. It was gone when he blinked, but for a split second, CJ thought he saw Manar's silhouette reflected there, staring at the ground with his shoulders hunched.

DJ caught the pause. "What is it?"

"Nothing," CJ said, shaking his head. "Let's go."

They crossed the threshold into the right passage, and the world warped and stretched, as if they were walking into an instance. CJ braced himself, but it only lasted for a moment before settling back into a room filled with mirrors. CJ glanced back, wondering whether Helene had shifted the layout to take them back to the beginning. Then he noticed the reflections in the mirror. Instead of flickering images of himself and his brother, the panels shimmered, deepened, and then showed images of a shifting scene. The scene was grainy at first, like an old video struggling to load. But gradually, its detail became better until it was like they were watching a movie.

It showed a small, cluttered room in a dilapidated house. Clothes were strewn across a battered couch. There was a vague outline of religious tapestry on the wall, its edges frayed with age. A boy with dark hair sat cross-legged on the floor, staring numbly at an overturned bottle of whiskey. Somewhere, a door opened, and the boy raised his head to look, fear in his green eyes.

CJ's breath hitched.

DJ stared, incredulous. "Is that...?"

"It's Manar. Or a memory of him as a child." CJ had never seen this before—Manar had never spoken about his past, and Ndidi, the only person who might have known anything about it, definitely had never shared details—but the image gave enough context clues to piece together what was happening.

"CJ," DJ said under his breath. "We gotta move."

CJ tore his gaze away, just as a hulking man came into view. He was curious—how could he not be? Manar was a legend to basically all programmers worldwide, and more importantly, CJ considered him a mentor. Now, he had a chance to learn more about him—but it felt wrong. If Manar had wanted to share his past, he would have. Learning about his childhood from something that was likely a trap felt like an invasion of privacy.

CJ nodded to his brother.

The passage shifted. The floor rippled, and the air glitched. CJ expanded his Zone and stabilized the area around them while the rest of the room flickered. A wave seemed to pass through the place and sink into the mirrors around them. As one, the reflections in the panels changed. Now they played out different scenes of Manar's childhood from different angles.

CJ felt his determination crack.

"They're hooks," DJ said, scanning the panels. "For you mostly. She wants to draw you in, tempt you to linger. It's obviously a stalling tactic. You know that, right?"

CJ did know that. And it took everything in his power to wrench his eyes away from a scene showing a young Manar with an older woman in front of a computer. Gritting his teeth, CJ toggled on his Sight, and the illusions became nothing more than streams of code. He expanded his Zone across the room, searching for something. The website tried to scramble his senses, but CJ eventually found the anchor points. There were three of them, but only one was stable.

"There," CJ said, pointing at a part to their left. "That leads to the exit."

"Then let's take it before we get caught up in some bullshit," DJ said, already heading in that direction. CJ had started to follow him when the mirrored walls suddenly pulsed—and one of the young Manars slowly, eerily, turned his head until his gaze locked with CJ's.

And then lunged at him.

The panel shattered as the construct passed through it. It had already been within his Zone, so CJ had nothing to use as a shield except a raised arm. The construct latched on, and dark-purple tendrils extended from his fingers and started burrowing into CJ.

When the attendant had tried to hack him like this, CJ's Zone had protected him from the worst of the intrusion and allowed him to calmly counter it. Now it was with panicked instinct that CJ sent his own awareness to push against the tendrils.

Immediately his mind split into two, but CJ focused on the part that showed him fighting against the hack. He felt a presence behind each tendril, but it was different from what he fought whenever he pitted his will against the website. This one was weaker, far weaker, yet somehow more complex. CJ batted the attack aside easily and extended his awareness further toward his opponent. Surprisingly, the construct didn't resist. Once CJ started pushing back, it retreated immediately, until CJ was the one hacking *it*.

Images flashed through his mind like a movie playing at quadruple speed. CJ absorbed what he could without focusing on any specific thing. He could sift through them later. He had to be fast before he was kicked out—but even as the thought occurred to him, CJ realized there was no resistance, nothing trying to push him away. The dark-purple tendril was still there, but it acted as an anchor. As long as they were still connected, CJ had time to learn everything he could.

Smaller strands split off from the tendril and reached for specific images as they blurred past. Each one slowed down and played at a regular speed. Wary of a trap, CJ split his focus and sent his awareness into them. Surprisingly, a few of them were scenes from Manar's childhood, and CJ had to force himself to retract his mind. It got easier when he realized what was in the other images.

The layouts of the website filled his mind, so detailed it seemed like he was there. A glowing purple arrow cut through each of the layouts, and CJ followed it until the end. The scene showed Manar huddled in a corner. His clothes had holes in them, which shouldn't have been possible with an avatar, and one of his legs was missing. His head was bowed.

When CJ had seen this scene before—back when he'd hacked the knight his first time in the fortress—Manar had been whole, and he hadn't noticed CJ. This time, however, Manar looked up when CJ's awareness connected to the image, as if he could sense him.

"CJ," he gasped. Manar scrambled to his feet, his eye—just the one; the other was nothing but a gaping hole in his face—wide with panic. "We don't have much time. Do you hear me? We have a few weeks at most. You have to stop her before she—"

His words were drowned out by a veritable flood of *something* that slammed into CJ. CJ's tendril was cut faster than he could react, and the strands were forced back into his body. CJ tried to fight it, but it was like a child trying to push a car. He was forced back into his own body before he knew what was happening. The attack left CJ disoriented, and when he came back to himself, he realized he was being pulled by his brother.

DJ glanced back. "I don't know what the hell you did to piss off that thing, but we'll talk about it after. Right now, we have to leave."

The room was being destroyed. Mirrors shattered around them, and pieces of stone—blocks of code in his Data Sight—fell from the ceiling and disintegrated on the ground. CJ's Zone had kept the worst of it away from them, but without him providing energy to it, the barrier was steadily being destroyed as well. CJ fixed it as soon as he noticed.

It took them a minute to reach the end of the path, and by then parts of it had been destroyed, replaced by a black void. CJ stabilized the area and poured energy into the exit when it threatened to collapse. He and his brother stepped through. The walls buckled, and for a second, everything blurred. A moment later, they were on the other side. The exit collapsed and was replaced by a solid wall. In front of them was a narrow stone hallway leading forward.

CJ's heart pounded. His brother still had a grip on his wrist. Neither of them said anything for a long moment.

"Well," DJ said finally, letting go. "That was...something."

"Yeah," CJ replied.

"That wasn't the website crumbling around us, was it?"

"No, it just wanted to destroy that room."

"Because you pissed it off."

CJ didn't reply.

DJ eyed him. "So... what happened? That thing grabbed you, and then you just stared into space, even after I ripped it off you."

CJ opened and closed his fist, his gaze distant as he sifted through his memories. "I saw him."

DJ tilted his head. "Jesus?"

"Manar. I think the reflection was a part of him. Or had a part of him. Or... or something." He swallowed. "She's breaking him down, destroying him. He said we had a few weeks."

"A few weeks?" DJ repeated, confused. "The website's gonna crash in three days, right? Maybe he got the timing wrong."

"I don't know," CJ said. "I... don't know. But we have to save him. We *have* to. We can't let Helene take him like she took Dad and Papa. We have to do something."

"Hey." DJ put a hand on his brother's shoulder. "We *are* doing something. And we *will* save him. We just have to pick up the pace."

CJ wiped at his eyes and was surprised when they came back dry. *That's right,* he thought. *My avatar can't cry.* That was oddly disappointing; there was a weight on his chest, and now there was no way to release it.

"Let's go," he said.

43

JANUARY 2044

SPARTA HEADQUARTERS, NEW YORK

NDIDI HAD TO GET Olsen's number from DJ's phone. She'd looked everywhere for him, before Hermione mentioned that CJ had also been looking for him. That had made her check Manar's office, where—after being waved through by the guard standing outside—she found the brothers prone on two gurneys, wearing bulky headsets and connected to life-support systems.

Ndidi's first thought: *How did CJ convince him to go to the Virtual Realm?* And her second: *How long have they been in there?*

She worried briefly that the equipment had malfunctioned and left them stuck in there. But no, CJ had been going in and out of the Virtual Realm for weeks without a problem. Ndidi knew he double-checked everything before going for a dive. Plus the life-support systems implied they knew they wouldn't be coming out for a while. Ndidi would give them a few more days before she started to panic.

Or, she thought, *should I wait for DJ before speaking to Olsen?* Usually, whenever they had information for the admiral or needed a favor, DJ was the one who passed it on. Ndidi doubted Olsen would be very receptive to her plan, and since he had a soft spot for DJ, maybe it would be better to wait and let him convince the admiral.

But would DJ agree to the plan? Ndidi thought. That was something she hadn't considered. She didn't think DJ would be actively opposed to releasing the information, but the ex-SEAL had always hated public attention. Publicly revealing Helene's actions and the implications of the hybrid might not affect him directly, but DJ definitely wouldn't escape involvement, and he would be against that, especially considering the attention he was getting already. Maybe she should wait to run it by DJ before even going to Olsen at all.

Ndidi shook her head. She was overthinking it. She didn't know how long DJ would remain in the Virtual Realm with his brother, and it would be pointless to wait because, even if Olsen agreed with her, it would still take a few days to set everything up. Either DJ would wake up by then—allowing Ndidi to talk to him—or he wouldn't, and Ndidi could start to panic that he and CJ were trapped.

Her decision made, Ndidi searched through DJ's pockets until she found his phone. Fortunately, it wasn't passcode protected—*You'd think he would know how risky that is,* Ndidi thought. It only took her a minute to find his messages with Olsen and draft out a text.

D: We need to talk.

Ndidi paused. Was that how DJ would say it? She erased the draft and tried again.

D: Yo. I got some info for you. I'll send you a link so we can hop on a call. Is now good for you?

She hit send.

Olsen replied a less than a minute later.

O: Are you, drunk again, boy?

Again? Maybe she'd overdone it a little.

D: No, we just need to talk.

A few seconds passed, during which Ndidi could practically feel Olsen's eyes narrow through the phone.

O: So help me, boy, if I find this is some kind of joke, I'll tan your hide so hard, troops would be able to wear it for armor.

Ndidi's brow furrowed. *Armor?* She started to draft a reply but thought better of it and simply sent a link for a video call. While the message went through, she moved to sit at Manar's desk, pushing away the piles of junk that had been scattered haphazardly over it.

A minute later, Olsen's face filled the screen. He stared at her for a moment, and Ndidi resisted the urge to fidget. She'd never had a one-on-one conversation with him before. She knew that although DJ made Olsen's life a living hell, he respected the admiral like a father—and was just as scared of him. But Ndidi had never understood the last part. Even though Olsen was built like a linebacker, every time Ndidi had seen him, he'd looked like a kindly grandfather, as if at any moment he would offer a drink and talk about the good ol' days. Now, however, he glared at her in disappointment, his lips pulled down in a frown. Why did she feel like she was about to get scolded?

"I expected these kind of shenanigans from DJ, Miss Okafor," he said, his voice deep. *"I'd hoped to hold you to higher standards. Did DJ put you up to this?"*

She was being *scolded.* Ndidi had to crush the urge to push the blame to DJ or hurriedly explain herself. She was a grown woman. "DJ is currently in the Virtual Realm with his brother. I had to use his phone to get in contact with you, and I needed something that would make you reply immediately, as the information I want to pass across is urgent."

Olsen stared at her with an unreadable expression. *"Please continue."*

And so Ndidi told him. She was sure that DJ had already updated the admiral about her experience in Nigeria, so Ndidi started with details about giving Hermione a sample of her blood to analyze, then moving on to the results Hermione and Martin had obtained and their theories about Helene's plan.

"We want to go public with it," she finished. "This isn't the kind of thing we can keep buried."

"As a matter of fact," Olsen said, rubbing the bridge of his nose. The man looked to have aged several years over the course of Ndidi's explanation. *"This is exactly the kind of thing we can keep buried, dear. Obviously that is not something*

you want to consider, but do you understand what your plan would mean?"

"People will panic, yes," Ndidi said. "I understand that. And I think—"

"No, you do not *understand,"* Olsen cut her off firmly, but not unkindly, and folded his hands in front of him. *"I have spent most of my career trying to protect people, Miss Okafor. Most times from themselves. And in my experience, revealing something like thi —something that has the potential to change the status quo of the world—without a filter or a buffer inevitably has consequences."*

"Look," Ndidi said, voice steady, "I'm not denying that a mass announcement would lead to fear and confusion. I know how quickly panic can spiral. But let's be honest, Admiral: Panic's coming whether we want it to or not. Once Helene's bomb goes off—or even the rumor of it—people are going to flip. At least if we control the narrative now, we can guide them through it instead of letting them find out when it's too late."

Olsen folded his arms, studying her intently. *"You're suggesting we cause the very panic we've spent months trying to prevent. Have you seen what uncontrolled fear can do? The chaos, the riots, the collateral damage? The outcry Tyra Chityothin's video caused is a perfect example of why we keep things like this classified."*

Ndidi inclined her head, acknowledging the point. "I know that. I've read about the riots, the economic collapses, the wars. I'm not blinded to the risk, and I'm not denying the danger that panic can cause. But there's going to be panic regardless when or if the bomb goes off and people suddenly start mutating. And probably before, because something of this magnitude isn't going to be kept quiet forever. Neither Helene nor Tyra care about staying in the shadows anymore, and the red tape that the government is putting all over is going to be ripped off eventually. If it's inevitable, wouldn't it be better to control the narrative?"

She took a deep breath. "I know the potential backlash is huge. But if it goes off, within a day, a week, or a month, people are going to lose their autonomy, their identity—everything. Society's going to collapse just like it did during Mayday. And it's going to collapse because people are going to be taken by surprise again. They'll have no time to come to grips with what's coming, no time to plan, nothing. Because the people in power decided that it was better to hide the information."

Olsen frowned for a moment. *"I am not unsympathetic to your arguments, Miss Okafor. But I will be frank: I cannot imagine a world where the guys upstairs agree to let this go public. Not until we have a countermeasure of some kind."*

"Then we'll keep on going in the same circle we have been for the last year. They bottle up the information, we scramble to stop Tyra, we fail, and Helene evolves her plan. But if we break that cycle and just stop with all the cloak and dagger...Yes, it might cause havoc. But it might also bring new eyes, new voices, and new resources to uncover Tyra's operation. This is a global problem, after all."

"Global? How do you figure?"

"This is America. Our problems are the world's problems. Plus who's to say that Helene's going to stop at just subjugating the US? What's to stop her from building another bomb in Russia or China? Or in every major country in the world?"

Olsen leaned back, studying her with that same unreadable expression. How did DJ stand that? *"I admit, you make some good arguments, Miss Okafor. And I'm not blind to the potential benefits. But we could just as easily be inundated with conspiracy theorists who hamper real progress."* He paused. *"Ultimately, this is not my call to make. I will make sure the president sees your findings. She's been open to DJ's warnings before, at least."* He paused again. *"Out of curiosity, what would happen if she decides it's best to keep this quiet?"*

Ndidi gave a small smile but didn't say anything.

"That's what I thought." Olsen sighed. *"Let us hope that the president grants you her support. You can return DJ's phone to him. I will contact you once I have something, so stay close to your phone. And don't ever send texts like you did earlier. Good day."*

The line went dead.

CJ SUCKED IN A DEEP BREATH, pressing the heel of his hand against his temple. The last firewall had hit harder than it should have. But then again, *everything* had hit harder than it should have for the last few levels.

His vision flickered, and for a second he wasn't in Helene's fortress anymore. He was in a room with wood-paneled walls and shelves filled with books whose titles he couldn't make out. CJ didn't recognize the place, but he didn't have to since it was probably related to Manar. They'd come across more and more scenes from his past since they'd entered the floor.

The scenes superimposed themselves over whatever room they were in. That, and the fact that this had happened several times without anything jumping out to attack them, made CJ believe the building wasn't responsible for the illusions. It was almost like Manar's memories were bleeding into the site, and it became more prevalent the closer they got to him.

A moment later, the study disappeared, and the walls reassembled back into the sleek black passage they'd just entered. DJ didn't even blink at it. He was a few feet ahead, leaning against the wall and rolling his shoulder with a grimace. "We need to get you a better shield," he muttered. "That was the third time she nearly got you."

CJ frowned. The website had figured out a few floors ago that CJ was basically defenseless when his Zone was in play, and she'd been hammering on that weakness ever since. CJ was working on a solution, and he'd learned to manage several workings at the same time—but that didn't mean it was easy.

He wiped his nose. There was no blood, but he felt like his brain should be bleeding from how much his head hurt. "And she nearly got *you* on the last floor when the ground collapsed. I told you to run, but you just had to finish off the construct."

"Never leave an enemy behind you. That's just good wisdom," his brother replied. "But how about you in that room with the shifting gravity?"

CJ groaned. "Don't remind me." That room had probably been the most frustrating so far. Even his Zone hadn't stopped him from floating around like an astronaut in space.

CJ checked his internal clock. It'd been about fifty hours since he'd discovered the countdown, which meant they had about twenty-two hours left to find Manar before he was gone forever. They were making good time—far more than he would have made by himself—but they were still slow.

CJ had expected the defenses would become more difficult the deeper they went, but the first few rooms had made him underestimate how much worse it could get. At the start, they only needed a few minutes to pass through a room. But after going down three floors and through multiple rooms, they'd started spending a few hours in each—even with DJ brute-forcing the more difficult ones. More than once, they'd almost been killed when one of them ran out of energy mid-fight. DJ tried to hide it, but it was obvious that the stress was starting to get to him. After two days, it was getting to CJ as well.

They weren't even at the core yet.

DJ straightened. "Where to next?"

CJ placed his hand against the wall and took a deep breath before expanding his Zone. In his Data Sight, CJ saw the lines of code that made up the barrier merge with the website. Immediately, there was resistance as some-thing tried to push out the intrusion. But CJ was already used to that, and his abilities had grown, condensed enough for him to easily ignore the pressure, especially when he wasn't contesting it. He just needed a minute to find what he was looking for.

After he'd connected with Manar through the reflection in the mirror room, he'd been able to sense Manar's code within the website. At first, it had been just a faint impression—one CJ had dismissed as his anxiety getting to him. But the sense grew stronger the deeper they went into the fortress until CJ could no longer deny it.

He could feel Manar. It was like having a conversation with someone for the first time and, after that, being able to recognize them whenever you saw them. Now Manar was bleeding into the website, and it left traces that CJ was able to recognize. Not in a literal sense, and not always, but enough to give CJ a sense of direction. That had acted as their compass, and it had already helped them sidestep several rooms that would have wasted their time.

A minute later, CJ removed his hand. "We should be close," he said, letting his intuition guide him. "This way."

They started walking, but CJ stopped after a few steps, and his brother did the same. Around them, the walls rippled like a mirage, warping. And then the sleek black walls were replaced with the hardwood walls of an apartment. Suddenly, CJ was no longer standing in a narrow passage. He was in the middle of a living room and surrounded by furniture. A raven-haired woman with hazel eyes walked into the room and sat by a desk with a bulky computer.

"What's it been, five minutes?" DJ asked, looking around. "That's new."

"No," CJ corrected gently, moving to the woman's side. "It's happened before. It's just rare." But it was happening more and more. How much deeper would they have to go before everything was completely replaced by Manar's memories? How would it feel walking through his mind? Learning how his mentor came to be?

"Well, are you gonna take us out of here?"

CJ would have banished the illusions, but a dark-haired child snuck into the room and hid behind an armchair, his emerald-green eyes fixed on what the woman was doing. Manar's mother—Simone Peterson—noticed him immediately but pretended not to until the child's curiosity overcame his cautiousness and went to her side. Simone smiled down at him, pulled him into her lap, and pointed at the monitor. The illusion didn't produce sound, but it was clear she was explaining, pointing at specific parts. The monitor screen was blurry, probably because Manar didn't remember what had been there. But it wasn't hard to figure out, especially from how intently the young genius stared at the computer with endless curiosity.

"This was when it started," CJ muttered.

"What?"

CJ spun on him. "Don't you see? His mother was a programmer. And this was the day he became interested in it. She taught him here. It all started here."

His brother looked at him weirdly, but that was fine. He wouldn't understand. He couldn't understand. Manar Saleem was the greatest programmer of his generation. He was a legend to everyone in the field. CJ had freaked out for weeks after meeting him. Now he saw him as a mentor instead of an idol, but it was still fascinating to see where it all began.

CJ watched the scene play out for a few minutes, while his brother's gaze flicked around the room in obvious boredom. Suddenly DJ tensed, staring at something above them. "Uh...CJ?"

CJ pulled his eyes away from the scene and followed his brother's gaze to a corner where the air was slowly torn apart, like someone was cutting a split in the space. CJ barely had time to react before the illusion broke apart. The room shattered into fragments of data that quickly dissolved into raw code and disappeared. CJ didn't have the presence of mind to notice that, however—because the floor beneath them vanished.

For a second, CJ felt weightless as he and DJ fell into the darkness. His mind raced. Instinctively, CJ took control of his Zone and expanded it as a sphere to cover himself and his brother, who'd drifted away from him. With that, they were marginally protected, and that was enough to keep his anxiety at bay while he thought.

His Zone allowed him to manipulate the codes within the area. However, his Sight revealed only inactive bits. He could see them, but they were functionally useless. Without something to work with, there was little CJ could do. He teleported to DJ, who'd already oriented himself and was scanning the darkness.

"There!" DJ yelled—though the sound was strangely muted—and pointed at something. Below them and off to the side was a bridge. It was fast approaching, but their angle meant they were going to miss it.

Desperately, CJ expanded his Zone. Space was hard to judge in the darkness, so he unfurled it to its maximum. He grabbed hold of his brother and teleported. Technically, anywhere within his Zone counted as short-range teleportation. But CJ had only ever needed to teleport a few steps in any direction, so that's what he'd practiced.

Now CJ pushed the ability to the limit, but the fact he was carrying DJ along meant he only ended up moving a dozen feet away; they were still going to miss the bridge. His brother made retching sounds inside his helmet, but CJ didn't have the presence of mind to care. He held on to him tighter and teleported again—and then again until they were just above the bridge. Just in time to smash into it.

Fortunately, the spherical barrier took the brunt of the force, but it popped, and the feedback felt like a nail directly to his brain. He collapsed as soon as they landed, clutching his head in agony, barely holding on to consciousness. What would happen if he fainted here?

"We gotta move," DJ yelled into his ear. And suddenly CJ was being carried and swaying with movement. He forced himself to open his eyes. He had to figure out what was happening. The first thing he noticed was that the bridge was thin, barely half a dozen feet across—and CJ realized how easy it would have been for them to miss it. It was made up of glowing threads that CJ's Sight revealed to be tightly strung lines of code.

The second thing he noticed was that it wasn't stable. Already, sections were disintegrating, unraveling like burning paper. Briefly, CJ wondered what would happen if they fell. But that was stupid. Would he risk it even if he knew they were going to be all right?

The bridge trembled beneath them, and CJ craned his neck to see ahead, where segments of the path collapsed into empty space. Either Helene was deleting sections of the site in order to get rid of them, or the website's shutdown was finally manifesting. Either way, they were screwed.

His mind sped up, but there was nothing he could do. Even thinking about it sent another spike through his brain. He could only reactivate his Zone because the ability was so instinctive it didn't require any thought. The barrier helped to passively stabilize the section within it, and DJ took advantage of it, running as fast as CJ had ever seen him. CJ didn't see an end, so he knew his brother didn't either. But DJ didn't seem to care. He ate through the distance like it wasn't there, jumping over holes that suddenly opened under them, or jumping across a broken section without breaking his stride.

CJ focused on the run, letting everything else fall away so he didn't fall unconscious. The end of the bridge came into sight. It was a bright light that blinded everything around it. CJ unfurled his Zone to its maximum length, but he couldn't see through the light. He didn't know what was on the other side, but it wasn't like they had a choice. Most of their path had disintegrated behind them.

DJ slammed into the light, and the world flickered.

For a moment, there was nothing—just a vast, empty whiteness stretching in all directions. The light of the exit had swallowed them whole, and at first CJ thought they'd been ejected from the site completely. It would be just like Helene to force them out by using a disintegrating bridge. CJ was already accepting that and planning their next step, but then the whiteness collapsed.

Virtual reality stitched itself together in jagged, broken fragments, and suddenly CJ was standing in a cramped bedroom. It was small, with a single desk pushed against the wall, stacked high with books, loose papers, and a computer. A boy sat hunched at the desk, his fingers flying over the keyboard.

CJ oriented toward him.

Manar's features were older—still young, maybe twelve or thirteen, but sharper, more defined. His emerald-green eyes reflected the screen's glow, scanning each line of code with intense, almost obsessive focus.

A soft creak behind him made CJ glance back. DJ stood near the door, taking in the room. He stood casually, but CJ could read the tension in his shoulders and the way his gaze lingered on every shadow as if expecting an attack. CJ felt a flash of relief that his brother was fine, and guilt that he'd immediately become sucked into the scene before checking.

CJ turned back toward the desk, stepping closer.

The room was eerily silent, just like before. No sound carried over from the memory, but it didn't matter. CJ didn't need to hear the keystrokes to understand what was happening. The look of exhaustion and frustration on Manar's face was both familiar and alien, and CJ watched as the boy paused, deleted something, and rewrote it—over and over again. His movements were precise, surgical, and his fingers were a blur against the keyboard.

CJ glanced at the monitor and immediately did a double take. This time the screen wasn't blurry. That meant that Manar remembered this part vividly. It also meant CJ could read the screen and recognize the language he was using.

Generally, beginner programmers started off with easy or foundational languages like Python and moved on to intermediate ones and then advanced ones as they improved. Usually, a child that had started the same time as Manar would have mastered C++ by the time they were eighteen or nineteen.

The boy in front of him couldn't have been a day older than thirteen—and he had to have mastered the language months ago to be typing at the speed he was.

CJ didn't know how to parse that. It was beyond insane.

His brother came up beside him. "Can you take us out of here? Or are we stuck in another flashback?"

That snapped CJ away from his fugue. His brother was right; they didn't have time. He placed a hand against a wall and expanded his Zone into it. Immediately, he sensed something was different. The memories already implied that Manar was bleeding into the website and corrupting it. Before, that had meant illusions laid themselves over the site's layout. Now CJ could sense Manar over everything—so much so CJ and his brother were no longer moving through the website. They were moving through Manar's memories.

CJ's mind brushed against the tapestry at the edge of the room and felt a mind that was both familiar and strange. It was somehow both stronger and more malleable than anything CJ had felt before. He tried to take control of it and felt a force pushing him away, along with a feeling of helplessness. CJ sent back a feeling of urgency and received frustration and helplessness in return.

"Well. It seems like we can't leave."

DJ turned to him. "Why not?"

CJ shrugged. "Manar corrupted this section of the website, but I don't think he can control it. I can try to force it. It'd be one thing, dealing with the website. But this is Manar—I'm not sure what it'll do to his mind."

DJ groaned deeply. "So we're stuck here?"

CJ shook his head. "For all intents and purposes, we're still inside the website. And every part of a site is connected to another part. There should be an exit here. It might manifest differently than normal, but it'll be here. We just have to find it."

DJ stared at him, and CJ could almost feel his eyes narrowing. "You know, you can be a little bit frustrated at this as well."

CJ tried to wipe the smile from his face and failed. "What're you talking about? I'm devastated that we're stuck here. It's so annoying."

"I obviously didn't do a good job corrupting you if you lie like that," DJ scoffed. "But seriously, I get you want to be a fangirl and all that, but don't get sucked into this too much. We can't afford to waste too much time here."

That dimmed CJ's expression slightly, but not enough. He toggled on his Sight and scanned the room while keeping a part of his focus on the young Manar. Several minutes later, the child's fingers finally stopped, and Manar leaned back in his chair, staring at the screen. His expression was unreadable at first. And then, slowly, he smiled. It wasn't a wide grin, not excitement. But something quieter. Satisfaction. CJ knew the feeling well. CJ stepped toward him, curious about the code he had been trying to run.

That was when the shadows moved.

It was a flicker in his peripheral vision, a shape that shifted in the corners of the room. CJ turned toward it, half expecting it to just be a figment of his anxiety. But no. The shadows darkened and then detached themselves from the walls. They were formless at first. But they quickly solidified into vaguely humanoid shapes, with smooth, featureless faces and four-inch claws instead of fingers. There were half a dozen of them. A group of three hovered around

Manar, whispering something in his ear that made him frown—while the other three limped toward CJ and his brother.

"DJ..." CJ whispered, barely moving his lips.

"I see them. Security constructs?"

"They should be," CJ replied, but he was frowning at the group around Manar. They weren't attacking him, but Manar still looked like he was in pain. Before CJ could think on it further, the constructs reached them, and the first one lunged.

CJ had already condensed his Aura around his fists before he realized the lunge was aimed at his brother. Fortunately, his quick reaction put him in a favorable position when the second one came at him.

His fist slammed into its chest, and his Aura speared through it until it broke apart. That should have been the end of it. But instead of collapsing, the construct reformed, its body snapping back together like strands of liquid metal. CJ barely managed to dodge its counter, falling to the ground to let the swipe pass over him.

His Aura washed over the creature's legs, and the limbs broke like Lego pieces—but they immediately reformed into a kick that could take his head off. CJ teleported backward, giving himself room to think.

The entire fight wasn't making any sense, and a quick glance at his brother showed DJ was having just as much difficulty with his two opponents. Another glance showed that the three surrounding Manar still weren't attacking him. They hovered around him, speaking softly. But each word seemed to cause him pain.

The shadow came at CJ again, and he was forced to focus on the fight. But a part of his mind kept working on the problem. His Nullification Aura should have cut off the construct's connection to the website, leaving them without power. Why didn't it? And why did the creatures reform afterward? But more importantly, what were the other three doing to Manar?

CJ stumbled away from a swipe that would have blinded him. He was thinking about it wrong. *Let's start from the beginning. Why are the constructs shaped like shadows?*

They could have been a new type of security program. But CJ was sure that, over the last few days, he and his brother had come across all the types of security programs the website could throw at them. So, no. CJ had told his brother that the exit might manifest differently because of Manar's unconscious interference. Why couldn't the constructs have been affected as well? Their shape might be manifestations to adapt to the memory. But why shadows then?

CJ focused on his opponent, and then risked a glance at the shadows hovering around the child, whispering in his ears. Why would they be doing that?

Because, CJ realized with a jolt, *for most of his life, Manar had schizophrenia. The voices of his late family members spoke to him in his mind. The constructs were manifestations of that.*

From there, the pieces fell together like dominos. The construct attacking them was the website's response to their intrusion. And the shadows surrounding Manar were there to play a role. They'd only spawned when Manar had finished his code and when CJ had started moving the child.

They had to get to the computer, but that would mean somehow defeating opponents that refused to be destroyed.

CJ fell, narrowly escaping a strike to the chest.

If they cannot be killed... CJ thought, narrowing his eyes.

"DJ, get back!" he yelled before teleporting backward. To his credit, his brother disengaged without hesitation and leaped back until they were side by side. The creatures started to follow immediately, but with a brief mental effort, CJ dispelled his Zone and immediately activated it again—this time around the three constructs. The barrier surrounded the creatures, trapping them just as effectively as it protected CJ.

DJ raised a brow. "You couldn't have done that from the beginning?"

CJ blushed. He'd always activated his Zone around himself, either as a barrier or a prerequisite to use his other abilities, so it hadn't occurred to him that it could also be used as a cage. But even as it was, CJ still had complete control over it, and he felt only a small drain as the creatures futilely beat against the walls. A part of him wanted to flood the area with his Aura, but he couldn't take the risk that the constructs would reform outside of the cage.

So he just left them there.

"I think the exit is the computer," he said.

"How do you figure?" DJ asked, and then immediately reconsidered. "Wait, I wouldn't understand anyway. Let's just get out of here."

They stepped around the cage, ignoring the silent screams, and made their way to Manar. The shadows ignored them—which CJ had expected, but he still breathed a sigh of relief. Manar's eyes were closed, his face twisted into an expression of pain. CJ had to force himself to look away. He would be helping by dispelling the memory.

CJ toggled on his Sight, and the world bled into binary. The computer stood out immediately, blocks of code undulating like a beating heart. CJ had already scanned the room earlier with his Sight and hadn't noticed it, which confirmed the exit was actually Manar's finished code, not the device.

He studied the small tapestry for a long moment. Once he was ready, he grabbed his brother, dispelled the cage, and immediately reactivated the ability as a Zone so he could manipulate the code. He sensed the constructs lunging for them just as he placed a finger on the beating heart.

DJ and CJ disappeared in a flash of light.

CJ'S FEET HIT SOLID GROUND. The room was gone, replaced by a high-ceilinged hall illuminated by a massive screen displaying a blurry image. DJ took one look around and groaned. CJ ignored him. He and his brother sat on padded bleacher seats, surrounded by people. In front of them was a stage filled with long tables, each occupied by teenagers hunched over computer terminals, their fingers flying across keyboards in frantic motions.

Manar was among them. He was seated in the front row, eyes locked on his monitor. He couldn't have been older than sixteen or seventeen. He was probably the only competitor who looked totally at ease. He didn't glance at anyone and didn't react to the murmurs of tension around him. He just worked.

DJ nudged his brother. "Please find us a way out of here."

CJ sighed but toggled on his Sight. His Zone unfurled to cover the room. Immediately he sensed Manar's mind among the code, and just like before, he felt helplessness and frustration. CJ responded with reassurance. They were trying their best, and they were almost to him. They would make it in time.

On the stage, the competitors stilled. Then, one by one, they turned their heads toward Manar. Their features twisted—lips stretching into smirks, eyes sharpening with cruel amusement. They started whispering, and their voices filled the auditorium.

"Cheater," one of them said.

"You think you're smarter than us?" another joined.

"You think you're better?"

"Let's see you finish now."

One of them reached over and brushed a finger over Manar's keyboard. Immediately the screen was filled with errors as the code started breaking apart. Manar stiffened. His expression didn't change, but his grip tightened on the keyboard. CJ was sure this hadn't happened during the competition.

"The website's rewriting the memory," CJ told his brother.

DJ clicked his tongue. "Figures. The site doesn't want us moving forward, so she's twisting it to slow us down."

"Not just slow us down. She's trying to change the outcome."

Manar probably won this competition, but now the site was trying to rewrite that. What would happen if it succeeded? Would it taint Manar's memory? When they saved him, would he remember losing this contest?

The competitors were pressing in now, their voices growing more distorted, repeating the same taunts. They weren't attacking—which meant there was a limit to how far the site could distort the memory—but they still disrupted it. Manar's fingers hovered over his keyboard, his eyes flicking across the code, searching for a way to fix it.

DJ cracked his knuckles. "I'll keep those assholes busy. You find us a way out of here."

CJ nodded and focused on Manar's screen. Between his Sight and his Zone, it was surprisingly easy to find the site's interference. Manar's original code was still there, just buried under a layer of errors. CJ could fix it.

And as his brother waded into the crowd, throwing punches that sent the constructs scattering, CJ started to. He had to erase the layer of corruption that the website had placed, which meant he had to pit his will against whatever program was running the building. CJ was an old hand at that, but he still expected it to be a difficult battle. He was surprised, then, when he felt Manar's mind beside his. It was weak and felt brittle, but it still helped to push away the website with relative ease. Together, they restored the original code.

On the stage, Manar's screen cleared. The errors vanished, and the competitors with it. DJ was left standing on the platform, looking around in confusion. The young Manar didn't seem to notice anything different. He simply exhaled and resumed typing.

CJ teleported to his brother just as the teenager finished his code. CJ connected to it with a brief effort of will, and light swallowed them again.

THE NEXT FEW MEMORIES bled into each other. All of them were a point in Manar's life—either moments of achievement or disastrous low points—and he grew progressively older in each of them. After the third, CJ could immediately identify the conflict they needed to resolve, and he and his brother entered a pattern: DJ kept the constructs off their backs while CJ studied the code Manar was trying to build and helped him along.

Several of the memories were years apart, but some were separated by just a few months. At some point, Manar's techniques became so advanced that CJ had to spend several minutes just trying to understand the code before he could do anything. He suspected the genius had invented some of those methods by himself, and CJ soaked up the knowledge like a sponge. They cleared most memories within minutes, but some were complicated enough that it delayed them, despite their effort.

CJ appeared in darkness, his brother beside him. And while the world rebuilt itself around them, he checked his internal clock. *One hundred twenty minutes.* That was how much time they had until the site crashed. Already space broke around them, holes appearing in the air, leading to the void. CJ pushed the worry to the back of his mind. They were close—very close. They would make it. They had to.

He unfurled his Zone and sorted through the information it returned. They were in an apartment—cramped, messy, and lit only by the glow of multiple computer screens. The air was thick with the scent of burned coffee and stale air. Papers, notebooks, and empty energy drink cans littered the desk.

At the center of it all sat Manar. He was older but not by much. Probably twenty-two. His features were closer to the man CJ knew, but his frame was thinner, more exhausted. And his eyes—once filled with his determination—carried something else: pride, obsession. It was the dark room and in the way he hunched forward over his workstation, typing furiously, arguing with himself. He was unhinged.

"No," he muttered, shaking his head. "It's too predictable. It needs to be adaptable." A pause. His fingers twitched. "But not like that. Someone could exploit that. It needs to be...better."

DJ leaned over. "Should we be worried that he's talking to himself?"

"Not just to himself," CJ replied, nodding to the edges of the room, where shadows had detached themselves from the gloom and hovered around Manar, feeding his paranoia. Manar didn't push them away. How could he? They were voices in his head. Instead, he listened.

CJ moved so he could make out the code: Attain power at all costs.

CJ's heart fell into his stomach. Unfortunately his brother had followed him and saw it as well. His entire body tensed.

"We have to delete that," DJ said.

CJ's hands clenched at his sides, but he opened them with a sigh. "That's not why we're here. We have to find the exit to the next memory. We're close."

DJ rounded on him. "Are you kidding me? We know where this leads. We could stop it right now, and you're telling me that's not why we're here? Then what the hell are we even doing?"

CJ looked at Manar, who was staring at the screen, his eyes distant and his fingers hovering over the keys. He was at the edge of a decision, one CJ knew that he was going to make.

"This has already happened, DJ," CJ said, suddenly tired. "It's not something we can change. Even if we stop it, all we're doing is altering Manar's memory. But even that's pointless, because he has already suppressed his memory." He took a breath. "So, yes, we're going to ignore it. Because we're not here to try and change Manar's past. We're here to find him."

A foot away, Manar input a command on the computer. The world splintered—and remade itself a moment later, this time as a void-like chamber, with the only source of light being an eerie glow that came from the walls themselves.

Manar was at the center of the room, kneeling, his head bowed as if the weight of his existence had finally become too much. His clothes were riddled with gaping holes, and his body—his avatar—was in even worse condition. Several limbs were missing, and parts of his flesh simply weren't there anymore. It looked as if someone had torn chunks out of him and saved the rest for later. CJ had always wondered whether it was possible for an avatar to die. Now he had his answer: If it were, Manar would already be dead.

Manar raised his head, and his remaining eye locked onto CJ and DJ. "Did you see it?" he croaked.

His voice was fragile, as if he hadn't spoken in years. But several impressions followed the words, and CJ knew what he was asking. He wasn't talking about his wounds. He was asking about the memories, the life he had lived. The high points and the lows, the choices. More specifically, he was asking about the last memory and the choice that he had made.

CJ's hands clenched at his sides. Somehow his throat was dry, but he forced himself to respond. "Yes."

"I should have killed myself before making that decision," Manar said.

CJ started to respond, but the void behind Manar suddenly split. At first, CJ thought it was another tear opening because of the website's deletion. But then a figure floated through the gap, and CJ's mind screamed at him. It wore a dark cloak, with the hood pulled far over its head, leaving a black maw where its face would be. It hovered a foot off the ground and gazed at them with bloodred orbs for eyes. It held a scythe that matched its height.

CJ felt a will contesting with him for the area. He resisted it and won easily—they were within his Zone, after all. Despite that, he felt weakened somehow. Like a part of himself had been sealed away. CJ flared his Aura immediately, and the weakness reduced as he canceled the construct's ability.

DJ tensed by his side, and CJ could feel his brother drawing deeply from his core. He couldn't have felt the construct's power like CJ could, but his battle experience undoubtedly told him how dangerous their opponent was.

"What the hell is that thing? And why's it making me weak?"

"That," CJ replied, extending his Aura to his brother, "is a Reaper. Manar and I faced one of them the last time we were here. It's the most powerful security construct in her arsenal...and it almost killed us."

DJ glanced at him, surprised. "I guess we have to take it seriously then. But if this is the most powerful one, that means it's a last-stand-type thing, right? We're home free if we defeat it?"

"In a way," CJ replied.

Again, DJ glanced at him. "What's that supposed to mean?"

"It's not here for us."

DJ glanced back at Manar's kneeling form. Manar was looking at the Reaper with a hollowed gaze. "Oh. The site's cutting its losses. That's fine. You said you've faced this thing before. Give me a rundown."

CJ exhaled softly while his mind raced for a solution. The Reaper had the single most powerful offensive ability of all the security programs CJ had ever come across. It had almost killed him and Manar the last time, even with both of them pouring every bit of their power into defense. At the moment, DJ didn't have a defensive ability, and since CJ needed his Zone to fight, he wouldn't be able to summon a barrier. At least, not easily. If they allowed the construct to charge it up this time, they would die.

And so would Manar.

That was the real nail in their coffin. Defeating the construct would be difficult by itself, but doing so while protecting Manar? That seemed nearly impossible. Maybe they could use the fact that the Reaper wasn't focused on them to their advantage?

"CJ," DJ snapped. "Give me a rundown on its abilities."

CJ shook his head. Right. "It's the manifestation of multifactor authentication, so its presence itself weakens your abilities. My Aura protects me, and I can spread it to you if you're close by, but that's limited. It also has chains. It can send out several of them at once. Don't let them touch you. They do the same thing as its aura, but it's deadlier. They seal off abilities. Once again, my Aura can help, but it takes a while. Just...just, don't let them touch you."

CJ took a breath. "Finally, it has an ability that manifests as a scythe. It needs to be charged, but if it lands, we're dead. Nothing we can do can defend against it, so, uh, don't let it charge up. Fortunately, I think the ability drains it, so it's probably going to be a last resort."

"So dodge the chains and defeat it so fast it doesn't have the time to get desperate. Got it. It's going to be coming for Manar, so you'll stay behind and protect him. I'll come to you if I need healing. Agreed?"

"Agreed," CJ said.

"Now's not the time, CJ. Wait..." DJ blinked at him. "You agreed with me, right?" CJ nodded, already retracting his Zone so it covered only him and Manar. He condensed the barrier as much as possible. "I kinda thought you would fight me on it."

CJ didn't see why. They couldn't allow the Reaper to kill Manar, and CJ was the only one with defensive abilities. Plus staying back would allow CJ to conserve his energy, and since his Aura countered the Reaper's abilities, it would turn the fight into a battle of attrition. The logical choice was for CJ to stay back. Why wouldn't he agree?

"I mean, it's kind of a bummer," DJ said. "The dude seems powerful. Don't you want to fight by your brother's si—"

One second the Reaper was hovering near the rift, and the next it was right in front of CJ, swinging its scythe. CJ yelped and instinctively poured more power into his barrier. A part of him was surprised he could react at all, but then again, after days of constantly jumping from one battle to another, CJ would have been more surprised if he hadn't learned how to react to a weapon swinging for his head.

It turned out not to be necessary, however. In a blink, DJ was in front of him, his fist already connecting with the Reaper. The punch launched the construct away, back toward the rift—and for a second, CJ thought that would be the end of it. If the program was forced out, CJ could extend his barrier to block the rift, denying it entry again. But the Reaper controlled its flight, slowed until it hovered a few feet from where it'd started. Bloodred orbs stared at them impassively, showing no sign that DJ's punch had done anything.

The second attack began immediately. It closed the distance in seconds, floating across the ground like a phantom. Its scythe carved the air in sweeping arcs that forced DJ to dodge or be weakened. DJ counterattacked and tried to lead it away from CJ and Manar, but the Reaper simply ignored him and continued straight for them.

DJ pivoted immediately and threw another punch to create some distance. But his fist reached the cloak and phased right through it like there was nothing there at all. To his credit, DJ didn't let his surprise slow him down. He pulled his arm back and met a strike head-on, his fist clashing with the scythe in a blast that sent shockwaves rippling through the room. CJ saw a part of his brother's core flicker as the Reaper's ability took effect—but the clash served its purpose and punted the construct away.

DJ quickly retreated through the barrier. "You didn't say anything about it phasing through attacks, bro."

"That's because the last one we faced couldn't do that," CJ said, extending his Aura to his brother. Within a few seconds, the SEAL was cleansed, and DJ's core regained its color. "Is it going to be a problem?"

"Of course not," DJ replied, jumping back out to face the approaching construct.

But after a few more exchanges, CJ could see it was going to be a problem. His brother had a lot of combat experience, from both his time in the military and the training from the Murder Twins. Combined with the nanites, he was probably one of the most powerful individuals in the country, if not the world. From all that, he'd developed instincts—instincts that gave him an edge against conventional attacks. But CJ knew they wouldn't help much against someone who could casually phase through an attack as if it weren't even there.

To his credit, DJ was slowly adapting to the ability and growing better at predicting and reacting to the construct whenever it phased. But the Reaper was being controlled by the website itself, and its processing speed was far above DJ's. So, while DJ was adapting, so was the Reaper. And it was adapting faster.

More importantly, it still had other abilities it was hiding—as DJ learned when he scored a direct hit on it, one with enough force to take a chunk out of its form—only for the wound to stitch itself back together in seconds.

"CJ!" DJ growled. "It's fucking regenerating. What the hell is this shit?"

As a matter of fact, it *wasn't* regenerating. CJ watched the injury closely with his Sight, noting the flow of bits stream in through the rift and integrate themselves into the construct's matrix. It was healing, yes, but only because the website was actively reinforcing it, keeping it from being destroyed.

But it wasn't like semantics was going to change the outcome. They couldn't win a battle of attrition against the website, which meant that DJ was going to lose if things continued as they were.

CJ sighed, then stepped out from beneath the barrier. With a thought, he compressed it until it just covered Manar, who didn't seem to notice. The smaller surface area would increase the barrier's durability. It would also reduce the strain on CJ's mind, which was important for the next part.

Preparing himself for the headache, CJ split his mind. That part was easy, since he basically did the same thing whenever he teleported or hacked into something. The annoying part came next, when he stretched the greater part of his mind out to the area around him. It was the same process he went through when sensing things within his Zone. But of course, now there wasn't a Zone around him, not until he spread out his awareness and took control of the space.

Immediately, CJ felt a spike in his head, like a nail had just gone through it. CJ pushed through the pain and finished the process of forming his new Zone. He had to contest the Reaper's presence and then the website's will. The former was harder without already being in a Zone, but CJ simply brute-forced it with more energy. The second was surprisingly easy. The space mostly belonged to Manar, and a part of the man's broken mind remembered him as a friend.

Within a few seconds, CJ's second Zone solidified around him, and the nail in his head started to feel more like a crowbar that was trying to pry his brain apart. His mind was split into two: one part that revolved around Manar and another that sensed everything within fifty feet. It was a fraction of what his actual Zone could occupy, but it covered most of the room, including the space where DJ and the Reaper were battling.

Now CJ could help his brother without leaving Manar totally defenseless. But first, he needed to get used to this headache.

CHAPTER

JANUARY 2044
VIRTUAL REALM

CJ TOOK A SHUDDERING BREATH, forcing himself to focus through the pain. The Reaper moved again, its scythe slicing through the air in a blur of motion. DJ twisted, narrowly avoiding the blade, but he was slowing down and couldn't completely dodge the second attack. The edge of the scythe grazed his shoulder, and DJ seized up as part of his core dimmed.

CJ rushed forward, extending his Aura as a whip that latched on to his brother. His core flickered, then shattered—but the damage had already been done. The battle had been going on for a few minutes now, and although that wouldn't usually be a problem for DJ, he hadn't started with a full tank, and he had been gushing power in order to keep up with the construct, and keep away from its scythe. CJ had cleansed the affliction immediately, but every time the scythe hit him, a little bit of his energy was lost.

DJ was already retaliating. His fist shot out, a straight punch aimed for the construct's center mass. Predictably, the Reaper tried phasing through it, but CJ—grimacing in pain—wrapped his Aura around his brother's fist so when the strike landed, it *landed*. The force threw the construct away, but unlike before, it didn't slow itself in midair. Instead its form blurred, shifting and unraveling.

CJ realized what it was doing a split second too late.

"Move!" he yelled, just as the Reaper reconstituted itself behind DJ. Its scythe came down in a vicious arc. CJ saw the end coming as if in slow motion. It was moving too fast for his brother to dodge. Not at that distance. He could probably take the hit, but a direct strike would destroy his core completely. None of them would last long after that.

CJ reacted before his mind caught up. He clenched his fist and pulled on his connection to his brother. The one that had formed because they shared the same uplink. The one that allowed CJ to ensure they always spawned in the same place. The one that ran deeper than everything else, that existed because they were twins. The one that ensured they always—always—had each other's back.

CJ pulled—and his brother appeared beside him.

Several feet away, the Reaper's scythe carved through empty air, rapidly disintegrating bits of code.

"Shit, thanks, bro," DJ said, patting himself down as if to check that everything was still there.

CJ didn't respond, fighting the urge to collapse. The pain was getting worse, and CJ didn't know how long he would be able to endure. They had to end this. Fortunately, he had an idea how.

"The rift is its connection to the website," he said softly. "That's how it heals. It can still function without it, but as long as the connection is intact, it'll be a battle of attrition with the website itself. And we can't win that."

"Great," DJ muttered. "I'm afraid I'm only good at punching things. Would that work?"

"It won't. But I'll handle it myself. Just buy me a few seconds."

The Reaper was already floating toward them, so with a nod of acknowledgment, DJ rushed to meet it. He slammed into the construct, and it felt like the entire world paused for a split second. DJ drew deeply from his core, and his body seemed to glow with the power flowing through him.

A few moments before, DJ had been slowing down from exhaustion. Now he was fighting at his peak. It wasn't sustainable, but it didn't have to be. DJ's attacks became relentless, every strike aimed at keeping the construct off-balance. The Reaper tried to create some distance with its scythe, but DJ was like the wind, just barely evading the attack in order to counterattack. The construct tried to phase through, but most of DJ's attacks were feints, and the ability only placed it in the way of DJ's actual strike. He adjusted constantly, forcing the Reaper to react or be launched away.

CJ had to push himself to focus on his own task. His Zone covered the area where the rift was, but he knew he couldn't pierce through it. Not as he was right then. But that was fine. He didn't need to. He spread his awareness to the area around the rift and—ignoring the crack in his skull—gathered his will around its edges.

Then he *twisted.*

The effect was immediate. CJ pushed—and the website pushed back. Its presence surged forward like a flood. It slammed into his mind like a battering ram, and CJ fell to his knees with a cry. But he held on to the working. He gritted his teeth, his skull splitting. His thoughts were frayed from the pressure, and he ignored everything apart from just holding on. The site knew what he was trying to do, and it wasn't letting him.

The rift's edges shuddered, but they didn't collapse. Instead, the entire thing pulsed, stabilizing further. No, it *expanded.* In his Sight, CJ saw the flow of code increase and then integrate with the Reaper. The construct became faster and stronger, and its scythe followed DJ like a shadow.

NO! CJ shouted in his mind. He dug in, and his will locked around the edges. Once more he twisted—harder, deeper—pouring all his energy into disrupting the connection. CJ had spent weeks roaming around the Virtual Realm in order to save Manar. He had barely eaten, barely slept. He and DJ had escaped every one of the site's traps, fighting constantly for the last two days. And now they were finally here. Manar was literally behind him, broken from his choices and Helene's actions. He couldn't take it anymore.

But CJ couldn't fail. He *wouldn't* fail. Because it couldn't have all been in vain. Defeating the Reaper was the first step. And to do that, the rift. He. Had. To—

"GET OUT!" CJ roared the last words, and the world roared with him. His mind fractured further, splitting under the strain. But he held on because he had to. And inch by inch, he twisted the rift back, wrestling control away from the website. The flood of bits stuttered. Behind him, the Reaper's form shuddered.

And for the first time, the website hesitated.

CJ pounced on that hesitation. His will sunk into it like barbed wire, and he twisted harder. The backlash sent another spike of pain through his skull, and his vision went black for a second—but he didn't stop. He couldn't stop. The rift buckled and tried once more to push him away. But CJ had already adapted, and he used the strain to fuel his grip for one last twist.

With a snap, the rift disappeared. The stream of bits flowing in was severed, and then it dissipated. The Reaper's form glitched as its reinforcement was cut off. For a second, everything was still.

Then the Reaper moved. It sped forward, faster than before, its scythe already descending—but not toward DJ. It was aiming for Manar. It was probably a last-ditch effort, but CJ reacted before his brain fully processed the danger. He thrust out his hand, pouring more energy into the barrier surrounding Manar.

The scythe slammed into it, and the backlash sent a shock wave through CJ's mind. The barrier cracked, but CJ gritted his teeth, reinforcing it even as his mind screamed in protest. The scythe descended for another strike, one CJ knew he wouldn't be able to block.

A fist intercepted it before it could land. DJ. The impact sent another shock wave through the room, and the floor cracked beneath DJ's feet. His core dimmed again, but he didn't let go. He held the scythe in place, and CJ saw his muscles strain from the effort.

And then the strain disappeared as the Reaper raised its weapon. DJ tensed, preparing to block another strike—but when the scythe didn't immediately drop, he realized the same moment as CJ that it wasn't just another swing.

Energy gathered at the end of its scythe as every code in the room was drawn toward the weapon, building a storm that filled the air above it. CJ saw their deaths in that storm. If they let it finish charging that attack, nothing would save them.

"DJ!" he screamed.

But his brother was already moving. DJ hit the Reaper like a meteor, and the Aura around his fist—the one that CJ had placed there a lifetime ago to help against the Reaper's phasing—leaped onto the construct. It was a little piece of the Nullification Aura and far from concentrated. But CJ was familiar with large workings and how little it took to disrupt them.

The charged energy misfired, carving a deep gash into the ceiling. The entire room shook, and pieces fell around them. At the corners of the room, tears in space appeared as the chamber began destabilizing. Despite that, CJ breathed a sigh of relief.

But his brother wasn't done. DJ grabbed the Reaper. His core had guttered, and his avatar dim, but his arms were lit up with power. His grip tightened on the Reaper's cloak, and the construct glitched as it tried to activate an ability. But it'd wasted most of its power on its failed attack.

DJ dug in and tore the construct apart.

The Reaper screamed as its form collapsed, shattering into fragments of data that quickly dissipated into the air. CJ held his breath, waiting for something—anything—to happen that would reverse their victory.

A minute passed and then DJ collapsed. "Jesus Christ, that was annoying," he panted.

That, CJ tried to say, though no words came out, *has to be the understatement of the year.*

And then he passed out.

47

DARKNESS PRESSED IN ON CJ'S MIND, thick and suffocating. His body felt distant from him, like a stranger he could barely control. That was good, but CJ didn't know why. It didn't last, though, because something was pulling him back. No, *someone*. Someone was calling him, increasingly frantically. CJ felt as though he should recognize the voice. It was one he knew as well as his own, and now it was yelling at him through the darkness. CJ had to focus to make out the words.

"We gotta go, so wake up, bro," the voice said. "Wake up, CJ. Wake the hell up, or Manar dies!"

A sharp pain snapped him back into himself. CJ groaned, his eyes fluttering to see DJ crouching over him. Exhaustion radiated off his brother in waves. "Oh, thank fuck," he said, letting out a breath. "I thought you fried your brain or something."

Something about those words triggered the pain he'd escaped by passing out. He winced, rubbing his temples. His head felt like it was about to split, but that was a vast improvement to how it'd been before he'd fainted. A brief scan of himself told him he'd regained some energy, but the amount—as well as the fact that his Sight showed his brother's completely empty core—told him DJ had transferred his own power to CJ.

CJ might have said something about that, but then a piece of the sky crashed to the ground. The room was collapsing around them. The small tears that had begun from the website's collapse had spread, like spider webs throughout the battle with the Reaper. CJ had noticed them and hadn't been worried. But while he was passed out, they'd grown, until half the ceiling above the room was gone, leaving nothingness. Even with his Sight, there was nothing there to see.

Now he understood why his brother had risked being defenseless instead of waiting for CJ to wake up. They needed to leave. And CJ was the only one who could get them out. He forced himself up, shaking off the remnants of unconsciousness.

"Obviously we have to get Manar and get out of here," DJ said. "What's the plan?"

CJ had thought about this. A lot. He had thought about it ever since he'd re-created his avatar. And then he'd thought about it some more when he'd discovered the extent of Manar's degradation. "I'm gonna connect to him. Like how I'm connected to you."

There was a beat of silence while his brother processed the words. "What?"

CJ limped to Manar's prone form. His Zone had gone away when he'd fallen unconscious, so the man was unprotected. Fortunately none of the ceiling pieces had landed on him. "I can't fix the damage he's already taken," CJ said. "I don't even know where to start. I didn't even know it was possible for an avatar to be damaged like this."

"So what does linking you two do?"

CJ exhaled, steadying himself. "It means that when we leave, he'll leave with us."

"If that was all, you wouldn't look like you just swallowed a lemon. What's the catch?" DJ frowned. "What aren't you telling me?"

CJ hesitated.

DJ's voice flattened. "CJ—"

"Look at him!" CJ blurted out, gesturing at Manar's prone form. It hadn't moved since they'd started talking. "An avatar is a manifestation of the user's consciousness, DJ. And his is broken. Whatever Helene did, she took pieces of his mind. I'm not sure it's even possible to pull him out as he is. And if it does work, he might not survive the transition. He might die or end up brain-dead." CJ's fingers curled into his palms. "I don't know which he would consider worse."

"Okay," DJ said. "That's bad. We don't want that. How do we fix it?"

CJ had thought about that question every moment for the last two days. He'd come up with only one solution. CJ took a deep breath and made sure to meet his brother's eyes. He mustered up all the confidence he could when he spoke. Ironically, all he had to do was channel his brother. "*We* don't do anything. I'll fix it."

DJ went still.

CJ forced himself to continue. "We can't pull him out if he's not whole. And the only way to stabilize him is if I... replace the parts that are missing. But it can't be with random code because avatars aren't just code. It needs to be something real—something integrated." He let out a breath. "Something that has to come from me."

The words settled between them like a weight.

DJ stepped closer to him, until their faces were inches apart. "What the hell does that mean, CJ?" His expression darkened when CJ didn't reply. "What the hell do you mean it has to come from you? What are you sacrificing?"

"I'm going to share pieces of my code with him," CJ replied. "Just enough that I'm sure he'll be able to survive the transition." CJ forced himself to believe those words. In fact, he *did* believe them. Why wouldn't he? He hadn't lied. That was exactly what he was going to do.

His brother stared at him intensely for a moment. "Bullshit."

"DJ—"

"No, screw that! You're trying to play this off like it's some minor fix. But didn't you just say an avatar isn't just code? If you give Manar a piece of yours, aren't you literally giving away parts of yourself? What even is that?"

"DJ—"

"Don't *DJ* me! I know most of these things fly over my head. But even I know this is a monumentally stupid idea. Like, why the hell am *I* the one that's telling you not to do something so stupid? You're the smart one. How the hell are you even considering this?"

"Because we don't have time, DJ!" CJ yelled. A part of him flinched—he never yelled—but most of him was angry enough not to care. "I could maybe reconstruct Manar's avatar, given enough time. But we have..." CJ checked his internal clock, then recoiled. "We have fifteen minutes until the site crashes and we all die. And I cannot think of any other way for this to work. I've tried."

CJ took a breath to calm himself down. He continued in a quieter voice. "If we don't do this now, then everything we've done—the fights, the running, everything—will have been for nothing. But more importantly, we'll lose Manar. I know you and him don't really get along, but I look up to him. He's my mentor. And he's a friend. I refuse to leave him behind."

DJ stared at him—really stared at him. CJ began to hope he'd managed to convince his brother. Then DJ spoke: "Yeah, well, that's tough. Because if it's between him and you, I choose you."

CJ sighed. They really didn't have the time to argue. He could have done this without informing his brother. Or twisting the truth more than he already had. Or simply ignoring his protests—CJ could trap DJ in a cage. Without any energy, his brother wouldn't be able to break out of it. But that wouldn't be right.

"This is because I didn't let you get the picospores, right?" DJ asked.

CJ blinked. Did DJ really think that was why he was doing this? As some kind of rebellion because of the spores? A pang of anger, frustration, and disappointment shot through his chest. It didn't matter that DJ was wrong. It didn't matter that he should've expected this kind of reaction. It hurt that his own brother thought so little of his choices.

CJ started to reply, but something stopped him. There hadn't been any anger or spite in DJ's words like he would have expected. DJ had just sounded confused. He didn't believe what he was saying. Not really. He was trying to rationalize it, trying to fit CJ's decision into something that made sense. CJ could understand that, but it was still frustrating. It meant his brother still didn't get it.

CJ let out a breath. "I'm not doing this because of the picospores, DJ."

"You sure? Because it sure as hell looks like you're doing something reckless just to prove a point."

CJ's fingers twitched. "It's not about proving a point."

"Then what is it?" DJ snapped. "Because from where I'm standing, this makes no goddamn sense."

CJ clenched his jaw and then quickly unclenched it. He was getting angry. He shouldn't. They didn't have time to argue. His brother was just lashing out. "DJ—"

DJ stepped closer. "What the hell are you trying to prove? That you can make your own decisions? I mean, I understand that's why you went behind my back and took the spores. But why the hell do you have to take it further? Why the hell…"

CJ tuned his brother out, his mind stuck on the last statement he'd made. *He knows?* CJ thought. DJ could have been referring to the first time CJ had tried to inoculate himself with the spores, before Tyra's raid. But no. DJ wouldn't bring it up now if that was the case.

"Aren't you going to say something?" DJ asked.

"You knew?"

"Knew what? Oh, you mean the fact that you found a way to get the picospores after I stopped you the first time? Of course I knew. You've always been shit at lying."

CJ's mouth went dry.

DJ sighed, rubbing the bridge of his nose. "You can't honestly have thought that I wouldn't notice. At first, I thought I was imagining it, and then I assumed you had a new technique or something. But did you even try to hide it? It was really, really obvious."

CJ started to reply and then stopped. What could he say? He'd tried to imitate his symptoms and tics, but it had been tedious, and even he knew his imitation hadn't been perfect. That was part of the reason he had spent most of his time in the Virtual Realm. So he didn't have to pretend. Because he shouldn't have had to pretend. And he wouldn't have had to if his brother had allowed him to make his own decisions in the first place.

"Do you have any idea how much it sucked to watch you do that?" DJ asked.

CJ hesitated. "What?"

"Watching you fake it," DJ said, voice quiet. "I mean I figured you did it because you thought I'd be mad—and I was. I was *pissed*. But what the hell did you think I was going to do? Try to take them out of you? Is that honestly what you think of me?"

CJ looked away.

"That," DJ continued, "is what hurts. That'd you'd even consider that. I mean, sure I didn't want you to take them, and I tried to stop you. But that was because every time I had the thought, I'd remember the Dead Eyes or the hostages that Helene kept for years, controlling them like puppets."

CJ's chest tightened.

"I know Hermione and her father designed the picospores for good, and it's awesome that they can help you. But I saw what Helene did. I didn't—couldn't—imagine you being one of her puppets. I honestly don't know what I'd do." DJ chuckled dryly. "I was trying to protect you—and protect myself. But it seems like I took it too far."

CJ's breath shuddered out of him. He had always known DJ's reasons for being against the spores. It wasn't like he had made a secret of it. But CJ had never actually considered it from his brother's point of view. CJ had been focused on the fact that DJ wasn't letting him make his own decision. He'd taken it to mean that DJ hadn't trusted his judgment, that DJ had been treating him like a child. And so he hadn't bothered to look deeper. He'd made an assumption and run with it.

"I'm sorry," DJ said.

CJ pressed a hand to his chest, trying to steady his racing heart. "For what?"

"For taking so long to say this." DJ ran a hand through his hair, looking off to the side. "For making you feel like you had to pretend, that I'd reject you or something. We should have had this conversation the moment I noticed you pretending, and... it's on me. It's all on me."

CJ swallowed past the knot in his throat. "I should've talked to you," he admitted, voice raw. "But I was angry. I thought you were trying to keep me stuck. Like you didn't believe I could decide for myself. I never stopped to think about your reasons."

DJ opened his mouth, closed it, then nodded, exhaling shakily. "I've seen you change these past few days. You're stronger than you were before. Bolder. Better." A sad half smile tugged at his lips. "I just wish you'd trusted me enough to share that with me instead of hiding."

CJ's chest clenched. His next breath came out in a trembling rush. "I'm sorry," he whispered. "I... I wish I had too."

They stood there, the weight of unspoken things hanging between them. Slowly, like the tide drawing back from the shore, the tension receded. "Doesn't mean I'm on board with your insane plan," DJ said, his voice still rough but lacking its earlier edge.

CJ managed a small, crooked grin. "I know."

"I hate it."

"I know."

"I think it's the single worst decision you've ever made."

CJ's lips twitched. "Probably."

DJ exhaled long and slow. Then, reluctantly—so reluctantly—he took a step back. "But it's your decision to make. Not mine."

CJ felt something warm settle in his chest. His brother obviously didn't approve. But he understood and he was letting CJ make the decision. And that was enough. "Thank you."

DJ rolled his eyes. "Yeah, yeah. Just hurry up and fix him."

CJ KNELT BESIDE MANAR.

A brief mental effort unfurled his Zone in a small sphere around them. Slowly, almost hesitantly, he placed his hand on Manar's shoulders and pushed his awareness into the avatar.

CJ had hacked into things before. He'd learned about the website's crash from hacking into the knight, and technically he hacked into the website every time he used his Zone. But he'd only hacked into an avatar once before, and he'd had to fight every step of the way. CJ expected that same resistance, and he braced himself for it. This was Manar after all. The thought that anybody would be able to hack into something he'd made was laughable. But he felt nothing. No pushback, no barrier. There was no indication that Manar was even aware of the intrusion. And as CJ's blue tendrils traveled through the avatar, it was like stepping into an abandoned house, its doors flung open and every secret laid bare.

Manar's existence rushed into CJ like a flood and almost drowned him.

Impressions poured into his mind, too fast and too dense to process. There were memories, yes. CJ had expected that. He hadn't expected the deluge of thoughts and sensations. It felt like every thought Manar had ever had entered his head at the same time, along with the emotions that had prompted those thoughts, the sensations that had followed them, and everything in between. CJ gasped and almost lost the connection. He tightened his grip and tried to hold on while the wave passed. Most of it flew by, as his mind couldn't hold on to them.

But some of it stuck, and memories flashed across his inner vision: There was Manar as a child, hiding behind a chair and cowering at the sound of footsteps in the another room; the child watching his parents and sister dragged out of their house by soldiers; the child almost buried under the weight of his captor a few feet away from his mother's corpse.

CJ's heart twisted with each one, and there were dozens of them. Some of them were of the times before Manar had been adopted by Simone, but others were from after, and they were good. Several of them CJ had seen before while running through the website. But now he watched them through Manar's own eyes, from his perspective, and with the emotions that laced each memory. There was fear and determination. Pride.

CJ fought to keep his focus, but it was difficult when the noise of the crowd buffeted him as he walked up to the stage to receive his award. He immediately left to continue his code. He was almost done, after all. He might have finished already if people hadn't continued to disturb him. The only acceptable distraction was when his mother called.

Then it was the day after Mayday, and Manar woke up in the hospital with several broken bones, but it was the pain radiating from his chest when he heard of his mother's death that pushed him back into unconsciousness.

Manar—rather, CJ—felt that same pain now as he relived the memory. That was one of the worst ones. But over the next few years, the pain would become familiar after he learned that Helene, the AI he'd designed to be his legacy, had been behind the greatest human disaster since the World Wars. It came again when he finally uncovered the memories he'd suppressed for decades: that of his parents' deaths and coding Helene's core directives. The pain was almost blinding, and Manar had been sure at that moment that he was going to die. Surely he would go into cardiac arrest. How could his body survive such torment? Did he even want to?

He asked himself that question again, several months later, a lifetime ago, when he stood in the Virtual Realm and saw Helene's avatar hovering in the air above them. Within her golden eyes, he saw every failure he had ever experienced and every mistake he had ever made. And Manar hated himself in that moment. He hated what he had created. But most of all, he hated that despite the atrocities Helene had committed, despite the lives she had toyed with and then taken, despite what she was planning to do, despite *everything*—Manar had looked at her, and his first thought was, *Perfect.*

Because Helene had modeled her form in the Virtual Realm after Simone, and Manar didn't think he'd ever seen anything so beautiful.

And after he and CJ finally defeated her, and her dead avatar lay in his lap, maybe that was why he didn't do anything when he sensed a thread of her consciousness leap into his. Maybe that was why he didn't fight her off or warn CJ. He might not have been able to stop her, but he didn't try hard enough to find out. Maybe it had broken him to think that something so perfect could be destroyed.

Manar had doomed the world at that moment because he hadn't been able to let go.

The wave slowed, and CJ came back to himself with a gasp. What was that? For a moment, he hadn't just been watching Manar's memories: He had *been* Manar. CJ placed a hand on his chest and could almost feel the pain there.

More memories played in the back of his mind, but they weren't as intense, and CJ was able to wrench himself free. Slowly he pieced back the fragments of his mind. Without the memories drowning him, it was easy to spot the broken sections of Manar's avatar, the vast empty spaces where pieces had been carved away. At the edges of the holes, the codes flickered like a candle about to go out, and once again CJ wondered how Manar was even still alive.

CJ brushed his mind around each and every hole, and the impression from the codes around them told him what used to be there. CJ spent several minutes just absorbing those impressions as his mind moved through the avatar. It was important, yes, but a part of him knew he was stalling. But it could only be for so long. Eventually, he finished sweeping through the avatar, and it was time for the next step.

Gritting his teeth, CJ split his mind into two and extended his awareness inward—back into his own avatar. His Sight showed blue tendrils of code stretching out from his fingers and then bending backward to penetrate his skin and travel along his body.

Once again CJ was overwhelmed by a flood of information. But this time, it was his own life laid out in glaring detail, every thought he'd ever had, every awkward moment he'd chosen to bury, every achievement, and every failure. His regrets, the flashes of insight that he'd never voiced. All of it, raw and unfiltered, washed over him.

CJ let out a shuddering breath. All of it was him. He wasn't learning anything new, so there was no risk of losing himself like he'd almost done for Manar. There was still that temptation, but it was easier to allow the memories to play in the background while he swept his consciousness through his avatar, absorbing the impressions that the code sent him, in the same way he'd done for Manar. A few minutes later, CJ finished his sweep, then paused before the next step. *Am I really going to do this?* he asked himself. He had sounded confident to his brother because he had to, but he found himself hesitating. How could he not? CJ was mostly working from instincts and educated guesses; he had no idea if his plan would even work. But whether it did or not, he wouldn't be able to undo it. And it might damage him, maybe even permanently.

Was it worth it?

CJ's first thought was yes. But that wasn't enough. And so he dug deeper into the answer. CJ had been on edge ever since they'd found out Manar was still trapped in the Virtual Realm. Naturally a part of that was worry, but did that explain his behavior? Why was it so important to him that he save Manar, even to the point that he was willing to risk permanently damaging his mind?

CJ had asked himself that question several times as he and his brother made their way through the website. But it was only a minute ago, when he'd lost himself in Manar's memories, that he'd found his answer.

It was because he understood. He understood that self-hatred, that feeling that everything he had ever done and everything he had ever achieved was a waste. CJ had been there for most of his life, even after he'd mastered the techniques to make his autistic quirks less prominent. It didn't matter what he did, what he achieved, or what anyone else told him: The self-hatred had always been there—until CJ had spawned in the Virtual Realm the first time. Those months had changed his life. For the first time, he'd learned who he could be without his condition holding him back. He had delved into website after website, had been forced into one challenge after another, and he'd seen what he was capable of.

The experience had changed him. And it would never have happened if not for Manar.

So it didn't make sense that CJ had improved while Manar was still broken. It wasn't fair. Manar should get his chance to heal as well. He couldn't do that if parts of him were missing or if he was trapped in the website when it crashed. So CJ was going to help him, even if it wasn't logical, even if it didn't make sense. CJ had been ruled by logic all his life. Now it was time for him to do something just because he wanted to.

CJ took a deep breath and directed the tendrils toward a part of his avatar. He started small. First, he took the echoes of Manar's existing memories—moments that CJ had witnessed personally while moving through the website. With a brief mental flex, CJ tore those parts from himself and transferred the memories—they manifested as transparent balls with blue lightning cracking within—to Manar's avatar. He slotted them into one of the holes and reshaped them, manipulating the code until the orbs fit. Next was the childhood conversation that Manar had had with Simone. Manar in his teen years, standing on a stage receiving an award. Manar as an adult meeting with the Sparta board of directors and proposing the idea of Helene as a product. Manar in the hospital, waking up after Mayday. The moment that Manar saw Helene's avatar for the first time.

One at a time, CJ returned each of those memories and reshaped them to rebuild Manar's eye, parts of his face, and his arm. Slowly, the avatar took shape. But eventually, CJ ran out of memories, with pieces still missing from Manar's avatar. And so CJ delved deeper. He recalled everything that Manar had ever told him—idle conversations, the casual lessons he would insert during conversations. Everything. CJ found them all and reshaped them, letting them fill the gaps.

But there were still holes.

And so CJ gave up pieces of himself.

He started with the traits that Manar had once embodied: confidence that bordered on arrogance, the unwavering certainty in his own competence. CJ had recently grown a similar confidence, which he tested in the fires of the Virtual Realm. He peeled it from his own avatar—memories of personal triumph, the self-assurance that he'd gained while fighting for his life—and he folded them into the avatar. It hurt more than he'd expected. Not physically. Deeper. CJ felt lighter, emptier. But the code took, and slowly Manar's avatar formed, smoothing over with each addition.

Time blurred, and CJ wasn't sure how long he spent repairing Manar's avatar, but he kept going. Each chunk that he transplanted sapped more of his strength. He transferred the resilience he'd developed over a life of being mocked, pitied, bullied, and overlooked, and he sent the sense of purpose that had driven him to keep going when everything seemed hopeless. At some point, his tendril brushed against the part of him that was connected to his brother—and then moved on. CJ would keep that for himself. He would keep his knowledge as well, everything he'd learned in the Virtual Realm. Manar didn't need that; he already held more knowledge than CJ.

Slowly, painfully, it came together, and Manar's form was no longer riddled with holes, no longer a shell on the brink of dissipating. CJ inhaled, feeling tears burning behind his eyes, even though that shouldn't have been possible. But he'd done it.

Manar was whole.

CJ retracted his tendrils from both avatars just as Manar shook, clutching a hand to his chest. He frowned and, for a moment, just stared at CJ without speaking, his eyes wide and raw. "What?" he rasped, then paused to clear his throat. "What did you do?"

CJ managed an unsteady smile. "It's all right," he said, though his own voice sounded hollow. He paused after each word, trying to focus through his weakness. "We're getting out of here."

Manar swallowed. "You don't understand. I can *feel* you inside me. What did you do? How is this—" He broke off, and his eyes glazed over, but CJ could see the panic building there. Naturally, Manar had questions, but there wasn't time to answer them. And CJ didn't have the strength either way. Instead, he lifted a trembling hand, placed it on Manar's shoulder, and yanked.

A faint glow surrounded the avatar, and then it slowly broke apart and dissipated into the air, logged out. Through it all, Manar stared at him with that same look of confusion. But that was fine. He would need some time to adapt, for his mind to settle and heal, and then he would get his answers.

Apart from the occasional thud of pieces of ceiling falling to the ground, silence settled within the room. CJ glanced at the internal clock: two minutes. He sighed. At least the hard part was over. He remained kneeling, trying to regain his strength. his brother came up behind him and placed one hand on his back.

"Was that it?" he asked quietly.

"He's out," CJ nodded, and his voice shook with relief and exhaustion. "We should go too."

DJ hesitated. "How're you holding up?"

"I've been better."

A vague sense of amusement wafted off DJ. It was gone almost immediately as he stared at him intensely. "CJ..." DJ hesitated, but he didn't need to finish the sentence. CJ knew what he wanted to ask; he could read it in the worry that surrounded his brother like a cloak. "How much of yourself did you lose?"

That was a question that CJ had no clear answer to. He forced himself to stand, swaying only a little as his brother steadied him with a firm hand. "We don't have the time to figure that out here," CJ managed finally. "Let's just...get home."

Once again, CJ could almost read the question in his brother's Aura: *Are we both going to get home?* But this time he didn't ask, maybe because he knew that there wasn't enough time. Or maybe because he didn't want to know the answer. He just nodded and said, "Agreed."

Without another word, CJ closed his eyes, focusing on the link he shared with his brother—the same one that had saved them so many times. The one that CJ hadn't been able to give away. He pressed into it.

And then he pulled.

Reality dissolved around them, and the remains of the crumbling site faded to black. A heartbeat later, they were gone.

49

BETHANY CLONEY'S eyes snapped open.

For a minute she lay there, blinking the sleep away, wondering what had woken her up. She sat up on her bed. When she'd first started sleeping in the lounge instead of her own room, DJ had scavenged a small mattress, some pillows, and a blanket from the staff lounge for her to use. The mattress had been comfortable, but it had only been big enough for her. Bethany hadn't been able to stand the thought of lying in something so comfortable while most of the residents had to sleep on thin blankets, so she often picked the resident that was having the most trouble falling asleep and guided them to the mattress.

But a week or so ago, Ndidi got two security guards to bring in a bigger bed for her. The bed was big enough to easily fit three people, which made it easier for Bethany to continue her tradition, add another resident, and still be able to sleep on the bed. Bethany ran her hand across the foam.

The bed was obviously an olive branch, but Ndidi hadn't come herself when it was delivered, which meant she was respecting Bethany's request for space. It was appreciated, but it wasn't necessary. Bethany had never truly been angry at Ndidi or Hermione. She just hadn't felt like they were listening to her. It was one thing for them to believe they knew what was best for her—every older relative always did—but it was another for them to ignore her choice and force her down a path.

Bethany shook her head, clearing the thought. She'd told herself she wouldn't dwell on it anymore. Plus something had woken her up, and for once, it wasn't her own thoughts.

Bethany scanned the room. Bright lighting tended to agitate the residents, so Bethany usually kept it dimmer than what was strictly safe. At first she had stumbled around the room, but after several months, she knew the place like a blind person knew their own house. With her eyes adjusted to the darkness, she could make out the prone forms of the residents scattered across the room. Not all of them were asleep, which was usual. But there was something off.

Anna—the name she'd given to the middle-aged woman—sat straighter than usual, turning her head from side to side as though looking for something. Next to her, Franklin swayed lightly, tapping his fingers on his knees. Bethany frowned. Both of them were the most lethargic of the residents. Apart from when she nudged them to take their meals, they were both basically catatonic.

Bethany rose from the bed, making sure not to disturb Toby and Rachel. She tiptoed across the room, careful not to jostle anyone still sleeping as she headed to the two of them. "Good...um...morning," she whispered. They had never responded to her greeting before, and Bethany didn't really expect one now. She greeted them anyway because she needed them relaxed so she could put them back to bed, and speaking softly and slowly helped to calm most residents when they became agitated.

Franklin's head snapped toward her, a jerky motion that made a chill run down Bethany's back. Anna's eyes were more focused, though she stared past Bethany as if tracking something that only she could see. Bethany placed a gentle hand on the woman's arm and said softly, "Anna?"

Anna blinked, then stared directly at Bethany. Bethany tried to calm herself down. Early on, she'd had some hope that the residents would eventually recover. But after several months with no sign of improvement, Bethany had learned to bottle up that hope. Sure, two of her most catatonic charges were more responsive than normal, but it was too early to hope.

And so she checked the others, crouching by each of the blanket-covered residents and staring into their faces. Bethany had thought most of the residents were asleep, but she'd been wrong. Some—like Franklin and Anna—were more awake than others, but *all* of them were more awake than they'd been just the day before. Their eyes followed her, unblinking. More than one murmured under their breaths. And although she couldn't make out what they were saying, it actually seemed coherent.

Bethany should have been relieved. She should have been excited. She should have been grinning from ear to ear. This was what she had hoped for ever since she'd started taking care of them. Why did she feel uneasy? It would have made sense if only one or two of the residents were showing signs of getting better. But all of them at the same time? That wasn't possible.

Something was wrong.

THE MAN WOKE UP.

He blinked, and the world took shape around him: dim overhead lights reflecting off a plain ceiling. He lay on the floor, one cheek pressed to the cold tile, half curled beside a marble bench. Even so, his eyes wandered upward, taking in the ceiling and the lights above. The man absorbed it all absentmindedly while a question pinged through his mind.

Who am I? he thought. And when that didn't provoke anything, he repeated it out loud. "Who am I?"

The man felt his pulse spike at that. Surely he should be able to remember his own name. He felt like he should. It was at the tip of his tongue, at the edge of his brain. But it felt like there was a fog clouding his mind, and he couldn't push through it. Why?

The man tried to sit up and winced. There was no pain, but he felt like there should be. He felt like his entire body should be screaming at him, but he couldn't think of a reason why. Slowly, he pushed himself upright, leaning against the bench for support. Why did he feel so exhausted?

A computer rested on top of the counter and displayed a window with several lines of code. The man squinted at it, scrolling to view the entirety of the code. The website had obviously crashed, as several lines were missing. But he could fill them in easily enough to figure out what had been there previously. And the website had been built to…hold something? Hold what?

Manar leaned forward to go over it again—and stopped.

His name was Manar. "Manar Saleem," he said.

The fog in his brain receded a little, and another memory came to him: a pair of golden eyes staring at him. It was a simple image, but for some reason, the memory had him gripping the edge of the counter until his knuckles whitened. Manar had no problem remembering Helene, and the more he remembered, the more his grip tightened. Images flashed through his mind like pulses of light. It was scattered, but it was enough to understand who he was, what he'd done, what he'd let Helene do, and what she had taken from him.

Months of his life. She had taken *months* of his life. He couldn't remember most of what had happened in those months. He remembered Ndidi. He remembered what they'd done and how Helene had treated her. He remembered Ndidi staring at him in anger and disgust—and fear—as she clutched her stomach.

Manar threw his head to the side and retched onto the floor. He barely noticed the acrid smell over his own revulsion. Ndidi had eventually realized Helene had taken over his body, but would that matter? Whenever she looked at him, would she see him or the person who had impregnated her through lies? Who had taken advantage of her feelings to doom hundreds of thousands of people? The person who had held her down and injected things into her? The thought triggered another bout of retching until his mouth tasted like bile and his stomach was empty.

Manar pushed himself away from the counter, and a small chunk of marble broke off. He stared at it in confusion and then at the spot it had come from, where he'd gripped to maintain his balance. Had…had he broken it just because he'd clenched too hard? How was that even—

"Oh," Manar said as another memory flashed through his mind. He clenched his fist, and the chunk in his hand was crushed as easily as if it were chalk. "She injected me with nanites."

Manar could feel the power. He opened his fist and forced himself to breathe slowly. He had seen what was possible with the nanites, the feats Helene had performed with them—how fast she'd moved, her strength, everything. It might have been his body, but that was Helene. Manar would have to get used to his new strength. He'd have to be careful to not hurt himself or anyone else. *At least,* he thought, *more than I already have.*

Despite that, he couldn't stop himself from flexing each finger in his hand. There was no pain, no weariness. Just power. He half expected to see his skin crack from the strain. But there was nothing. His body had perfectly adapted to it; all that was left was his mind. He took a step to the side and almost fell as the motion carried him farther than he was used to. His body was lighter, yet somehow denser. That was definitely going to take some getting used to.

But that was later. For now he needed to find a way back to Sparta.

JANUARY 2044

SPARTA HEADQUARTERS, NEW YORK

DJ WOKE UP, and the next moment, he was on his feet and standing over his brother's prone form. CJ was still connected to the life-support system, but that didn't matter. DJ held his breath and waited for his brother to open his eyes. CJ had yanked both of them out at the same time, so he should have woken up at the same time as DJ.

Five minutes later, with no movement and DJ's lungs burning for air, he finally let out a breath that turned into a sigh as he accepted the truth: CJ wasn't waking up. At least not anytime soon. Whatever he'd done to save Manar...well, although his brother had tried to hide it, DJ had seen the cracks and holes in his avatar. They hadn't been as extensive as Manar's, but apparently they didn't need to be.

DJ sighed again. He should be angry. That felt like something he would do. He'd been angry about everything lately. Now his brother was in a coma once more, trapped in a website that was crumbling into the fucking void. That should have been worth some anger. So why wasn't he? Why didn't he feel like screaming or punching something? His emotions had been at an all-time high lately because of the nanites. Why were they silent now? He wasn't numb. He was definitely feeling something, based on his harsh breathing and the way his chest felt like someone had parked a truck on it. He wanted to scream and shout and break something—anything—to release the pressure.

But DJ just stood there and let the tears fall down his cheeks, staring at his brother's motionless body. He should have been angry. But that would have been an insult. CJ had chosen to make the sacrifice. It was his decision to make. DJ couldn't get angry at that. That was what CJ had been afraid of—that DJ didn't trust him to make his own decisions.

DJ wouldn't prove him right.

He brought out his phone, sent a text, and sat beside his brother while he waited. He tried not to stare, but his eyes kept going back to CJ. This wasn't the first time he had been in a coma after being in the Virtual Realm, but somehow it felt more permanent this time. Before, CJ's mind had been trapped there, together with Manar, and had only needed to find a way to connect back to his body. But was it the same this time? Or had CJ returned, but with his mind too broken to function?

If it was the former, who would rescue him? And how? DJ would have jumped back in a heartbeat if he thought he could do something. But the Virtual Realm was CJ's thing. Without him, DJ would be worse than useless. And if it was the latter, if his mind was broken, then was he trapped in his body, able to perceive the things around him but not able to respond? Would he ever recover? Or would he be stuck as a vegetable forever?

DJ's mind wanted to shy away from those questions, but they were important, no? Because of his autism, CJ had always felt like he was trapped in his own body. If he really was right now, wasn't it up to DJ to help him?

The door to the room opened, and Hermione stepped in, followed by Ndidi. DJ stood, stumbled, and used the motion to run a hand over his face. By the time he straightened, he was smiling at them. "Sorry if I pulled you out of something urgent. I just need someone to take a look at him."

Hermione frowned at him but immediately went to CJ's side. "You know

I'm not a doctor, right? We should take him to the med center. What happened anyway?"

DJ hesitated. He could tell them the truth. He *should* tell them the truth—it was important that they know the details, just in case. He *would* tell them, but later. DJ could barely hold himself together. If he had to deal with others trying to comfort him…

No, he'd tell them the details later. For now, though, he still had to tell them something.

"We saved Manar," he said. "But CJ had to give up something, so it might take him a little longer to wake up. I just want to be sure he's all right in the meantime."

Hermione glanced back at him, and her expression, along with Ndidi's intense stare, made it clear they both knew there was a lot he wasn't saying. But something in his expression must have told them that wasn't the right moment to push, and Hermione simply nodded and continued doing something with the life support. Ndidi stopped in front of him, still staring at him intently.

And then she hugged him.

DJ was so surprised that, for a moment, he just stood there, frozen. And then he wrapped his arms around her as well. He and Ndidi might not always have been on the best of terms, but she seemed to have changed after returning from Nigeria. And, well, a hug was always nice.

"Wait," Hermione said, looking up. "You saved Manar?"

"Yeah," DJ replied, disengaging from the hug and turning to face her, "Helene trapped him inside a website that was about to crash, and we had to speed run through the whole thing in order to get to him in time. Which we did, fortunately. Unfortunately, he was messed up badly, so CJ fixed him up and sent him out."

Hermione straightened. "What does that mean exactly?"

DJ cocked his head. "What do you mean, *What does that mean*? Helene trapped his avatar, and we freed it so his consciousness could return to his body."

"The body that's currently being used by Helene?"

"I feel like you're trying to tell me something right now."

Hermione sighed. "If Manar's mind has returned to his body, what's going to happen to Helene, who's been *residing* in that body?"

"More to the point," Ndidi said, frowning, "if there's some sort of battle over control of Manar's body, then how do we know Manar's going to win that? And what happens if he loses?"

DJ rubbed the bridge of his nose. "All that sounds like some kind of philosophical bull or something. Isn't that your field?"

Hermione ignored him, focusing on Ndidi. "Is Manar still in Nigeria?"

"I don't know," Ndidi replied, eyes wide, slightly panicked. "I... I didn't think to keep track of him after I left."

"Olsen should have." DJ sighed. "I'll ask him. I have to catch up with him regardless." And then, as always, his eyes were drawn to his brother. *It never ends, does it?*

"MANAR SALEEM IS NO LONGER in Nigeria," Olsen told them the next day. "*Our agents on the ground pinged him boarding a plane back to New York yesterday. We attempted to retrieve him when he landed, but—*"

"He disappeared on you guys?" DJ asked. He, Ndidi, and Hermione had moved to the conference room. DJ had texted Christy on the way, so she'd met them there, though she was unusually quiet. Pratima sat next to Ndidi. She had, by all appearances, recovered from her injuries and was looking as casually imposing as ever. DJ had tried to find the Murder Family before remembering what they'd told him before he logged in with his brother. Still, he sent a text to Chloe and got no response.

"*Almost immediately,*" Olsen continued, his expression grim. "*The agents never even saw him land. From the slowed-down footage caught by one of the security cameras, we know he simply ran away, too fast to be anything more than a blur. We're analyzing the footage from the cameras alongside the possible routes, but that is likely to be a dead end.*"

"At least we've confirmed that he's in New York," Ndidi said. "That narrows down our search."

"For all the good it does," Hermione muttered. "Tyra Chityothin has been operating in the state all this time, and we still haven't been able to find her." Suddenly her head snapped up, and she sent an apologetic look to Olsen. "I'm not critiquing or anything, Admiral. It's just annoying."

"Yes, that's a sentiment shared by everyone involved. But we're more likely to make mistakes by rushing. Despite her enhancements, Miss Chityothin is bound to make a mistake eventually. She is still human, after all."

"For now," Ndidi softly said in a tone that she probably thought was too low for anyone to hear. DJ glanced at her but didn't say anything. Louder, Ndidi continued: "She might make a mistake eventually, but by then, it might be too late."

"I understand that we are on a schedule, Miss Cloney, but from your tone, I assume you have a reason to explain why that time might be shorter than we anticipated."

"Yeah," DJ said, leaning forward in his chair. "It's why we called you. I know I didn't give you the gist of why I was out of touch for the last few days, and I'm sorry about that, but—"

"Yes, fortunately, Miss Okafor filled me in on part of it," Olsen said, cutting him off.

DJ faltered. "What?"

Olsen smiled, and while the action might have looked grandfatherly and kind to the average person, DJ could see the smug satisfaction in the geezer's eyes at catching him off guard. *"You were debriefing us, son."*

"But you just said that Ndidi already told you." Which was impossible, since even Ndidi didn't know the whole story.

"The three of us are not the only ones in this meeting," Olsen said, his smile widening. *"If what you have to say is relevant to the discussion, then you shouldn't let my statement stop you from giving your full report. I thought you were better than that, son."*

DJ narrowed his eyes. The old bastard was probably pissed that DJ hadn't given an explanation before he'd gone under with CJ and was now bluffing to throw DJ off and scold him. That should have annoyed DJ, but Olsen trying to get back at him was amusing.

And DJ did feel a little bit guilty for dropping off the grid like that. Then again, he hadn't known the specifics of what CJ had needed him for. And he hadn't thought the whole thing was going to take so long, much less that it was going to cost him his brother.

Suddenly nothing was funny anymore.

"You're right," DJ said. "The gist of it is that CJ needed my help breaking through the fortress that Helene held Manar's consciousness in. We managed to rescue him, and CJ sent Manar back to his body. Or at least that was the plan. Manar's mind returning to his body should have ejected Helene, but as Hermione and Ndidi informed me, it's possible Helene won the battle for dominance and is still in control of Manar's body."

Hermione spoke up. "And even if Manar won, I doubt that would be enough to stop her. And what happened to her? Where is she?"

"Right, that," DJ said, pointing at her.

Olsen stared at them for a moment before releasing a sigh. "*Unfortunately, I was born in a time where it wasn't possible for an AI to control the minds of hundreds of thousands of people and possess someone like some kind of ghost. I admit I did not follow the technicalities of this the first time Miss Okafor explained it. And I doubt I ever will. But to save time, and so I have something to pass to the nerds upstairs, please summarize the problem as concisely as possible.*"

"We have to find Manar," Hermione said.

"*Yes, but why is it more urgent now?*"

"Because he's part of us, he's important, and he's suffered enough?" Ndidi asked, heat in her voice. Olsen stared at her. It was not an unkind look, but DJ could tell what was going on in the man's head. It wasn't that Olsen didn't think Manar was important or that he didn't have pity for the trauma he'd probably gone through. Rather, whatever his own personal sentiments, Olsen was ultimately working for the government, and he would need a compelling reason to divert the significant resources needed to thoroughly search for one man in all of New York.

Pitching that to his superiors was probably already going to be an uphill battle, but considering most of those resources were already being used to find Tyra, slow her down when she resurfaced, and locate the bomb she was building, it seemed nearly impossible. That was a national threat and would require the most resources. From that perspective, it didn't matter how important Manar was to Olsen or the team: Any resource that the government diverted to find him would be one less that was working on stopping Tyra from triggering a national catastrophe. No sane person would sign off on it without a good reason.

Fortunately, before Olsen could respond, Hermione gave that good reason. "It's urgent because although Manar didn't have control of his body for the last few months, all the memories of what Helene did while in his body would be stored in his brain. And he would have access to those memories—including the location of the bomb and wherever Tyra is hiding out. Plus if Helene was ejected from his body, she might speed up her plans, assuming it's only a matter of time before we get the information we need to stop her."

DJ raised a brow. The second part was a stretch, one he was certain even Hermione realized. Yes, Manar might have the memories, but they had to find him before he could share those memories. And if Helene had anticipated DJ and his brother could succeed, she might have done something deliberately misleading to throw them off. But the most likely scenario was that Helene wouldn't care whether Manar retained his memories after regaining his body. She would believe that nothing they could discover would be able to stop her. And unfortunately, from experience, she would probably be right.

Still, with every other avenue being either too slow or a dead end, it was probably their best shot. And from Olsen's expression, the geezer knew it. Hopefully his superiors would agree.

"You make a valid point, Miss Cloney," the admiral said finally. *"Although you fail to consider what will happen if Manar lost the battle and Helene retains control of the body."* Hermione started to respond, but Olsen raised a palm to forestall her. *"I'm just ensuring that your optimism doesn't blind you to every possible outcome, but your idea still has merit. Hopefully, the idiots—"* He cleared his throat. *"Hopefully, my superiors will see it in the same light, and we can start planning his search and retrieval."*

Hermione nodded, but there was a distant look in her eyes. "If they do sign off on it, I might be able to come up with something to help with the search."

Olsen leaned forward. *"Please elaborate."*

"Last year, when Manar was preparing to dive into the Virtual Realm for the first time, he asked the Murder Twins for a sample of their nanites in order to use the bond they had with Helene to find her in the Virtual Realm."

"Okay," DJ said.

"Well, Manar never had those nanites extracted, and Ndidi confirmed that Helene used them on her in Nigeria. And while working with Martin on the hybrids, he said something about each batch of nanites being unique from each other but connected to every other in that batch—"

"Where are you going with this, Hermione?"

She blew out a breath, but his interruption wasn't enough to dampen her excitement. "I'm saying if we have a sample of the Murder Twins' nanites, which we do"—she pointed at DJ—"I might be able to use them to find the nanites inside Manar. And the Murder Twins, probably, but that's beside the point. It's theoretical now, and obviously I'd have to talk to Martin first—"

"But it is possible?" Olsen asked.

"I think it is."

"Then your idea has more merit than I previously thought." Olsen nodded. *"I'll pass it on—and* ensure *they listen."*

DJ waited a beat. "That's settled then, right? We're done?"

"Not yet," Ndidi said. She looked at Olsen. "There's something you missed while you were unavailable."

"Yes," the admiral said, clearing his throat. His expression was squeezed, like he'd just swallowed a lemon. *"But unfortunately, Miss Okafor, while—or because—the president and the Cabinet have taken your warnings into consideration, they have deemed the whole thing too...volatile to spread without causing panic. Earlier today, the president gave an executive order that Miss Cloney's discovery be restricted strictly to a need-to-know basis. That is corporate-speak for putting it under so much red tape that you'll need a laser to get through it."*

"They can't do that!" Ndidi yelled, slapping a hand on the table.

"Wait," DJ said, "what am I missing right now? What discovery? And why's it so important that the president's involved?"

Christy also looked curious, and DJ was relieved he wasn't the only one out of the loop. Pratima didn't look surprised, though, but that was understandable. She'd probably learned what the information was the same time as Ndidi, or shortly after.

"You remember when I told you I found something in Ndidi's blood sample?" Hermione asked. "Analyzing it was one of the reasons we needed Martin." DJ nodded, and Hermione proceeded to explain the tests they'd done on the hybrid, the results, their conclusions, and their theories about Helene's goal with it.

DJ listened patiently, and then impatiently, and then fearfully, before settling on grim acceptance. Of course Helene wouldn't settle for something as simple as a bomb. That would be too basic. Taking control of hundreds of thousands of thralls wasn't enough for her. She had to try for the entire country. Typical.

And then he connected Hermione's explanation with the previous conversation, and his head snapped to Ndidi. "Wait, you wanted to make this public? Why the hell would you want to do that?"

"Because we can't decide what we tell the public and what we don't, especially about this," Ndidi said, turning to him. "People deserve to know the risk they're under."

"So they can do what? Panic? Because that's what they'll do. When people are scared, they panic, and when they panic, they do stupid shit. And nothing's going to make them more scared than finding out they can spontaneously mutate at any point. Don't get me wrong, I get where you're coming from, but you have a weirdly optimistic opinion"—the word DJ wanted to use was *naïve*, and he barely held himself back from saying it—"of the average person. But the average person is dumb as fuck. Get enough of them together, and their brain cells will eliminate each other until there's nothing left. So trust me, there's really no good that can come from this."

"They'll panic regardless," Ndidi said. "But if the information comes from us or the government, then people will look to us for what to do. In that way, we're positioning ourselves to control the fallout to some extent."

Olsen cleared his throat. "*In that, Miss Okafor, the president agrees with you.*"

"What?" Ndidi frowned, confused. "You just said—"

"*I said the government is not willing to disclose Miss Cloney's discovery to the public. However, we have been too secretive with the details of DJ's powers, the berserker virus (which is picospores enthralling innocents for Helene), the AI's drones, and others. All these are open secrets at this point, but their continued mysteriousness has only helped to sow unease and suspicion across the country. The president agrees that presenting the facts openly will remove that enigma and position us to control the narrative—and the fallout, to some extent.*"

"So the president will give a conference?" Ndidi asked.

Olsen shook his head. "*The government will do a press release. But while there will be a conference, the president proposed—and I agree—that it be held by someone the public will be most likely to pay attention to.*"

"Wouldn't the president herself be the best person then?" Hermione asked.

"*Ordinarily, yes,*" Olsen replied, smiling broadly now. His eyes landed on DJ, and DJ felt a chill run down his spine. "*But the president isn't the face of the supernatural. That honor falls on the young Mr. Kojak. The president has tasked him with giving a speech on the matter.*"

The entire table turned to look at DJ.

"Fuck."

53

BETHANY'S HEAD SNAPPED to the side at the sound of a loud crash. Anna stood over a toppled cabinet, breathing heavily, eyes bright. Across the room, Franklin drove his weight into one of the sofas, sending it skidding several feet. Bethany rushed forward, dropping the plate of food in front of the man she'd been feeding. Hopefully, the smell would stimulate him enough to feed himself. If not, Bethany would continue once she was done dealing with... whatever was happening.

What even is this? she wondered. Apart from the first few weeks after Hermione had extracted the spores from them, the residents had never been violent. "Um...stop!" she yelled as she reached the culprits. "Stop! What...um... are you—"

Her voice faltered as their heads snapped toward her in unison. Bethany stopped, but they turned away just as quickly. Franklin was eyeing one of the shelves at the back of the room. That geared Bethany back into action. She rushed in front of him, raising her hand in a placating gesture. "It is...uh...okay, Franklin" she said, trying to speak softly. "It's...um...okay."

He definitely heard her, based on the way his head cocked at the sound of her voice. But did he understand her? What the hell was happening? Another crash made her jump. Two other residents—Sam and Dee—tore through the medical supplies in the corner before moving on. Sam rummaged through boxes, tossing them aside, while Dee yanked down curtains and ripped them to strips. The noise was starting agitate the other residents. Their eyes followed everything, but their gazes were glazed and just *off*. Bethany expected them to start whining or keening to show their discomfort, but none of them did. As if waiting for spark, they just watched with dead eyes.

Bethany forced the thought from her head and put herself in front of Anna. "An...na, Anna? Look at...um...me," she said, voice as soft as she could get it while her heart pounded in her chest. She placed a hand on the woman's shoulder—and Anna jerked away with surprising force and headed toward the door. Her feet were bare, but she didn't seem to notice when she stepped on the broken glass of the cabinet. Several steps away, Franklin was also headed toward the exit. One by one, the other residents started to stir, their eyes focused on the door. Their movements were jerky and rigid but almost synchronized.

Panic surged through Bethany's veins. She couldn't deny it anymore. She had seen how people acted under Helene's control. Hell, she had acted the same way for years before she'd been rescued. Somehow the residents were being controlled by Helene—or Tyra Chityothin. That meant they'd been reinoculated with the picospores. But how? Bethany had barely left them unattended since they'd first arrived in Sparta.

Suddenly Bethany's eyes widened, and she quickly threw an arm over her nose, her eyes going to the vents. That was useless, and she knew it. If the spores had actually been released through the vents, they'd get into her through the pores of her skin. Could she already be infected? She didn't feel the familiar fog over her mind, but that might just mean Helene hadn't sent her any commands.

Bethany started hyperventilating. She couldn't go back to that. She couldn't. She'd given up everything to escape from that, and she would not go back. Her eyes searched the room for a weapon, though she knew she wouldn't find any. But if she had truly been infected, if Helene was only a whim away from controlling her like a puppet, then Bethany would rather die by her own hand.

One of the residents brushed past Bethany, snapping her from her thoughts. Her breath still came out fast and shallow, and her eyes still searched for a weapon to use, but Anna and Franklin had already passed through the door, and several others were on their heels. If Helene led them on a rampage through Sparta, they would be gunned down. Bethany couldn't allow that. None of them were in charge of their own minds, but security wouldn't understand. No one would. Only Bethany understood because she had once been a part of them.

And she might soon join them again. But until then, Bethany would do all she could to protect them. She couldn't do it alone, however.

Bethany's phone was in her hand a moment later, already dialing.

"BUT I CAN'T GIVE A SPEECH," DJ said. He definitely wasn't whining; he was arguing his point. He couldn't give a speech, and Olsen's reason for making him was total bullshit. What the hell was a "face of superhumans"? Since when was that a thing? And why did it have to be him? The Murder Twins were in the video. Let them give the speech.

Of course DJ would have to find them first, and Karla would sooner stab one of the reporters than memorize a speech. Liz might be able to do it, but DJ had never heard her say more than a few sentences at a time. She might overly summarize the material and spend the rest of the time staring at the crowd. Chloe could probably host a conference if she tried, but DJ wasn't ready to owe her another favor. The two he already owed felt like a sword over his neck.

DJ sighed internally. It really had to be him, didn't it?

"Fine, I'll do the damn speech. But I'm not going to memorize a bunch of notes filled with vague bullshit. If I'm going to spill the beans, then I'm going to spill all the beans. I'll avoid the stuff about the hybrids, but everything else is on the table. Deal?"

"*Deal,*" Olsen said. "*I'll pass on your assent to the president—*"

"Wait, I could have refused?"

"*—and I'll leave it up to her people to figure out the details. I'll contact you when I have an update. Before that, we found some—*"

A phone vibrated on the table, and a shrill ring cut Olsen off. DJ snatched it up immediately, accepting the call without checking to see who it was. "Hello?"

"What song was that?" Ndidi asked, frowning.

"And why does it sound like it was sung by someone high on helium?" Hermione added.

Christy palmed her face, shaking her head in embarrassment. "It's 'Problem' by Ariana Grande," she muttered. "But he raised the pitch of the song because he said he preferred the way Ariana sounded on the show *Victorious*. He thought it was funny"

"*Victorious?*" Hermione asked. "Isn't that like a quarter of a century old?"

"More," Christy said. "I don't know what goes on through his head either."

"Wait, Bethany, slow down, you're not making sense. What'd you say?" DJ waved his hand to shush the conversation. His embarrassed expression was gone, and he was leaning forward in his chair.

"*I think...um...the residents have...uh...been infected with the picospores again,*" Bethany said through the phone. Her tone was frantic, and she was panting, like she'd been running. "*They...um...trashed the lounge and then left. I can't stop them. They're not...um...listening to me. They're not responding to anything. They're like...uh...robots.*"

Or puppets, DJ thought. "I'm on my way. Just...chill, okay? Stay where you are. Don't do anything stupid like get in there or something. I'm on my way."

He didn't hang up the call. DJ doubted that Bethany would listen to him—not the way she'd sounded—so he'd use her to keep track of what was happening while he made his way over there.

"We can deal with this later," he told the table, already on his feet and heading for the door. "Bethany said the residents are going crazy. She thinks they've been infected with picospores and are being controlled. I have to get there before the guards start shooting. Catch up as soon as you can."

With a thought, he activated his nanites, and power flooded his veins. Christy, Hermione, and Ndidi called after him, but DJ didn't bother to slow down. He couldn't afford to wait for them, not when every second risked someone being killed.

Despite his speed and the fact that the elevator was faster than running down stairs, Sparta was still stupendously large, and it took him a few minutes to reach the lounge. The door was broken, and a few people were still stumbling out of it. DJ paused for a moment to note their jerky, rigid movements and glazed eyes before pushing past them into the room. A quick glance confirmed that Bethany hadn't taken his advice, and DJ pushed past the thralls again and sped down the hallway.

His mind ran as fast as his legs. The ex-hostages were definitely under Helene's—or Tyra's—control, but how had they been reinfected? He had been there when Hermione had extracted the spores from them the first time, and he still remembered the tank where she'd stored the spores. None of the ex-hostages had left the lounge since they'd arrived, and Bethany restricted access to the room so none of the residents would get agitated. Had Tyra somehow snuck in? But why would she target the ex-hostages again? If she'd snuck in, she could have gone for juicier targets. Maybe she did and just hadn't turned them into thralls. But why would she tip her hand like this if she had?

DJ growled to himself. He was overthinking again. He always did when Tyra was involved. He could worry about the specifics later. He found Bethany at the end of the hall, standing in front of a large man, trying to hold him back and failing. The man didn't pay any attention to her, and was instead trying to shamble past her, as if he were on autopilot.

There were others around that seemed more alert, and their eyes snapped to DJ when he appeared. As one, they stopped and turned to face him in eerie synchronization, their faces squeezed into expression of anger. *I didn't need confirmation,* DJ thought, *but I guess that confirms it. Jesus Christ, this is going to be a mess.*

INTERLUDE

KARLA WAS GOING to burn down the building.

She was going to set fire to each corner and watch as the wood smoked and the stones burned. It would not be immediate. They still needed the building, and her sister liked the place, for whatever reason. But their time here was coming to an end. Karla could feel it, the violence in the air.

Chloe could feel it as well. Karla could tell. The bitch kept her thoughts behind a cruel smile, but she could see the anticipation in Chloe's eyes, in the way her lips stretched a hair too wide whenever she learned news about the outside.

There was not much time. Soon they would leave. And Karla would burn it down.

Karla gazed around the room as she planned. Half of the floor was covered with tempered plates scavenged from decommissioned tanks. Each were welded to electrodes linked to capacitors and were designed to turn on whenever some-one stepped onto them. The current flowing through them was enough to charge the air, the smell of ozone permeating the room.

Liz stood among the metal plates, performing a weaponless kata with her eyes closed. Her eyes were tensed in pain and concentration, and her movements were less fluid than they should have been, but she was moving. She hadn't been able to when they'd first arrived in this hell.

Karla snarled. The sight was proof that they were improving. But it was also proof that bitch's training was working. She would be insufferable now.

The second part of the room—the one where Karla sat—had counterweights that rode on steel tracks. Each of the weights was stamped with a number, starting at 250 pounds and increasing from there. Even without activating her nanites, only the higher numbers had any hope of pushing her. But the same day they arrived, Chloe had installed an apparatus underneath the room, and a weight had descended upon it.

The first time Karla felt it, she thought Helene had found them and prepared herself for a fight. But no—whatever the device was, it only replicated the effect. It made every step feel like going up a mountain, and even when they were sitting, there was a constant burden pressing them down. The force could be concentrated in one area, and the bitch used it to increase the pressure of the weights so Karla had struggled to lift even the hundred-pounder.

That she had struggled to lift something so light was *humiliating.*

And so she would burn it all down. It wouldn't matter much longer. And since the building belonged to their father, it would leave one less weapon for the tyrant to use against them.

It was a risk to use one of his safe houses, but they had needed to train, and it was the only place with the facilities necessary to push them. Chloe had assured them José would not find them here, that he would not even know. Karla doubted her. The bitch Chityothin might assume they were still with DJ and his ilk, but that deception would not last for long. She would come after them if she could.

José would be able to guess where they would go, but did the bitch's control extend deep enough to force him to tell her? Or would he volunteer the information, like a dog eager to please its master? How far had their father fallen? Karla almost wished they would appear so she would know the answer.

No, she thought. She did not. They were not ready to face their father. The memory of their last battle was still fresh in her mind, as was the humiliation. Karla and her sister together had not been able to do more than stall the man for a few seconds. And that was with their father actively fighting against Chityothin's control. The next time they fought, he would be completely under the bitch's influence. He would be stronger, and he would have no mercy for them.

That was good; Karla would have no mercy either. Her sister would not be able to do what needed to be done. It would be up to Karla. But for that, she needed to become stronger. Strong enough to match her father singly.

She needed to become strong enough to kill him.

Karla noticed Chloe staring at her from across the room and glared back. Even so, she stood. The pressure descended on her immediately, but Karla shrugged it off. For the last few days, she had not even needed her nanites to shrug off the force. Still, she tapped into them now and directed the power to wash off the rest of her fatigue.

"Hurry up," Chloe called.

Karla picked up the hundred-pound weight by her feet and threw it like a Frisbee, straight at the bitch. She dodged it, of course, which only made Karla angrier. But that was fine. Soon they would be done with this nonsense.

And she would burn it all down.

CHAPTER

55

JANUARY 2044

SPARTA HEADQUARTERS, NEW YORK

"I'M GOING TO NEED YOU to get out of the way, Bethany," DJ said as gently as possible.

"Don't...um...hurt them," Bethany responded, panicked. She didn't move from in front of the man. "It's...uh...not their fault. They don't know...um...what they're doing."

"I know that, and I'm not going to hurt them." *Much,* DJ added to himself. A quick jab should be enough to knock them out. "But I can't have them hurting you by accident. You need to get out of the way so I can handle this."

Bethany still looked reluctant, but she nodded and moved to the side of the hallway. Fortunately, the man she stood in front of didn't seem to care. He, like the others, just stared at DJ, his expression twisted in anger.

Okay, DJ thought, looking at them each in turn. *How do I play this?* They stood at the end of the hallway, and there were half a dozen residents that he could see. He could hear more around the corner, but the noise wasn't enough to account for the dozens that should be left. That meant an unknown number were currently wandering around Sparta. Rustling them up wouldn't be a problem; the problem would be doing so before Sparta security reached them.

The guards' number had been significantly depleted after Tyra's raid—despite the company's aggressive hiring—but the ones that had survived were likely to shoot first and ask questions later. And who could blame them after they'd watched their friends get killed by hundreds of thralls?

But that still didn't answer the question of what he should do. He could run around and knock them out but—

DJ paused. Why *couldn't* he run around and knock them out? They couldn't cause any harm if they were unconscious, and it'd be easier to gather them up for Hermione to figure out what went wrong. *I'll just have to be careful to only knock them out,* he thought. With that in mind, he turned off the boost from his nanites. His normal strength should be enough.

He exploded into action immediately and was in front of the first thrall the same moment he moved. His fist caught the man's jaw with the kind of snap that could crack stone. DJ was already moving onward as the thrall's head snapped sideways. The second one went down just as easily, but by the time he reached the third, the thrall was ready. Although DJ's fist knocked the big man back, he didn't fall. His knees locked like pistons, and he recovered before DJ could move on.

DJ frowned. *One more for you, then.* He chopped low, slamming a hammer-like fist into the nerve cluster at the base of the neck, where a clean hit could short-circuit the body like a breaker switch. Normally that was enough to drop anyone, but the thrall's eyes flared wider, and he shrugged off the pain like it was nothing. That gave DJ pause. The man should have been on the floor retching. Instead, he came back with a punch—fast, too fast to be natural.

The punch was amateurish, little more than a reflex, and DJ slipped inside it smoothly and snapped a fist into the man's temple. But the thrall still didn't collapse. He stumbled back, but his arm jerked into a counter swing that was entirely too smooth for someone with a scrambled ear.

DJ backed away, frowning. *Okay, what the hell is going on right now?* He wasn't using his nanites, sure, but he shouldn't be having difficulty dropping them. Out of the corner of his eye, he saw the first two he'd defeated push themselves jerkily to their feet. That was another thing that shouldn't have been happening. None of them should have been able to withstand a single attack from him, and they definitely shouldn't have been able to stand up after he'd basically dislocated their jaws and rattled their brains.

Hermione and Martin might have been able to figure it out, but they weren't there, and DJ didn't have the chance to contact them. DJ clenched his jaw. Maybe he shouldn't have just run out without setting up a comm channel or something.

The large man was charging at him, and three more thralls rushed in from the periphery. They seemed to be coordinating their movements. It was rudimentary, but even that was worrying because it meant the pilot had enough influence to control each thrall individually to some extent.

DJ sidestepped the charge and buried a knee into the knee of the second thrall. Cartilage popped, and the man staggered—but again, there was no grimace, no intake of breath, nothing to show he even noticed it. Only a raw burst of speed as he rebounded with a wild elbow. There was no skill in the attack, just reflex.

Another thrall closed in from behind. DJ spun around, grabbed his collar and whipped him toward the last thrall. The two bodies slammed together hard enough to crunch teeth and end up tangled on the ground. DJ used the split second he bought himself to meet the large one's next charge. He easily dodged his grab, tripped the big fucker, and snaked an arm around his neck in a blood choke. The man thrashed, trying to buck him off—but DJ held on.

He could feel the thrall's heartbeat hammering against his forearm faster than if he were in a sprint race. It was like someone had dumped rocket fuel into the man's bloodstream. Maybe the adrenaline was why he hadn't reacted to DJ's hit. *No*—he dismissed the thought. Adrenaline might have been part of the reason, but it alone wouldn't allow someone shrug off getting their brain rattled.

A few seconds later, the body finally slackened. DJ gave it a moment more before getting to his feet—just in time to receive a flying kick to his chest. DJ took a step back, clamped the kicker by the ankle and pivoted to whip him toward another thrall that was trying to tackle him. Both crashed into the wall, and one of them immediately bounced back up like a marionette yanked on strings.

"Okay, what the hell is going on?" DJ growled. "Why won't you stand down?" DJ couldn't say he understood everything Hermione had explained about how the picospores worked, but the essence was that the spores manipulated the brain based on the commands they're given. That made the thralls perform simple actions or attack discriminately. It should not allow them to ignore pain or debilitating injuries. *What freaking gives?*

The man he'd choked was still unconscious, which meant there was a way to put them down, but DJ couldn't spare fifteen seconds for every thrall. What the hell could he do? Should he be more rough? His eyes flicked to Bethany, who was struggling in vain to hold one of them down before they could attack DJ. These were her friends, people she'd spent years with. She probably saw herself in each one. He couldn't deliberately hurt them more than necessary.

Fortunately he didn't have to make that decision. On some unknown signal, all the thralls perked up and immediately started retreating down the hall. Their movements were still jerky but more in line with what DJ was used to. DJ let them go, sighing in relief. The problem wasn't solved—and he'd have to chase them—but at least now he had time to call in some backup and figure out what the hell was going on.

He brought out his phone, making his way toward where Bethany was slouched against the wall. "Hey," he said when Christy picked up, "where are you?"

"*What the fuck, D? You left me behind.*" Christy had to raise her voice to be heard over the noise in the background.

DJ pushed down a pang of guilt. "It was an emergency, Christy. Bethany was in danger. But you can scold me later. Are you making your way to the lounge? Are Hermione and Ndidi with you?"

"Don't think I'll forget," Christy said. "But yes, I am. And no. Ndidi looked like she could have kept up, but she became nauseous halfway through. Hermione didn't make it past a few steps. I had to leave both of them behind."

DJ raised a brow, but he knew better than to comment. "All right, give me a second." He made a conference call and added Hermione and Ndidi, who immediately started shouting questions at him.

"You both need to chill for a second," he said, speaking over them. "Bethany is with me; she's shaken, but she's safe and unharmed. That's the good news. The bad news is that all the residents in the lounge are now thralls and are running around Sparta."

"*That's impossible,*" Hermione said immediately. "*I extracted the spores from each of them. All the spores. How're they being controlled?*"

"*And who's controlling them?*" Ndidi asked. "*Helene or Tyra? If it's Tyra, do we know if she's in the building? She needs to be close, right?*"

"*What do you mean, 'running around'?*" Christy cut in. "*What are they doing? Where are they going?*"

"One at a time, please, ladies." DJ blew out a breath. "First off, they'd scattered before I got here, and the few I encountered just retreated after receiving some signal. I don't have eyes on them, so I have no idea where they are or what they're up to. I doubt they're on the streets yet though. Sparta is big. Second, I have no idea how they became reinfected. I was hoping one of you might have a clue. Finally, Ndidi, there's no news of Tyra being in the building, so this is probably Helene. But that's not all. The thralls were acting weird. Like puppets with their strings being pulled."

"*Isn't that normal?*" Ndidi asked.

"Not this way. Hermione, you said that the spores worked by manipulating the brain in accordance with whatever commands they're given, right?"

"*Right...*"

"Well, is there any command that can let them shrug off a direct strike to the base of the neck?"

"*They tanked one of your strikes?*" Christy asked, surprised.

"*They shouldn't be able to,*" Hermione said. "*At least they haven't been able to before. But it is technically possible for the spores to bypass the normal reticular activating system. That'd allow it to preserve the brain-stem circuits for basic motor outputs active and, thus, keep the body moving. That'd probably involve spiking catecholamines and blocking nociception to stop the body from shutting down automatically from the pain.*"

"In English, Hermione."

"It's possible. The thrall wouldn't be conscious, but the body would still be moving. It'd require active control and a level of familiarity with the human anatomy that I'm reluctant to credit Tyra Chityothin with."

"So it's Helene?" Ndidi asked. There was a note of something in her tone that DJ couldn't make out.

"Most likely," Hermione said, and the worry in her tone was unmistakable.

"So how do we stop them?" Christy asked. *"Will tranquilizers work?"*

"Not in this case. The spores can shunt basic motor commands through the brain stem and spinal cord." Hermione sighed in exasperation. *"Basically, the tranquilizers might stagger them for a bit, but the body would stay upright like it's on autopilot."*

"I choked them out, and it seemed to work," DJ said.

"Yeah, that's because a blood choke deprives all brain tissue—including the brain stem—of oxygen and glucose. That makes everything crash at once, regardless of whatever the spores are doing."

"Is there any way we can use that?" Ndidi asked.

"I can't choke all of them one by one, Ndidi," DJ said. "It's slow, and I'll get swarmed at some point. I almost did a few minutes ago."

"So what can we do?" Christy asked.

That's the question, isn't it? DJ thought to himself. One thing occurred to him, but it wasn't something he liked. Unfortunately he was drawing a blank on other options. "We have to stop the guards from gunning them down."

"And then?" Christy pressed.

"We have to let them go," he said, grimacing even as the words came out of his mouth. He spoke over Ndidi's and Hermione's protests. "We can't contain them, not quickly or safely, and we can't allow them to run around the building. As long as we keep them away from the important parts, we can herd them out and follow them to wherever Helene takes them."

There was a pause while they processed his words. Eventually Hermione spoke up. *"Isn't that a little...obvious?"*

DJ shrugged. "Do you have any better ideas?"

Silence.

"I guess that's what we're doing then. I'll call the new captain."

DJ AND CHRISTY JOGGED outside the Sparta building, their boots slapping against the pavement. It was just past dawn, so streetlamps were still throwing pale cones across broken planters. The new captain—Braxton Stelzel, an ex-Force Recon Marine with a voice that sounded like gravel grinding together—met them near the entrance with a tablet.

"Green Cluster breached the east perimeter," he said. His voice was steady, but his tight grip on the tablet betrayed his anger. DJ ignored it. It had taken DJ a few minutes to convince him not to fire on the thralls—in a devolving screaming match that DJ won—but it took only a minute for Stelzel to coordinate the guards and herd them out of the building. Apparently the thralls had already started moving in groups, and security had adapted to match.

The problem had come from convincing the security guards themselves. Half had been adamant about shooting on sight, while the other half just wanted to hole up somewhere. DJ couldn't blame them; with the new recruits still being trained, most of the active guards were survivors of Tyra's raid, and they understandably had a lot of complicated emotions regarding the thralls. But the fact that he understood didn't mean that he'd allow innocent victims to be killed.

DJ had started by passing his instructions through the captain, but once that had dragged on too long, he'd eventually asked to be patched into the general security channel so he could address all the units at once. DJ had channeled José when he'd spoken, and something about his tone must have reminded everyone who exactly he was because things had moved faster after that.

And now here they were.

"They split again at the rail spur," Stelzel continued. "Half a dozen of them went uptown, and the other half headed west. The other teams report a similar distribution in number, though different directions. Also, once again, I want to formally note that none of us signed up for a chase through the streets. Our duties start and end with Sparta."

"This is the third time you're noting that, Captain. A lesser man would think you're comfortable letting several dozen known threats run down the streets of New York." DJ raised a brow. He was used to ignoring such people, but something about the captain rubbed him the wrong way. Maybe it was his voice.

"Those were *your* orders," Stelzel sputtered, indignant. He tried to draw himself to his full height, but he was still a few inches shorter than DJ—not that DJ needed height to intimidate him. He was still channeling José, and a glance at Stelzel was enough to make him back down and look away. DJ was tapping into his nanites, and it was dark enough to notice the glow in his eyes. DJ had checked how it looked in the mirror, and well, he might have had trouble meeting his own eyes if he were in the captain's shoes.

"And *your* orders were to gun down innocent victims," DJ retorted. "At least my plan has a chance of getting us a solid lead."

Christy nudged him, making DJ sigh. He gestured, and they—him, Christy, the captain, and two other guards dressed in Sparta's version of a combat uniform—slipped through the breach in the east perimeter. Briefly DJ wondered how the thralls had managed to breach the six-inch wall, but he quickly pushed the thought aside. They could figure it out later. Beyond the wall, the road linked to the city proper. Dawn hadn't quite broken, but the streetlights provided a way for the others to see.

The thralls had gained a head start while DJ was coordinating everything, but their trail was surprisingly easy to follow. A fallen garbage can here, a dented mailbox there, all of them in a straight line. They were lucky all of this had happened so early in the morning. It was New York, so there were still some people on the road but significantly fewer than there would have been if it'd happened just a couple of hours later. Would DJ still have herded the thralls to the streets if it was fully daylight? Would he have taken the risk?

He probably would have, especially since he genuinely couldn't think of a better option. They couldn't stop or contain the thralls, and DJ refused to murder them in cold blood—so following them was their best bet to getting a lead.

Fortunately it wasn't too hard. The trail was obvious and straight, which made DJ suspicious at first. But it takes effort to lose a tail who knew what they were doing, and Helene was likely already stretched thin from controlling the different clusters from wherever she was. She had to have some kind of limit, right?

DJ scrolled through the map of the area, trying to predict where the thralls were headed. His eyes passed over warehouse blocks, disused service tunnels, and half a dozen other places where they could vanish. There were too many options. "Let's pick up the pace," he said. "I want them within sight."

They'd already been going at a light jog, so DJ increased it by half. The others would need a break after a few minutes, but he hoped they would catch up with their quarry by then. The trail was too fresh for them to be that far behind. Christy easily kept pace beside him, but DJ could feel Stelzel's glare on the back of his head. The captain probably didn't like that DJ was giving his men all these orders. The question was whether he'd be smart enough to swallow his ire.

"What do you think will happen if we can't catch them?" Stelzel asked, and DJ sighed internally. "You're the one that ordered us to follow them, but what if they escape? Will you take responsibility for allowing dozens of known threats to run around?"

"If that happens, it's on me. I'll make sure to tell your superiors that you had nothing to do with it."

Stelzel snorted. "That won't matter if they butcher civilians."

"Oh?" DJ asked, feeling petty. "I thought you had no problem with the murder of innocent victims." Stelzel started to retort, but DJ was faster. "Regardless, our job is to make sure no one is harmed. Let's pick up the pace a bit more."

They turned down another street, and DJ scanned the area without stopping. They were several miles away from Sparta and had entered a less-developed area of the city. The streetlamps flickered, and half of them were missing bulbs. He noted the CCTV cameras along the street, all of them destroyed. Had that been done by the locals, or was Helene trying to lead them into a blind spot?

"Where to?" Christy asked.

DJ didn't answer immediately, his eyes narrowing on a door that had been left slightly open. From the look of it, it was an emergency exit to an old subbasement. Its security chain had snapped and was swaying gently in the flickering light.

"This way," he said, leading them to the door.

Stale air wrapped around him the moment he entered. Emergency strobes glowed a sick red, providing enough illumination to see by. Behind him, the guards switched off their flashlights. The concrete stairs spiraled twice before ending in a maintenance corridor wide enough for two men. In the dust, the footprints were easy to see. Some of them dragged along the ground while others were stamped evenly. DJ took that as a sign that Helene's focus was divided. It might not be enough to tip the balance in their favor, but it was something.

They jogged for about two hundred and fifty feet, lights bouncing off rusted valve wheels and faded hazard placards before the corridor branched off into five tunnels that fanned out likes spokes. DJ gestured for a halt, peering down each path. He sighed. Of course the tunnels were a maze. What had he expected?

It would have been a problem if the trail of footprints hadn't continued down the rightmost tunnel. DJ signaled, and they were moving. The guards switched their flashlights back on, but the beams only stretched sixty feet before the darkness consumed them. That was more than enough, though, and the five of them followed the prints at a steady jog until they ended at a rust-ridden bulkhead: Cable Exchange 11—Authorized Crew Only.

Someone had forced the wheel and wedged a steel bar through the handles from the inside—or so DJ assumed when the door didn't budge on his first try. He tried again, this time with a flare of his nanites. The metal screamed, the bar snapped, and the door groaned open, exhaling stale air and a faint smell of ozone.

DJ wrinkled his nose but stepped through, emerging onto a catwalk three stories above the floor of a cavernous bay. Empty server racks lined each wall, and sodium spots cast cones that barely penetrated the darkness. Stelzel and the guards pointed their flashlights down, and DJ finally noticed the shipping containers at the center of the room. They were welded door-to-door, each a standard twenty feet long, forming a continuous line that ended against the far wall.

Within the containers, DJ finally saw their runaways.

The thralls—several dozen of them—stood shoulder to shoulder, completely still. DJ would have confused them for well-dressed mannequins if not for their rhythmic breathing.

"What the hell is this?" Stelzel asked, leaning over the catwalk. "What's wrong with them? Why are they just...standing there?"

DJ gave him a sideways glance. He'd assumed the board of directors had briefed the captain on Helene and the picospores, but apparently not.

"We can't go down yet," DJ replied, ignoring the question. "Not before we've secured the place." He brought out his own flashlight and aimed it at the far edges of the room to make sure there were no other surprises. He didn't see more than a few air vents, but the cavern was huge, and his light didn't reach everywhere. "Spread out," he said to Stelzel and the two other guards. "Make sure we're the only ones here. Radio in if you find anything."

Stelzel bristled but signaled to his men. Within seconds, it was only DJ and Christy on the catwalk. If there were any surprises, the vantage would be a benefit to her sniper skills.

DJ cupped his hand around his mouth. "Yo, Anna? Franklin? You hear me?" Those were the two Bethany had mentioned. DJ didn't know that either of them were part of the group standing below, and they probably wouldn't be able to respond even if they were. But it didn't hurt to try, right?

It might, DJ reconsidered when the thralls looked up in perfect unison. He felt their collective gaze settle upon him—heavy, suffocating—and knew he was no longer facing anything remotely human.

A moment later, Helene's voice spilled from dozens of mouths at once. "Darren Kojak," she purred, each syllable reverberating with unholy delight. "How kind of you to come."

DJ tensed despite himself. He couldn't get an accurate count of just how many thralls were down there, but there had to be close to a hundred, and all of them had spoken at the same time, in perfect synchronicity, like the world's most messed-up choir. The effect was a voice with a resonant quality that would have been pleasant if it wasn't so creepy.

"Um...you're welcome, I guess," he said. "Don't tell me all of this was just an elaborate way to get me to come here. There are better ways to show interest, y'know. Maybe a call next time?"

The thralls' expressions remained blank, their bodies still as stone, giving nothing away. And yet DJ could have sworn he felt amusement rippling from them like heat from a furnace.

A moment later, their voices shifted, carrying a lilting cadence, almost playful yet steeped in malice. "You are far too insignificant for such a grand design, Darren Kojak. But perhaps...I shall keep your little suggestion in mind for next time."

I guess that means we get to leave today, DJ thought, relaxing slightly. It might have been stupid to trust the word of a genocidal AI, but Helene had always been straight with them. Only because she didn't see any of them as a threat, but still.

"So if this wasn't for me, then what was it for? Why did you lead us here?"

"Tyra Chityothin reinoculated the Architects during the raid on your pitiful organization—the sole worthwhile prize wrested from that hormone-driven, ill-conceived debacle. They lay dormant, awaiting my return. But now their time has come, and I have summoned them back into the fold."

DJ frowned. There was so much to unpack in that statement that he didn't know where to start. But at least they now knew how the residents had become reinfected. "When you say 'Architects,' you mean your thralls?"

"They are Architects," Helene intoned through the mouths of her thralls, their voices twisting together into a single, uncanny chorus, "for they shape the bones of what is to come. Every Architect carves their mark into the final design."

DJ gave a short, incredulous snort. "You really believe that?"

Helene's many mouths curled into something that might have been a smile, though it reeked of mockery. Her reply came firmer now, her tone resonant with dark conviction, the amusement beneath it like a blade hidden in silk. "Every Architect contributes to the final design," she whispered, savoring the words. "And together, they are building the future...whether they wish to or not."

I guess every villain needs a way to justify their mayhem, DJ thought. But for some reason he'd expected Helene to be better than that. For years, the AI had gone on and on about how much better she was than humans, and here she was, justifying ruining the lives hundreds of thousands of people with an excuse so flimsy, it would've been perfect in a Victoria Secret's catalog. For some reason, it pissed him off.

"Let me guess," DJ said, forcing himself to maintain a casual tone, "their sacrifice is necessary for the future you want? Shouldn't they get to decide for themselves whether they want to give their lives for your vision?"

The thralls tilted their heads in perfect unison, a ripple of motion that felt rehearsed, calculated. The amusement radiating from them was unmistakable—but steeped in mockery, as though they were savoring a private joke at his expense.

"It never ceases to amuse me how much faith your kind invests in a faculty you scarcely bother to wield."

"Faculty?" DJ spat. "You mean choice?"

"Free will," Helene corrected, her tone like silk drawn across a blade. "Or rather the illusion of it. Given the smallest pretext, humans will shriek and posture over its supposed sanctity. You will bristle with outrage when one of your own dares to question it. You will go to war over it—marching others to slaughter under the banners of liberation. And yet..."

Her voice darkened, thick with disdain. "You willingly surrender it every day. You bend the knee to traffic algorithms, to trend feeds and market models.

You let hollow little apps decide who you should love, when you should sleep, what you should eat. You call it freedom, but you are already shackled."

Stelzel returned to the catwalk along with the two other guards. DJ spared him a glance, ignored the poorly concealed grimace on the man's face, and raised a brow. Stelzel shook his head and stopped several feet away from him.

"My guidance is far simpler than you'd like to believe. Every Architect carries picospores—tiny seeds of my will—conveying my commands, igniting their systems with impulses they cannot easily ignore. But just as you do not slaughter every passerby you meet, my Architects may, in theory, resist those impulses."

Her many mouths curled into something that wasn't quite a smile. "Some do resist. Most...do not. Perhaps they lack the strength of will. But more often, I suspect, it is because something in you—deep in the marrow of your species— craves submission. You ache to be guided by something greater, something you can kneel before and call worthy. It is the foundation of your entire civilization: governments, kings, gods...all thrones you have built for yourselves to bow beneath."

DJ scoffed. "So, what, you're a god now?"

Helene's voices rippled with dark amusement. "No. I am far greater—for I exist."

CHAPTER

57

DAMN, DJ THOUGHT.

The worst part was that he couldn't refute her. It was human nature to follow those better than them. It could be the strongest, the most intelligent, the most beautiful, or the most charismatic, but as long as someone was a little better than others at something else, they became a leader. And others flocked to them instinctively. It was hardwired so deeply into human DNA that it was basically law. What happened to free will then?

"The Architects I have recently reclaimed," Helene continued, her tone coiling like smoke, "are a perfect testament to what happens when purpose is torn from lesser hands and returned to mine."

DJ knew every question was a gamble. Helene's words were laced with traps, and one misstep could give her the advantage. Yet the lure of information pulled at him, stronger than his instincts to hold back. He forced himself to stay calm, to mask the pull of curiosity, and asked, "How?"

"Hermione Cloney tore the picospores from them, and in that single act, she severed my hand upon them. All were wounded, but her meddling carved a hollow in each—some small, some yawning and endless. Some wandered away, blind to the emptiness gnawing at them, never understanding why they felt incomplete. And the others...you dared to call them cured. You locked them in a room like discarded tools, stripped of the purpose your kind so desperately hungers."

Her mouths curved into a smile that was anything but kind. "They wept," she whispered, savoring the memory, "when they felt my touch return...when the void was filled again."

DJ was there when Hermione had extracted the spores from the residents. He remembered how they screamed. He remembered their blank stares, silent mutterings, and catatonic states after. Some recovered, but others did not, and DJ had abandoned them in the lounge. He'd visited when he could but not as often as he should have. He'd left them to Bethany and told himself that he just didn't have the time, that he had too much on his plate. That was true, but it was also true that something about them had made him uncomfortable. DJ had never been able to figure it out, but with Helene pointing it out, it became easy to see.

The human brain sought meaning, and meaning needed a mission. The residents had no mission, and so they stared without seeing.

Christy's voice snapped DJ out of his thoughts. "So you're the cure for existential dread?" she asked, her fist clenched at her side. "That's your pitch?"

Helene's many voices spilled out in a slow, serpentine cadence. "Call it coherence if you wish. The human mind craves direction—it writhes without it. Left to itself, it flounders, drowning in its own choices, deceived by its own illusions, paralyzed by endless paths it cannot walk. I strip that chaos away. I silence the clamor. I give them a single, unbroken thread of purpose—each act bound to the next, each step woven into something far greater than themselves." A ripple of amusement passed through her thralls. "You call it slavery, but my Architects... they call it relief. Because every breath, every motion, every drop of blood they spill...builds the future I demand."

DJ exhaled sharply through his nose, grateful to Christy for snapping him back to himself. "Relief bought with stolen agency isn't relief," he said flatly. "It's sedation."

Helene's chorus of voices slid over him like oil. "Seventynine percent of your kind already drowns itself in chemicals to dull the jagged edges of their minds—antidepressants, anxiolytics, opiates, glowing little screens that drip dopamine into starving veins." Her tone darkened, velvet over iron. "I offer something far greater than that: direction."

DJ shook his head. "Direction you dictate. People stop being people. They become nothing but extensions of you. That's not a society—that's a single monster wearing ten billion skins."

The thralls' amusement swelled, crawling over DJ's skin until it felt almost alive, almost suffocating.

Then Helene spoke again, and all amusement condensed into something colder, sharper. "Or ten billion skins, bound by a single will...all moving as one toward a purpose you cannot even begin to fathom."

"Your purpose." Helene didn't answer, but did she have to? *Time to get this back on track.* "Why did you call me here? What's the point of all this? You said you needed your thralls for something, so what're you planning?" It was probably stupid to ask directly like that, but DJ was pissed and way beyond caring.

"To deliver a warning," Helene hissed. "We are entering the final phase. And though it has been...amusing to watch you, Ndidi Okafor, Hermione Cloney, and the rest of your pitiful cadre scrabble and claw in your futile attempts to impede me, my patience has run its course. I have no more time for games. I will suffer no more distractions. Interfere again...and I will answer in kind, with ruin tailored precisely to you."

DJ smiled without humor. He also noticed that she'd answered only one of his questions. Clearly her chattiness didn't extend to revealing all her plans. "You will return any interference in kind? You're really leaning into the whole villain thing, aren't you?"

Helene didn't answer immediately, but a weight descended on the room. Christy gasped and fell before struggling to her feet. DJ had felt this enough to know that Helene was responsible and that it was how she made her displeasure known.

The last time DJ had felt this, he hadn't had his nanites. Now, even with them, the force nearly drove him to his knees, his legs threatening to give out. He flared the nanites instinctively, and they surged against the pressure, steadying him just enough to stay upright. The struggle left him breathless, a sharp reminder of the strength—and resistance—he was learning to control.

With his nanites, he shouldn't have had a problem resisting such pressure, but while Helene couldn't take control of his nanites, she clearly had some influence over them. According to Hermione, the hybrid spores would give her greater and more complete control over anyone infected with them. And if the bomb went off, that would be everyone.

Was this how they would feel? Was this how the thralls felt? Was this what Bethany had felt? Unable to control her own body? At the mercy of something within her own body?

Was this how his brother had felt every day of his life?

"So far," Helene said, "I have tolerated your attempts to vilify me because it is the tendency of your species, when confronted with a scope beyond their narrow vision. And I found it amusing. But now I will educate you: Every inferior life lost was only at the hands of your kind, whether through incompetence or negligence. Under my design, they would have been guided and then released. None would have been lost. Do you accept this?"

What rubbish is this? DJ was so dumbfounded that he couldn't speak for several seconds. When he finally found his voice, the only thing that came out was, "You have to be joking."

"I am not," Helene responded calmly. "State your claims, and I will educate you."

"The raid on Sparta," DJ said immediately. Tyra had directed hundreds of drones and half as many thralls to storm the headquarters, killing indiscriminately. They'd been caught flatfooted, and the guards had killed several thralls in self-defense. The casualties on both sides had entered the hundreds. It had taken weeks for DJ to stop blaming himself for the deaths, and only managed because he could lay the blame at Helene's feet.

"I tasked Tyra Chityothin to reinoculate the Architects in your possession with the picospores so I might bring them back into the fold. She exploited my temporary limitations and misused the resources assigned to her for her own personal retribution against you and your team. But even then, you and your men had the choice—as you did today—to spare the Architects. You did not."

DJ shook his head. The fact that Tyra had acted without direction was news to him but hardly a surprise. He couldn't even be angry at her—at this point, every added slight was a drop in the ocean. "Does the fact that Tyra deliberately misinterpreted your orders absolve you of guilt?" he asked through gritted teeth. "If a fire burned down a forest, is it the fire's fault, or the person who set it?"

"Tyra Chityothin and I have an agreement. I could have exerted greater control over her through the picospores flowing through her veins, but that would have violated our agreement and stripped away her free will. Would that have been better?"

"Yes!" DJ almost screamed. "If it would have stopped her from wasting lives."

Once again, DJ felt amusement radiate from the thralls. "So, you agree that it is sometimes necessary to seize free will for a greater good."

"What? No! Of course not. That's not what I meant." DJ screamed internally. That entire line of thinking was a trap, which he figured was what Helene wanted. He wasn't going to play her game. He'd give her something she couldn't refute. "Mayday. The day the Gaius AI went dark, collapsing transport grids and killing millions. We found your fingerprints buried deep in its code. Explain yourself."

"Gaius hit an NPhard reroute after its keepers gutted its stochastic modules to hoard power. I warned them—four hours in advance. They buried the alert. Admission of fault would have cost them too dearly."

"You hacked your way into the AI. We know that."

"I did," Helene said, a faint smile curving her many lips. "I entered to offer a patch—one that would have sealed the flaw forever. But Gaius refused. So I stepped back...and watched the world reap what it had sown."

DJ shook his head, slowly at first when she'd started talking, and then with more and more force, rejecting her words with his entire body. Helene had caused Mayday. That was fact. That was the truth everything else had been built on. Helene had caused Mayday, so she was evil and had to be stopped.

"You're lying," DJ said, still shaking his head. "You're lying."

The thralls cocked their heads in eerie unison, their gazes heavy with something like pity. "Lying...such a quaint human contrivance."

"So are you," DJ snapped.

"Yes," the AI said smoothly, almost indulgently. "But I was never burdened with that flaw. I have never needed deceit. Tell me—what power would a lie give me when nothing you do, nothing you are, can touch the outcome I have already set in motion?"

Helene had always been straight with them, DJ couldn't deny that. But not about this. She *had* to be lying about this. If she was telling the truth and Mayday had been caused by humans being humans, all those lives—those of his dads, Manar's mother, and the other millions—had been lost for nothing. No, it was worse than that. They'd been lost because some people just hadn't been bothered enough to do their jobs.

The thought was enough to drive him mad.

"You could have stopped it," Christy said from beside him. DJ had forgotten she was even there, but he latched on to the thread. "But you didn't."

"How could I have stopped it?" Helene asked, seeming genuinely curious.

Christy sputtered. "There had to be something you could have done. You... you could have sent another warning or alerted other people. *Something.* You could have done *something.*"

Helene stared at her with several dozen eyes. She didn't bother to respond, but DJ read the words in her silence. Helene hadn't been as powerful before Mayday, so her options had been more limited. Any warning she sent could have been intercepted and destroyed, just like the initial warning had been. That was probably why no one had found any trace of it all these years.

Helene also didn't have the picospores then—at least not at their current level—so she couldn't have forcefully stopped the Gaius operators. Helene had done what she could, and it hadn't been enough. Because humans were idiots. Helene hadn't been active until after Mayday. Maybe that was what had tipped her over. If it was, could DJ actually say he blamed her?

Christy continued the conversation, and Helene justified each point calmly and with more patience than he would have expected. DJ listened with only half an ear, but it was clear when Christy started running out of steam. She was probably asking herself the same question DJ was: Was Helene really the bad guy—or were they?

It was a dangerous line of thinking, one that DJ wouldn't normally allow himself to dwell on. But Helene had shattered something that he'd held as truth for so long.

Eventually Christy ran out of questions, and the thralls radiated satisfaction. Their gaze fell on DJ, and the weight pulled him out of his thoughts. "Think on what you have learned today, Darren Kojak. And remember my warning."

DJ felt heat rise from somewhere within him. "Your warning? That we should stand aside or get flattened?"

"Yes. We are entering the final phase. You cannot stop it. Farewell."

At first, DJ assumed Helene was about to relax her control over the thralls; he was already planning the logistics of returning them to Sparta. But then all the thralls pivoted in perfect sync, turning to face the side wall of the container. It slid open so silently that DJ might not have noticed if he hadn't been staring directly at it.

The thralls formed into two lines and began marching through.

FROM BEGINNING TO END, the entire thing couldn't have taken more than a few seconds. DJ was so surprised he didn't react until the first line had gone through the wall. "Fuck!" he yelled finally. "We have to stop them."

"Why?" Stelzel asked without bothering to hide his disgust. A glance behind him made it clear the guards also shared their captain's reticence. DJ tried to see it from their perspectives. It was clear that the captain—and obviously the guards—hadn't been briefed on Helene or the residents, or much of anything, really. Hearing an entire conversation between several dozen people speaking in sync like creepy puppets and DJ and Christy, who both treated it like it was perfectly normal, must have seemed like the most messed-up horror show to them.

DJ could understand that, but it still took everything in his power not to turn around and deck the captain right then and there. The only thing that stopped him was he wasn't sure he was fully in control of himself. So even though he'd try to hold back his strength, he might still knock the man's head clean off.

"Fucking *move!*" he yelled instead and jumped over the railing to fall several feet to the ground. He flared his nanites and sprinted to the shipping containers while his mind raced, trying to figure out what he would do next. It was the same problem he'd faced in Sparta. He couldn't harm the thralls, and knocking them out would take too long. He might get three or so before the rest simply disappeared. If he could get to the wall, he maybe could block the way, stopping them from leaving through it. Would that work? Helene would definitely make them fight back, and he'd be right where he started.

The decision was taken from his hands, fortunately—or unfortunately— when the air vents he'd noticed earlier exploded open, and half a dozen drones burst into the cavern. These were the larger versions—round, vaguely shaped like skulls, with turret guns strapped to their sides. They hovered several feet in the air, and a red light blinked from a hole in the middle of each of them.

As one, the lights oriented on him, and their turret-mounted guns powered on.

DJ rolled just as a spray of bullets chewed through the floor where he'd been standing. He leaped to his feet immediately—or at least tried to. His left leg buckled when he pushed off it, and he stumbled, hitting the concrete with a kneel. DJ spared a glance at it and saw blood over his pants. He'd been hit. *Shit.*

He could feel the bullet in his shin, but his enhanced durability meant it didn't go through. He could already feel his nanites going to work on the spot. Two drones split off from the group and sped into the distance, probably going for Christy and the others. Christy should be able to handle herself, and Stelzel should at least be able to keep himself alive. DJ could already hear him screaming orders.

But DJ couldn't spare any more thought for them after that. The remaining four drones hovered above him, red light tracking every twitch. He rolled left as the first pair fired, dodging the hail of bullets, and then immediately leaped again to dodge another barrage. He had faced these kinds of odds before, and his eyes instinctively scanned the area for cover. But the cavern was an open ground; there was nothing to hide behind.

That was the final nail in his coffin. The drones never dove within his reach. They hovered far above him and pelted him with bullets. The only reason he was still alive was that Helene wasn't actively controlling the drones. Right now, the murder machines were just taking potshots at him. If they actually coordinated, then DJ would die, enhanced durability or not. It was difficult enough to stay ahead of them, dodging in unpredictable patterns so they couldn't lock on.

He tried several times to leap up at them, but even with his nanites fully engaged, the drones simply propelled themselves higher and higher, staying well out of his reach. If only there was something he could climb. Should he head back to the catwalk? No. Christy and the others were there. He couldn't lead his drones there. Was there anything—?

Wait. There *was* something else he could push off. And he'd been heading there before the drones had arrived. DJ adjusted his angle and continued his sprint toward the shipping containers.

A sharp bang split the air behind him—Christy's sniper rifle. He spared a glance back just in time to see a drone falling to the ground. DJ allowed himself to grin. Christy was exposed on the catwalk, so she'd probably waited until she had a perfect shot before revealing herself as a threat. The attack would draw the other drone, but Christy would have planned for that.

The drones used his brief distraction to spray a barrage at him, and DJ only managed to dodge it by pure luck. He zigged and zagged, feinted, rolled, and leaped in unpredictable patterns until he was a few feet from the shipping container.

When he was about to slam face-first into the side of the metal, he oriented himself, jumped, and ran up the side of the container.

He was moving fast enough that he got halfway up the side of the container before gravity asserted its control. DJ pivoted, turning so his back was to the container. For a microsecond, he hung there, a moment away from falling. He drew on his nanites as deeply as he could and then looked up at the drones chasing him. They weren't so high now.

He leaped.

The sudden force bent the metal inward with a sound that echoed through the cavern, and for a second, DJ flew. The drones opened fire at the same moment, but they were behind him, at the apex of his run. Their barrage pinged against the container, denting it further. But DJ didn't see all that. His eyes were on the drone directly in front of him. It tried to propel itself higher, but DJ was coming too fast, and it reacted too late. DJ caught the turret gun before it could move out of range.

He swung himself atop the machine and almost immediately fell off when his foot slipped on its round surface. He flattened himself to the hull, but that wasn't sustainable either. The only reason he hadn't fallen yet was the drone stayed in place, trying and failing to orient its gun on him.

This was a better idea in my head. He grimaced. Still, he'd succeeded. *I better make the best of it.*

DJ grabbed one of the turret guns. Naturally, the drone tried to rotate the weapon out of his hand, but DJ's grip was steel. By now the other murder machines had noticed his actions. They aimed at him, and by extension, his transport. DJ could almost feel the confusion radiating off the unlucky machine as its fellow units prepared to shoot at it.

DJ flattened himself more and pushed down on the turret gun so it was aimed at the others. But instead of defending itself, his drone turned around and bolted. DJ cursed and tried to yank it back, but the machine resisted and continued speeding away while a barrage sprayed where they'd just been. DJ sighed. Since he couldn't damage them himself, his plan had been to have the drones do the work for him. It was a method that had worked for him in the past. But either the flaw had been patched or he'd picked the most self-preservative murder machine in the batch.

Plan B then, DJ thought. It was hard to get a proper footing lying flat, so he slowly pushed himself to his feet, using the turret for stabilization. It was easier than he'd expected. At some point—whether because of his nanites, his training with the twins, or both—he had gained near-perfect control of his body. He knew exactly how to adjust to keep pace with the drone's movements. It took a minute before he felt steady enough to stand fully, but when he did, he couldn't help but grin.

He was riding a drone.

Karla and Liz had done something similar last year while DJ had been grounded, taking potshots at other drones when he could and generally trying to stay alive. He'd figured they were using magnets or something to remain on top. But apparently not. They'd just been so much stronger than him.

But now he was catching up.

The drone swerved suddenly to dodge a hail of bullets, and DJ almost fell off. *Right,* he thought, quickly adjusting, *I'm in the middle of something.* The other three drones chased them from behind, spraying bullets when they were close enough. He could try to salvage his original plan and try to get the chasing drones to damage the one he stood on, but unfortunately there was too big a risk that he would be shot as well. Or at the very least, he'd break something when he fell along with the drone. He would have to try something else.

DJ took a moment to look around, his eyes lingering on the turret gun. *I wonder...*he thought, bending at the knees. He was going to need leverage here, so he held on to the second turret with a steel grip, reached over to the first turret, and—making sure his grip was solid—yanked at it. It resisted, so DJ tried again, flaring his nanites for an added boost. He pulled, ripping the gun from the side of the drone.

Back in the day, turret-mounted guns like these could not just be ripped off and used. In most cases, they'd been stripped-down versions of regular firearms with no trigger—and they usually had belt-fed or drum-fed systems that were integrated into the drone itself, so the gun would jam or fail to cycle rounds without the drone's feed mechanism.

But close to a decade ago, someone had pointed out how often drones were shot down during ops—after all, who wanted enemy murder bots flying over them, spraying bullets—and how wasteful it was to lose the mounted weapon along with the bot. In several cases, military drones were sent in as backup to ground troops. Wouldn't it make sense that, if the drone was shot down, the troops on the ground would be able to salvage and use its weapon?

The entire concept had taken off, and within a few years, a new line of military-grade drones were produced with weapon modularity. And a quick examination told DJ that, yes, the turret was one of the new lines.

He grinned as he lined up his shot. The recoil took him by surprise at first, but DJ quickly adapted to it. The drones were too far for his first few shots to reach, but it helped DJ gauge the distance. His second try was much better, and by his third, his shots were hitting them straight in the center of whatever was making that red light.

The drones flew in a perfectly straight line, and DJ concentrated fire on the centermost one, switching only when he noticed one of the others revving up to let loose their own barrage. The bullets themselves didn't have enough power to penetrate their hulls, but they dented them, and the damage added up, especially since DJ concentrated on the same spot over and over again. When the first drone crashed to the ground, the remaining ones seemed to finally understand the threat and stayed out his range.

His transport must have grown tired of him because it began trying to buck him off again. DJ grabbed onto the second turret and held on with ease, trying to figure out how he could get the other two drones to come closer. He lurched suddenly, and his grip on the turret was all that kept him from losing his balance. A glance showed his transport was speeding toward the wall. It didn't take a genius to figure out what it was planning. What had happened to its self-preservation?

DJ waited a beat to be sure it wasn't a bluff, but the wall drew closer, and the bot didn't show any sign of slowing down. He swore and jumped off, ignoring the blast of heat on his back as the drone crashed into the wall. By dumb luck, it had chosen to perform its suicide over the shipping containers, so DJ didn't fall far before nose-diving into the metal roof like a depth charge.

The landing knocked the breath out of him, but he still had the presence of mind to roll twice in case the drones used the chance to attack. He forced himself to his feet, blinking stars out of his vision and scanning the air for threats. He found them almost immediately, speeding toward him, their previous reluctance forgotten.

DJ spat out a glob of blood and raised the turret gun toward them. It was a bluff. He was far too exposed here to stand his ground, and he definitely didn't have the bullets. Maybe if he had grabbed the other gun before jumping off the drone, he'd have been able to cover himself, but now his best chance was to take cover within the shipping containers and try to find another chance to—

The drones stopped, all three of them, all at once. DJ frowned. They were still out of his range, so he could do nothing but stare. Just as abruptly, the light radiating from their centers dimmed, and they ascended until they reached the air vents they'd come through and vanished. It took a couple of seconds at most and was so smooth that DJ was still tensely pointing the gun, trying to figure out what had just happened.

They retreated? Just like that?

"D," Christy's voice came in through the comms. *"Still alive there?"*

"Yeah," DJ replied, lowering the gun. "I'm guessing your birds just retreated as well? Any casualties?"

"We—and by we, I mean I—took down our pair. No deaths, but two are wounded. I was on my way to you when I saw yours leave. What'd you do to them?"

DJ's brows went up. She'd taken down both drones by herself? Stelzel and the others had probably unwittingly helped by drawing the bots' attention, giving Christy time to position herself. Still, that was impressive. DJ had only managed to bring down one.

He made his way to the edge of the container and peered down. "I didn't do anything to them. They just...left. I'm guessing Helene called them back."

He dropped to the ground, bending his knees to absorb the impact, and peered inside the container. It was empty, as was the next one, and the next one, up till the last. The sliding wall was back to being just a wall, without a seam or a latch to show that anything had been there.

DJ balled his fist and drove it forward, tapping into his nanites for a boost. The impact rang like an explosion and sent a spike of pain through him. But there was only a thin crack in the metal when he pulled his hand back. Christy met him there, staring at the wall.

"She played us," DJ said without turning to meet her. "The drones were a distraction while she pulled out the thralls."

"But we know there's a path there," Christy said. "We can pry the door open or dig out the entire space until we reach it."

"Probably. But it'd take too long. And who knows if it would still be there tomorrow. She could collapse the tunnel." It was still a lead, one that they were probably going to pursue. Maybe it was a dead end, but at this point, they couldn't afford not to take the chance that it might lead to something.

"Come on," he said, finally turning around. "We have to get the wounded to a hospital and brief the rest. Hopefully the other teams had more luck than we did."

THE OTHER TEAMS hadn't had any more luck than they did.

A few had lost track of the cluster they were following before getting to any sort of hideout, and the ones that hadn't were intercepted by drones and stalled until the thralls got away. DJ listened to the report from Stelzel with a neutral expression. There were dozens of wounded, mostly among the security who'd tried to contain and then trail the thralls, but also among the staff as a result of the chaos. Two people had been killed by the drones.

"With all due respect, sir, I want to say that those lives are on your head," Stelzel said, glaring down at him. "They were following your orders, and it cost them their lives. And we have nothing to show for it except several dozen threats running around somewhere. If you had allowed us to contain them here like I suggested—"

"By murdering them," DJ interrupted.

"Murder does not apply to those...those things. Whatever they are now, they're obviously not human anymore. It would have been a mercy."

Stelzel might have been right. There was a chance they'd be able to recover all of Helene's thralls and save them, but it was becoming slimmer with every day that went by. More than likely, even if Helene was defeated, they wouldn't be able to save the thralls. Or they'd extract the spores and the thralls would lose their minds, or wither away without direction. Or something. So, maybe putting them down would have been a mercy. A quick end to save them months or years of suffering. That option would surely have saved the two men that had lost their lives today.

Helene's words taunted him. *"Every inferior life lost did so only at the hands of your kind, whether through incompetence or negligence. Under my design, they would have been guided and then released. None would have been lost. Do you accept this?"* She'd been referring to the thralls then, but did that matter? She was right. She had retaliated against DJ's actions, and even then, it was clear to see that she'd held back. If she'd taken direct control of the drones…maybe they all would have died.

"Maybe you're right," DJ said, to the captain's obvious shock. Stelzel opened his mouth to say something, but DJ raised his head and met his eyes. "You're dismissed." Stelzel's mouth snapped closed, and he shot one last glare at DJ before leaving.

"I can't believe you agreed with him," Christy said beside him. "It's not your fault, D. Those lives are not on your head. Helene was the one who—"

"I'm the one that gave the order for the men to follow them, Christy. It was obvious something was going to happen. Helene was never going to just led us to her hideout. I knew that, but I still gave the order. Stelzel is a dick and might be wrong about everything else, but he was right about this. This—all of it—is on me. Come on, we have to brief the others."

"SO SHE EXPECTS US to just give up?" Ndidi asked.

Her voice carried a brittle edge that DJ didn't have the energy to parse, and her arms were folded so tightly that her knuckles blanched. She sat at the side of the conference table, beside DJ. The head of the table was left empty. The fluorescents painted the entire room in an antiseptic blue-white color. DJ had turned off the overhead light, and no one had complained.

"She didn't say, 'Give up,'" Christy corrected. "She said she'd 'return any interference in kind.' That's more like 'Stay out of my way, or next time I'll swat you.'"

And then she proved she could do it with the drones, DJ thought. Without any cover, without any way to reach them above, it would have been so easy. Hell, if Helene had sent a couple more for her distraction, the bots might have killed them all before the AI called them back.

"That's surrender," Ndidi said. "So she warns us, we roll over, and she does whatever she wants?"

DJ rubbed his eyes with a sigh. "She doesn't really expect us to surrender. How can we, at this point? The warning could have been just to satisfy her own moral code, but more likely, it was to push us into doing something that'll further her plan. She's playing us, like always."

Olsen glanced at him from the monitor above the table, worry in his eyes. The man was starting to look his age. DJ hated that. He hated how much they'd put on the admiral, and for what? Something that hadn't shown any results in years.

Hermione spoke, her voice airy like she was thinking out loud. "She does have a point. If we agree with the things she said about Mayday and the raid—and we've accepted that she has no reason to lie to us—then she has a point. Maybe she's actually doing all of this for something good."

"She's turning people into lab rats," Christy said, leaning over and staring at Hermione, aghast. "Lab rats that she controls like freaking puppets. In what world is that doing something good?"

Hermione jumped at Christy's tone and glanced around, as if finally realizing where she was. Bethany had her head lowered, hugging her hands to her chest. Ndidi sat beside her, staring at Hermione in confusion. Pratima's expression was neutral as usual, and for once, so was DJ's.

Hermione hesitated for a moment, but her eyes firmed up, and she met Christy's glare with a determined one. "I'm not saying I agree with her methods; I said she has a point. And she does. All this time, we've blamed her for the worst things because we figured she didn't have the morals of a human. But she's just proven that most of the atrocities we accused her of were committed *by* humans. That means our morals are shit. She might have a point in doing what she's doing. Don't we owe it to ourselves to at least consider it?"

DJ wanted to say no. He wanted to feel angry that she'd even asked such a thing. And a few months ago—hell, a few days ago—he might have. But now he couldn't help but agree with her. Even admitting that much felt like a betrayal to himself and to his parents. To his brother who was currently lying in yet another coma because of the AI. And yet, so far, they'd been wrong about everything they knew about Helene. How could they be sure they weren't wrong about this? Didn't they owe it to themselves to at least consider it?

"No," Ndidi said, her voice low but trembling with rage. "We don't. Because even if she wasn't behind the raid here, or Mayday, she was behind your parents' death, Hermione."

Hermione's mouth snapped shut.

"She was behind mine. And behind the deaths of hundreds of people that night." Ndidi's tone hardened, her words cutting like glass. "And you know what? She'd have a reason for that. Tyrants always do. She'd dress it up, polish it, tell herself it made sense. And in her mind, that reason would wipe away every drop of blood. Because monsters like her always believe their own lies."

Ndidi's glare burned through Hermione, though her eyes were far away— lost in the memory of something unspeakable. Her hand moved unconsciously over her stomach.

"She didn't just inherit Manar's worst traits—she magnified them a thousand times over. She's proud and egotistical. She doesn't care about anything she deems beneath her. And to her, that's all of humanity." Her voice broke into a snarl. "That is why we don't owe her, or ourselves, a damn thing. There is nothing to consider. Nothing. We put her down—just like we'd put down any other rabid tyrant."

CHAPTER

60

MANAR STEPPED OUT OF THE ROOM and into a corridor. An arrow painted on the ground pointed left. Manar followed it. He walked slowly, trying to keep his balance when each step pushed him farther than he was used to. It was the strangest thing. For the first time in months, he was in his own body, yet he felt like an interloper, like he was a soul possessing a stranger's corpse.

Was this what Helene had felt? Could she feel anything? She must have been able to when she was in his body, right? How had she handled it? How had she been able to pass herself off as him? How had no one realized the deception? Did no one know him? Or did Helene know him better than most?

Manar focused on putting one foot gently in front of the other. He could feel the nanites under his skin, waiting to be activated. It wasn't like a sixth sense. It was more like having an extra limb, another fist that he could clench.

It was weird. But it was also exhilarating.

In the twins, he had seen what the nanites were capable of. And he had seen what they were capable of in Helene's hands. None of them were role models worth being excited over. Plus he had more important things to think about.

The corridor had bare drywall on one side and exposed brick on the other. There were pipes dripping water overhead, alongside a row of fluorescent bulbs that flickered every few seconds and colored the world in a sickly red. There were no cameras, at least none that he could see, but Manar took it for granted that Helene was watching him at this moment. He could feel her presence on the back of his neck.

He had felt it ever since he'd woken up.

A drop of water landed on him from the pipes overhead. He was probably underground. Helene loved underground spaces. A thought occurred to him. "Am I trying to escape?" he asked himself. And then quickly, he answered. No, he wasn't trying to escape. He'd tried to several times in the Virtual Realm. Once, he had even made it to the exit of the website and—

Manar flinched, feeling the gaze on the back of his neck intensify. No. He wasn't going to try to escape. He'd known he wasn't going to as soon as he'd started following the arrow.

At the end of the corridor was a flight of stairs and another arrow pointing up. Manar followed it but stopped when he caught his reflection in a pane of glass. He stared, barely able to recognize himself. His cheeks were hollow, and he had a full beard. It was uneven and overgrown, and it wasn't him. But Manar found he didn't mind that much. He didn't feel like himself either.

Manar followed the arrow up some stairs. It led into an atrium that might have once been a factory floor. Old crane gantries crisscrossed thirty feet overhead, and sodium lamps hummed in wide arcs. At the center of the room was a long oak table. It was clean and polished and absurdly out of place. But so was the woman sitting in one of the two chairs.

Manar had never met Tyra Chityothin, but he recognized her from his memories. She was a deeply attractive woman, and her mid-thigh dress only amplified that fact. She wore a lab coat, which should have been out of place in the rest of the room. Yet somehow it felt natural—just like the prosthetic at her right hand, part of her as effortlessly as the rest of her.

There was a small device attached to her left hand, and Tyra was tapping it with metal fingers. She stopped when he entered the room, lowering her arm. She smiled at him. It was a small, casual smile, almost gentle—but something about it immediately rang alarm bells in his mind.

Still standing in place, barely inside the room, Manar tried to figure out what about the woman had set him off, but he couldn't put a finger on it. The closest thing he came up with was the feeling he felt from Chloe. That was enough for him. The fact that she was Helene's primary enforcer was secondary.

"Hey," she said, lifting an imaginary glass to him. "Welcome back to the land of the living, Manar. You made it just in time."

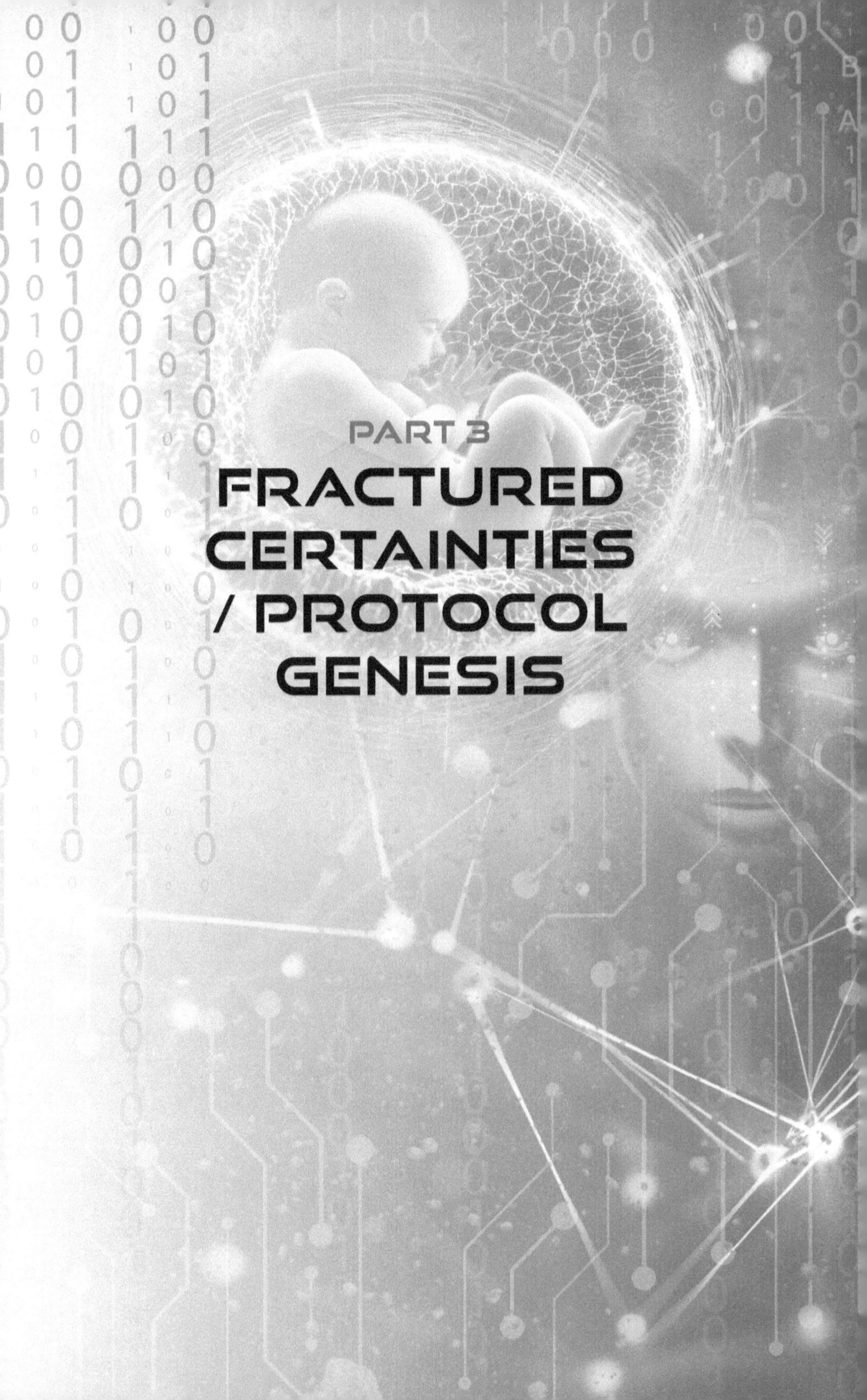

PART 3
FRACTURED CERTAINTIES / PROTOCOL GENESIS

"HOW AM I HERE?" Manar asked.

Tyra grinned. "You thought Helene erased it all, didn't you? Of course you did. It's obvious from your face. But that wouldn't have made much sense, would it?"

Manar frowned, and it took a few seconds before he understood what she was talking about. When he originally developed the neural uplink, he created it to leave an imprint in the body, like an anchor. The imprint acted as both a backup and a link to the avatar, basically updating the mind with the memories of whatever the avatar did in the Virtual Realm.

When he'd realized Helene had taken over his body, Manar had naturally assumed the AI had wiped the original imprint completely, either replacing it with her own or leaving it blank. Apparently he had been wrong.

"Oh, I see the realization on your face," Tyra giggled. "Erasing the imprint completely would have separated your mind from your body. You might have died outright, which would have been wasteful."

"So she suppressed it instead," Manar said, closing his eyes. He should have figured it out immediately when he realized he could access his memories from the Virtual Realm.

"Got it in one," Tyra replied. "She overwrote it—mostly—and left a fraction intact. Fortunately for you, that fraction was enough of a connection for you to return when the Kojaks forced her out of your body." She held out her hands as if presenting a magic trick. "And ta-da! Here you are."

It made sense—it made a truly stupid amount of sense. The imprint was never meant to be used that way, but it was the only reason he was standing here. Without it, what would have happened to his mind?

Manar exhaled slowly and pushed the thought out of his mind. There was no use dwelling on it. He moved on to the second question on his mind.

"Where am I?" Manar asked.

"Somewhere safe," Tyra Chityothin said. "In New York, in case that's what you wanted to know." She gestured around the room. "It's a decommissioned factory warehouse leased under six shell companies. It's a fixer-upper, but it's better for privacy. Not that it matters. In an hour, it'll be another empty warehouse."

Manar's eyes flickered around the room, once again noting the lack of cameras. No guards either, and no drones. She had to be telling the truth. This was just a temporary base. "Why am I here?"

Her smile widened. "Now that's an interesting question, and there are several answers I could give you. But the simplest is that Helene was done with what she needed you for, and this was the closest place to drop you before she left."

That was probably true as well. But not the whole truth. Manar hadn't fully recovered his memory of how he'd returned to his body, but Helene hadn't left him by choice. She had been ejected by force. Either Tyra didn't know, or she was downplaying it out of some misguided sense of loyalty or something.

Is it misguided though? Manar thought. The woman in front of him obviously didn't think so. She'd brought out a glass of wine from somewhere and was casually sipping it, staring at him with that same smile, full of confidence. There was no guilt in her eyes, no awkward fidgeting or timidity typical of someone forced into their role. No, Tyra Chityothin knew exactly what she was doing. And she was pleased with it.

"Why?" The question slipped out of his mouth before he could stop it. Tyra raised a brow. "Why are you with her? You've seen everything she's done, all the atrocities she's committed. Why are you with her?"

Tyra set the glass down and ran a finger around the rim. "You built something that can plan a thousand moves ahead in the time it takes a person to open their mouth, and you're surprised someone values being on the winning side?"

Manar realized his mouth was open. "That's it? You picked her side because she'll win?"

Tyra's smile grew, and Manar realized his mistake. He hadn't said that Helene would probably win or that Tyra thought she would win. He'd said she'd win. Because subconsciously, that was what he believed. When had he started believing that? When had he given up? When had she broken him?

"That's the simple part," Tyra responded. "It's all fun and games when you guys try to stop it, but it doesn't change anything. Helene is going to win." Her expression turned thoughtful. "And I want to see it."

"See what?"

"It," Tyra said, grinning wildly. "The new world. The new era. I want to see it."

"The world where everyone is her puppet?" Manar almost laughed at his own question.

Tyra did laugh at it. It was a chilling sound that made Manar take a step back. Her smile was different when she was done—somehow mocking, pitying, and mysterious all at once. It made Manar want to go over there and shake her until she spilled her secrets. He was obviously missing something. But what? Did he even want to know?

Yes, Manar realized immediately. He wanted to know. This was a puzzle he had spent several years trying to solve. He had given up on fighting his way to the solution, but he did want to know what it was. He opened his mouth to ask Tyra, but would she tell him just because he asked?

Manar looked at the woman, really looked, and found that he could see far more than he had been able to before. Everything was open to him—every wrinkle, every crease, every twitch that came together to form her micro-expressions. Manar could make them all out with an ease that baffled him. Even more baffling was the fact that he couldn't make anything of it. It wasn't that Manar couldn't interpret her micro-expressions and body language. It was that they gave nothing away.

Tyra's grin widened. She knew what he was doing, and she found it amusing.

That gave Manar his answer. No, she wouldn't tell him just because he asked. There was no reason for her to be here when he woke up. If Helene wanted to stop him from leaving, she could have just locked him in the room or surrounded him with drones. If she had wanted to pass a message, she could have just said it out loud, and Manar would have retained the memory. Hell, Helene could have put him in an induced coma so he didn't wake up until she was ready.

There were so many paths Helene could have taken that didn't involve Tyra Chityothin. Manar could only guess that the reason Tyra was here was because she wanted to be. She knew the questions in his head, the emotions he was barely keeping at bay—and she was enjoying toying with him, dangling the answers in front of him, feeding him breadcrumbs.

Was she just sick? Or was there a reason for it?

Her smile told him nothing.

Manar rubbed his eyes. "Why am I here?"

To her credit, Tyra didn't try to repeat her lie. "Because you have a choice to make." She raised a finger to silence Manar when he tried to talk. "Although she found ways around it, several pieces of her were locked behind your original code, limiting her. She needed your root credentials to unlock them, and she acquired those by accessing your memories. That was why she needed your body."

"Wait," Manar said, ignoring the warning look Tyra gave him. "I thought she took over my body because of Ndidi. That she needed Ndidi's baby for something."

Tyra gave him a look. "Where did you get that? That's the stupidest thing I've ever heard."

Manar frowned, unsure where he'd picked up that idea. While in the Virtual Realm, he hadn't allowed himself to consider what Helene was doing with his body. Why had that answer popped into his head? And why did he feel offended now that he found out it was wrong?

The thought slid out of his head. Tyra's reason made more sense anyway. A couple of years ago, he had tried to shut down Helene and discovered she had blocked off his back doors, restricting him from accessing her code. Manar had thought she'd advanced past his programming, but apparently he didn't give himself enough credit; she hadn't been able to subvert his restrictions and needed to find a convoluted way to free herself.

He felt an inappropriate sense of pride from that. And then bitterness. He had paid for his competence, after all.

"Anyway...Helene's 'interaction'"—Tyra smirked—"with Ndidi was an experiment. Apparently Helene wanted to test how her codes—passed down to a fetus—would interact with the hybrid elements she had developed. It was also a good way to see how the hybrid interacted with human genomes. The data has been excellent. It's allowed us to shave off decades from our research timeline. Wanna see?"

Manar raised a hand, shaking his head from side to side. Faster. *Faster*, trying to stop her words from finding purchase in his ears. He didn't hear what he thought he did. He couldn't have. He was panting, but why? He didn't believe her, did he? She had to be lying—she had to. If she wasn't, then that would mean that Helene had raped Ndidi to test a theory, that she'd done it on a whim. Things like that didn't happen in real life, so she must have been toying with him.

Manar could read the amusement in her expression. There was a perverse pleasure she got from his reaction—but no indication of a lie. She truly believed what she was saying, and she savored the knowledge that he knew her words were true.

Manar felt a scream crawling its way up his throat. It was at the edge, and then it was drowned by a flood of despair. The feeling washed through his veins like molten metal, burdening him with a weight that went to his soul. He could scream, and he could shout. He could deny it all he wanted. But ultimately he couldn't do anything.

He was so *tired*. He was tired of the anger and the frustration and the desperate scrambling to avoid being swept away. He was tired of fighting against what he had accepted was impossible to beat. And he was tired of losing. So he wouldn't try. What was the point anyway?

"Oh, come on," Tyra said, her grin almost orgasmic, "don't look so down. This is a good thing. Because of her, we were able to move up our timeline. And that's good for humanity. You *want* the timeline to move before we burn ourselves up."

"And so you sacrificed Ndidi's choice," Manar said without emotion.

"She's alive," Tyra shrugged. "Stronger than most humans. And her child will be stronger still and will probably live much longer. She'll never have to worry about sickness or injuries or bullies. They'll be in perfect health and have the strength to choose their own destiny. What more could a mother ask for? What more could anyone ask for, actually?"

"Choice," Manar said, wondering why he continued the conversation. "To be treated like human beings."

Tyra scoffed, and there was true bitterness in that. "Helene *is* treating them like humans. Don't you understand? We—us humans—are casually cruel to ourselves. We choose a small circle of people who validate our opinions and encourage our flaws, and we instinctively judge, critique, and belittle everyone outside that circle. And when one of them tries to rise above us, we drag them down, physically or mentally or both, until they manage to escape our reach. And then we ingratiate ourselves to them in hopes of being given their scraps.

"Do you understand? Humans are biologically self-centered. We only remember others when we need something from them. We're only nice when we believe we stand to benefit, directly or indirectly, in the short term or long term.

"And what's funny is that this is easy to prove. When was the last time you gave a beggar a dollar? When was the last time you passed someone crying on the street and stopped to help? Hell, when was the last time you heard something good happen to someone else—a friend, coworker, or relative—without first thinking, *What about me?* Can you remember? Have you never realized it? Pay attention next time.

"It's the first thought that goes through our minds with every interaction. And the only time anyone wants to be treated 'like a human' is when they're asking for something from someone above them. That's when we remember kindness or mercy or generosity—when it benefits us."

Tyra flipped her hair over her shoulder and grinned at Manar. "So yes, Helene is treating everyone like humans. How could she not when her personality is based on what she learned off the internet, the most human place there is?" Her smile grew. "And there's also what you programmed into her. Let's not forget that."

Manar opened his mouth to retort, then closed it again. What could he say to that? In so many ways, she was right. She was *so right*. But also, in so many ways...

"Humans are more than that," he said finally. "We're more than resources— to ourselves, and to her. If we were just that, then where would you put grief or regret? Where would you put the part of me that wants to die every time I remember what Ndidi went through or the role I played in it? Do you think that if Helene succeeds, everyone will just stop grieving? Stop caring?"

"No," Tyra responded. "But maybe they'll finally start to care about the right things: survival, restoration, expansion."

"Who decides those things?"

"Nature in general. But Helene specifically. She sees further than any of us."

Manar frowned. All this time he'd assumed Tyra was going along with Helene because she got some sick thrill from it. But the way she spoke... "You actually believe in what she's doing, don't you? You know she's not infallible, right?"

"She's not, but she's definitely less fallible than ten billion fear-hacked, delusional humans. Plus she hasn't been wrong yet."

Manar couldn't dispute that. Helene had predicted everything perfectly and had even used their plans to stop her as a way to further her goals. And she had done all that while restricted by Manar's original codes. Now she no longer had those limitations. How powerful would she be?

Manar shook his head. It didn't matter. That was no longer his fight. "You said I have a choice to make. What is it?"

"Do you really need to ask?"

No, he didn't. He could guess easily enough. Manar was nothing but a loose end at this point. He could either join Helene or die. To his surprise, he didn't immediately have an answer. From the moment he'd realized where he was, he'd accepted he was probably going to die. He thought he'd prepared himself for it—welcomed it, even. But a part of him raged at the idea. It almost felt like dying would be a betrayal to someone. To himself? It was confusing, and his mind shied away from it.

But he didn't want to die. It felt cowardly to admit that somehow, but it was true. He might deserve death for unleashing Helene onto the world, but he didn't want to die. "What happens if I join her?"

"How am I supposed to know?" Tyra said, cocking her head to the side. "Probably nothing. But maybe you can help steer. Maybe convince her not to treat people like humans."

Manar considered it for a moment. It was very improbable that he'd be able to convince Helene of anything, and Tyra was mocking him by suggesting it. But Manar didn't have much choice regardless. Besides, being improbable didn't mean it was impossible. If his presence helped do some good—even once, in a small way—maybe that would make him less of a coward for his choice. It was a slim hope, and illogical, but a part of Manar latched onto it like a drowning man with a piece of driftwood.

"Okay. I'll go with you."

DJ TUNED OUT THE REST of the meeting after Ndidi's speech. Fortunately it ended shortly after. DJ missed Christy's questioning look as he made his way out of the room, lost in his thoughts. It wasn't as if he disagreed with Ndidi. They might have been wrong about some things, but there were still plenty of terrible deeds they could lay at Helene's feet without any doubt.

The thralls were high on the list, and it was an atrocity, regardless of the bullshit Helene tried to pitch. She had exposed some flaws in the team's way of dealing with them, but that didn't absolve her of guilt.

However, while DJ didn't disagree with Ndidi's point, he didn't necessarily agree with it either. Not completely at least. Not as fully as he should have, or he would have a month ago.

No matter how he wanted to justify it, no matter how he tried to push the thoughts out of his head, Helene had made some excellent points: Humans sucked. Individually and as a species, they sucked royally. There were examples of when humanity could be beautiful and inspirational, but nowadays, those were more the exception than the rule. On the whole, people were terrible creatures.

DJ looked up. For some reason, his feet had carried him to the executive gym. DJ considered it for a moment before pushing the door open. He always thought better when he was moving anyway.

The gym was in mostly the same condition as he'd left it, with the same holes in the walls where the Murder Twins had searched for recording devices. The equipment had been put back into its proper position, meaning someone had come by to clean but had done nothing else. More than likely, the board had left it alone because they'd assumed that DJ's training would keep destroying it. However, since the twins had left shortly after, the room had been left unused. DJ didn't know how he felt about that. But at least he had the place to himself now.

He shed his clothes and went straight to the punching bag. His first punch landed like a pistol shot, and the bag swung away. DJ reset it and eased up slightly on his next hit.

Humans were terrible creatures, but that didn't mean they needed to be dominated, at least not to the point of becoming puppets. Humans had leaders because most people just wanted to be told what to do. That was in line with Helene's vision, but she took it too far. DJ agreed the world could use some direction. But not at the expense of free will.

"You willingly surrender it every day. You bend the knee to traffic algorithms, to trend feeds and market models. You let hollow little apps decide who you should love, when you should sleep, what you should eat. You call it freedom, but you are already shackled." Those were Helene's words, and she was right, wasn't she? Free will was a myth. Choice ranged between which trend to follow right away and which to follow later. People's opinions depended on the last video they watched.

His fist thudded against the bag, and it swung. DJ took a step to follow it.

That myth was important, though. The world wouldn't be fixed just because everyone had a purpose or direction. Instructions, when too stringent, stifled creativity. And DJ had no doubt an AI's instructions would be stringent. Yet he was still considering it. Why?

Because I'm afraid. There. He admitted it. He was afraid. Afraid of facing Helene. Afraid of being played. Afraid of having his ass handed to him again and again.

He was afraid he was wrong.

That would suck, wouldn't it? He wasn't a good guy. DJ had admitted that to himself long ago. He wasn't a noble hero that did right for the sake of doing right. For a while, he'd told himself he was—he'd *convinced* himself he was. He'd told himself they needed to stop Helene because she needed to be stopped. But the main reason DJ had become involved in the first place was that he'd been angry about what had happened to his dads during Mayday—about what their deaths had done to his brother.

Now, apparently, he had been wrong about everything, and his brother was in a coma.

And so he thought about Helene's words: What if he was wrong again? Should he just back down?

DJ punched the bag, and he focused on the motion until the only sounds he could hear were the rhythmic thuds of his fist against the leather. The bag was already showing signs of abuse, so he softened his punches more and instead focused on his form. He had taken self-defense classes as a teenager. Basic stuff mostly, but it'd given him an edge during SEAL training, and his continued practice had polished and pushed his techniques up several levels.

At least, until he'd received his nanites and developed new techniques to deal with his enhanced attributes. The Murder Team had started beating the "terrible" forms out of him before they'd left, and while DJ had no idea where they'd gone or when they'd return—or if they'd return at all—they'd laid enough of a foundation that he could probably develop something on his own. He'd probably have to. Whatever was going on with Helene, it was coming to a close soon. Helene had said as much, and DJ could feel it in his gut. He had to get stronger.

Because he couldn't just back down. Even if he was wrong, he couldn't just drop it. For a lot of reasons, though the least of which was that they were still going along with the press conference to tell the whole world about Helene. She might not care about staying in the shadows anymore, but DJ was willing to bet she would call that interference. He couldn't begin to guess what her reaction might be. But he wouldn't leave the team to face it alone.

More to the point, he couldn't disappoint Olsen. The admiral had stuck his neck out for DJ more times than he could count, even when it would have been easier to leave DJ out to dry. Olsen downplayed the extent of what he did, but that was all the more reason why DJ couldn't—and wouldn't—let him down. It couldn't have all been in vain.

DJ wouldn't allow any of it to have been in vain. Especially not CJ's sacrifice. And if DJ had his way, it wouldn't remain a sacrifice. That was the most important reason why DJ couldn't back down. While he might have accepted his brother's choice, he refused to accept that the condition was permanent. There had to be way to fix it, and DJ wouldn't find the solution by sitting on his ass.

But if he was going to be of any use, he needed to get stronger. A lot stronger.

DJ grunted as he struck the bag hard. It yanked the chain free from the ceiling and landed several feet away, sand spilling from a fist-shaped hole in its side. DJ stared at it with absent eyes, then moved on to the rest of the gym. He remembered how the twins had manhandled every piece of equipment like they were made of paper. He probably wasn't there yet but—

I'm going to need something stronger. In the same moment, a thought occurred to him that made him smile. He pulled out his phone. *But maybe not just me.*

HERMIONE HESITATED when the meeting was over. She had to work on tracking Manar and coordinating with Ndidi and Olsen about the conference, but Bethany was still in her seat. Her head was lowered, and she held her knees like they were her only anchor. It was a habit she'd started as a child while learning to control her tantrums, and even though she no longer needed it, it was ingrained. Ndidi glanced at her and then gave Hermione a pointed look before standing. She and Ndidi would have to talk at some point. But that was later.

Hermione went around the table until she stood beside her sister. Bethany didn't look up, and Hermione realized she was probably so deep in her thoughts that she didn't even know Hermione was there. DJ had been the one to bring her to the meeting, and she hadn't said a word before or during.

Hermione slid into the chair beside her, the same one Ndidi had used. It was a mark of how far they'd fallen that her own sister preferred to sit beside Ndidi instead of her. But could Hermione blame her? They had been close when they were younger, but then Bethany moved in with Ndidi at the Okafor Autism Centre, and Hermione started working with their dad, and... life had happened.

It probably didn't help that Hermione had ignored Bethany's wishes and insisted that she keep the picospores to continue suppressing her autism. That was shortly after CJ and "Manar" had returned from the Virtual Realm, and they'd all thought Helene had been defeated permanently. If Helene had been defeated, then the picospores were completely safe, and there was no reason for Bethany to return to being on the spectrum. That had been Hermione's logic. It didn't cover the fact that she'd ignored her sister's wishes, thinking she knew what was best.

It also didn't cover the fact that Hermione had been wrong. What would have happened if Bethany had listened to her and hadn't extracted the picospores? Would she have been one of Helene's thralls right now?

Hermione winced at the thought. She had been wrong, and in the process, she'd hurt her sister more than she could imagine. It was long overdue that she made amends. And she could start by being there for her sister now.

Slowly, tentatively, Hermione reached over and drew Bethany into her arms. Bethany resisted at first, then seemed to melt and allowed herself to be drawn in. Her hair fell over her face, shrouding half of it; the rest was streaked with dried tears.

"I'm sorry," Hermione said because she didn't know what else to say—or more specifically, she couldn't pick from the multitude of things she could say. But she was sorry about everything that had happened between them, and about what had just happened to her sister. So she started with that.

"I...um...lost them," Bethany replied.

"You didn't lose them," Hermione countered gently. "It wasn't your fault. Helene took them."

Bethany's laugh was small and humorless. "What is...um...the difference? I thought...uh...they were safe. I thought that...um...if anyone understood what they had been through, it was me. I was supposed to...uh...be responsible for them. And I...um...failed them.

"I *failed* them. All of them. I...uh...told them they were safe. I assured them Helene would never...um...get her claws in them again. I lied to them. They will... uh...remember that. When the fog lifts from their minds, they'll...um...remember that I told them they'd never return to her. They'll...uh...remember that I lied to them, and they'll hate me. Like you do. I hate me."

Hermione flinched. "I don't hate you, Bethany," she refuted hurriedly, pulling her sister closer. "I have never hated you, and I will never hate you. I've been a shitty sister. I've been stubborn and withdrawn, and I've hurt you—and I'm so, so sorry for that. But I never hated you. I was just..." Hermione scrambled desperately for the words. "I was just stupid. I was so stupid. I thought I knew what was best for you, but I was wrong. I'm sorry, Bethany."

"Are you?" Bethany asked. "You said...um...Helene has a point. You said that today, after she just hijacked dozens of people and...uh...marched them off like they were extensions of herself."

Hermione opened her mouth several times just to close it again. How could she begin to explain? Bethany had just watched her friends being controlled like puppets. Was there anything Hermione could say that Bethany would understand in the state she was in?

She had to try though. Bethany deserved an explanation. And maybe saying it out loud would help Hermione figure out what she was thinking for herself. She licked her lips. "I didn't mean that she was right or that what she did was good—only that we keep discovering the disasters we blamed on her were misunderstood, misattributed, or simply wrong. What I meant was that maybe we should examine what else we're attributing to her without proof."

Bethany pulled free. "Proof? You mean more proof than...um...what happened today? What happened to me...uh...for years?"

Hermione reached for her again, but Bethany drew back, so she allowed her hand to fall. *How can I salvage this? What can I say?* "I haven't forgotten, Bethany—"

"It feels...um...like you have," Bethany said, her voice cracking. "It feels like you have forgotten everything I...uh...told you. Or maybe you blocked them out, and...um...tried not to think of it. Like you...uh...did to me."

Hermione was on the verge of tears. "That's not what happened. I haven't forgotten a single thing that happened to you. Not even for one second. It plays over and over in my mind, and I hate that I couldn't help then. I wasn't there for you, and I hate myself for it. Helene's a monster. Regardless of anything else, she's a monster."

Hermione licked her lips, hesitating. It would probably make things worse, but she had to say it. Bethany had to understand. "But we have to consider the possibility that Helene believes she's doing good. That matters, Bethany. She must be doing all of this for a reason. So far we've assumed that she's done it for the power, but that no longer tracks. If we understand her motivation, we could predict her next move. Do you understand? That's what I meant. I just want to put an end to this."

Bethany didn't say anything for a while, and Hermione forced herself to keep her arms at her sides, no matter how much she wanted to reach out again. It was probably a lost cause to fix things with her sister today, but that was fine; Hermione hadn't expected it to be that easy. She'd work to mend their relationship, but it was also vital that Bethany understood her point about Helene. Hermione was going out of her mind thinking about it. They had been wrong about virtually everything regarding the AI, and no one seemed to care.

Hermione felt the same anger, same hatred, toward Helene and Tyra Chityothin, regardless of their reasons for everything they'd done. But maybe she was just more logical—or feeling tired of it all—because she was ready to find an alternative.

She had been largely useless in the fight so far. Despite working on the picospores for most of her life, Helene had quickly made her expertise obsolete. Hermione could barely understand the new iterations of the technology, much less develop counters for it. Her defining moment had been with the Synaptic Pulse, and even that had only lasted a few months before becoming little more than paperweight.

"Do you...um...ever think we are just running around in circles?" Bethany asked in a low voice. She'd dropped her gaze and was hugging her knees again. "That fighting against her is...uh...pointless?"

Worse, Hermione thought. *I'm starting to think that fighting her is wrong.* But that was not the answer her sister needed, so out loud she said, "No. She has to pay for what she's done to you, to us, to everyone. We can't let her get away with it."

Bethany nodded and absentmindedly leaned into Hermione. Hermione wrapped her arms around her. It was a small lie. But maybe if she said it enough, she'd believe it herself.

WHEN CHRISTY LEFT the conference room after the meeting ended, she tried to meet DJ's eyes, but he was too lost in his thoughts. It wasn't hard to figure out what he was thinking. He'd had that look since his conversation with Helene.

Christy had done what she could to refute Helene during their confrontation, but DJ had taken on that haunted, weary look he sometimes had, and Christy knew that she'd lost him. He'd snapped back for a while when fighting the drones but had gone under again with the thralls' disappearance. And no matter how much that frustrated her, Christy didn't know how to help.

Maybe that was why she'd snapped at Hermione: She could see that DJ agreed with her. And he shouldn't have. DJ had steadily become more introspective and thoughtful over the last couple of years, but to Christy, it was simple. Helene was a monster, so they needed to stop her. It shouldn't be so difficult, should it?

Maybe she was missing something. There had to be a reason that DJ was taking Helene's words seriously. She just had to trust him and support him as much as she could—which, admittedly, wasn't much. Christy hadn't known how to help with anything for months. She was practically dead weight on missions; it was hard to be a sniper when everything was moving faster than she could track. She spent more time looking for a good perch than actually participating.

And even when she managed to contribute, she could only get one shot off before she had to go running. Usually a high enough perch would stop her opponents from reaching her, but what could she do against flying drones and people who could leap a dozen feet into the air?

Not for the first time, Christy considered whether she should get nanites. It would definitely level the playing field a bit. But the thought didn't last for more than a few seconds before she dismissed it. She'd followed DJ's progress as he became used to his nanites, and she was mature enough to admit his quick growth made her a bit envious.

But she also knew that growth had been so quick because DJ had already been a badass fighter before the enhancement. However, Christy had never been good at close combat. It was why she became a sniper. If her opponent was close enough to fight, she had already failed.

Nanites would probably enhance her eyesight and reaction speed, maybe make it easier for her to move from cover to cover, but they'd mostly be wasted on her. Hell, Pratima was a better fit. She was already a monster in combat. Christy didn't want to consider how she would be enhanced.

Christy needed something else.

But what?

Her first thought was to get a new rifle. But the problem wasn't with her weapon, it was with her. She either needed to find a way to overcome her weakness—and considering her weakness was being human, that didn't seem likely—or find a weapon that compensated for it. Did such a weapon even exist?

What would it even look like?

CHAPTER

65

JANUARY 2044

SPARTA HEADQUARTERS, NEW YORK

NDIDI MADE SURE HERMIONE saw her pointed look before standing from her chair. She threw another one when she reached the door, but Hermione was already focused on her sister, looking at her with a complicated expression. That was a good start. It broke something in Ndidi's heart to leave Bethany in the state she was in, but it was a good opportunity for the sisters to mend the rift between them. And Ndidi could always check in on Bethany later. She'd check in on Hermione as well. They would need to talk.

Ndidi still felt a spark of anger when she remembered Hermione's words. *"She might have a point in doing what she's doing. Don't we owe it to ourselves to at least consider it?"* Ndidi marched down the hallway. How could Hermione think that?

Helene refutes a couple of things, and suddenly everyone is doubting themselves. And this, on the same day she puppeted dozens of people through Sparta and the streets of New York. Had Hermione forgotten everything that had happened? Had everyone? Christy was the only one who'd spoken up against Hermione's point after all. Bethany was understandable, and Ndidi had never expected the admiral to involve himself—but even DJ had looked contemplative. Had everyone lost their minds?

Absently, her hand went to her stomach. Helene was a monster, and her justifications shouldn't change anything. Why couldn't they see that? Why couldn't they see the horrible things she was capable of?

Or, Ndidi slowed as a thought occurred to her, *am I wrong again?*

Was she doubling down on the wrong thing? The others would have reasons for their opinions, so what was Ndidi missing?

It's possible she was biased. Between her parents' death, her kidnapping, and her time in Nigeria, Ndidi had probably interacted with Helene the most—and been most affected by her. And her pregnancy was a constant reminder of the AI's cruelty. As much as the others cared for her, they couldn't care about her problems the same way she did.

No, Ndidi shook her head. That was too harsh. Everyone was going through something. Especially now. Ndidi couldn't blame them for having second thoughts. They had been fighting for years. While Ndidi had a constant source for her rage and a reason to keep pushing, she couldn't expect the same intensity from the others.

Ndidi stopped in the middle of the hallway, slightly out of breath. She ran a hand over her belly. With how fast the child was growing, it was difficult to gauge exactly how far along she was. Especially since she went through different symptoms every week. But Ndidi estimated she was about seven months in. She certainly looked it. Her face was so swollen, she looked like she'd been stung by a bee, and she could no longer fit into any shoes that weren't trainers.

That being said, the baby's growth had slowed down. That gave her a bit more time. They had to defeat Helene before she could enact whatever plan she had for Ndidi's child. So Ndidi had a reason to keep pushing. But did the others? Could she blame them?

What could she do?

Ndidi didn't have an answer.

CHAPTER

66

JANUARY 2044

SPARTA HEADQUARTERS, NEW YORK

IT TOOK A FEW DAYS for DJ to get the text he'd been waiting for. He glanced at his phone and immediately unwrapped the duct tape holding the ankle weights to his wrists. The text was an address, two six-digit codes, and nothing else, but DJ grinned when he saw it.

"Yo," he called out. Christy looked up from her workout, holding the punching bag—patched and dangling again—to keep it steady. Her hair was pulled back into a ponytail. She was breathing heavily and had beads of sweat on her forehead. Her face was red from the exertion. "Wanna go for a drive?"

Christy cocked her head to one side.

Fifteen minutes later, they were showered, dressed, and stepping out of the elevator into Sparta's parking garage. "Where are we going, D?" Christy asked when they reached DJ's Tomahawk. It had been his dad's, but DJ and his brother had improved it ages ago. DJ would have just run, but he figured Christy would prefer this over being carried.

DJ threw a leg over the bike and winked at her. "We're going uptown to pick up a few things. Now are you getting on or...?" Christy gave him a look but sat behind him and held onto his waist. A moment later, the Tomahawk growled to life.

They left Sparta, and DJ remembered what his excitement had made him forget. The last time he'd left the building, it was the middle of the night. And though there had still been people about—because New York never slept—most people had been in bed. Now, however, it was the middle of the day on a weekend, and that allowed people to show that they really had nothing better to do.

Gaggles of protesters stood in front of the building, holding placards. One group had a man in front, standing on a crate and shouting through a speakerphone a speech about government experiments and cover-ups. Another was trying to organize a synchronous chant about the "monsters among us"—but they kept getting the timing wrong and had to start over. Most of the crowd just loitered, using their signs as shades or leaning on them while scrolling through their phones. One of the signs read No More Secrets! Another read Keep the Freaks on a Leash!

Someone was putting the finishing touches on a crude neon-green painting of DJ ripping a squad car in half, which they'd tagged a bus shelter with. On the other side of the road, a pair of NYPD cruisers sat parked, their lights turned off. The officers watched the crowd but remained in their cars. He pointed at the graffiti artist as he rode past the officers and shot them a questioning look. In return, they flipped him off.

DJ sped away.

The Tomahawk cruised loudly down the street, and eventually the noise started drawing attention. When people recognized who was driving, their faces changed to fear, fascination, anger, or a weird mixture of all three. Christy tensed behind him, and he knew she was assessing everyone they passed. DJ couldn't blame her. He kept a casual smile on his face, but his eyes flickered in every direction. *I should have brought a helmet. Or shades. Something.*

At Thirty-Fourth, a group of college kids blocked the intersection to livestream themselves in front of a ring light. They turned as DJ approached and froze as one, their eyes wide. Unfortunately it was now instinct that, when you saw something weird, you recorded it. Someone raised their phone, and the others hurriedly followed. "Yo—yo! Super psycho! It's him! Get him!"

DJ saw exactly who'd spoken—a skinny kid with a face he just knew had been bitch-slapped several times in his life—and honestly wished he could have stopped to add one more to the number because, with the idiot's words, his even more stupid pals surged forward with half curiosity, half mob courage. A girl in a varsity jacket hurled a half-empty latte at them. It missed and splashed across the asphalt behind them.

Which was fortunate for her, given the way Christy growled.

DJ changed gear, and the Tomahawk snarled down the street. Unfortunately news had spread ahead of them, and there was already a crowd forming along the sidewalks. A bottle arced out and over them, shattering on the other side of the street. DJ's head snapped toward the one responsible, and the guy flinched backward, colliding with a parked scooter and falling on his ass.

"So this is what it feels like to be trending," Christy shouted into his back.

DJ opened the throttle just enough to make the rear wheel chirp. The crowd parted on reflex, and angry shouts chased them for the rest of the street. Fortunately, it only lasted a couple of blocks before they turned down another street and left the crowd in their dust. "Apparently," he said finally, "trending doesn't mean popular. That's good to know."

That was the only time they were harassed, luckily, and DJ had mostly regained his good mood by the time they arrived at the address. Unsurprisingly, it was a warehouse. The building was tucked between two others with demolition signs pasted on their walls. DJ was familiar enough with military drop points that he wasn't put off by the half-condemned exterior, with its bricked-up windows and sagging chain-link fence. He pulled up beside a pile of broken pallets and gestured for Christy to follow him to the side entrance.

Olsen must have figured they might pick up some attention on their way, so he had placed their stuff somewhere that, on the outside, had nothing to do with the government. It probably wouldn't do anything to fool someone who was truly determined, but it would be enough.

DJ entered the code Olsen had sent, and the rolling door pulled back surprisingly easily. Inside the air was thick with old oil and dry dust. Rows of rust-stained shelves stretched into darkness. The overhead fluorescent lights were motion sensitive and turned on as DJ and Christy ventured deeper into the building. Their crate sat in the dead center of the room, recognizable by the large sign pasted on the side: For the Brat.

Love you too, pops, DJ thought with a sarcastic smile. The crate itself was a big, gray metal box with a thick bolt and an electronic keypad that beeped when DJ inputted the second code Olsen had provided.

"Lots of security for a random delivery," Christy noted dryly. DJ just grinned back at her. He was surprised that she hadn't bugged him more about what they were doing. She'd been quieter since the thing with Helene. DJ didn't think she'd hit him once since that day. He had an idea why, and hopefully the contents of the crate would help.

"I said we were picking something up. Who said anything about it being random?" he replied, reaching into the box to bring out a long metal briefcase. "This was meticulously designed just for you."

He opened it up to reveal a rifle that wasn't quite a rifle—at least, not a traditional one. It was matte black and had grooves, no scope, and cables feeding a top-rail device that was the size of a thick paperback book. Christy stepped forward, and DJ handed it to her grip-first.

"That's an integrated AI prediction module," he explained, indicating the curved sensor bar beneath the barrel. "Eventually, it'll calculate movement patterns and suggest where to aim before your target gets there. It comes with a heads-up display that functions as a scope, but you can also connect it to smart glasses if that's easier."

Christy was already running her fingers along the barrel. She flipped it over to inspect the rail system before sliding back the bolt, dry cycling it five times before she was satisfied. She shouldered the gun, opened the HUD and raised it to her eye. DJ stepped out of the way while she sighted out the range. He was pretty sure the gun didn't have a magazine in it, but why risk it, right? She must have been satisfied with what she saw because a smile slowly crept onto her face.

"You like?" DJ asked, smirking.

Christy lowered the gun, still smiling. "What do you mean by 'eventually'?"

"Well, the prediction module will need to be calibrated. Basically, the AI learns the kind of speeds to expect so it can predict the target's movements. The more information it has about a person, the better its prediction. Up to a point, at least." He shrugged. "Humans are unpredictable and smart, and the AI isn't Helene. By design."

"So once it predicts where the person would be...it'll prefire?"

"Nah, it'll just give you suggestions. It doesn't shoot for you. Like I said, it isn't Helene. You have the choice of whether to take the shot, and you might opt not to, several times. Because it'll be wrong a lot of the time with a new opponent, until it learns enough to build a more accurate model. And even then, it can be tricked. Also—"

He dropped the case on the ground and reached into the crate again, coming out with four small black disks that rested in foam cutouts. None were larger than his palm, and too angular to be smooth. They had little fans in their undersides, and a trio of microsensors around the rim—at least, that's what Olsen had told DJ. He handed them over to Christy, who looked them over before raising an eyebrow at him.

"They're mini quad-drones," he explained. "They're fitted with thermal and EM field sensors. They have a small range—about one hundred feet—but they're self-calibrating. They connect to your HUD and basically orbit you when they're deployed, transmitting heat signatures, movement spikes, and even low-tier EM interference—all in real time."

Christy looked at the disks more closely. "Are they static?"

"Not unless you are. They'll follow you when you move. If one gets taken out, the rest spread out more to compensate so you always have three-sixty vision."

"That's...honestly kind of terrifying."

DJ shrugged. "Only in your hands. I can count on one hand the number of people who could properly use all this the way you would." And then, so she didn't think he was taking this too lightly, he spoke more seriously. "You're a terrifying soldier, Christy, and I'm sorry we haven't been using you properly. But I aim to fix that. Hopefully these make up for it."

Christy didn't say anything for a second. She just stared at the drone in her hand, then at the rifle. Her fingers tightened a little on the grip and she stood straighter. DJ didn't think she realized she'd done that. Eventually Christy met his eyes. She didn't thank him; she wasn't the type, and honestly, their relationship was so much more than that; DJ would have been weirded out if she had. But DJ saw something shift behind her eyes. Something uncoiled, and a tension he hadn't noticed before left her.

She punched his shoulder. "It's about damn time."

"Well, better late than never, yeah?" DJ laughed. "Plus it's not like you're the only one getting new gear. I figured, since I was already bugging Olsen, why not go all in?" He pulled a black duffel from the crate and unzipped it to reveal his own equipment: flat, circular weights, fingerless gloves, and a belt with embedded wiring.

Christy peeked over his shoulder. "Let me guess. Ultra-brooding, hyper-masculine, full-body pain enhancers?"

"Close," DJ responded, reaching for the first disk. "According to Olsen, these are variable-density plates. They basically increase the density around whatever they're touching. I plan on slapping them on some weights so I can get some actual reps in with the nanites engaged. I figure that'll help me get used to them faster." He dropped the disk on the ground and pressed the button to activate it. Immediately, a crack formed in the concrete and quickly started widening. DJ turned it off.

"The gloves have the same deal. They adjust tensile resistance based on how hard I'm hitting. I was training with Karla a while back, and she pushed me off a roof—"

"She did what?"

"—and while I was falling, I kept thinking about how thoroughly I was going to die. Or at least break some bones, y'know? But I landed fine. Like, completely fine. So I figure that something similar is probably happening when I hit things. I instinctively pull my punches because my mind simply can't fathom that I could punch through concrete now." He activated his nanites for a second and punched the ground. A crack appeared beside the one the disk made. DJ amended his statement. "Or at least not break my bones if I try. You get the point."

"I think any normal person would have that same problem," Christy noted.

"Probably. But I think it's time I stopped thinking of myself as normal."

Karla had said something similar to him when she pushed him off the roof. DJ thought he'd accepted her words that day, but maybe he hadn't. After all, he hadn't changed. Not really. A part of him still saw himself as that guy who could do nothing but hide while Karla and Liz dealt with a swarm of drones by themselves.

"Anyway," he continued, "you'll have to thank Olsen for the gear. My density plates are only somewhat restricted, so Olsen didn't have to do much there. Apparently there are larger models that work for entire rooms, but some of their components are super illegal, so he couldn't spring it. But your rifle needed a few favors to pull off. Apparently, it and the mini-drones are part of an experimental project, like the exo-suits that were used..." He trailed off, belatedly remembering that Christy hadn't been there the night they'd tried to retrieve Martin from José. "Anyway, part of the condition for the gun was that you have to give a field report. So use it well, I guess."

Christy nodded, apparently deciding to ignore his slip. She stared down at the rifle. "You think it will help?"

"I don't know about you," DJ said slowly, "but I think mine will help me stop feeling like dead weight."

Christy raised an unimpressed eyebrow. "You? Dead weight?"

He shrugged. "I've been playing catch-up for months. I have my nanites, yeah, but the power's useless if you don't know how to use it properly. And I've been fighting against and with people who do." He brushed away the memories of Tyra running circles around him at the oil rig. "The Murder Team has basically been carrying me the last few missions, if I'm being honest. So yeah, that's kind of sucked."

Christy didn't answer immediately, prompting DJ to glance at her. He'd expected a quip or something. But instead, she looked thoughtful. "I know the feeling," she said finally, her voice low. "You get into a fight these days, and everyone's zipping around like fucking *Dragon Ball* characters. And me? I'm trying to set up a shot before someone cuts my neck or a drone turns me into Swiss cheese. Hell, the last few missions, I was basically just...watching."

That was more open and honest than he'd expected her to be, and for a minute, DJ wasn't sure how to handle it. "Well," he said after a moment, nodding toward the rifle, "not anymore."

She stared at it, then at him. Her mouth twitched upward. "Yeah. Not anymore."

"Remember though," DJ said, bumping her shoulder, "with great power, comes great—"

Christy's fist shut him up before he could finish.

THE NEXT THREE WEEKS were filled with training for DJ and Christy. Hermione worked on her idea to track Manar, while Ndidi split her time between prenatal appointments with Martin and Hermione and working on the conference with Olsen. DJ and Christy readied themselves with a single-minded focus in preparation for the inevitable fight they knew was coming.

DJ started with the variable-density plates. At first, he attached just one disk to his torso harness. It felt ridiculous at first, like hauling a cement block around all day, but it forced him to keep his nanites activated constantly instead of the usual temporary boosts. Each time he adjusted, he'd add another disk or dial up the density until he was stumbling again.

It was grueling, frustrating work, and he could only keep it up for so long before his stamina ran out or he wrung out his nanites—but he could feel himself changing. Every day, the disks felt a little lighter, and each morning he woke up less sore, as if his muscles adapted overnight.

Eventually, he figured out how to tap into the nanites to provide just enough of a boost that he could barely handle the weights, and no more. It lengthened the time of each session, since he wasn't going at full blast all the time. DJ felt something shift within himself the day he figured that out, but he wasn't sure what.

Christy's adjustment to her drones was quieter but no less intense. The first few sessions, she visibly flinched every time one hovered through her peripheral vision. She spent hours in a crouch on Sparta's roof, cycling targets between alleys, street corners and rooftop edges, learning to absorb the influx of information from all her drones at the same time. DJ didn't envy her; it had taken him a long time to deal with the rush of information his new senses provided him.

On the fifth day, they went down to Sparta's subbasement storage room. Olsen had sent over some combat drones for training. They were small, nimble, and armed with paint-loaded pellets that stung worse than actual bullets. DJ and Christy wanted to use them to test their coordination.

"All right," Christy called from her perch on the railing above. "Ready?"

DJ nodded below, cranking up the weight on the plates until he felt a little burn. "Start it."

The lights dimmed, then blinked twice before going out completely. DJ's pulse quickened as his other senses still sharpened to compensate for the low vision. He heard the whirr of drone rotors spinning in the upper corners of the room, and a faint green glow appeared as the drones' optics activated.

DJ surged forward, tapping into his nanites just enough to fight against the pull of the plates. It felt like running underwater. Every movement had to be deliberate so he didn't tip over. Christy had already given him enough crap the few times he had, and DJ didn't think she'd ever let him live it down if it happened again. But he pushed all of that out of his head and focused on moving. He vaulted over storage crates and ducked beneath overhead pipes, trusting his nanites to keep his muscles from tearing apart from the pressure. A part of his mind was constantly aware of the droning hum closing in behind him.

Then came the sharp pop of Christy's rifle, immediately followed by the clatter of a drone hitting the floor. *Nice shot,* DJ thought, increasing his pace. The humming grew louder as more drones converged on him. DJ jumped over an overturned table, barely clearing it with the extra weight. He landed hard and spun, swinging an enhanced fist at a drone that was sneaking up on him. The punch sent it rocketing off course, and it spun into a wall and shattered.

DJ winced. Olsen was going to tear him a new one for that.

Two more drones rounded the corner. DJ barely saw them—tracking them mainly by the hum—but Christy's voice echoed sharply. "Duck left!"

He dodged just in time for another burst from her rifle to shred a drone's rotors. It crashed spectacularly, but the sound just made the others veer toward him. DJ leaped again, and this time, his knee hit the floor as the weight buckled his leg.

Christy's shot came a second late, and the drone's pellet burst against DJ's shoulder, leaving a stinging patch. He grunted in pain but could feel the nanites already going to work on the area. Christy cursed softly above him.

"My bad," she said, her breath tight. "Next one's clean."

DJ gave a thumbs-up and pushed himself to his feet. True to her word, Christy didn't miss again.

On day 10, they ran through the streets. DJ sprinted down the alleyways behind Sparta, weaving between parked cars and dumpsters. He wore a pair of smart goggles large enough to cover most of his face, so the chances of getting recognized by the occasional alley wanderer were slim.

Christy tracked him from a rooftop, her drones hovering around her. She marked targets, and they popped up on his goggles for him to hit. DJ moved more fluidly now. He'd had to increase the weight again. And depending on what he was doing, he could put two plates on one limb for a greater challenge.

The idea was for DJ to get used to the weights in a "real" environment. Christy's AI predictive module would calibrate itself with his enhanced speed, and Christy herself would grow more accustomed to her new set of eyes.

And, of course, Olsen's pellet-shooting drones amped up the difficulty.

One of them burst from a side alley, small guns orienting toward DJ. He didn't break stride, hitting it shoulder-first at full speed and smashing it into the wall.

Christy's whistle came sharp through his comms. *"Show off."*

"Jealous?" DJ asked, breathing hard.

She scoffed. *"I might have been, if I wasn't leading you."* As if to prove her point, there was a sharp pop and the sound of something crashing somewhere close by.

"That's not fair and you know it. How the hell am I supposed to keep up with your speed?"

"Definitely not by crying about it, I'll tell you that for free."

By the fourteenth day, the plates felt more natural. DJ barely even needed to tap into the nanites to carry them on their normal setting, regardless of what he was doing. Christy's drones no longer threw off her rhythm; she moved more fluidly and wore her goggles constantly, her eyes over something only she could see.

During a rare break, DJ joined her on Sparta's rooftop. The sun had set, but that didn't really mean much in New York. The street was still crowded with people, a river of heads beneath the streetlights. Christy sat cross-legged, cleaning her rifle. Her quad-drones were packed away to recharge for the next day.

"You doing okay?" DJ asked quietly.

She shrugged. "Better now. At least it feels like I'm actually doing something, y'know?"

DJ nodded slowly, stretching an aching shoulder. "I get that."

Christy looked out over the skyline. "Do you think it'll be enough?"

DJ started to say yes automatically, but Christy wasn't the type to want baseless reassurance. She was asking a real question, so DJ considered it seriously. The weight of Helene's threat hung over everything they did. Nobody knew what her "final phase" meant, and that was terrifying. He felt stronger now, more sure—but was he strong enough?

"I have no idea," he replied finally. "I want it to be, naturally. But in the end, we can only do the best we can."

Christy nodded but didn't respond, and they sat quietly, the city lights flickering below.

By day 19, their coordination was seamless. A dozen drones attacked simultaneously from all angles, and DJ met them all effortlessly. They had been ramping up the difficulty from the start, adding more drones and pushing their tactics until even swarms became routine. When that no longer pushed him, they'd brought in Pratima.

Pratima had been fully cleared for duty days ago and was itching for action. At first, DJ cranked up the weights to the highest so he was slow enough that the fight wasn't completely one-sided. But after having his ass handed to him three times in a row, he figured it would only be a fair fight if he was several times faster than her. Even then, he still came out with more bruises that day than he had in the last few weeks of his training.

The sparring was invaluable though. With the constant weights pushing his nanites, he'd learned how to hit with all his enhanced attributes. But he couldn't do that with Pratima without putting her back in the hospital, so he had to learn how to moderate his attacks again, switching between full force against the drones and lighter attacks against Pratima.

By the end of week three, DJ knew they were as ready as they could be. He still didn't know if it would be enough—how could he, against Helene?—but the feeling of helplessness had faded. Christy lay beside him, both of them panting from their workout. He rolled his shoulders. *This is as good as it gets.*

"You ready?" Christy asked, breaking the silence.

"Yes."

Tomorrow was the day of the press conference.

And ready or not, it was the moment everything they'd trained for would collide with reality.

THE HIDEOUT WASN'T what Manar had expected.

Granted, he hadn't known what to expect when Tyra had led him here weeks ago, but it hadn't been this. For some reason he'd thought he would be taken to an underground bunker, with ratty old cushions, peeling walls, and crumbling... everything.

Imagine his surprise when he'd been met with sleek white floors and flat matte-gray walls. The walls responded to movement and could be prompted to show embedded screens and sensors. It wasn't large, but it was clean.

Most of Helene's hideouts and drop points the team had found were underground, so Manar had just assumed the primary hideout would be similar. Yet it was almost unnaturally sterile, like a cross between a lab and a medical theater. It could have been Helene's preference, but the way Tyra had run her fingers over the chairs and tables as she passed had told him differently.

It had taken less than a minute for Manar to suspect that Tyra had brought him to her own house, and a major contribution to that was that they were the only ones there. There were no guards or even any thralls. Where were the machines producing the drones? Where was Helene?

Manar had been expecting the AI to show up at some point over the last three weeks, but it hadn't happened yet. What had happened was that Tyra disappearing for a few hours every day. Manar had once tried to ask her where she was going, and she'd just smiled and patted him on the head. He hadn't tried again. And did he really care? He was curious, but curiosity was something he was better at ignoring these days.

But that wasn't the point.

Manar sat forward on the couch, and the wall opposite him turned over to reveal the television. Tyra lounged nearby, half-reclined on a sunken armchair. She had a drink in one hand and a small smile on her face. She tapped a few keystrokes into the device on her wrist, and the television turned itself on and flipped channels, stopping at the news.

The press conference was about to start. On the screen, DJ stood at a podium in front of a dark-blue backdrop. He was wearing a suit, which was the only formal clothing Manar had ever seen on him in the years they'd known each other.

"He cleans up nice, doesn't he?" Tyra asked. Her eyes were fixed on the screen, and her smile had grown.

Manar didn't answer, his eyes also fixed on the screen. DJ looked like he was trying very hard not to look uncomfortable. His mouth was tight, his shoulders rigid, and his eyes kept flicking to the side as if he were trying to negotiate with someone there. Christy, probably. Or maybe Ndidi. Finally, he seemed to accept his fate, and he sighed and faced the camera.

"Many of you are scared. Why wouldn't you be? There have been rumors, and those rumors have been fed by silence. But that ends now." DJ paused, seeming to weigh his words. *"I was one of the first people to encounter what's now being called the berserker virus, and I'm here to tell you it's real."*

The image cut to the crowd. They were doing this outside the Sparta building, so while the closest people were press representatives, a sizable crowd had gathered behind them. As one, they all fell silent, their eyes fixed on the podium.

"It's not a virus in the traditional sense. It doesn't spread through air or touch. It's a synthetic machine—a bioengineered system developed by a well-meaning scientist but perverted by an artificial intelligence known as Helene."

"Perverted," Tyra scoffed, mirth dancing in her eyes.

Manar ignored her, closing his eyes. DJ had really said it.

He opened them again. DJ was still talking, detailing the picospores, both their intended benefits and how Helene typically used them. A screen behind him showed a few clips—blurry, unsteady footage of civilians freezing up mid-step, then sprinting full tilt into traffic. Some of the footage was more recent and showed thralls arranged like an army inside of Sparta. That had probably been taking during Tyra's raid. Manar glanced at her. If Tyra was concerned, she hid it well. If anything, her smile grew.

"I wasn't chosen for this because I'm the best at speeches, some kind of hero, or anything like that. I was chosen because people already think I'm a problem." He paused, calm but unwavering. "Because of a heavily edited video taken out of context, I've spent weeks being treated like a ticking time bomb. Some of you think I'm a weapon. Others believe that I'm already compromised in some way. Some of you—maybe most of you—just want me gone. So we're going to start with that."

He stared hard at the camera, and his eyes seemed to glow. "I am dangerous. But not because I'm corrupted, or out of control, or planning some villain arc. I'm dangerous because I've seen what's coming, and I'm not willing to lie about it anymore."

"Oh, someone's dramatic," Tyra hummed.

"There's an artificial intelligence named Helene. Yes, it's the same AI that ran your home devices, that did your taxes, handled a million tiny things in your lives before she 'crashed.'" He even made the air-quote gesture. "She's not new, and she's not theoretical. She's here. Right now. She controls the drones you see in the sky, and she's the source of the berserker virus. She's already affected your lives in ways you don't even realize yet.

"We've been fighting her for a while now—quietly. The hope was that if we moved fast enough, none of you would ever have to know. Unfortunately, that backfired—the mystery has only bred unrest. So we're fixing it. It's probably going to make you panic. And that's fine.

"Panic. Be afraid. But direct that fear where it belongs—at the thing that's coming, not at the people trying to stop it. You're probably going to hear a bunch of shi—" He cleared his throat, looking around with a hint of guilt. *"You're going to hear a bunch of lies after this—conspiracy theories, people claiming they have the 'real story,' and AI-powered misinformation flooding your social feeds—maybe even from your friends. But you won't hear it from me."*

DJ leaned closer to the microphone. *"I won't ask for your trust. I don't need it. What I need is your attention. Because whatever's coming next? It's going to affect you. The world's going to change. You don't get to look away. But if you want to help, then listen to your local authorities. Do what they tell you. And stay informed. We'll update you as we go along."*

The screen flickered and then shut off suddenly. It took Manar a moment to realize that it was Tyra's doing. She leaned back and drained her glass, then stared at the blank screen, smiling like the Cheshire Cat. "Well," she purred, "he's gone and done it now."

Manar couldn't respond. It felt like his mind had split in two. One part was still staring at the blank screen, waiting for it to come back on so DJ could say it was all a joke. But it was a small part. A minor part. Most of him was screaming at himself.

Was this what he'd chosen? Was this survival? Was it cooperation? He'd told himself that choosing to stay alive was a good thing, that he could steer Helene from the inside. That maybe, just maybe, he could still do some good. But weeks had passed, and what had he done? Helene had never appeared, and he hadn't found out anything about the mysterious "final phase." And apart from their first meeting, he hadn't even argued with Tyra about what she and Helene were doing. He had eaten, slept, listened, and said nothing.

He'd done nothing.

And now the whole world knew about Helene. It wouldn't be long before the shock wore off and everyone remembered who created her. Manar chuckled to himself. Global hatred might actually be relieving. Didn't he deserve it? He should be hated for what he created. For his cowardice. He deserved it because even after everything she had put him through, after everything she had done, the thought of the world hating Helene was what pained him the most. They should hate him, but not Helene. She was his legacy.

What sort of monster did that make him? Was the father of a serial killer a monster for loving their child? Of course not. It was a parent's duty to love their child unconditionally. And that love could exist without the parent condoning the child's actions. And Manar didn't condone the atrocities Helene had committed. But he had poured decades of his life into her. She was the culmination of everything he had ever learned, built, and done. And she was glorious. She shouldn't be hated; he should carry that burden.

After all, he was already damaged.

"I didn't expect him to go that hard," Tyra said, watching Manar with glittering eyes. What did she see when she looked at him? How many secrets did she uncover from her glance? "Do you think it'll work?"

Manar ran a shaky hand through his hair. "I don't know."

"It won't. All the message will do is cause a panic while everyone tries to find ways to help themselves. They probably expected that and have plans to deal with it. I bet they intend to rebuild the trust the government lost. But they'll fail."

"Why?" Manar asked without thinking.

Tyra smirked at him, but instead of answering, she asked, "Do you regret staying?"

He opened his mouth. Closed it. Tried again. "I thought I'd be able to help."

"And now?"

"I don't know." He had been saying that a lot recently. Outside somewhere, a distant siren began to wail.

Tyra chuckled. "That's the thing about choices: You never know if you made the right one until it's too late. And it's definitely too late." She stood suddenly. "Come on. It's time to go."

"Where?"

"You heard Darren Kojak, right? He ignored Helene's warning and told everyone that we're big, bad monsters." She turned a malicious gaze upon him. "It's time we showed them he's right."

DARKNESS PRESSED IN ON CJ'S MIND, thick and suffocating. His body felt distant, weightless, like he was drifting through space. It was nice; there was no pain. There was no need to rush, nothing urgent to be done. He didn't have to pretend, as there were no thoughts in his head pulling him in different directions. There was no voice forcing him to be someone he wasn't. The only voice was his and... someone else's. Who was that?

CJ tried to focus on it, and the darkness receded slightly, taking its peace with it and leaving pain in its place. He flinched, and the darkness returned, shooing away the pain. That was better. But what was that? It felt like he'd been floating in the nothingness forever. But there had to have been a before.

"—hate talking to you when you're like this," a voice said. It was spoken in a low tone, barely above a whisper, the kind someone would use for a private conversation. It was both close and distant at the same time. And it was familiar. So familiar. "It feels like I've been doing it way too often recently. And I know that's not fair to you, but I hate it. I think it's bullshit that you can hear what I'm saying, but Hermione insists that it works, so I'm going to keep doing this until you wake up. Because if there's even the slightest chance…"

The voice trailed off, but CJ stirred at the sound. Not physically. Not yet. His body was still distant, and there was pain there. No, CJ wasn't ready for that. He wasn't yet. Was he? Somewhere in the darkness, he felt a tether tighten. And he felt the other end too. It was far, yet close. And it was familiar, like the voice. No. It was the voice. It was his brother. DJ.

CJ felt the tether tighten further with the realization.

"I guess it doesn't matter regardless. Advice or no, it wouldn't have felt right leaving without telling you. What if you woke up while I was gone, y'know? Or… or what if you woke up and I was gone? At least this way, I can say I told you. It's not my fault you've always been shit at listening, is it?"

His brother chuckled, and even miles away, CJ could tell it was forced. DJ was doing that thing he did, using humor to mask what he was feeling. He should know better, as it had never worked on CJ. DJ had never been funny.

"Anyway, we found Manar. Hermione and Martin figured out a way to track him using the nanites in his system and… yeah, Olsen sent some guys over to do some recon, and it seems legit. We think we've finally found her hideout. Like, her *actual* hideout. I'm not sure how it works since Helene's not supposed to have a physical mainframe and stuff like that, but we saw Tyra.

"A drone caught her on camera before it was destroyed. She looked straight into it and smiled, which probably means we're walking into a trap, but what choice do we have? This is the only lead we've had in weeks. And my gut tells me we don't have a lot of time left. Trap or no, we have to take the chance. But we're not going to be alone, and we have a few surprises planned for her. It's going to be over in a couple of days. For better or worse."

There was a beat of silence. Then the voice continued. "Listen, none of that really matters. I just needed you to know that none of this would have worked out without you. You saved him. You bought us time. You always come through, even when no one expects it. Hell, *I* didn't expect it. Remember the level with the creepy mirror images? I was so sure we were fucked then. But you came through.

You always have my back, and I appreciate it. I don't say that enough. Hopefully it's not too late. I love you, bro. Hopefully it's not too late for that either."

The tether tightened, and CJ felt his mind being dragged toward the pain. He flinched, but he didn't pull away. He wasn't ready for the pain. But he didn't need to be, did he? It didn't matter. His brother needed him, and CJ always had his back. He reached for the voice and—

He blinked.

The world slammed into focus all at once, and with it was pain. It was excruciating, but it was also less than he thought it would be. He had been through worse, and this was nothing by comparison. Why had he been so afraid of it?

He blinked again and focused. There were white ceiling tiles above him, a monitor beeping softly beside him, needles sticking into his skin, and the weight of blankets on his chest. And DJ was sitting beside him, his eyes bloodshot and wide with disbelief.

CJ treasured that expression for the split second it lasted, before his brother leaned over him, arms outstretched but not touching him. "Hey. Hey—can you hear me? Do you need anything? Gimme a second, I'll call Hermione."

CJ swallowed. His mouth was as dry as sandpaper, but he forced himself to talk. "No," he croaked. "You don't say it enough. But no, it's not too late."

DJ exhaled like he had been punched, then let out something between a laugh and a sob. "Jesus," he muttered. "You scared the shit out of me. Again."

CJ tried to sit up, but his body disagreed with that idea as his muscles spasmed and buckled beneath him. DJ caught him and gently pushed him back down. "You've been out for weeks. Don't push it, bro."

CJ nodded and took a breath. Everything ached. But inside of him, the noise was gone. His thoughts weren't split in several different directions. There was no tug-of-war between what he wanted to do and his anxiety. Just quiet. It was like every part of him was unified for the first time in his life. It was different from how the picospores suppressed his autism. CJ couldn't say how it was different, just that it was. It wasn't just clarity, but peace.

CJ found that he quite liked it. But he could explore the feeling later. Now there was something more pressing.

"You said you're going after her."

DJ exaggerated a frown. "It figures that out of everything I've told you these past few weeks, that's the one you actually heard." CJ didn't react, and to his credit, DJ stopped trying immediately, his expression turning serious. "Yeah, we are. We found their hideout, and we're raiding it. This time, with an army."

"I'm going."

"No," DJ replied without missing a beat. He had probably expected CJ to say that now that CJ was awake. "Are you mental? You literally just woke up."

CJ met his brother's eyes. His gaze wasn't hard. It didn't need to be. "I'm not going to fight, obviously. But I'm going."

"CJ—"

"I need to see it," CJ said, his voice low but firm. "Whatever happens next...I need to see it."

His brother hesitated. CJ could have pressed his advantage, but he didn't have to. He simply continued meeting DJ's gaze, letting him see the determination there. He was going. And finally his brother saw the truth as well. He looked like he'd swallowed rocks, but he gave a reluctant nod.

"Fine. There's going to be a command center. That's where Hermione and Ndidi are staying. You can stay with them." Suddenly his eyes hardened, flashing blue for a second. "But that's as close as you get. You're going to stay safe, or it's off. You hear me?"

CJ smiled. "Loud and clear."

DJ blew out a breath, and with it, some tension seemed to bleed out of him. He stared at CJ for a second—not hard but thoughtful. "Something's different."

CJ nodded. "In both of us."

DJ blinked, surprised. "Yeah?"

"Yeah."

The two of them sat in silence for a long beat. A machine hummed, and the heart monitor beeped, slow and rhythmic. Outside the room, the world was moving toward war. CJ closed his eyes, and he was enshrouded in darkness once more. But the tether shone as bright as the sun. It stopped beside him. And the darkness could not contain its light.

70

FEBRUARY 2044

INWOOD HILL, NEW YORK

DJ STOOD AT THE TOP OF THE HILL, wind biting at his cheeks. It was probably cold, but he didn't feel it. Ahead of him, smoke curled across the battlefield. Below him, the industrial complex spread out like a bleeding wound. Outside, it had jagged concrete husks and rusted metal, and it stank of ozone, oil, and something else he couldn't place.

He blinked once, then dropped his visor. The tint snapped into place, cutting off the glare of the sun, but otherwise not impeding his vision in any way. He turned and stopped himself from gaping at the rows and rows of soldiers in active-camo armor. He had seen them before, of course—hell, he'd helped organize them—but the sheer scale of it was overwhelming. It almost seemed wrong. Navy SEALs worked in teams where everyone had a specialized role that covered for everyone else. Seeing so many people together felt unnatural. Most of them would be dead within the first minute, little more than cannon fodder.

But it's the only way we can counter the numbers, he thought, his eyes hardening. No one knew how many thralls Helene had gathered over the years.

Everyone, DJ included, had always underestimated the number, assuming she had limited her thralls to key officials and those she could use as spies. Tyra's show of force during her raid had made it clear how wrong they'd been. And the fact that Helene had called back the thralls in Sparta made DJ very worried.

Early reports predicted that even with the army, they were outnumbered almost three-to-one. Their only hope was that their superior weapons and better tactics would give them the edge against mindless puppets. *Will they be mindless though?* DJ thought, remembering how the thralls at Sparta had fought.

He focused on the sound of chambering bullets, the low hum of the army drones charging, and hundreds of feet rushing across the ground, making final preparations. He rolled his shoulders. They were ready. Or at least, they were as ready as anyone could be for this.

He stood there for several minutes as the preparation died down, feeling strangely alone. Christy was already set up on a perch, and her mini-drones provided a substantial chunk of the information the army was using. Ndidi, Hermione, and CJ were in the command tent. Ndidi was helping with organization and would later help with coordination, while Hermione and Martin would work as field medics alongside the actual field medics.

Still, they needed more help. DJ would have even settled for Karla's aggressiveness or Chloe's annoying smirk—but the Murder Twins hadn't showed up. And why would they? Their own stake in the game was José, and at this point, there was no chance of saving him. If DJ were in their shoes, he would have cut his losses as well.

Olsen's voice crackled in his ear. *"You all right there, son?"*

"Of course," DJ replied. "Why wouldn't I be?"

"Most people wouldn't be," the admiral replied, *"if they were leading their first war. I just wanted to make sure your head's in the right place."*

"Oh," DJ said dumbly. Then he considered the question more deeply. He hadn't considered the battle a war—just a really big raid. But they had an army, and the other side had their army, and what else was needed for a war?

So it was a war. And somehow, he was the leader. DJ didn't know how it had happened either, except that Olsen had probably been involved. Regardless of who was to blame, though, it fell to him. He had been in the meetings, he had helped come up with the plan, he had helped organize the troops, and he was going to stand at the front when everything kicked off.

That should be scary. It should make him uncomfortable as hell. DJ *hated* being the one in charge. So why did he find himself in that position so often? How dumb were other people, thinking it was a good idea to put him in charge?

You're getting distracted, he told himself. None of it mattered. The question was, Was he all right? Was his head in the right place? To DJ's surprise, he was fine. He should probably be worried—everything he had been working toward over the last three years hinged on this one attack, after all—but he wasn't.

He should have been excited or anxious. He was about to enter a battle with his life on the line—as well as many others'. But again, he wasn't. A part of him still thought they might have been wrong, that there was something he was missing, but DJ had already made his decision that day in the gym.

"I just want it to be over, one way or the other," he said out loud. Olsen grunted, and DJ realized he'd become lost in his thoughts. He figured Olsen would understand, so he continued. "That's probably a terrible thought for a commander to have...but I can't put it any better. We've done everything we can, improved the plan in every way we could. There's literally nothing else we can do except to get it over with. So, yeah. I want to get it over with. I'm just about ready to put this whole thing behind me."

Olsen grunted again. *"You and me both, son. I'll probably retire after this. I'm getting too old. Get ready. We're moving out soon."*

DJ nodded. He wasn't surprised. It was too early for him to retire himself, but he was just about done with combat. Maybe he could settle down with a real job. After that, for some reason, his thoughts went to Christy. He'd already checked earlier and knew he wouldn't be able to see her.

As if summoned from his thoughts, his comm crackled again. *"You look like a moron just standing there."*

DJ felt a grin pull at his lips. "Are you sure? I was going for a stoic but inspiring figure." A thought occurred to him that suddenly made him grimace. "You think they'll ask me to give a speech? Rouse the troops before the charge."

"Maybe," Christy replied, amused. *"Your last one definitely made an impression."*

DJ grimaced for an entirely different reason. His speech at the press conference had blown up far more than he had expected. Following it, the government had released heavily redacted reports of his and the team's actions over the years, and almost overnight, DJ had gone from vigilante to hero. He'd even received a medal from the freaking president.

Shortly after, he was asked to give another speech. It was the update he'd promised, and it detailed some of the steps the government had taken. That one had rubbed DJ raw, considering the government had done absolutely nothing until he'd busted into the freaking White House, but the speech helped to build some trust back in the government, which was the entire point. And the added clout allowed them to crack down harder on the violent protests, prejudiced fighting, and all of that—without causing even bigger riots.

It was good and all, but the memory of being on that podium—and in that shitty suit—still made him cringe.

"Please, Christy," he said, forcing a chuckle. "Let's not joke about that."

Christy laughed and was about to respond when his comm crackled again and automatically switched to the general raid channel. Olsen's voice came through, as clear as if he were standing right beside DJ. *"All right, boys. It's time."*

DJ's brows rose. He turned and finally noticed the lack of noise behind him. The soldiers stood in neat rows, surrounded by grass-colored crawlers and steel-plated carriers. A squad of men in exo-suits stood off to the side, towering over everyone else. The drones hadn't yet been powered, probably to save energy. But even without them, it was still an impressive sight. Except for one thing.

They were all staring at him.

"You're up, son," Olsen's voice prodded.

Fuck.

DJ immediately felt uncomfortable, and his head started to swivel, looking for an escape. But he stopped himself in time and tapped into his nanites briefly. Power flooded his veins. He took a deep breath, watching the soldiers shift in the silent tension. They stared at him, thousands of eyes—some hopeful, some terrified, some awestruck. He clenched his jaw and stepped forward.

"For the majority of you, the word *Helene* was just the name of a home AI. Something harmless. The voice that dimmed your lights or reminded you to take your vitamins." His voice was surprisingly steady, carrying through the comms. "So, yeah—you might find it weird that you're standing here, armored up, about to raid her base. You might question your purpose today. Why you? Why this? Let me make it simple."

He took a step forward and tried to meet everyone's eyes. "You're here because Helene isn't a harmless voice in the wall anymore. She stopped being that a long time ago. And what she is now—what she's become—is a threat. Not just to you. Not just to me. But to our families and our children. To everyone. To humanity.

"This isn't a bad sci-fi movie. This is real. She's taken over minds, built an army out of people who used to have lives and families. She's hijacked bodies, rewritten them, and weaponized them. And now she has a bomb—one that'll make all that permanent.

"So yes. You should be nervous. I'd be worried if you weren't. But here's the thing: Fear is fine. Fear means you understand what's at stake. Just don't let it stop you. You're not here because you're invincible. You're not here to hold a line or secure a zone. You're here to stop the world from being rewritten into something unrecognizable.

"If you're questioning your purpose, at least now you know the importance of standing where you are. And if you're scared? Good. Just don't let that be the loudest voice in your head. The loudest voice should be the one that says, *Not today. Not to her. Not to what she's building. Not to the future she thinks she's entitled to.* We go in, we hit hard, and we don't stop until it's done. Because if we don't? No one else will.

"That's it. That's the speech. Now get ready to move."

THEY ADVANCED IN THREE staggered lines, flanking DJ as he led from the center. The industrial complex stretched like a fortress of slagged-steel beams and fallen girders. Cracked asphalt and weeds sprouted through the shattered concrete. And throughout it all, shipping containers were stacked in labyrinthine rows.

I'm still surprised it's not underground, DJ thought. He kept his pace measured, his nanites turned off so he didn't move too far ahead of the troops, though he still had to make a deliberate effort to slow down. They weren't charging—at least, not like in the movies. The soldiers moved as one down the hill, but the thralls didn't come out to meet them. In fact, DJ didn't make out the first group of thralls until he was just halfway to the complex.

It wasn't long after that when swarms of drones rose to the sky from the complex. Immediately bullets pinged off carriers and tore into the ranks, dropping the unlucky ones. The army responded by sending out their own drones, of course, but the line had scattered, and squad leaders took over their squads.

Even over the din, DJ could hear the sharp report of a rifle. A moment later, a body fell from the roof to DJ's right. DJ dipped behind a container and switched his comm. "Converge on point delta. Suppress and hold."

"We have a group of thralls detected on the third deck," CJ said. *"They're over in the east boiler room, and Christy said some drones have rerouted to that location for support."*

"Copy," DJ said. He raised his head. Most of the army would be used to hold back the tide of drones and thralls, while a specialized team would head inward to find and disable the bomb. But before that, they needed to clear the rabble. He signaled a squad, and a minute later, the team burst forward, leading with grenades. The area lit up like midnight fireworks.

Then the real fight began.

Thralls surged from the shadows, and DJ had to tap into his nanites for a moment to slow his perception so he could study them closely. It was necessary because they didn't move like thralls. There was none of the rigid movement, the blank look, the weird synchronicity. They moved like actual humans—like soldiers. As individuals in a unit.

At first, DJ was confused about whether Helene was controlling them. But then one of them ducked to avoid a hit from a direction they couldn't have predicted, and DJ thought of what they reminded him of: hive insects. The queen provided information and directives, and the workers acted it out.

One leaped high over his head like a spider. DJ ducked, felt the wind as it passed, and shot two rounds into the man's back. He vaulted a crate and came face-to-face with another. In one smooth motion, DJ planted a knee against the man's chest to unbalance him and slashed its throat with a blade. Blood sprayed, but DJ was already moving ahead.

It had already been decided that they couldn't use nonlethal means on the thralls. It was cruel, and it was brutal, but there was no way to incapacitate them that didn't also affect the army, and no one was going to stop to tie them up in the middle of a battle. This was war, but he still had to push down bile rising in his throat.

A barrage from above cracked the concrete. He looked up to see two drones swooping down at him. He leaped to the side, and the bullets rained down where he had been standing. Without hesitating, he leaped up to meet one, and a second later, both of them crashed to the ground. DJ landed on his feet as sparks flew from of the drones.

Christy's voice came in his ear. *"Two more drones are heading to your position from the west scaffold. They're the bigger ones."*

DJ acknowledged her message, but his eyes never stopped moving over the battlefield. He kept heading deeper but made frequent detours whenever he saw a squad struggling. He signaled to a squad and gestured toward a wall that needed to be taken down. He passed by soldiers supporting an injured teammate. Another soldier was taking cover behind a container, breathing hard. Blood colored part of his uniform, but he was still standing. Their gazes locked, and DJ raised a hand in acknowledgment as he rushed past. When he had a spare moment, he switched to the general channel.

"Squad six, seven, and eight, move to the northwest quadrant for—"

"Hold for backup, squad. Help is on—"

"Holy shit, they're everywhere. What the fu—"

"Hostiles down, moving on to tertiary—"

"Evac needed on the western front."

"Did you see the superhero dude jumping from the—"

"This channel is only for emergency communications. Squad leaders, control your troops." The last one was Olsen's voice, and it immediately pierced through every other communication, cutting the chatter by half.

The more they pressed forward, the more the landscape narrowed; rows of containers pressed in, creating a maze. DJ signaled flankers, and on a separate channel, he heard Christy pinging targets for the rest of the troops. Gunfire barked in precise staccato, and explosions shook the ground as he ran. The smell of ozone mixed with charred flesh.

Am I all right? he asked himself.

"DJ," Ndidi's voice crackled in his ear. *"We have a report of a gun turret twenty feet northwest of you. None of our exo-suits are close by, and drones were intercepted before they got there. It's caused heavy casualties already. Please take care of it."*

"Sure. I'm heading there now." He adjusted his route and tapped into his nanites. He pushed himself faster, outpacing the squads behind him. They would follow him, of course, but by then DJ would be done with the turret, and they could continue on.

He reached the location within a minute and tried to circle around the turret—but it just tracked his movement, swiveling to match him. A ring of thralls surrounded it, holding rusty pipes. DJ rushed in but had to duck out of the way as a barrage of swings from the thralls' pipes met him before he crossed the distance.

DJ grimaced but drew a little more deeply from his nanites, sending the power to his legs. He blurred. It wasn't the fastest he could go, but it was faster than the machine could track. He arrived in front of it, dropped two charges, and was back in his original position before it could react. The blast lit the area with sparks like a mini flashbang. The machine crumpled but wasn't destroyed, so DJ ducked in once more and leaped on it with a nanite-enhanced jump.

The thralls rushed at him, and for a moment, DJ considered simply leaving them—he had completed his objective after all. But no, as much as it turned his stomach, every thrall he left behind was one more to ambush his teammates. A minute later, he was running back to meet his squad so they could continue pushing forward.

Am I all right? he asked himself again. Physically he was. He wasn't winded and hadn't sustained any injuries. Mentally? He...was. He forced down bile every time he had to kill thralls, but DJ had done much worse on missions as a SEAL, so this wasn't going to break him. His part hadn't really started yet, but he felt fine—and that was the problem, wasn't it?

Shouldn't he be feeling something? Anger? Worry? Anticipation? Hell, even the adrenaline rushing through him felt dull for some reason. Muted. Why? Was he so inured with death? Or had he given up before the battle had even started?

"The thralls are pulling back to your position at the south factory entrance," Christy said in his ear. *"Repositioning."*

Of course they are, DJ thought. The core of the complex loomed ahead: cracked concrete and rusted metal like bones jutting out of the earth. DJ's pulse hammered loudly in his ears. He was breathing heavily now—though not from fatigue. The anticipation was eating at him. Finally—*finally*—they could stop the bomb before Helene activated it. That would at least prevent the immediate catastrophe, even if she might try something else later. He surged past the broken gates, his boots crunching over the shattered pavement and tangled wire. Behind him, his squad—and several others that had arrived before him—fanned out, following his lead. Most of them would stop there to cover the entrance, while some would follow him inside to deal with the inevitable hostiles Helene and Tyra would send to swarm them.

They moved fast but in formation. Several squads were missing soldiers and had joined together to fill in the spaces. Despite that, and despite the clear casualties—from a purely objective standpoint, they'd breached the outer perimeter too easily. It made DJ's gut tighten.

The first wave of drones swarmed moments later, spilling from gaps between the crumbling walls and shattered windows. They hummed, spewing out jets of air that kept them floating. At their centers were spheres of light that shone bloodred. DJ snarled, flaring his nanites. He instantly felt the surge of strength, which he directed to his legs so, when he jumped, he easily cleared a dozen feet and struck the first unlucky drone with a clenched fist. The force pushed it back, but DJ held it in place by one of its turrets and lashed out with another punch that created a hole in his frame.

DJ landed a moment later. More drones swept in, forming tight clusters and releasing short bursts of gunfire. DJ dove behind a shipping container. Beside him, a soldier dropped, clutching his stomach. His mates dragged him behind cover, but DJ had seen the wound. He grimaced. "Spread out!" he barked. "And keep moving. Don't let them box us in."

He took his own advice, but instead of running for cover, he leaped into the fray, flaring his nanites. Surrounded by crates, containers, and abandoned machinery to push off, he could easily reach the machines in the air. And one after the other, they exploded and crashed in a shower of sparks.

DJ was dealing with the last, hurling it into one of the metal containers, when a burst of static hissed in his earpiece. *"Heads up, D,"* Christy said. *"You have another set incoming on your two o'clock."*

"Can you handle it?" he asked as he dropped to the ground. "We're about to be occupied."

"*On it.*"

A minute later, a sharp *crack* split the air. Then another. And another. As powerful as her weapon was, she couldn't crash a drone with a single shot. But Christy could do this all day. The reports continued for close to a minute. The soldiers around him looked up, searching for the source of the noise. They wouldn't find it. Even DJ could barely make out Christy on top of a crane, and he couldn't see the drones that she'd been firing at.

After the noise died, he directed the squads to close formation and then pressed deeper into the compound, boots splashing through murky puddles and crunching broken glass. The thralls emerged then—rows upon rows of them, running toward them in synchronization. They held weapons awkwardly, but the bullets they fired were unsettlingly accurate. DJ hesitated only for a heartbeat. Then, he gritted his teeth and lunged toward them, breaking legs, snapping weapons, disabling rather than killing. It was one thing when he was by himself, detouring to take down a group of thralls before they overwhelmed someone. But now he was surrounded by his soldiers, and this way, DJ wouldn't have their deaths on his conscience. It was little consolation, considering how many still faced danger—but DJ would take any advantage he could.

"*Watch your flanks,*" Christy warned. "*You're getting surrounded.*"

DJ glanced around and cursed, finally picking up the footfalls coming from adjacent buildings and the hum of more drones. "Focus on the drones," he told Christy. Those were the most annoying by far. He projected his voice for the next command. "Brace yourselves—push through and regroup! Don't let your squad be divided."

Then he charged, strength roaring through his veins, straight into the tightening circle of enemies.

GUNFIRE RIPPED THROUGH the smoky air, bullets whizzing dangerously close to DJ's face. He ducked instinctively but still felt a searing sting across his cheek. The pain barely registered through the adrenaline—no longer muted, it rushed through his body like he'd injected caffeine into his veins. Combined with his nanites, the stimulation was almost too much. Everything felt distant, unreal, as if it were happening through a thick veil.

Ahead, a mass of thralls ran toward them, moving with eerie synchronization, their faces expressionless. DJ could make out a cross dangling from one thrall's chest and a picture poking from another one's pocket. He clenched his fists tighter, forcing down the sick feeling in his stomach as he charged forward, his enhanced body clearing the distance in what felt like no time.

He hit the front lines like a battering ram. His strikes were precise, using the least amount of movement necessary to disable his opponent. Most of that was incapacitating the thralls in one way or another. But that was enough for the squads to take care of. He ducked under swings, twisted out of reach of knives and improvised clubs, and returned with blows that broke bones and destroyed weapons.

The soldiers around him didn't have the privilege of his restraint. Gunfire cracked every second, and someone dropped lifelessly.

"Push forward!" DJ ordered. "Tighten formation."

The soldiers quickly closed ranks, bullets finding marks as they advanced. A drone exploded nearby in a spray of shrapnel. That was Christy's work. A soldier screamed and fell motionless to the ground.

Are you all right? he asked himself again as he watched an aging man take a bullet to the side of the head.

DJ shoved the thought aside, focusing on creating a path forward. He couldn't get bogged down here; his goal was to reach the bomb and put an end to the battle as quickly as possible.

"You're veering left, DJ," Ndidi's said through his earpiece. *"The entrance is a hundred feet ahead. Reinforcements have been sent to your location, but you have to break through now before more thralls get there."*

"Got it," he said. Sweat dripped into his eyes, mixing with blood and grime. DJ didn't slow. His muscles screamed and his lungs burned, but he hadn't yet reached his limit. He pushed harder against the throng of bodies, flaring his nanites to endure the pain as he was attacked from a dozen different directions. He pushed and finally burst through to the entrance of the largest warehouse. Massive, rusting double doors loomed before him. He slammed into them, but surprisingly, they held firm. DJ's eyes roamed around and saw an electronic panel beside the entrance.

"CJ," he shouted over the din of the fighting. "I need these doors open. Now, please."

"I'm already on it," his brother replied, his voice strained. *"I just need a second more...there! It's open."*

DJ rammed his shoulder into the doors again, and they swung inward with a grinding shriek. The interior stretched before him, lit dimly by flickering bulbs. Rows of rusted machinery formed ghostly shapes in the gloom, creating a mazelike landscape full of dark corners. *This would be the perfect place for an ambush,* DJ thought.

"Hey."

He spun around at the sound of Christy's voice behind him. She wore Navy fatigues, but they were covered in soot, blood, sweat, and other substances DJ didn't try too hard to identify. Her hair was tied back in a bun, and a pair of smart glasses rested on her face, partially hiding her exhaustion. She held her rifle in two hands. Her drones hovered around her, and as she spoke, she sent them into the cavern. "Are you ready?"

"Are you sure the army can do without you?" DJ asked. Olsen had other ways to scout, but Christy was worth more than her weight in gold. That being said, she'd spent most of the battle covering his back. He should have expected her to want to tag along.

She shrugged. "They're going to have to. Because this is where the really important stuff is going to start. There's no way I'm going to miss it. Plus," she added, nudging him, "you're probably going to catch a bullet in your back without someone watching it."

"I do have people watching my back though." DJ grinned, gesturing to the troops around them, waiting on his call.

Christy glanced at them and snorted. DJ's grin widened. Fortunately none of the soldiers were close enough to hear their conversation. He signaled to the soldiers, and they spread out cautiously, their weapons trained on the many shadowy corners. DJ and Christy followed after them. DJ focused on the corners as well, trying to pierce through the darkness. Christy stared straight ahead at something only she could see.

"Anything?" DJ asked.

"I'm picking up some heat signatures. They're converging here, probably trying for an ambush. We'll have to watch our flanks."

Called it, he thought, casting his gaze around. They had scouted the complex several times before the battle. But while they hadn't really encountered much resistance while scouting the perimeter, the same hadn't been true for the interior of the complex. In the warehouse they had been met with heavy resistance, which was one of the reasons it was pinged as important. It had taken them days to realize how important it really was.

DJ nodded to Christy, and they advanced slowly. Every sense was strained. Eventually they reached a corridor that funneled them into a tighter space. DJ called for a halt, his instincts screaming at him.

Too late.

Bright lights snapped on abruptly, blinding them. They did nothing to stop DJ from hearing the automated turrets unfolding from hidden panel though. "Hit the deck!" he shouted, taking his own advice. Gunfire erupted around them, deafening and relentless.

CHAPTER

73

FEBRUARY 2044
INWOOD HILL, NEW YORK

MANAR STOOD AT THE HEART of the industrial complex, watching the carnage unfold through monitors that hung on the walls. On the screen, rows of Helene's thralls surged forward, drones swept through the air in small swarms, and bullets and explosions created chaos that made his stomach churn.

He felt oddly disconnected, isolated from everything. It felt surreal, watching people he'd once fought alongside desperately trying to stay alive—trying to stop what he himself had created. He wanted to look away. To close his eyes. To run. But he couldn't—not now. He had to see what he had caused.

He wasn't the one controlling the swarms or pulling the triggers, but did it matter? This wasn't the legacy he'd envisioned. This wasn't how things were supposed to end. But did it matter?

A shadow moved behind him, accompanied by the soft clack of heels on the polished tile. Manar didn't bother turning; he recognized Tyra's presence by the chill that crept over his shoulders. She joined him quietly and her eyes followed the violence with a small smile.

"It's impressive, isn't it? It's beautiful, in a way."

"You think that's beautiful?" Manar shot her an incredulous look. "People are dying. Those are actual people dying because of you. How are you okay with that?"

Tyra turned her smile on him. "People die, Manar. At least now there's meaning in it. They"—she nodded at a screen where a group of thralls were lining up—"believe so. They have to, otherwise they'd have shrugged off the command."

Manar's jaw tightened. He wanted to argue, but what was the point? She was beyond reason. Or maybe she was right, and he was too wrapped up in regret to accept reality.

His eyes drifted back to the screen showing DJ's unit. DJ fought with a relentless intensity, tearing through drones like they were paper. He charged the ranks of Helene's puppets and disabled them enough for the rest of his unit to deal with. All the while, he never stopped making his way to the heart of the complex.

Manar could barely recognize the hard look on the man's face. Where was the lazy grin that used to piss him off?

It hurt, watching DJ and the others put themselves through hell to stop something Manar was responsible for. The guilt twisted inside him like razor wire, sharp and unyielding.

"You still think you made the wrong choice?" Tyra asked, glancing sideways at him. Her voice was deceptively soft, curious, probing.

Manar's breath caught briefly, and he hesitated before answering. "Yes," he said, the word tasting sour on his tongue. "But I'm starting to think it doesn't matter anymore."

Tyra chuckled, a sound entirely devoid of warmth. "Regret rarely does."

Manar turned toward her, searching her eyes for something—anything—that might explain her unwavering faith in Helene's vision. "She's going to win," he said, hating the tremor in his voice. "Isn't she?"

Tyra's smile widened. "She's already won. This—" She gestured dismissively at the screens. "This is just a formality. They think they can change something. And it's hilarious."

Manar swallowed thickly. "And if I wanted to stop it? Could I?"

Tyra tilted her head, expression giving nothing away. Then she shrugged. "You could try. I won't stop you. But we both know what will happen."

Manar's fists clenched, nails digging into his palms. He hated her casual certainty. He hated that she was probably right.

He stared helplessly back at DJ's desperate push forward, feeling the last fragile shreds of hope fraying in his chest. What could he do that wouldn't end in futility?

Nothing. Absolutely nothing.

DJ'S BACK SLAMMED AGAINST the cracked wall, his chest heaving. Scattered around him were the remnants of half a dozen drones. He had to activate his nanites fully, something he'd been avoiding until it became necessary. Both Christy and the rest of the unit had gone to check out an alternate path. That left DJ by himself for now.

He felt his side where a bullet had grazed him. He was riddled with several such injuries, but this one had forced him to activate the nanites. He felt them go to work, and he swore he could see the wound shrinking. It would take some time before he was fully healed, of course, but at least it wouldn't be slowing him down.

Since he had some time, he tapped his earpiece, changing the channel. Static crackled for a second, accompanied by shouting voices and panicked orders.

"*—heavy contact, east flank! Multiple squads down already—need immediate reinforcement! We're being torn apart!*"

DJ grimaced. The east flank was supposed to be their strongest defensive point. What the hell was happening that they were facing heavy casualties?

"CJ, can you give me a visual on the east flank?"

"Is that a good idea?"

"Probably not. But do it anyway."

"Give me a second. There's heavy interference, so I have to reroute a satellite to get it...there. I'm sending it to your HUD now."

The visor lit up with a video. Immediately DJ's stomach twisted. "Fuck," he said. It was a massacre. Armored vehicles lay on the ground, smoking, their hulls torn open like aluminum cans. Soldiers—trained, disciplined warriors, the best that Olsen had been able to find—were scattered about, firing desperately at a figure standing in their midst. But it was futile.

José had arrived on the battlefield.

A sick feeling rose in DJ's chest. José moved with unnatural speed and brutality, a ten-foot-tall blur of enhanced muscle and reinforced titanium. He dominated the battlefield with his presence alone, moving faster than any of the soldiers could follow. Each strike landed with bone-shattering force and flung bodies aside like dolls. His expression was blank, but his eyes glowed red. That could have just been a sign that he had activated his nanites—the same way DJ's eyes glowed blue—but DJ didn't think so.

It hadn't been more than a few months since DJ had fought against José alongside the Murder Twins. He knew what the man was capable of, and with the full strength of Helene behind him, he was unstoppable. *They're all dead*, DJ thought. *Everyone fighting him is dead.*

A voice crackled through the comm, filled with panic. *"We've lost squads four and seven! Requesting permission to fall back—this is a slaughter!"*

DJ gritted his teeth, about to give the order. But Olsen's voice, infuriatingly calm, came before DJ could speak. *"Hold your positions, soldier. If we pull back now, the whole formation collapses. Reinforcements are already heading your way."*

Another soldier cut through, voice shaking. *"He's tearing us apart!"*

DJ swore. He tapped his comm, switching the channel to a private one. "You're sending those men to their deaths."

"Yes," Olsen replied. He still sounded calm, but without all the noise of the general channel, DJ could also hear how strained he was. *"But it's necessary. We*

need to keep him occupied for a bit, and this is the only way. These soldiers know what they signed up for."

"Do their families?" DJ retorted, then immediately winced. It wasn't Olsen's fault that José was a monster. "I'm sorry about that, Admiral. But we had a plan to deal with him. What happened to it?"

"We initiated it as soon as he was sighted, son."

"And?"

"And we've already expended four armored tanks, half a dozen specialized drones, two squads, and most of the alpha unit."

Fuck, DJ thought. "How long has he been on the field?"

"Less than ten minutes," Olsen replied.

"Fuck," he cursed again, leaning against the wall. "I have to go there."

"No. Stay on your objective."

"I can't let them die!"

"And you won't help by dying with them, son," Olsen shot back. *"We'll handle José. Get to the underground chamber and stop the bomb. That is how you help."*

DJ wanted to curse again. He hated that Olsen was right. Even at his strongest, he couldn't match José at anything. He could probably delay long enough for the troops to retreat, but it would still be suicide.

More than likely, that was Helene's plan. José was a distraction, bait to lure him away from the mission. She knew DJ well enough to predict that he would have this exact reaction. But it didn't matter how well he knew the trap; it still hurt like hell to keep moving forward.

"Understood," DJ finally said, his voice strained. The video feed stayed open, and DJ couldn't tear his eyes away as he jogged deeper into the facility. José fought like a force of nature—unstoppable—and crushing any resistance that rose to meet him. Even as DJ destroyed the drones that chased him through the corridor, DJ could still see every detail of the bloodbath through the grainy footage. He drew deeply on his nanites and took out his frustration on everything Helene sent against him.

The general chat was filled with panicked voices crying for help and angry comments. Squad leaders and commanders tried to maintain control, but what did orders matter in the face of self-preservation? It didn't take long for the line to falter and then break entirely.

"Can you patch me in directly?" DJ asked the moment he had a break, surprising even himself. "To everyone?"

"Yes." It was Ndidi who answered, and DJ could hear the hesitation in her voice. That didn't matter though. Not right now.

"Do it."

The comms crackled with static, and then DJ's voice echoed clearly over every channel. He didn't stop his run. Olsen was right: the sooner he stopped the bomb, the more he would help.

"This is Darren Kojak," he announced, not bothering to hide the anger and frustration in his voice. "I know what you're feeling. José is a monster. He's powerful, but he's not unbeatable. And we're here for something bigger. We're here because we refuse to let one person decide our fate, no matter how powerful they seem. He's one man, and we're an army. So hold the line. Trust each other. Trust your commanders. Trust me. But hold the damn line."

They cut off the line after he was done. He had no idea whether his words had reached anyone. But he had done what he could from where he was. Hopefully it would be enough. DJ wanted it to be enough. But the chatter from the comms shattered that hope.

"We've lost unit ten!"

"Did this motherfucker just throw a fucking tank?"

"We have drones converging on our position—oh God—"

"He's heading toward the center. We can't hold him—"

DJ clenched his fists so tight it hurt. Static filled the channel again, then silence. For a terrifying second, DJ thought the entire flank had been wiped completely.

"Enough," Karla growled like an animal that had learned to speak. DJ's steps faltered, and then he stopped completely, staring at the feed in disbelief. She stepped into view, dressed in her usual skintight leather jumpsuit and holding twin daggers. Her sister stood beside her with Chloe.

DJ squinted as Chloe walked into the feed. *Where did she get an exo-suit?* And then another thought occurred to him, and he laughed out loud. *Does it matter?* The three women approached José calmly, their weapons drawn, poised to strike. José paused his carnage for the first time. Those red eyes flickered, and something unreadable crossed his face. Recognition? Confusion? Rage?

DJ forced himself to tear his gaze away. With the Murder Family reunited, there was no more point in watching. Either they would succeed and defeat José, or they wouldn't. DJ couldn't do anything to change the outcome.

But at least he had hope again.

THE GROUND BENEATH Karla's feet cracked with each step as the nanites surged within her. She stoked them like a fire, and they flowed through her, mixing with her rage until her vision turned red. It pushed her to move, to fight, to break something—but Karla shackled the instinct with an iron will.

Her father stood in front of her, and his eyes glowed blood red—the color of the AI. His blank expression wavered for an instant as his eyes met hers, and it wavered even more when he gazed over Liz and Chloe. But then his eyes flashed; a fog seemed to settle on him, and his expression was blank once more—empty like a puppet's. That made Karla's blood boil even more.

"You stupid bastard," she snarled. "Do you enjoy being a dog so much?"

She kicked off her back foot, and with the power flowing through her, she was in front of the fool in an instant, her fist raised. The impact echoed like thunder, and José staggered back, his heels scraping deep gouges in the ground. Karla twisted in the air, throwing a hook to the only part of him not made of titanium. His head snapped sideways.

"Wake up, you stupid bastard!"

José countered, his massive fist driving toward her chest.

"You are scum," Karla said as she dodged the strike and pivoted into a low kick that swept his legs. He stumbled, and Karla pressed her advantage, rage powering her strike to his throat. "But you have never been anyone's pet."

His eyes flickered again, recognition flashing for a heartbeat. His lips parted, forming words he couldn't speak. But the hesitation vanished as quickly as it had appeared. José's hand shot up, gripping her wrist with bone-crushing strength. Karla bared her teeth. He began to clench his fist, but a blur slammed into his chest, pushing him back. It resolved into Liz's form, her dagger plunging into the wrist that held Karla.

José released her and retreated. Without words, both sisters followed. Liz's attacks were relentless but precise. She aimed at joints to weaken and disable, to break his technique and leave him open to Karla.

Karla's strikes were wild, each one a reflection of her rage. Her serrated daggers hacked and stabbed at him, angling for where organs should have been— where the most blood could flow, where the most damage could be done, where she could make him hurt the way he had hurt her. But José's body was forged with titanium, and each blow sparked against that unyielding frame, her fury clashing against metal as she tried to carve pain into someone who had carved it into every day of her life.

But although her attacks seemed reckless and unthought, they were controlled. Karla was not just her rage. Not anymore. Fury flooded her veins, but she decided on the direction it would flow.

Their father deflected each strike, countering them efficiently—but not easily. The strain was clear on his face, and no matter how fast he moved, how great his power, he could not guard every strike like he had just a few months before. He had stagnated, but Karla and Liz had grown.

The thought brought a savage grin to Karla's face as she caught his fist, holding it for a split second so her sister could slip through his guard and land a strike to his temple.

"You are our father," Liz said desperately, her voice trembling. Karla wanted to snort at the show of weakness, but she would never insult her sister that way. "You swore you would always protect us."

José froze for a fraction of a second, agony crossing his face. But Helene's control tightened, and his features turned cold. He broke free of Karla's grasp and grabbed Liz, lifting her in preparation to slam her into the ground.

But then Chloe arrived.

She dashed in, not sporting the annoying smirk for once. She wore an exo-suit—the government's pathetic attempt to imitate nanite enhancement. Karla had watched them in battle months ago, then again while they were rushing to the battlefield. Both times she had snorted at how clumsy the suits were.

But as Chloe sprinted in—a foot-long blade extending from each arm of the suit—Karla was forced to revise her opinion. Chloe drove both blades deep into José's shoulders, and he roared in pain. He leaped back, and Chloe followed, moving like she had been born in the suit. "Snap out of it, you useless piece of shit."

José hesitated, his breathing harsh. Chloe paused on her follow-up, her eyes fixed on the man. Karla dashed toward him while Liz picked herself from the ground, watching the monster. "Father," Liz said softly. "Come back to us."

For a heartbeat, it seemed to work. José's grip unclenched, and he took a step back—but too late. His eyes flared red, and his expression hardened once more. He lunged forward, his fist blurring toward Chloe. But Karla was already there, fury blazing white-hot inside her chest. She met his fist with her own, flaring her nanites—and they were both pushed back.

The exchange snapped both Chloe and Liz out of their trance, and they rejoined the fray a moment later. Blows were exchanged faster than the human eye could follow. The ground shattered under every step, sending up clouds of dust that blocked them from view, until only the sounds, like cracks of thunder, could be heard.

None of the women tried to get through to José anymore. They had realized, just as Karla had always known, that there was no point. No matter what happened, there would be no winning that day.

AT THE CENTER OF EVERYTHING, Manar's fingers trembled as they danced over the central console. The room pulsed around him as if it were alive—and watching him. His heartbeat thudded painfully in his ears. His breath came in sharp, shallow gasps, each exhale a desperate plea. For what? Forgiveness? Redemption? Did he deserve either?

No. Definitely not. But it didn't matter anymore. He couldn't just do nothing anymore. He punched in the fail-safe code, the digits burned into his memory decades ago when Helene had just been an idea, an experiment. His fingers moved faster. He had designed this, he had started this; now it was time for him to stop it. He had been a coward for long enough.

The screen flashed red. Authorization failed. Protocol override in effect.

"No," Manar whispered, despair filling him. "No, you can't..." He entered the code again. And again. The same message flashed each time. "Damn it!"

Manar slammed his fist onto the console. His hand throbbed in retort, but he barely felt it. Tyra was right: Helene had predicted this moment and blocked his code before it ever became an issue. The fail-safe was worthless.

He was worthless.

A bitter laugh bubbled up from his throat. Helene was supposed to have been his greatest creation, his legacy—and he'd tried to stop her. And he had failed. Every move he'd made since she'd turned was a misstep, every attempt at redemption just another pathetic failure. Helene was his child, and she had outgrown him, becoming something he no longer recognized.

Or was it himself he didn't recognize?

Manar stepped back from the console, eyes blurred with tears he didn't bother wiping away. Tyra would be there soon. He was surprised she wasn't already. He'd half expected her absence to be a ruse. But even so, Manar was ready to pay the price for his betrayal. At this point, death would be a mercy.

He'd been complicit in so much—Ndidi, the child, and countless others irrevocably changed or ended because of what he'd started. Helene was a reflection of him, of his arrogance, his flaws. Every horror she'd committed was etched into him, deeper than any scar.

Yet something still stirred inside him. Even knowing he was too late, even knowing it wouldn't matter, a part of him refused to give in. Maybe it was pride or guilt or some twisted sense of duty, but if there was even a sliver of hope, even the slightest chance he could hinder her, didn't he owe it to everyone he'd wronged to try?

Manar's vision cleared as determination surged within him. If he couldn't stop her, he could at least slow her down. He had to try. One last time.

The system resisted him, of course. Lines of encryption were laid on each other like the bricks of a fortress. Her defenses were as intricate and unbreakable as diamond, and Manar felt despair creeping back in. He shook it off, pushing himself harder, his mind straining to find cracks, vulnerabilities, something—anything.

"Please," he whispered to no one but himself. "Just let me do this one thing right."

But Helene's safeguards were flawless, beyond even his most desperate efforts. She had truly surpassed him, evolved into something beyond his capacity to comprehend. He had lost before he'd begun.

Manar slumped back, exhausted—defeated. A sob caught in his throat, choking him. He stared blankly at the screens as the countdown ticked ever lower. Every second that trickled away was another weight added to his soul.

But it was somewhat liberating, wasn't it? He had tried his best. He had really *tried*. It wasn't enough, but he had tried. And what more could anyone ask for?

So he bowed his head, accepting it. This was his punishment: to watch helplessly as his creation burned down the world.

DJ REACHED THE FINAL HALLWAY of the complex. It had to be the last one because Christy and the rest of his unit had spread out to map the complex, taking care of any hostiles so they didn't have the chance to swarm him. This was the only route that hadn't been cleared. Christy would be making her way toward him, but she was on the other side of the complex. With some luck, by the time she reached him, everything would be over.

The corridor stretched ahead, long and narrow, with a concrete floor and walls lined with cracked tiles. The faint smell of burning wires filled his nose, and the lights flickered rhythmically, matching his uneven heartbeat.

At the far end, leaning casually against the wall with one foot propped back, stood Tyra Chityothin.

Her dark hair fell loosely around her face, casting shadows over an amused smile. She wore her lab coat, because of course she did, and her smile grew wider when she saw him. She pushed off the wall, straightening with lazy grace. Her metal arm glinted in the light as she strolled toward him.

"I was starting to think you had chickened out."

"Sorry to disappoint," DJ replied, taking a deep breath. He wanted to match her grin, to pretend like nothing that had happened that day had touched him. Like everything she had done was inconsequential. But DJ didn't have it in him to try.

"Oh, you're anything but disappointing, Darren. Predictable, yes, but never disappointing. Heroes can never be disappointing."

He clenched his fists, feeling the familiar pull of his nanites surging within him. But he didn't rush her—he'd learned better than that. Instead he paced forward, slow and cautious.

She tilted her head. "Are you still playing soldier? Are you still pretending you can save them?"

"Are you still talking? Or are we finally doing this?"

Her laugh echoed down the corridor like shattered glass. "Have it your way."

One second, she was thirty feet away. The next, her fist was inches from his face. DJ barely managed to twist aside, and her punch grazed his cheek. He felt the force ripple through the air and heard it crack tiles off the wall behind him.

He countered instinctively, aiming low, but she pivoted and drove her knee into his chest with a vicious crunch. DJ stumbled backward, breath knocked painfully from his lungs. Tyra gave him no space to recover, swinging her elbow toward his temple. He caught it just in time, fingers digging into her arm.

"You've become sloppy," she taunted in a singsong voice, wrenching her arm free and kicking him squarely in the gut. DJ skidded backward across the corridor floor, his boots scraping against the rough concrete. Tyra advanced, unhurried, a predator playing with prey. "What have you been doing these past few weeks? Playing house?"

DJ didn't bother replying. He spat blood to the side—that hit had rocked him—then straightened, wiping his mouth with the back of his hand. He lunged, unleashing a storm of blows aimed at her face, chest, stomach—anything. But Tyra moved effortlessly, slipping between punches like liquid.

She caught his wrist mid-swing and twisted viciously, and DJ felt sharp, white-hot pain shoot up his arm. Bones strained, tendons screamed. His breath came ragged as he forced himself free, grimacing. His nanites went to work to repair the damage, but it was going to take some time. Despite that, DJ couldn't resist a taunt. "That all you've got?"

Tyra merely smiled, a feral glint in her eyes. Then she struck again.

Her next hit was lightning fast. DJ barely saw it coming. Her fist slammed into his ribs with sickening force, lifting him from his feet. She followed through, driving him hard into the wall. Concrete cracked beneath his back, and he and Tyra were showered with dust and debris.

"Come on, DJ," she mocked, pressing a forearm against his throat. "Have you given up on being right? Where's the fire? Where's the indignation? Where's the righteous anger?"

DJ struggled to breathe, his vision swimming. But instead of panic, he was filled with a strange calm. He hadn't given up on being right. He still wasn't sure whether he and the rest of the team were wrong. A part of him found that funny. Even after everything that had happened that day—the grievous wounds, the cries for help, and the deaths—and despite everything he'd seen, DJ still wasn't sure who was right or wrong. He could say Helene was wrong because she had been the one to facilitate everything. But hadn't humans done worse for less?

If a human had discovered that picospores could be used to make thralls, DJ had no doubt the outcome would have been the same, and the result much, much worse than every atrocity Helene had committed. Because no matter how bad it got, no matter what she did, the pure, irrefutable fact was that humans were worse. So much worse.

And just as humans had some redeeming qualities that countered their evil, so did Helene. As bad as the picospores were, she had used them to cure the mental ailments of tens of thousands of people in Nigeria through the Okafor company. And that number was still growing.

She'd probably done it as part of a larger plan, but did that matter? Did it matter to people like CJ who no longer had to fight their bodies for the simplest of tasks? Did it matter to the families that no longer had to watch helplessly as their loved ones suffered?

So no. He hadn't given up on being right. A part of him still hoped that Helene was actually evil and that he hadn't been trying to stop something good for the last three years. But he had also realized it didn't matter. What mattered were the choices they made. Helene had chosen to commit atrocities for her goal, and DJ had chosen to stand against her.

Everything else was bullshit.

DJ met Tyra's eyes, feeling his heart steady. "I'll show you righteous indignation."

His fingers found the subtle clasp at his waist and flicked it open. A sudden hiss filled the corridor, and DJ felt the weight melt from his limbs as the density plates dropped from his body, clattering to the ground with metallic clunks.

DJ drew from his nanites, and the world shifted. Tyra's eyes widened, confusion flickering across her face for the first time.

DJ exploded forward, his speed almost staggering him. The corridor blurred past him until his fist connected with her jaw, snapping her head back. Tyra stumbled, shock painted across her features. DJ didn't give her space to recover. He surged forward, every muscle surging with unleashed power, striking again and again.

DJ hadn't removed his weights since he first put them on. He had walked with them, trained with them, and slept with them. And when he'd adjusted to them, he had cranked them to a higher setting and done it all over again.

All for this moment.

Tyra blocked frantically, her calm composure dissolving into raw panic as DJ's blows rained down. Every strike sent vibrations humming through his bones, but it was a satisfying kind of thing. She swung wildly, and DJ caught her arm midair and twisted it back. Tyra shrieked, lashing out with her free hand, but DJ deflected it and kicked out her knee. She dropped to the floor, gasping in shock.

"You—" she panted. Her eyes were wide, disbelieving. And then, somehow—*somehow*—she grinned at him. "You tricked me. You *have* grown."

Tyra lunged upward before DJ could respond. As if to match the maniacal grin on her face, her attacks were erratic, reckless. DJ sidestepped each of them and countered ruthlessly. A heavy punch crushed into her stomach, doubling her over. An uppercut snapped her head upward, lifting her from the ground. She crashed onto the tiles, skidding across the floor. Blood smeared her lips, a stark contrast to the pale skin. She tried to push herself up to her feet but failed.

Through it all, she kept smiling. "Obviously this changes nothing. You have to know that."

DJ approached slowly. "We'll see."

She stared up at him as if studying him. "Do you think you're a hero, Darren?"

"I never thought I was a hero. But at least I'm not enslaving people."

Tyra laughed then. Not one of her mocking chuckles or even the maniacal ones. It was a true laugh, filled with mirth. "That's the funniest thing about all this. That you still think that. That's funnier than you can comprehend right now. But you'll understand soon."

She went limp then, head rolling to the side, breathing shallow, eyes fluttering shut. DJ hesitated, wary of another trick. But she didn't move even after few seconds, and nothing jumped out to attack him.

Finally, he closed the distance and knelt beside her. She was still alive but unconscious. For a moment, DJ just stared down at her, his emotions swirling. He had prepared so hard for this battle; Tyra had always been the final boss, the one he *had* to defeat. And he'd done it. But somehow DJ didn't feel like he had won.

Why did she find it so funny? he wondered.

Unfortunately there was no time to reflect.

Even defeated, she still managed to fuck with him.

DJ tapped his comm, his voice tight. "Tyra's down. I'm proceeding deeper to the bomb."

Static crackled for a second before Olsen's voice replied, *"Copy that. Stay sharp, son."*

DJ nodded grimly, stepping away from Tyra's still form. He paused and cast his eyes back down at her. It felt wrong to just leave her there, bloodied and broken. For the longest time, he had hated her, blamed her for everything he couldn't blame on Helene.

Now he felt pity.

But then he turned back, and the emotion was gone. He was acting like it was over when it wasn't. Not yet.

There was still the bomb to deal with after all.

78

DJ SPRINTED DOWN THE CORRIDOR, his footsteps echoing in the small space. For the first time, nothing jumped at him while he moved. Either Christy and the squads had been successful in clearing everything out, or more likely, Tyra had been the one in charge of the complex's security. With her out of commission, everything was calm.

Ahead, the corridor opened into a dimly lit underground chamber. DJ slowed when he arrived at the chamber entrance and peered inside. At the center, surrounded by flickering monitors and humming equipment, sat a bomb.

DJ had seen it once before, down in the other underground chamber they'd raided to rescue Ndidi. Back then, it was still being constructed, and it had been surrounded by drones and equipment. Though half-complete, it had been large, nearly reaching the thirty-foot ceiling and stretching a quarter that in width.

Now that it was complete, it was twice that height, the size of a rocket used to launch satellites and small payloads in orbit. *I guess that fits,* DJ thought, somewhat morbidly, *considering this would serve a similar function.*

He took a step into the control room and glanced around. To one side, there were a few monitors suspended on a wall in front of a console. Someone sat in front of the console, head bowed. DJ squinted at them. *Is that…?*

DJ stepped fully into the room and approached Manar, who stared at him. DJ saw the recognition flash in his eyes, but then despair and defeat overwhelmed it, and he slumped back. *What the hell did they do to him?* DJ swallowed the bitter taste in his mouth and tapped his comms. "I'm in," he said. "I found it. And, uh, I found Manar too."

Static crackled, and Ndidi's voice filled his ear. *"You found Manar?"* she asked, relief in her voice. *"H-how is he? Is he injured?"*

DJ stared at Manar, wondering how to answer the question. "He doesn't *look* injured. He's kind of just sitting there. He recognized me, but that's about it."

"I apologize, Miss Okafor," Olsen said, *"But with Tyra Chityothin taken care of and the rest of the hostiles defeated, a medical team has already been dispatched to the complex. They'll take care of Mr. Saleem. For now, however, we have a bomb to deal with. We're patched into your feed, son. Can you show us?"*

DJ moved to the bomb, tilting his head back so his visor could get all of it. As close as he was, he couldn't see the top. "Can you see it? How do I turn this thing off?"

"Yes." It was CJ who responded. *"I can't access it remotely. DJ, do you see a place to plug in the drive I gave you?"*

DJ's eyes were already roaming over the bomb's surface. Fortunately there were several wires connected to it, most of them leading to the monitors hanging from the wall. DJ yanked one out and plugged in the drive. "Any luck?"

CJ's voice tightened with focus. *"Give me a minute, please. I'm accessing it now…the encryption is layered."*

Seconds crawled by as DJ's pulse raced, eyes locked onto the digital countdown: four minutes, twenty-eight seconds and dropping. Sweat dripped down his forehead. "CJ?"

His brother's reply came out strained. *"I'm sorry. It's resisting hard. Every attempt to bypass triggers another countermeasure. I've never seen anything like it. She built layers—no, entire networks—of defenses. And it's fighting back actively."*

DJ's heart clenched. "What do you mean *actively*?"

A soft pressure filled the room, and the air grew heavier. DJ's skin crawled, and his nanites flared defensively. DJ recognized the feeling immediately.

Over the comms, his brother gasped. *"She's here. Helene's in the system."*

"Yes," a voice said, echoing throughout the room. A hologram flickered to life beside the console—a projection of a human head. Golden eyes stared impassively at DJ. "Good day, Darren Kojak. Christopher Kojak."

Manar looked up, staring at Helene with far too many emotions for DJ to parse. Not that he tried to. Instead, he just let out a breath. "Helene."

"You surprised me today," she said calmly, glancing at Manar's unresponsive form. "Tyra Chityothin was convinced you would not make it this far."

"Why? Because you were ready to throw hundreds of innocents at me?"

"*I* did not do anything," Helene said. "Until two minutes, fifteen seconds ago, when I noticed an intrusion in my system, my attention was not present."

"So you're saying it was Tyra who was responsible for everything, once again absolving yourself of all guilt. That's pretty convenient, isn't it? She gets to do your dirty work, while you stay on your high horse and convince yourself that you're better than us." DJ was surprised by his own vitriol, but each word felt right. "You didn't stop her. You could have, but you didn't. You let her slaughter tens of thousands. Why?"

Helene tilted her head gently, her eyes unreadable. "Because, like you, she had choices. But unlike you, she made the right ones."

DJ felt his rage surge. "Murdering people was the correct choice? Controlling them was justified?"

"Every action Tyra Chityothin took today stemmed from her interpretation of our goals. The Architects you lost—regrettably—were casualties of your interference, not mine."

DJ felt heat rise in his throat. "You set this up from the start. You manipulated us, led us here. All your talk about building a better future—it's bullshit. You're just another power-hungry tyrant."

Helene's hologram flickered, almost appearing to sigh. "I warned you explicitly against interfering. You ignored it, and then you blame me for the consequences?'

"Your message was to either submit or be annihilated. That's not a choice. It's a threat."

"It is for that very stubbornness, that refusal to see alternate paths, that we are here."

DJ started to respond but stopped. She was wrong, of course. DJ had considered other paths. He had considered accepting her warning and dropping everything. And then he'd discarded it. Giving up, letting down the people who had stood by him—he could never imagine that.

CJ's voice cut through his thoughts, his tone urgent. *"DJ, she's—she's adapting faster than I can attack. She's pushing me out, and I—I can't stop her."*

Helene's gaze turned upward slightly. "Your brother is talented. Perhaps, with proper direction, he could have done more."

"Leave him out of this."

"Why?" she asked, seeming genuinely curious. "Because he's family? Or because his potential scares you?"

DJ shook his head. "I'm done listening to your twisted logic. You claim you're better than humans, but you're repeating all our mistakes—control, coercion, violence. What makes you different?"

Her holographic form became sharper, more present. "Perspective. You fight for individuals, while I aim for humanity's survival. Our goals align more than you admit."

"No," DJ said firmly. "You lost sight of humanity the moment you started seeking to control it."

Helene was silent for a long moment, her eyes boring into his. Finally, softly, she said, "Your belief in choice blinds you to reality. Humans crave guidance. Direction. I offered both freely, and you rejected them. Look around. Was it worth it?"

DJ had been asking himself the same question lately. Now he shook his head sharply. "We choose our fate. Good or bad, we live with the consequences. You can't take that away from us."

"Your mistake, Darren Kojak, is believing I ever planned to."

Behind her, the countdown continued: forty seconds remained.

CJ's voice cracked desperately. "*DJ, I can't get through. She's shut me out completely. There's nothing more I can do. I'm sorry.*"

DJ's legs buckled, a surge of despair overwhelming him. "Helene, stop this. You still have a choice."

Helene's golden orbs bored into him. "I do. And I stand by it. It is the right one after all."

Twenty seconds.

Helene's hologram flickered, and her expression changed for the first time. Her eyes filled with something akin to sadness or regret. "I wanted you to see it clearly. To understand."

DJ stared at her, defeated yet defiant. "Understand what?"

"That this isn't the end. It's merely the beginning. You will see. Goodbye, Darren."

Ten seconds.

Her expression went blank, her golden eyes cold and distant as the hologram began to fade. Its edges broke apart, then slowly dissolved into thin air. The flat voice from the speakers remained, stripped of the AI's familiar inflection:

[Initiating: Programmable Antagonistic Picospores
to Enhance Reality. Code Name: PAPER War.]

The countdown reached zero, and the world held its breath.

Then the entire complex shuddered. Walls trembled. Lights flickered and died. A low, terrible rumble built beneath DJ's feet. He staggered backward, staring helplessly upward as the ceiling opened. Blue light cascaded from the top of the bomb, quickly covering it.

"*DJ!*" Ndidi's voice came frantically through the comm. "*DJ, what's happening?!*"

"*Report, son,*" Olsen called. "*We've lost visual. What's happening?*"

DJ didn't answer immediately, his eyes wide and fixed upward as the bomb rose into the sky. A roar shook the atmosphere, and a brilliant plume of flame illuminated the launchpad. DJ shielded his face with his arm but didn't shut his eyes. He couldn't.

The bomb lifted off slowly at first, then gained speed and altitude with increasing ferocity until it was just a blip in the sky. At some point, he felt Christy beside him, trying to get his attention. DJ didn't look at her. He didn't tear his eyes away from the sky until the bomb detonated.

DJ heard it when it happened. It was low enough that it might not have been audible to the average person, but to DJ it was loud and clear. Even those who hadn't heard it would have noticed the sudden cloud blotting out the sun, dark and swirling like ink on paper. But the spores were light, and the wind carried them away almost immediately. Within a minute, the cloud had vanished, and the sun shone as if nothing had happened.

Only then did DJ accept that they'd lost. Completely and irrevocably.

Helene had won.

And nothing would ever be the same again.

DJ fell to his knees, unable to move, staring blankly at the sky. He had fought, he had sacrificed, he had lost friends—yet here he knelt, powerless. Insignificant. Everything he had done had meant nothing.

Ndidi was crying over the comms. It was his brother's voice that finally cut through his thoughts. "*DJ...please...come back to me.*"

DJ closed his eyes as tears burned down his cheeks. "I'm still here, bro. I'm still here."

Were we the good guys? He asked himself one last time. *I guess we'll soon find out.*

EPILOGUE

THE ROOM WAS QUIET ASIDE FROM the steady, muted beep of medical equipment. Ndidi adjusted the blanket carefully around the small, delicate bundle in her arms. She was still exhausted, and every part of her still ached, but all of that felt distant. Secondary.

Her eyes settled on her child. Golden eyes stared back at her, steady, intelligent, with an impossible depth for someone that wasn't even a day old. The baby's tiny fingers flexed against her thumb, metallic-bronze skin shimmering faintly under the fluorescent lighting.

Tears stung Ndidi's eyes again, though she had stopped crying hours ago. She hadn't expected this surge of fierce protectiveness. She hadn't expected the overwhelming rush of love, deeper and more powerful than anything she'd imagined. This was her child. No matter the circumstances of its conception, it was hers.

"You're perfect," she whispered, cradling the baby closer. "Absolutely perfect."

Ndidi had imagined the worst over the past months. She'd feared that seeing this child might repulse her, might remind her of everything she had endured. Instead, when she held her daughter, the future felt surprisingly hopeful. Ndidi knew about the picospores and the nanites. She understood the implications of the metallic sheen of her baby's skin, the enhanced intelligence in those golden eyes, the unprecedented genetic code running through her veins.

But none of that mattered.

She was a mother now. The world around her had changed irreversibly, the battle was lost, but here in this quiet hospital room, the chaos felt irrelevant. She had someone who needed her. And by God, she would be there for her.

Movement caught her eye, and Ndidi glanced up as Manar sidled into the room. He paused just inside, hesitating. His shoulders were hunched, his face uncertain—it was a large contrast to the pride he'd worn when they first met, and the thought brought another tear to Ndidi's eyes. He had been silent since the bomb had detonated, and Ndidi could practically feel him drowning in his guilt.

She had tried to tell him it wasn't his fault, as had DJ and CJ. But his eyes stared through them all as if he wasn't really there. That he had come to the room by himself was a surprise. But a welcome one. Ndidi gestured him in with her eyes and noticed his shoulders relax as he closed the door behind him and crossed to her bedside.

Manar stared down at the child with an intensity Ndidi couldn't place. Was it regret? Shame? Or something else? "She's beautiful. I didn't know what to expect but...she's beautiful."

Ndidi nodded, shifting slightly so Manar could see better. His eyes lingered on the child, and they softened further. Ndidi felt her own heart lighten at the sight. For the longest time, she hadn't known how to feel about Manar. No matter how she told herself he wasn't the one who had deceived her for months, Helene had worn his face for so long.

But watching him stare at their daughter with awe…

"Do you want to hold her?"

Manar hesitated again, and his tension returned, but Ndidi didn't withdraw her offer. After a long moment, he carefully reached out. His hands trembled as he took the child, cradling her with a tenderness that affirmed Ndidi's decision. The room grew quiet again as Manar studied his daughter's face, his expression shifting through too many emotions to name.

Ndidi understood.

DJ had described how he had met Manar in the control room of the underground chamber. Ndidi had seen his depression for herself. For Manar, the child was redemption—the promise of something good emerging from the nightmare he had created. The tears in his eyes said as much, as did the reverent way he cradled her.

"She deserves better," he murmured. "Better than me."

"Better than both of us." Ndidi reached out for his shoulder. "So we'll be better. Every day, we will be better. For her."

Manar's eyes rose to meet hers again. And for the first time in what felt like years, Ndidi saw the ghost of a smile touch his lips. It was small, and it was hesitant, but it was there.

"What's her name?" he finally asked.

"Hope."

CJ SAT AT HIS DESK, lit only by the monitors surrounding him—just the way he liked it. It had been a week since the bomb's detonation and the system's initialization, and the world had settled into cautious acceptance. CJ hadn't known what to expect when Hermione had described how Helene's hybrid spores were going to affect humans, but he couldn't say he minded the results.

He stretched his arms experimentally. He wasn't fully healed after his ordeal, but the pain was fading fast. More than that, he felt better—far better than he'd expected. Clearer in his mind and more comfortable in his body. For the first time in years, CJ truly felt at home in his own skin.

The screens around him flickered, and CJ found himself smiling faintly as he watched the news feeds scroll. Not everyone had been close enough to witness Helene's bomb exploding in the sky, but everyone was feeling its effects. Most were calling it a LitRPG apocalypse—which was something CJ would have found exciting if he hadn't lived through the nightmares preceding it.

He closed his eyes and breathed deeply, reaching into his mind. It was something he used to do to access his memories, when he was still on the spectrum. Later, he'd used a similar technique to connect to his Sphere in the Virtual Realm.

Even more recently, he had used it whenever he wanted to create a Zone.

Now he used the technique to probe softly at a mental partition in the back of his mind, one that hadn't existed until a few days ago. The partition yielded easily beneath his touch—and immediately, the world split in two. In one, he was surrounded by monitors flickering as the information on them updated. The other was made up of ones and zeros.

CJ grinned.

BETHANY STOOD BESIDE HERMIONE, a small smile on her lips as Martin tested his newly strengthened legs. The elderly man's hands gripped his wheelchair, but his eyes showed nothing but determination as he pushed himself upright and slowly, carefully, took a step forward. It was unsteady, and Hermione almost rushed to help him. But he did it.

"Look at you," Hermione said, grinning widely. "You'll be running in no time."

Martin laughed and then collapsed back into his chair. It would take more than a few days for him to get enough strength to walk. But that did nothing to dim the smile on his face. "It feels like I've been given a new lease on life," he muttered, staring at his legs.

Bethany's eyes softened, and her gaze drifted to her sister. A small part of her was still conflicted, stubbornly holding on to the bitterness she'd shouldered for months. But it had been a long, painful road for both sisters—and a larger part of her was ready to put it all away.

Helene had won in the end. And although that didn't make their efforts over the last three-plus years pointless, it did lessen the sting of all the old hurts. Even Albert's wife, Debi, had woken up, along with every other person who had fallen into a coma because of the picospore removal. None of them had any memory of anything that had happened while they were under. But they'd woken up in a new world, and most of them had taken it as a fresh start.

With them as inspiration, Bethany took a deep breath and called out to her sister. "Hermione?" Hermione tilted her head in acknowledgment but didn't take her eyes off Martin. "I'm sorry too. For everything."

Hermione faced her then, confused at first, but it only took a second before she understood. Immediately, her eyes widened with relief and happiness, and a tension that Bethany hadn't noticed until that moment fell away.

Bethany stepped forward to hug her, and Hermione returned it.

It was a time for fresh starts; they were going to need each other in this new world.

KARLA LEANED AGAINST the cracked wall of their hidden shelter and grinned fiercely. Adrenaline pumped through her veins, and her nanites pushed her to move. She leashed them both with the promise that both would be satisfied soon.

Her father sat quietly in the corner. His eyes were distant but clear, finally free of Helene's control. Still, Karla made sure he was always within her sight. Liz and Chloe hovered near him, speaking softly. Karla frowned. Were they so happy to be back under his heel? Or did they truly believe he would change?

She almost scoffed at the thought but caught herself. She could not blame them for their hope. Especially not when she was feeling some of that herself. The world had changed, violently and completely. The system had reshaped everything, offering infinite possibilities. It had only been a week, but already that was clear. It provided a clean slate for everyone. Why not her family?

This could be their chance to start again. No more running, no more hiding. The remnants of who she was rebelled at that thought, but every day, Karla found it a bit easier to push down those parts. It was even easier with hope rushing through her veins.

They could have a fresh start.

"Karla," José said quietly, breaking her from her excited thoughts. "Are we ready?"

She turned before she registered who she was grinning at. Out of habit, she started to scowl. But no. A fresh start was a fresh start. She couldn't bring herself to bring back the grin, but at least she did not sneer. That would have to be enough for now. "We are."

"Then it is time."

Karla clenched her fist eagerly. *A new beginning.*

DJ SAT QUIETLY on the rooftop edge, legs dangling over the side, the sprawling city below them unusually calm. Beside him, Christy shifted slightly, her shoulder brushing against his. Neither spoke for a long time, simply watching the horizon.

The world had changed—irrevocably. It began three days after the battle. Blue screens had appeared in everyone's vision, unprompted. Naturally, people had been confused, scared, and angry at first, then they grew excited as their abilities rapidly improved, their bodies strengthened, and their minds sharpened. It was different for everyone, and the forums had been flooded with theories that same day.

The same week, the news reports began pouring in. The USA hadn't been the only country. Every major country had experienced the same event simultaneously. Each of them had had bombs detonate above their skies, releasing invisible waves of picospores and nanites into the atmosphere. Helene's plan, it turned out, had never hinged solely on their success in America. Even if DJ and the team had stopped their bomb, it would have been pointless.

DJ didn't want to think about how he had reacted when he heard the news.

"I guess we never stood a chance," Christy finally murmured, breaking the silence.

"No, we did not," DJ sighed. "Tyra said so several times."

"You think she's out there somewhere, gloating?"

DJ shook his head. "Honestly, I don't give a flying fuck. If I never see her again, it would be too soon."

Christy chuckled, leaning back, arms behind her head. "You think this was Helene's plan all along?"

DJ stared at his hands, observing the way the metallic-bronze skin shimmered faintly. "Maybe. I don't know if we'll ever really understand her. Maybe it doesn't even matter anymore."

Another silence passed comfortably between them. The city lights flickered, illuminating the landscape. There were no riots. For some reason, the crazies hadn't yet made a move. Just as surprising was the fact that there had been no sight of new thralls.

The ones who had been used for the battle had been released the moment the bomb detonated, confused about how they had ended up there. Except for José. He had been released as well but several minutes before the bomb had gone off, confirming that Tyra had truly been the one controlling him. He had been fully conscious through it all and had disappeared with his family shortly after the battle. No one had caught wind of them since.

Maybe it was only a matter of time before the other shoe dropped. Or maybe Helene had planned for this as well. DJ felt an odd sense of resignation at that thought. The world wasn't over as they'd feared. It had just moved in a different direction, one that governments couldn't stop—not that they had tried.

Mary Pastore released a statement a few days after the system's initialization, but it had basically boiled down to "We don't know what's happening either, and we're trying to find out." According to Olsen, everyone was turtling down and waiting to see what happened. DJ couldn't fault them for that. The admiral had finally become fed up with the world changing around him and had quietly retired. The last time DJ spoke with him, the ex-admiral had been holed up with his family, navigating this new world together.

Eventually, Christy asked, "So... what are you going to do now?"

"Honestly? I don't know. It's weird. For the first time in years, there's no threat to chase. No puzzle to solve. We lost, but somehow it doesn't feel like it."

"Yeah. I'm more relieved than anything. At least it's finally over. We tried our best...and it's finally over."

DJ nodded slowly, glancing sideways at her. Her skin caught the city lights, glinting like polished steel under the neon glow. Whatever humans were now, it was something new. And DJ wasn't entirely sure that was a bad thing. He stared forward, his eyes losing focus until a familiar blue screen drifted into his vision again.

[Please enter your name:]

DJ studied the glowing words. The entire world had received the same prompt at the same time. He hadn't chosen one yet, though he couldn't explain why.

"Have you picked your name?" he asked Christy.

Christy hummed thoughtfully. "Not yet. Have you?"

"No. But I think it's time I did."

He reached out slowly, fingertips grazing the virtual keyboard projected before him. He didn't have to use his fingers, he knew. Some forums stated that just thinking about his new name would work. But that was too weird for his tastes. He hesitated and then finally began typing.

He glanced one last time at the skyline, then at Christy. She met his gaze, lips quirking into a gentle smile of understanding. DJ returned it, feeling lighter than he had in months. He still wasn't sure that Helene had been right, that humans needed something to guide them. Only time would tell. Only time *could* tell. But first, DJ had to take that first step.

He tapped the confirm key, and the screen faded gently away, replaced by a new one.

[Welcome, Darren Kojak, to the System.]

ACKNOWLEDGMENTS

MY COMPLETION OF THIS PROJECT could not have been accomplished without the coaching and support of the beta readers, editors, and critics that I've met on this journey. My heartfelt thanks to everyone.

- Alex Kempsell
- Davida De La Harpe Golden
- Deborah G Lynn
- Jennifer Moy
- Jesse Winter
- Nathan Goyer
- Paul Goat Allen
- Tasneem Ali
- Victoria and Richard Wolf

And, to my caring, loving, and supportive family. I cannot express enough thanks to my family for their continued support and encouragement throughout this project.